For Ron
enjoy the book
All the best
your good friend

Doug Bicknese

THE

NIGHT

HAS

GREEN

EYES

Doug Bicknese

The Night Has Green Eyes
2021 Doug Bicknese

Print ISBN: 978-1-66780-414-9

eBook ISBN: 978-1-66780-415-6

PART I

CHAPTER 1

Sunday, Oct. 3, 7:45 PM
Milton, Mass. Near Boston

Detective Eddie McGowan raised his arm in front of his face and pushed the wet pine branches to the side. He held a flashlight in his other hand and kept it trained on the policeman in front of him. Eddie did his best to keep his balance as the two of them pushed deeper into the woods.

"How much farther is it?" asked Eddie, sounding tired and frustrated.

"Only about another hundred yards or so. We're almost there," replied the officer.

Eddie was not a particularly agile man and was about twenty pounds too heavy for his frame. Every step of the way was a struggle for his 45-year-old legs. Fatigue and pain were beginning to rule. The smell of moist soil and decaying leaves filled Eddie's nostrils. He could almost taste it on his tongue. His pants and jacket were now totally soaked and a chill ran through his body.

"Slow it down a bit. What the hell were those kids doing this deep into the woods?" cursed Eddie.

"Apparently they have a secret hideout where they party and drink beer. They were playing some sort of hide-and-seek game with flashlights when one of them came across the body," replied the officer. "She's pretty shaken up."

"Did you get a look at the body?" asked Eddie

"No. My partner did. I went back to show you guys the way out here. We figured the fewer people screwing up the crime scene the better. I watch CSI," said the officer, doing his best to appear professional.

"Hah, you guys aren't as dumb as you look," joked Eddie, trying to show some appreciation in his tone.

A large branch swung backward and slapped Eddie across the face, and he lost his footing. He tried to break his fall on a rotting log but it crumbled beneath his weight and he stumbled headlong into a soggy patch of mud, dirt and pine needles.

"Shit. I should have been a real estate agent like my father told me."

Eddie righted himself and wiped the muck from his hands on a wet pine branch. He then finished by drying them on his pants. He picked up his flashlight and shined it on the officer's face.

"The clearing is just up ahead. The body is another thirty or forty yards beyond that," reassured the officer, trying to conceal a grin.

"Can't come too soon," groaned Eddie.

After a few minutes they began to hear voices. Eddie pushed his way through the few remaining branches that blocked his way. The glow of flash-lights revealed a group of people standing in a circle around a small stone fire pit. They did not appear to be a happy crew. They stood there in silence and looked as if they were chilled to the bone. A small campfire was still smoldering in the damp evening air but it offered little heat to the shivering party. A few gray curls of smoke rose slowly in the air like ghosts above the dying fire. They lingered for a moment like souls reluctant to depart their world and then vanished in the darkness. A number of dilapidated chairs covered with plastic sheets surrounded the campfire. They looked like they had been there for several years. Dozens of beer cans were strewn about the area. On the edge of the clearing stood a small lean-to constructed from sheets of plywood, two-by-fours and tree branches that had been lashed together with twine. It was also covered with a taut plastic sheet. Raindrops dripped slowly from the trees onto the plastic tarp like cold, somber tears, each one making a distinctive plunk in the cool night air.

Eddie pushed through the thick brush and entered the clearing. The group consisted of two police officers, four boys and two teenage girls.

"I'm Detective McGowan," announced Eddie. I'm in charge of this case and I need to ask some questions."

Eddie began by taking the names of the two officers on the scene.

"We would have put some wood on the fire but we didn't want to disturb any evidence," explained one of the officers, rubbing his hands together and blowing warm air from his mouth.

"Good thinking. I'm glad you guys know what you're doing."

He then turned to the kids and said, "I know you're all cold and uncomfortable but I have to ask a few questions first. You'll be out of here very soon."

He looked at them and noticed the look of gloom and sorrow in their eyes. "Which one of you found the body?" asked Eddie in a sympathetic tone.

"I did," replied one of the girls nervously. Her eyes were still red and swollen and a tear rolled down her cheek.

"What's your name?" asked Eddie, trying to sound compassionate.

"Cindy."

Eddie took out his notepad and scribbled down the name.

"Last name?"

"Cunningham."

"How old are you?"

"Fifteen."

"Did you touch the body at any time?"

"No! Oh God, no!" replied Cindy with a look of horror and disgust.

"How long were you all here before you found the body?"

"A few hours," replied the oldest boy.

"Did any of you touch the body?"

They all looked at each other and shook their heads.

"Okay," said Eddie, speaking to one of the cops. "I'll be done asking questions in a few minutes. Then you can escort them out of the woods and take them home."

Eddie continued to interview the teenagers.

"What's your name?" he said to the oldest boy.

"Kevin. Kevin Cunningham, sir."

"Your sister's the one who found the body?"

"She's my cousin, actually"

"And how old are you?"

"Nineteen, sir."

"Okay. You can take us to the body. You know the area."

Eddie continued questioning the teenagers, as he began to hear voices coming from the woods Soon another police officer entered the clearing, accompanied by a forensic team.

Eddie recognized most of them immediately. Bill Donnelly and Dave Whitmore were two photographers who had made the trek into the woods. Eddie had worked many cases with both of them. Too many. Together they had more than twenty years of experience between them. Doug Morse and Gary Mayfield were experts in collecting evidence. They were all good at what they did. Eddie walked over and greeted them.

"I haven't been up to look at the body yet. I was waiting for you guys." Eddie took command and started giving orders. "Dave... I want you to come with me to photograph the body. Gary, you come too. Kevin here is going to lead the way." He nodded in Kevin's direction. "Bill and Doug... I want you to process the campsite. Bill... first make sure you get pictures of the bottom of everyone's shoes. When you're done those kids can go home."

"Okay," said Bill and he began to take pictures.

"When my partner, Detective Morrow, gets here send him our way, but keep everyone else out," Eddie instructed the officer who had led him into the woods. "And thanks for your help," he added.

"All right then. Let's go. Be sure to take plenty of evidence bags and that high intensity flashlight, Gary. You guys with the body bag wait here till we're done with the crime scene. We'll let you know when we're finished. Try not to touch anything here in the campsite."

"Okay, Kevin. Lead the way," said Eddie with a wave of his hand.

"Yes sir," said Kevin, feeling somewhat important. He began to lead the group into the woods.

The four of them set off in direction of the body. Eddie told Gary to tie small pieces of white cloth to the trees as they walked on. After a couple of minutes of slogging through the dense brush they began to smell the unmistakable stink of death.

Then they were upon it.

There, partially concealed, they could see two legs dressed in blue jeans protruding from underneath a bush. They all stood for a moment and took time to prepare themselves.

"Whoever did this went through a lot of trouble to make sure the body wouldn't be found for a long time," said Eddie. "I doubt if they knew that campsite was even there. We got a break with you kids finding the body when you did."

Kevin nodded and flashed a smile, feeling appreciated.

"Take pictures from a lot of different angles, Dave," ordered Eddie. "I need you to take close ups of the body. You know, the usual stuff. Gary, use your flashlight and look for footprints in the immediate area. Let me know if you see anything that could be of value. I'd wait till morning but it might rain again tonight. Okay, Dave. Let's get started." After a complete set of photographs had been taken of the surrounding area, Eddie pulled the brush away from the body. The flashlights revealed a body that was apparently female.

Her throat had been cut.

"Get a good close-up of the face," instructed Eddie. He put on a pair of latex gloves and pulled the corpse out from underneath the brush. He jotted down several notes and began to make a careful examination of the body.

He noticed that the extremities and face of the victim had been chewed and partially eaten. The fingers had been completely stripped of flesh.

Raccoons, thought Eddie.

Although it was October the body also showed signs of insect activity. Eddie rolled the body slightly over on its side to reveal a pocket of maggots boring into her flesh just above the hip.

"More pictures over here," said Eddie, trying to hold his breath.

It had rained hard several nights before but her shirt and jacket were still stained red with blood.

"Get a good picture of this," demanded Eddie. "Shine that flashlight over here. Get another close-up of the face."

The eerie light revealed the mottled gray pallor of her skin. Her dark hair was wet and matted down across her forehead. Eddie brushed it away to get a better look.

A small scarab beetle raced across her lips and disappeared into a hole in her cheek. Her pale eyes remained motionless. They offered no objection and stared blankly at the tree tops.

"Oh Christ!" said Dave as he briefly turned away.

"Yeah. You never really get used to this," Eddie sympathized.

The two of them looked at each other and then continued to do their work.

"Hey McGowan. I might have something here."

Eddie looked over to see Gary about twenty feet away holding up a piece of torn clothing.

"Looks like part of a shirt or something. It's soaked through and through."

"Okay. Mark the position and bag it," said Eddie.

"Looks like the brush has been beaten down around here. There might be some footprints, too. At least partial prints. It's hard to tell. Looks like maybe a struggle went on here."

"Good! Just what I was hoping for. Dave, take some shots of all those prints. Make sure you keep track of which are yours and Gary's."

"McGowan, where are you?"

Eddie immediately recognized the voice as his partner Rob Morrow.

"Over here, Rob."

Moments later Morrow appeared on the scene.

"Hell of a trek out here, Eddie," he remarked.

"Don't have to tell me twice. We still have to walk back out of here," grunted Eddie.

Rob was only thirty-two and in excellent shape. He was far more capable of making his way through the thick underbrush. The detectives had been partners for more than two years.

Eddie was happy to let Rob take on the more physically demanding aspects of the job when they presented themselves.

"What we got here?" Rob asked.

"Apparent homicide. Female. Throat cut. Probably late twenties or early thirties. Hard to tell at this point. Been dead at least four or five days," suggested Eddie. "Maybe more. This is Kevin. One of his friends found the body and called 911 on a cell. That was about two hours ago."

Rob leaned over the body and began to take his own notes.

Eddie noticed that Kevin was staring at the body with a look that suggested both fascination and horror.

"Kevin, thanks for your help," he offered. "If you can think of anything that might help us, you know how to get in touch. You can go home now, and thanks again."

Kevin reluctantly started to walk away, looking back at the body several times.

"Forensics will have to stay on all night and go over everything. I want to know if she was killed here or at the campsite," insisted Eddie. "See to it, Gary. This is your show now. I also want to know if there are any more footprints leading to this area. It rained pretty hard last Wednesday, but maybe we'll get lucky. We might at least find out something about the size and weight of our perp," he added.

"Look at the way her throat was cut, Eddie. Almost took her head clean off," remarked Rob. "Remember the body they found last week? "Same M.O. Head nearly severed. But that was a male victim. Never did get an ID on the body."

"Yeah," replied Eddie. "Might not be any connection but we'll have the M.E. look into it."

Half an hour later they were done with the body and called for the bagmen.

Eddie and Rob parted company with Gary and the other members of the team and began their return to the campsite.

"I'm sure Jimmy's going to assign this case to us," said Rob.

"That's almost a given," said Eddie "Meet you at the M.E. tomorrow morning."

"You got it," said Morrow.

"Better we get some sleep tonight and start fresh in the morning. We've done about all we can for now."

"Are you sure you don't want to stop at Zan's for a drink?" asked Rob.

"I don't know. I'm pretty tired."

"Come on. Just one. I swear," pleaded Rob. "I'm buying."

"Okay. I guess I could use one," admitted Eddie.

The two of them looked around the campsite for another ten minutes and began their retreat from the woods. Eddie complained all the way back. An hour later they were sitting at the bar at Zan's.

"You look miserable, Eddie," said the barmaid sympathetically. "Having the usual?"

"Make it a double, Zan," said Eddie.

Zan poured a double bourbon for Eddie and looked at Rob. "Becks for you, Rob?"

"Make mine a double, too, sweetheart."

Zan gave him a wry smile. "What happened to you guys? Did you get caught in the rain?"

"Long story, Zan. Trust me. You don't want to know," said Eddie.

Actually, she did want to know. Zan was always intrigued by police work. Boston P.D. were some of her best customers.

"Come on, guys. You never let me in on anything."

Eddie was all too aware about loose lips in a bar.

"Maybe another time, Zan."

Zan's real name was Alexandra Salerno. She was only thirty-six but already owned her own bar, building and all. She worked six days a week and was a wiz at running the business. Her goal was to be a multi-millionaire by the time she was fifty and then retire and travel the world. Zan's was a favorite hangout for cops in Hyde Park. Eddie and Rob often went there to talk about a case they were working on.

Eddie's legs were still sore. He took a gulp from his glass. The bourbon was starting to kick in. The warmth spread through his body and he let out a satisfied sigh.

Zan drifted down to the end of the bar and the two detectives began to talk.

"What are your thoughts, Rob? It's kinda strange finding a body way out in the woods like that."

"I agree. Somebody didn't want her to be found."

"Well, hopefully we can get a quick I.D. tomorrow and get a jump on things." Eddie looked at his watch. It was 9:30. "If we want to get an early start we better get out of here soon."

"Okay, just one more for the road," suggested Rob.

Eddie finished his bourbon and said, "Okay. I could certainly use it."

It was eleven o'clock when they finally left.

CHAPTER 2

Sunday morning, Oct. 3, 8:10 AM
Forest Park, New York

Mike Davis awoke to the sound of his two little girls fighting over the control of a cell phone.

"Delete it!"

"Delete it now!!! Jamie, I swear to God I'm gonna kill you."

"You look just like a chipmunk. You're sooooo cute."

"Hey Dad. You've gotta see this video of Roni," Jamie yelled up the stairs. "Daddy! You've gotta see this"

A smile came to Mike's face as he opened his eyes.

What sounded like World War Three downstairs was actually good-natured fun as always, and Mike knew it. Jamie raced up the stairs, with Roni close behind. The two of them jumped on the bed on either side of him.

"Look at this, Daddy." Jamie began to play the video. "Isn't she cute, Daddy?"

"Shut up, Jamie. I'm gonna get you," Roni said with a half-smile and a sense of futility.

Mike rubbed his eyes and dutifully began to watch the video.

Roni had tried to gobble down the last three Oreos in the box all at once, before her sister could have dibs. The video was Jamie's revenge.

Roni had her mouth stuffed full. She couldn't swallow them all and now Jamie was making her laugh. Roni tried to turn her face away from the camera but Jamie kept after her.

She was beginning to drool small pieces of cookies and tears were coming to her eyes. Jamie wouldn't let up. She kept making faces, trying to mimic Roni's predicament. Finally, Roni ran to the sink and had to spit them out.

Mike chuckled and gave them both a hug.

"You girls. What am I gonna do with you two silly creatures? Hey! Today is Sunday. Isn't it?" Mike exclaimed, eyes widening with enthusiasm.

Hiking in the hills behind their house was something the family did together every Sunday morning.

"Who's going walking today?" Mike asked.

"Me. Me," the girls both answered eagerly.

"Okay. Go see what Mommy's making for breakfast and I'll be down in a couple of minutes."

Jamie and Roni jumped up and ran back down the stairs.

"Mommy, Daddy wants to know what's for breakfast" shouted Jamie, running toward the kitchen.

His wife Brittany called up the stairs, "I haven't started making anything. What would you like? I can do pancakes or bacon and eggs."

"Both sound great. Whatever you and the girls want," Mike replied. "Surprise me."

He got up, took a shower, and got himself dressed. He trotted down the stairs and into the kitchen. Brittany was frying up some bacon and sausages and a pan full of scrambled eggs. Besides many other talents she was a pretty good cook. There was, of course, the time she tried to make the chocolate soufflé. It seemed she had opened the oven too early and the soufflé had collapsed. It was totally flat.

It was still the source of occasional family jokes.

Mike and the girls would sometimes sing, "Beware of the blob" from an old sci-fi movie and tease her. Brittany would laugh it off.

Mike grabbed some plates from the shelf and began to set the table.

"Girls, can you get some silverware from the drawer?"

"Okay, Daddy." The girls were always eager to please their mom and dad and jumped into action.

Breakfast was soon ready and they all took their places at the table.

"So, how is everything at school, girls?" Brittany asked. "Have you made any new friends?"

"They're the same as last year, Mom," Jamie replied. Jamie had just turned nine years old and was now in the fourth grade.

Roni was a year younger.

"What about you, Roni?" Brit followed up.

"There are some new kids in the class. I'm just starting to know them," said Roni.

The girls did occasionally have friends over. There was Rachel from down the block and Tony from across the street. The four of them sometimes played in the woods behind the house with the family dog, a yellow lab. Jamie had named the dog Kardashian because she liked to chase cars.

Mike thought that was hysterical.

Truth was that Jamie and Roni were inseparable best friends and spent most of their time together. Brittany wished that they would make more friends but was not overly concerned. When Roni was born, she became sick. She had contracted pneumonia, mostly due to the negligence of the hospital. There was a virus going around and many of the elderly patients were infected. Roni caught it almost immediately. Her breathing had been labored and she had spent the first two weeks of her young life aided by an oxygen tent. She overcame it and was now perfectly healthy, but it had an effect on her early years. As a result, the family had always been somewhat protective of Roni… especially Jamie.

Mike stretched his arms over his head, looked out of the window, sat back for a moment and reflected on how lucky he was. Mike was a computer systems wizard and specialized in accounting and banking software. Many financial institutions now relied on the software he had helped to develop for their systems.

Things were going well.

Five years earlier Mike had been given the choice of working in New York City or moving to the company branch upstate just west of Albany. He and Brit had talked it over and they had decided on upstate even though the job paid about ten thousand dollars less per year. They both felt that it was a better place to raise the girls and they both had their own love for skiing and outdoor adventure.

Neither of them regretted the decision. Jamie, Roni and his wife Brittany were the best thing that could have ever happened to Mike, and he knew it. Things were not always so bright for him. In his early college years, he could have gone either way. Mike sometimes hung out with some wild friends and a few very questionable girlfriends. It was Brittany who had lured him away and toward success and happiness. They had gotten married when Mike was only a senior in college. Their first child was on the way before he even graduated school. Brittany had stayed at home and raised the two girls until Roni was ready for school. The last eight years had been more than he ever could have hoped for.

Mike loved where he lived. It was almost four years since he had moved into his new home with Brittany and the girls. The house was near the edge of the woods and there was an unobstructed view of the hills a quarter mile away. Mike and Brittany both loved the outdoors and had raised their daughters to appreciate nature as well.

The view through the picture window was like a postcard. It was early October and the leaves had exploded into color. The hills had become a beautiful tapestry of fiery reds, yellow, orange and green. The rain from the previous night gave the wet leaves an electric glow. A path led from the back of the house toward the woods and could be seen rising into the hills.

It was like an invitation to paradise.

After they had finished breakfast, Jamie ran to let the dog out of the extra room near the garage. Kardashian ran into the kitchen and greeted them all with overly enthusiastic jumping, licking and tail wagging. Of course, there was the mandatory bacon strip that Roni had carefully concealed under the table.

Kardashian gobbled it down as if it were trying to escape.

Roni took another piece of bacon off her plate and tried her best not to be obvious. Mike smiled and winked at Roni as if it were their special secret.

Brittany did not approve of feeding the dog at the table. She glanced over at Roni with a disapproving eye roll.

Roni flashed an impish smile, put her hands up in the air and said, "What?"

Mike and Brittany had raised their two daughters well. There were some hard and fast rules but they did make some allowances. Feeding the dog at the table was not a battle they chose to fight. The girls cleared the table and the four of them got ready for their Sunday walk. Brittany had prepared sandwiches for lunch and packed them in Mike's backpack.

Roni grabbed a tennis ball. Kardashian was almost psychotic when it came to playing her role as a retriever. Jamie opened the back door and they all headed outside. Before they could even set a foot on the porch Kardashian raced past them as if her tail were on fire. Mike put on the backpack and locked the door behind them.

They started toward the woods with the dog far in front and the girls running behind.

Mike gave his wife a big kiss on the cheek and said, "I love you, Brit."

"Love you, too."

The two of them walked slowly toward the hill.

Brittany called out, "Slow down, girls. Don't get too far ahead."

It was a perfect morning, with a promise of sunshine and warmer than usual temperatures. The morning dew still clung to the tall grass and a light mist still danced playfully in the trees, helping nature carry its own patented perfume. The smell of wet grass filled their senses and a faint smell of pine hung in the air as they approached the woods.

"I can't believe they're thinking about developing this place," sighed Brittany.

"It won't be for at least a few years," replied Mike, reassuring her. "We have it for the moment. Let's enjoy it while it's still here."

"Of course. You're right. You know, we can always burn down any new houses they try to build," joked Brit.

The two of them laughed and walked on. They reached the edge of the woods and paused for a moment.

Mike drew a deep breath and allowed the aroma of pine to fill his lungs. He took Brit's hand and they continued to walk on.

Beneath their feet was a carpet of newly fallen leaves and pine needles. The cool morning breeze played with Brit's hair as she turned and smiled. She was absolutely beautiful, even without makeup. Mike was tempted to tackle her and spend the day right there frolicking in the leaves, and would have done so were it not for the girls.

After a few minutes they arrived at the foot of the hill and the path began to rise. They could see the girls about fifty yards ahead, climbing steadily upward. Kardashian was racing back and forth, stopping occasionally to get some affection from Jamie and Roni.

"Slow down a little, girls. Wait for us," shouted Brit.

The girls pretended not to hear and continued to race up the hill.

About twenty minutes later Mike and Brittany reached the top of the hill, where they found the two girls waiting for them.

"What took you so long?" mocked Jamie. "You guys are as slow as molasses."

"Yeah. We thought you got lost," Roni added.

"Very funny, girls," retorted Brit.

From here the trail was level and followed the top of the hill for about three miles. For the first mile they could see the development in which they lived about two hundred feet below. It was called Forest Park. All the streets were named after trees. Mike and Brit's house was 42 Birch Street. It was one of two streets that bordered the woods. When they had company over there was always the inevitable comment on how nice it was to have a house on the edge of the woods. Mike would always reply that he liked living on the edge and Brit would roll her eyes. She had heard it several thousand times already.

The four of them walked along together. Soon the houses were out of sight and the trail became less obvious. Mike and Brit talked about their plans for the future. Brit had a steady job as a marketing consultant. She was also a licensed real estate broker.

The girls took turns throwing the ball for Kardashian to retrieve. Every once in a while, Jamie would pretend to throw the ball and hold onto it instead. In the past the dog would fall for it but she was now getting wise.

About two hours later they arrived at their destination. The trail ended in a clearing overlooking a pristine lake. It was the perfect place for a picnic. The sun was high in the sky now and the temperature was a comfortable 70 degrees. They spent the next hour there enjoying nature and each other's company and playing hide and seek. Mike and Brit would take turns hiding in the woods and it was Kardashian's job to track them down.

The day passed on and it was now about two in the afternoon.

"What kind of sandwich would you like?" asked Brit. "I have ham and cheese or chicken salad."

"Chicken salad," all three called out at once.

"Well, I have two of each."

"I'm having chicken salad," Mike insisted. He made a face and stuck his tongue out at his daughters.

"Oh Daddy," Jamie moaned and stuck her tongue out at him in retaliation.

Roni giggled and said, "You're so silly, Daddy."

Brit just smiled.

Of course, Mike relented and settled for the ham and cheese.

After lunch they took one more look at the lake and Jamie took some pictures with her cell phone. They then started back home. By the time they arrived it was after five o'clock. The sun was still just visible above the hills. It was the end to what had been a perfect afternoon. They all walked back together through the woods and across the field. As they approached their house Kardashian suddenly turned and began to bark in the direction of the woods.

"What's the matter, girl? Is there a raccoon or a bear out there? What's out there, girl?"

Kardashian continued to bark and run nervously back and forth behind the house.

Mike unlocked the door and they proceeded inside.

"Come on, girl," insisted Mike. The dog reluctantly obeyed.

That evening the girls did their homework and after dinner they all sat down for an hour of television and some well-earned rest and relaxation. Mike and Brit suffered through the end of a Harry Potter movie they had already seen at least twice before. After the movie the girls got ready for bed and kissed their parents good night. They were asleep within minutes. Mike and Brit spent the next two hours watching TV and fooling around on the couch. They then headed for the bedroom.

The next morning Brit awoke to the music of Kitaro. It was mood music and reminded her of being in the mountains. She called to the girls to get up and get ready for school.

Mike's feet also hit the floor and they all went through their routine. It was just after seven. The girls would catch the bus for school at 8:15 AM. It conveniently stopped about 20 yards away. In the afternoon the bus would drop them off at 3:10 PM sharp. Rachel's mom, Mrs. Avery, who lived down the block, would look after them until Brit returned home at 4:30 PM. Mike had to be at the office at 9:00 AM. He had to leave the house at about the same time as the girls. Brittany's hours were somewhat more flexible and she could wait until the girls were on the bus before she left for work.

After breakfast Mike got his attaché case. The girls grabbed their cell phones, backpacks and books. Brittany accompanied them all outside. Mike kissed his wife and daughters goodbye and jumped into his car. He pulled out of the driveway and drove down Birch street ..... totally unaware of the binoculars on the hill that were following his every move.

CHAPTER 3

Monday, Oct. 4, 7:06 AM

FBI Headquarters, Boston, Mass.

Don Corlino walked down Atlantic Avenue and through the doors of Boston's FBI headquarters. Don had been an agent for ten years and had been promoted two years earlier. He was now a detective in the homicide and major crimes division.

"Good morning, Steve."

Steve Hronin worked the front desk at night and was just ending his shift.

"Yeah," Steve grunted facetiously. "Another beautiful day in downtown Boston."

Don continued down the hall toward the elevator.

"Hold the door," he yelled to his friend Benny, running the last few steps. "Thanks, buddy. How was the weekend?"

"You know… the usual … The wife… the kids. It's all good. How about yourself?"

"Cheryl and I had dinner and caught a movie. Some chick-flick. Forgot the name of it already."

"When you gonna marry that girl? What's it been? Almost three years now?" asked Benny.

"One of these days, I guess. I really haven't thought about it seriously yet."

"Isn't she starting to drop hints? A girl can't wait forever and she's got plenty to offer."

"Yeah, I know. You're right. I probably should give it more thought," agreed Don.

Benny just laughed and said, "Sure… sure… sure."

The elevator door opened on the third floor and the two of them stepped out into their office.

"Catch up to you later," said Don as he walked toward his desk. On the way he stopped and poured himself a cup of coffee from a freshly brewed pot. He took the paper from under his arm and casually began reading the headlines of the *Boston Globe*.

He sat down and rested his head in his hands, staring at the stack of dossiers in front of him. It was Monday morning and it had been a busy weekend. Don had been assigned to investigate the disappearance of a bank executive and his wife.

George Barnett, the FBI coordinator for the Boston area, tapped him on the shoulder and tossed another folder on his desk.

"Jack wants you to look at this one right away. A body was found Sunday night. Female, late twenties-early thirties. She was found by some kids in a remote wooded area in Hyde Park near Milton off Route 138. Best guess is she's been dead about a week. Hard to say until the M.E. finishes examining her, but at first look it fits the description of Jennifer Reardon. If it is, the FBI is gonna handle it."

"Who was the lead detective on the scene?"

"Eddie McGowan," replied George. "I hear he's a good man. They want you to work together on this one. At least until we can get a positive I.D."

"Do you have a number where I can reach him?"

"Yeah," said George. "He's from the E18 Hyde Park Precinct. Their number is 617-343-5600. But he's probably catching a little sleep right now. He wound up working very late."

"What else can you tell me now?"

George frowned and said, "Her throat was slit. Sound familiar? The John Doe that's still in the morgue? If the M.E. confirms that the same weapon was used in both murders Boston PD is gonna assign a special task force."

"How long until we get a definite on Mrs. Reardon from the M.E.?" asked Don.

"With any luck we'll have a positive I.D. in a couple of hours," replied George.

"All I want to know right now is if it's her. Jack is getting pressure from the big guy and I'm getting it from Jack," complained Don.

"Understood. The M.E. is running a check with dental records as we speak. My money says it's her. The physical description matches and the time frame fits. But who knows? Could be some prostitute that met the wrong guy," suggested George.

Don opened the folder and took out a stack of 8" by 10" glossy photos. First, he looked at the pictures of the crime scene. He studied each one with a keen eye, looking in detail for forensic clues.

"Probably killed at the scene."

George leaned over Don's shoulder, looking at the picture.

"That's what Detective McGowan said. Either she went out there voluntarily or she was forced to walk out there and then butchered."

He then looked at the pictures of the body. That was always the most difficult part of the job.

The pictures revealed a body with significant decomposition. The features were still recognizable as female and confirmed by the long hair. The face suggested a moment of horror and fear. The gaping canyon in her neck showed that her head had been almost completely severed. It was images like this that gave Don nightmares and kept him awake at night. It also caused him to spend some time drinking with his fellow colleagues in the local bars.

Don was one of six detectives that the FBI had assigned to investigate the disappearance of Kevin Reardon and his wife eight days earlier. Technically, Don had a partner, a black man by the name of Tommy Brown. They were both alpha personalities and preferred to work independently. They had agreed, however, to share any relevant information.

"All right," said Don, getting to his feet. "I'm gonna pay a visit to the M.E. I want to know as soon as possible if it's that Reardon girl. Get in touch with Detective McGowan. I'll want to talk to him right away. Give him my number."

"Will do. Tommy is still in Chicago following up on that lead we got about Reardon's business contact. He won't be back until Thursday or Friday. I'll call him if it turns out to be Mrs. Reardon."

"Good, George. I'll give you a heads-up as soon as possible."

Don took his coffee with him and headed for the door. On the way out he walked past Benny's desk.

"What, leaving already? That was quick."

"Gotta run downtown. They might have Mrs. Reardon down at the M.E. at the hospital. I want to know as soon as possible if it's her."

"Catch you later, Don. Go catch the bad guys."

Don skipped the elevator and trotted down the stairs to the parking lot. He jumped into his car, drove down Atlantic Avenue and headed for Boston University Medical Center. Boston traffic on Monday mornings was a bear. After a half hour of torture, he made it to Albany Street and found a spot in a no-parking zone. He put his parking permit on the dashboard and made his way to the Medical Examiner's Office. It was a trip he had made many times in the last two years. Don pushed open the doors to the autopsy room, where he was greeted by the M.E.

"Hello Don."

"Hi Erica. They put you on this one, eh?"

Erika Koenig stood at the autopsy table and meticulously studied the body. She had begun with the wound in the neck and recorded her observations as she spoke into a microphone. She was now working her way down the body, looking for anything that might help I.D. her. She had already checked the teeth and compared them to missing persons' records.

"Here," she said, offering Don a mask to cover his nose.

"Thanks. What can you tell me?"

"Well, I can tell you that she's dead. Also, I can tell you that it's not that banker's wife, Jennifer Reardon. Dental records rule her out."

"I don't know if that's good news or bad," replied Don.

"Well, it's certainly good news for Mrs. Reardon," stated Erika sarcastically.

"How long has she been dead?"

"Best guess is about a week to nine days. After the first four days things get a little more difficult to determine."

"Anything you can use to determine her I.D.?"

"Body's undergone considerable decomp. Fingerprints won't help much. She was no streetwalker. I can tell you that much. Expensive jeans, blouse and shoes. Teeth are in good shape. Looks like she took good care of herself. I talked to Missing Persons but there's no one fitting that description who has gone off the radar in the past two weeks."

"So now we've got a Jane Doe to go with our John Doe," sighed Don.

"For the moment. Something's bound to give us a clue. Boston P.D. is expanding their missing persons search statewide. We're also checking New Hampshire, Vermont, Maine and Connecticut," said Erika encouragingly.

The doors of the autopsy room opened again and Eddie McGowan walked in with Rob Morrow.

"You're Don Corlino, right? They told me you would be here. Eddie McGowan," he said offering his hand. "This is my partner Rob Morrow."

Detective Morrow reached forward and shook Don's hand.

"I'm sure we all know Erika," stated Eddie.

Erica Koenig was the senior M.E. in Boston.

"It's not Jennifer Reardon. We still haven't got an I.D.," said Don, bringing the two detectives up to speed. "What about the murder weapon, Erika? Can you tell us if it's the same weapon used on our John Doe?"

"Nothing conclusive yet. There's too much soft tissue decomp on the male victim. What I can tell you is they were both killed with a very sharp blade. Might be a hunting knife or it could be military issue. The person who did this was right-handed in both cases and probably about five feet, eight inches tall—give or take a couple. They also had to have considerable strength or anger to cut that deep with one pull. Right now, I'd give it better than fifty – fifty it's the same type of knife. But that's speculation.".

Erika continued, "The weapon left some distinctive marks on the neck vertebrae of the male victim. There are also some microscopic metal fragments in both cases. If it left any marks on her I might be able to give you a better guess. It'll take most of the day for me to get that far."

"Okay," said Don. "I guess there's no point hanging around here for now." Don did not like to witness autopsies and the smell was making him gag. "Keep us all posted as soon as you know anything," he added.

"I'll let you know, Don. I've got all your numbers."

"You had breakfast yet?" asked Eddie, turning to Don.

"No, but I'm not real hungry after this. I do want to talk with both you guys. My boss, Jack Sullivan, wants us to cooperate and share information. I'll join you and settle for coffee."

"Okay. You know that little luncheonette up on Concord Street near Washington? What's it called again?"

"Charlie's," Rob chimed in. Rob knew every restaurant and bar in all of Boston.

"See ya later, Erika," said Eddie and the three of them left together.

"You want to follow us?" asked Eddie.

"I'll just punch it into my GPS. See you guys there. I've got your number just in case."

"Okay, give me yours too."

"I'll just call you and you'll have it." Don punched in the number.

"Okay. Got it."

"Give me yours, too, Rob. It's best we all keep in contact."

CHAPTER 4

Charlie's Restaurant, 9:32 AM

Don walked into Charlie's and found Eddie and Rob already seated at a table, each with a cup of coffee in front of them.

"Hey Don. Rob and I have already ordered. Are you sure you don't want something to eat?"

Don wrinkled his nose and said, "Yeah, I'm sure. The smell of a week-old body sort of kills my appetite."

"All right. I get it," sympathized Eddie.

"Look guys. Let's get right to the point. The only reason I was called in was because of Jennifer Reardon. Her disappearance, as well as her husband's, is still being treated as a double kidnapping for now. If the body found in Milford had been hers the FBI would be in charge, but right now this is your case. Still, I think somehow these two cases might be connected," suggested Don.

"Yeah, why's that?" asked Rob.

"Just a hunch. Could be totally wrong. But the Reardons are rich upper-class types. He's a top executive at Lexington Finance. She's pretty well connected with some important people," explained Don. "Nobody's heard anything in eight days. They just dropped off the radar. If they were kidnapped, we would have heard something by now but there's been no ransom note. Nothing! If it was a robbery, they would either be alive or we would have found the bodies. So where are they? Someone wanted to make sure our Jane Doe wasn't found anytime soon."

"That's exactly what we were thinking," agreed Eddie.

"Like I said: could be nothing," said Don, shrugging his shoulders.

"Got to be thorough," said Rob, giving him support.

"Also, we have a John Doe. It's the same in many ways. Slit throat and buried deep in the woods. Again, whoever did it wanted to make sure the body wasn't discovered. The body was found by a guy walking his dog in a very remote area in the woods out toward Westwood. The dog kept whimpering and trying to dig it up from under a pile of rocks. The guy got suspicious and called the police. Again, we were lucky the body was ever found," suggested Don. "The Westwood police department had the body shipped to our M.E here in Boston. They figured we would have better chance of making an identification. If the Reardons aren't being held for ransom and they weren't victims of a mugging then, where are they?"

"I see your point," said Eddie.

"According to Erica this girl was well-dressed and took care of herself. I've checked with Missing Persons at the Bureau and there's no one of that description missing. At least not in Massachusetts. I'm good friends with the head of computers and statistics in that department. I'm gonna try to get them to do a nationwide check on Jane Doe and John Doe as well."

"Sounds like a long shot but if she comes from money like Erika suggested, it might be a little easier," suggested Rob.

"All I want from you guys is for you to keep your eyes open and keep me in on anything that might help. Jack Sullivan, my boss, is getting antsy about this case. He wants something he can give the press. You know how it is," said Don, looking straight at them, knowing they had been there themselves. "All we know is that they disappeared about eight or nine days ago," he added. "They went out to dinner at Terrell's. You know that upscale place in the Back Bay area? They were seen there having dinner and after that, nothing. Their car was found at their house so they were almost certainly abducted there."

"The Reardons have been all over the papers for the last week," remarked Rob.

"Yeah. That's right. Jack wants to keep it as low profile as he can. Of course, we want the public's help on this but the longer the Reardons are in the news, the worse it looks for law enforcement."

"I'll have to say, it's pretty strange," remarked Eddie. "There's been no attempt to extort money. No ransom note. If it's not about money, what's going on?"

"That's been on my mind for the last week," said Don, sounding frustrated.

Breakfast arrived at the table and Rob said, "Thanks Meriam".

He gave her an affectionate wink.

"You're welcome, Rob. Will there be anything for you, sir?" asked Meriam in a soft, sugary voice.

"Just coffee, thanks," replied Don.

Rob looked at Don with a knowing smile on his face. Eddie just shook his head.

Meriam smiled and walked away slowly, moving her hips with just a little more accent than usual. Rob and Don let their eyes follow her all the way to the kitchen. Eddie feigned a disapproving eyeroll.

Meriam was a tall, pretty 24-year-old blond. Nature had blessed her with long legs and thighs that meant business. Her perpetual mischievous smile made guys wonder what was on her mind. She was one of Rob's favorites.

"So... Where were we? Oh right. I'm gonna drop in on Greg Phillips over at Missing Persons. I want this case to be a priority. If you guys could help expedite this with Boston PD, I'd appreciate it."

"We'll do our best, Don," said Eddie. "I feel your sense of urgency on this thing. I've gotta agree. Who knows how many more bodies might be out there?"

"Right now, we've got over 2000 missing persons this year in Massachusetts alone. Most of them are teenage runaways, but a lot of them are still a complete mystery. There are several college students and just ordinary people. It's kind of scary," commented Don.

"Yeah. Makes me sleep really well at night knowing my wife and kids are safe and sound," scoffed Eddie.

"One more thing, Eddie. I know it's standard procedure and I don't mean to tell you guys your business, but I'm under pressure and I need it ASAP. Please see if there are any surveillance cameras on the streets close to the woods down in Milton. Go through anything from about a week ago if they still have it. Also check with parking violations to see if any summonses were issued around that time. It's a long shot but we have nothing else right now and I need anything I can get."

"We're already on it, but it's probably gonna take a lot of man-hours before we find out anything," said Eddie.

"If we find anything," added Rob.

Don called Meriam over and asked for a second cup of coffee.

"Hi. My name is Meriam. I know Eddie and Rob but I haven't met you before."

Don was held captive for a moment by her emerald green eyes. "My name is Don," he managed to get out. "It's nice to meet you."

"My pleasure. I hope you become a regular like these guys. Are you a detective too?"

"Yes. But I'm not Boston PD. I'm with the FBI."

"Oooh… FBI!" said Meriam, sounding impressed as she let her eyes grow larger.

"It's not that special, really," replied Don, trying to appear modest.

"Well, you're always welcome here." she said, holding his eyes as she turned to walk away.

Meriam had a way of encouraging guys to visit Charlie's. Charlie, the owner, had no complaints.

The three of them continued to talk about the case and thought about what else they could do.

Don might have ordered a third cup of coffee but too much made his stomach queasy.

"I know you guys were up most of the night. You're probably running on fumes right now. Let me know if you find something; otherwise, get a good night's sleep tonight and I'll see to you tomorrow."

"Okay, Don. Good hunting. I'll give you a call this afternoon and let you know if anything interesting turns up. We'll check out if there were any parking violations or traffic infractions in that area in the last week. As for those cameras, it's going to take some time to go through all that tape. If we knew what we were looking for it would be easier but this is just random."

"I know," said Don. "It's like looking for the proverbial needle in a fucking haystack."

Don gulped down the rest of his coffee, took one last look at Meriam, said goodbye to Rob and Eddie and walked out the door.

Eddie and Rob continued to eat their breakfast and began to plan the rest of the day.

"I'm dead dog tired," complained Eddie, "but I guess we should get started on this right away. The longer we wait the colder the trail is going to get. What do you say we get back to the office? We can get Sarah to upload the surveillance camera footage from the Internet. That's gonna take some time. Meanwhile we can start with the DMV and check out parking tickets."

Rob rolled his eyes and sighed. "Sounds thrilling. This is the kind of excitement I was told about when I decided to become a detective."

Eddie laughed and said, "Yeah. Enough to drive you to drink."

Rob came back with, "My mother always worries that I might get shot, but I think I'm gonna die of disgust or just plain boredom long before that."

Eddie reached into the front pocket of his pants and pulled out his wallet. "I think it's my turn to pay," he offered.

"Gee, I think you're right," replied Rob, trying to sound convincing. "I'll leave the tip."

Eddie had been married for nineteen years. Happily, for the most part. He had a daughter in college and two younger sons. Eddie was totally faithful to his wife, Lisa. He appreciated looking at girls but never considered crossing the line.

Rob, on the other hand, was single and made a point of flirting with every girl he met. He had a square jaw and good old Irish charm. He did quite well with women in general. He had acquired quite a reputation in the department as a ladies' man. He had also been reprimanded for showing up late on Monday morning on more than one occasion. He was, however, an excellent detective and had been cited several times for his performance in the field. It was his hard work that broke the case in a double homicide two years earlier. In spite of his transgressions, he had a great deal of respect among his fellow detectives.

Rob called Meriam over to the table and said, "We're ready to settle up, sweetheart. You know I'd love to stay longer but we've got a real busy day. Leaving you is always difficult, but Eddie told me he would beat me up if I didn't come with him right away."

Eddie rolled his eyes and looked at Meriam with incredulity.

Meriam laughed and said, "I'll miss you too, guys."

She batted her eyes at Rob and planted a kiss on his cheek.

The tab was $32.56 and Eddie put thirty-five dollars on the table. Rob put a crisp new ten on the table and said, "Keep the change, Meriam."

Eddie and Rob headed for the door.

Before they reached it, Meriam called to them in her most seductive voice, "Come back soon, boys. Promise me."

"You can count on us," said Rob proudly, giving her a wink and a smile. The two detectives walked through the door and turned the corner. Rob looked through the window. His eyes never left Meriam until she disappeared into the kitchen.

· · · · ·

Mike stopped at the 7-11 convenience store and poured himself a cup of coffee to keep him company on his ride to work. He picked up a copy of the *Times Union,* a popular Albany paper, and proceeded to the checkout counter.

"Good Morning, Raj."

"Good morning, Mr. Davis. No corn muffin today?" asked Raj with a strong Indian accent.

"No. I seem to put on weight every fall. I've got to be more careful and watch what I eat," sighed Mike.

"I know," said Raj, patting his chubby stomach and widening his eyes. "I should do the same."

Mike smiled, paid for his coffee and paper.

"See you tomorrow, Raj," he said and walked out the door.

Mike drove his Subaru Outback down Route 90 toward Albany, taking in the colorful foliage on the way. His commute took about 45 minutes. He arrived at his company, Affirmed Software, and turned into the driveway. He parked his car in the lot, grabbed his attaché case and the newspaper and walked through the front door.

"Good morning, Mike," said Diane cheerfully greeting him as he walked inside.

"Good morning, Diane," echoed Mike.

"How was the weekend?" she asked.

"It was delightful. I had a great time with Brit and the kids. How was yours?"

"I went out to a show with my new boyfriend. I think I'm falling in love."

"Sounds wonderful, Diane. I'm happy for you. Is Donna here yet?" asked Mike.

Donna was Mike's secretary.

"Yes. She's in your office getting everything ready for your meeting with Danson and Lawrence."

"Okay, great. Are you coming with us for lunch today?"

"Of course, I am," she replied, smiling sweetly at Mike.

Lunch was a regular thing on Mondays and Fridays for Mike, Donna and Diane.

Mike walked down the hall and into his office.

"Good morning, Mike."

"Good morning, Donna."

They asked each other the usual questions about the weekend and proceeded to get down to the business of the day. The meeting was scheduled for ten o'clock. Danson & Lawrence started as one of their smaller accounts but had grown significantly in recent years. They had requested certain custom modifications to the software that would allow them to accommodate special clients and facilitate the transfer of funds. Mike was one of four software engineers in the firm and it was his assignment to make the necessary changes. It was easy for him to do. He was one of the best in his field.

At 10 AM the representative from Danson & Lawrence appeared at Mike's office. He introduced himself as Aaron Williams and said, "Good morning, Mr. Davis. It's nice to finally meet you."

Aaron was a software specialist for his corporation and had heard a great deal about Mike.

"Call me Mike," he offered with a smile.

The two of them discussed the modifications to the software for the next couple of hours until their business was completed. Mike invited Aaron to join him for lunch with his two regular companions. Aaron said he would love to but politely said no and explained he was running on a tight schedule.

Mike gave him an estimate as to when the new software would be ready to install and told Aaron to contact him if there were any questions. They shook hands and concluded the meeting.

At 12:30 Mike told his secretary, "Go tell Diane we're ready for lunch."

The three of them decided on Italian food and went to Angelino's a few miles down the road. Donna and Diane both loved Mike. He was very generous and had a way of making them laugh with his corny sense of humor.

After lunch Mike offered to pick up the check.

"Oh Mike, you're too good to us," complained Donna with a chuckle and a smile.

Diane agreed and thanked him heartily.

After lunch Mike called Brittany as he always did. The phone rang and Brittany answered.

"Hi Britski. How's everything going with you?"

"The usual. Just the same accounts I've been working on the past few months. Then of course, there's Mrs. Cooper. She's this sweet old 85-year-old lady who doesn't understand that we're a large company with major accounts. She keeps calling me to get my advice on how to market her little

Christmas and Valentine's Day Cards. I don't have the heart to send her away. I'm trying to help her set up a website. She's so adorable, Mike. I wish you could meet her."

"She can't be as adorable as you, sweetheart. Nobody is."

"Oh Mike. Are you trying to play me? Did you do something you need to apologize for? What did you do, Mike? Did you buy yourself something we can't afford? Just kidding. I really do appreciate that you appreciate me. Just to prove it I'll make you something special for dinner. When will you be home?"

"I'm not sure yet. If I don't have to work too late tonight, I should be outta here just after six. Figure about seven o'clock."

"Okay honey. I'll see you then," Brit replied. "I love you," she added.

"Right back at ya."

CHAPTER 5

Don walked into the Missing Persons division of the FBI.

"Hi Toni. Is Greg here?" he asked the receptionist.

"Yes, he is. He's downstairs right now. I know he's still busy with the Reardon case. He checks every new case that comes in. He's trying to match up anything that fits the Reardon's description. I assume that's why you're here."

"Yup. Jack is pretty hot on this one."

"He's doing a nationwide search. I can't believe how many unidentified bodies are out there," said Toni with a disconcerted look.

"They've sent Mrs. Reardon's dental records to every Medical Examiner in the country now. Either she's being held against her will or the body has been very well concealed. That's why I want to see Greg. If the Reardons are still alive every minute counts."

"Okay. I'll buzz him and let him know you're coming down."

Don trotted down the stairs and into the computer room, where he found Greg.

"Don Corleone. Welcome to my house. Please be seated, Godfather," said Greg, putting on his best Marlon Brando voice. Greg always greeted him this way when he had cause to drop in.

Don would usually laugh but this time he took a more serious tone. "Hi Greg. Where do we stand?"

"Kinda busy right now. You guys a-make-a me crazy," Greg replied, gesturing with his hands and still trying to sound Italian.

"Well, sorry, but it's gonna get worse," replied Don.

"Shit. Okay what is it now?"

"We've got two bodies at the M.E. No ID. Both victims killed the same way and found deep in the woods. I have a hunch they may be connected to the Reardon case."

"No shit. Really?"

"Well, think about it. There's no ransom note or attempt at extortion. We haven't heard anything. There's no trace of either of them. I haven't put all the pieces together, but I suspect the worst. I'm having the M.E. send over dental records. I want you to put them on the computer and put out a nationwide alert."

"Did Jack OK this as a priority?"

"Not yet, but I'll convince him. Trust me. When I give him my theory, he'll go for it."

"Well, I'll try."

"Also..." added Don apologetically.

"Oh God. There's something more?"

"I want to know of any cases nationwide that involve unsolved murders where the victims had their throats slashed. I need an account of all cases in the last six months."

"Jesus, Don! We're already stretched thin. We keep asking for more personnel and funds."

"Please, Greg. It's important."

"Okay Don. I'm crazy busy but I'll get on it. Only because it's you, Godfather. It's going to take about an hour before I can compile it and send it to your email."

"Thanks, Greg. I owe you one."

"Dinner would be nice," suggested Greg.

"Little busy right now, Greg."

"So make me an offer I can't refuse."

"I'll think of something. I gotta run right now. Thanks again, Greg."

It would be at least an hour before he could do anything constructive so Don decided to take a walk in Malone Park. The sun had warmed the air and it was a beautiful day. He knew that soon he would be stuck at his desk trying to put the pieces of the puzzle together. He could use the downtime. Don walked outside, took a deep breath of crisp autumn air and strolled down Spruce Street toward the park.

He took out his cell and decided to call Erika to see if there was anything new.

Erika picked up the phone and stated, "Medical Examiner. Erica Koenig speaking."

"Hi Erika. Sorry to bother you so soon, but I'm trying to get this case moving as quickly as possible. Anything new you can tell me?" implored Don.

"I was able to examine the wound to her neck more thoroughly. I could identify several distinctive marks on the vertebrae where the knife left an impression. I've put them under the microscope. The body of the male victim was, of course, much larger. The female's head was almost completely severed, but the knife didn't cut quite as deep with our male victim so it may not be easy to make a correlation. We also sent some hair samples to the DNA lab for analysis. I found some strands that didn't match hers. It's going to take time, Don. It will take at least a day before the DNA test comes back and at least a few hours to complete my autopsy. I'm trying to determine if the same weapon was used from the soft tissue. Believe me, if I can give you anything new, you'll be the first to know."

"Okay. Thanks, Erica. I'm sorry to be such a pain in the ass."

"That's okay, Don. I understand completely. Let me get back to work now. Goodbye."

Don entered the park and walked toward the flower gardens. The park was beautiful at this time of year and he wished that he could just blow off the whole day. For the next half hour, he walked aimlessly around and took in the sights and sounds of people enjoying themselves. A young couple ran by, laughing and smiling. A girl had stolen her boyfriend's hat and playfully held it behind her back, taunting him to try to get it back. It was nice to see people so happy. There were still good things in the world, he thought to himself. After a while he found a bench in the sun where he could relax. He thought about calling McGowan but it was still too early for that. Don let his thoughts wander. He thought about his girlfriend Cheryl. He was always happier when she was around. She had a way of bringing calm and stability to his life. The past two weeks had been rough. He could tell that the long hours he was putting in were beginning to affect their relationship. They were still good but how long would that last? Cheryl was a strong girl and understood Don's commitment to his job. She wasn't interested in expensive dinners or presents. She was never concerned with social status or fancy cars and big houses. If he was going to get married, she would be the one. Still, they were spending less and less time together and he could see the unhappiness beginning to show in her eyes and her mood. To her credit, she said nothing. Don thought to himself that when this case was resolved he would take off some time and surprise her with a two-week Hawaiian vacation. A smile began to grow on his lips as he thought about getting away.

Don's phone rang to the tune of "Missing you," an old John Waite song.

"Hi Greg. What have you got?"

"So far nothing on those dental records. It's not like fingerprints. The computer has a database that can analyze them automatically. Dental records are different. They need a person to actually compare them. X-rays are taken from different angles and our computers are not yet sophisticated enough to match them. Especially if it's been a few years and the victim had dental work done. But I have a list of murders where a knife was involved and there were severe injuries to the throat."

"Okay. How many?"

"Nationwide, 86 in the last six months. Most of them were solved. We've got 42 still on the grill. And get this: Besides the two in the morgue, four others were in Massachusetts, one was in Vermont, one in New Hampshire, one in Connecticut, one in Rhode Island, six in New York, and five in New Jersey. That's twenty-two bodies in the New England area. That's more than half of all the cases. May just be coincidence. Maybe not."

"It's definitely worth looking into. I'm surprised no one raised an eyebrow sooner," lamented Don.

"Funding and personnel, Don. Computers are great but somebody's got to sit down and analyze the data. We have 'red flags' that will alert us for suspected terrorist activities but that's not going to help us in this case. Truth is since 9-11 we've turned most of our resources in that direction. Chemical sales … money transfers … Internet communication … encrypted files. It all takes time. We're just plain overwhelmed."

"I hear ya, Greg. Everyone is stretched thin. Can you get me a detailed report on those 42 unsolved murders? I'll also need photographs of the crime scene and the bodies."

"Already done. I've sent hard copies to your office."

"One last thing, Greg. I need a list of all the women between 20 and 35 reported missing in Massachusetts and all the bordering states."

"That I can do for you. Should be ready in an hour. Two at most," promised Greg. "I've sent all the basic info on the unsolved murders to your email. I'll update it as soon as I can."

"Thanks, Greg. I really appreciate it."

"I am honored to be at your service, Don Corleone. May your first child be a masculine one."

"Talk to ya soon," replied Don with a sigh.

He hung up and called McGowan. The phone rang twice and Eddie picked up.

"McGowan."

"Hi, Eddie. This is Don. Did you check with parking violations yet?"

"Yep. Checked a window from twelve days ago till four days ago. We looked at summonses that were issued on streets that bordered the woods or anything close by. We have about fifty violations. There aren't a lot of parking restrictions in that area before five o'clock PM. If you want, I'll fax the plate numbers and vehicle descriptions to your office."

"That would be great. How's it going with the surveillance cameras?"

"I have a couple of officers looking at them right now. We have to go pick up some of the tapes from private businesses. Some gas stations and convenience stores on Brush Hill Rd. I'm on my way down there myself. It's gonna take a while to round them all up. But remember, Don, even if we get more tapes it's going to take hours to go through them all. We have to have some idea of what we're looking for. We just don't have that kind of manpower."

"Understood, Eddie."

"How's it going on your end?"

"I'm heading back to my office. I have 42 unsolved murders to look through. If I find a connection, you'll be the first to know."

"Okay, Don. Good hunting."

That was Eddie's usual sign off whenever he was working together with someone on a case.

"You too," replied Don.

CHAPTER 6

Police Headquarters Precinct E18 Hyde Park, 10:40 AM

Eddie and Rob drove from Charlie's back to their precinct headquarters in South Boston. They walked through security and greeted Sergeant Kinnear at the front desk.

"Good morning, Chris," said Eddie.

"Good morning, detectives. Jimmy is looking for you."

"No surprise there," said Rob. "He's gonna ask us to work overtime until this case is cracked."

"All part of what you signed up for," Eddie came back.

"Good luck, guys," said Chris.

Rob was only thirty-two years old, very young for a homicide detective. He was moved quickly up the ladder for his excellent performance when he was a rookie cop. He was instrumental in breaking a high-profile case that had stumped several detectives. He had followed up on a lead that led to the arrests of two suspects that had committed several armed robberies in the Hyde Park Precinct. Morrow had a reputation for being tenacious. He had even been honored by the mayor on television.

Eddie and Rob walked into Jimmy Dugan's office expecting the usual pep talk and spiel about how this case was special. They had heard it all a hundred times. Was any day really different from another. Both of them always gave it a hundred percent. Jimmy had a way of making his detectives feel guilty if they did anything less.

"Good morning, detectives. I know you guys are already assigned to this case but some special circumstances have presented themselves. I want you to work with the FBI in solving this Jane Doe case. This is a high priority and I need your total dedication. I'm sure you guys will give it your best effort."

Eddie and Rob just looked at each other and back at Jimmy.

"Of course," they both said at the same time.

"I got a call from Jack Sullivan over at the Bureau. Apparently one of their detectives assigned to the Reardon case thinks that this case might somehow be connected," continued Jimmy. "His name is Don Corlino."

"We're way ahead of you, Jimmy," said Eddie. "We met him this morning at the M.E.'s office. He explained his theory about Jane Doe's connection to the Reardon case. I don't know if he's right but it seems to be worth looking into."

"Okay then. Let's jump to it. The mayor is up my ass on this. He wants something yesterday if not sooner."

They made their way to their desks, knowing full well what was in store for the remainder of the day. Detective Morrow took his place at his desk, keyed in his password and accessed the Traffic Violations Bureau.

Eddie checked the in-basket at his desk and then walked over to the computer center to put in a request with Sarah, the crime lab's computer and Internet specialist.

"Hi Sarah. I've got an urgent request for you. I need you to upload all video surveillance from cameras in the Blue Hills Reservation area in Milton. I also need you to find out if there are any other cameras in the area that can't be accessed by the Internet. I need a list of those cameras ASAP. I'll be at my desk. Please let me know when you're done. I promise I'll treat you to lunch real soon.

"No need for that, Eddie. This is my job. It won't take too long. The State Motor Vehicle operated surveillance cameras were uploaded last night when we got the news about Jane Doe. We have a whole data bank already, but it's going to take some time for me to track down private commercial cameras. I'm sure there are gas stations and stores that keep that footage for some time, but after ten days it might be iffy. I'll do my best. I'm gonna have to start making phone calls to those local stores and gas stations."

"Okay. Thanks a million, Sarah. You're the best. And don't make me twist your arm about lunch."

"Okay. Okay," said Sarah, looking up from her computer with a smile.

Eddie walked back to his desk which faced Rob's and said, "Where we at?"

"I began a search for summonses issued in the Milton area during the week of September 20 through September 28. There are four roads that border the Blue Hills Reservation that are close to where the body was found. I narrowed the search for Canton Avenue, Blue Hills River Road, Unquity Road and Hillside Street. There were thirty-eight parking summonses issued during that period that need to be checked out."

"Good," said Eddie. "We'll start there. We should probably also check out summonses for speeding, but that will have to wait."

"Right. Let's run the plates with the DMV and match them with some names. Here's a list of plate numbers that have been issued summonses."

Rob gave half the list to Eddie and they began entering them into the computer. After a few minutes they had come up with a list of names.

"Okay. Let's cross reference these names with the database of known felons," said Eddie.

He punched in the search parameters and the computer started doing its thing. After about thirty seconds a message came up on the screen that said NO MATCHES FOUND. It had turned up nothing.

"Strike one," sighed Rob, sounding disappointed.

"Let's widen the search for arrests of any kind," said Eddie.

Rob punched in the information and waited for the results. This search turned up four DWI arrests. One of the drunk drivers had two DWIs and also had several misdemeanor arrests for domestic violence, drunk and disorderly, as well as resisting arrest. Morrow wrote down the name Peter Robertson.

"Well, this will probably lead to a dead end, but we need to be thorough," Rob said.

Eddie and Rob both knew that good detective work was often tedious and frustrating and they had very little else to go on. They decided it would be a waste of time and resources to personally interview everyone so they got the home and mobile numbers of all those on the list.

Eddie and Rob prepared themselves for a long day.

Rob took half the names, put his feet up on his desk and began making phone calls. He began with the following questions:

"Why were you at the Blue Hills Reservation in Milford?"

"How long were you there?"

"Were you alone or with someone else?"

This was followed up by:

"Did you see anything suspicious or out of the ordinary?"

"Do you remember seeing a dark-haired girl about twenty-five to thirty, wearing blue jeans and a black blouse, possibly accompanied by a man?"

Almost all the explanations were that they were hiking or jogging in the area. Some people were taking pictures of the beautiful fall foliage that this area was famous for. Most of the violations were issued during the day between 10 AM and 4 PM. No one remembered seeing anything suspicious and couldn't remember if they had seen a girl of that description. After three hours and several more cups of coffee they were no closer to a lead than they had been that morning. They had spoken to all but six of the people on the list. They either had their cells turned off or too busy to pick up. There were also three additional summonses that had been issued to rental cars. Two were from Enterprise and one from Avis. They could not get the personal information directly from the DMV. They would have to get their identities from the rental companies. They had saved Peter Robertson, the drunken wife abuser, till last.

"What's the date on that summons issued to Mr. Robertson?" asked Eddie.

"September 25," answered Rob. "And its time of issue was 10PM. Maybe we should check this one out in person."

Meanwhile Sarah had successfully uploaded all the surveillance videos and had a list of eight private cameras from the stores and gas stations on the roads bordering the reservation.

Eddie assigned a couple of rookie cops to look at the tapes and write down anything that might be useful. He told them to make a note of any girl wearing blue jeans and a black shirt. He also told them, if possible, to write down the plate numbers of any cars, but this was an enormous task. He told them to concentrate their efforts on September 24 through 26. That was the M.E.'s best estimate of time of death so far. If Erika Koenig could give a more precise TOD they might again be able to narrow their search. At this point they were grasping at straws for any possible lead.

CHAPTER 7

FBI Headquarters, 12:15 PM

Don tried to think of any other possible ways he could throw more light on the Reardon case. That was what his actual assignment was supposed to be. For all he knew, these murders weren't even related. He then went back to the list Greg had sent him and began the long, arduous task of trying to put the pieces together.

Might as well begin with Massachusetts, he thought.

He opened the dossier for the most recent murder.

The document described a man in his early thirties. He had been found in an alley in one of Boston's more notorious crime districts. The victim was described as a homeless man and was probably murdered over something trivial like a bottle of cheap booze. Don looked at the photograph of the knife wound. It was a single stab to the jugular. There were also stab marks to the abdomen.

Probably not connected to the current investigation, thought Don.

He set it aside and began with the next case.

The case involved a man and a woman found in a car north of Worcester.

The dossiers contained a standard federal form which had to be submitted to the CDC. There were also county and state forms. The basic M.E. forms from different counties and states were all very much alike, with only a few variations. They all gave a description of the deceased including age, height, weight, eye color, hair color and cause of death. The county forms gave more detailed information such as distinguishing characteristics, occupations, and marital status. A brief synopsis of the lead detective and description of the victim and cause of death was included in each dossier.

The report described the victims as two illegal immigrants from Honduras. Following their murder, they had been linked to a cocaine smuggling operation. The wounds on their necks did not seem to match up closely to those on the bodies currently in the morgue.

Just a drug deal gone wrong, he thought.

Don set it aside.

The next dossier concerned the body that was now in the morgue at Boston University. It described a man in his 60s. No identification had been made and the body was listed as a John Doe. The body had been found under a pile of rocks in a rural area near Westwood not far from Boston. Don was almost certain the murder in Milton was tied to this one. The attempt to conceal the body and weapon used were too much of a coincidence to ignore. Somebody clearly had a definite M.O.

Definitely have to drive out to Westwood and talk to Detective Cluff, thought Don.

Lead Detective: Gary Cluff	Date 9/29 2021
Name	Unknown
Age	60-70
Height	5' 11"
Weight	85 lbs.

Hair	Gray
Eyes	Brown
Cause of Death	Cardiac arrest due to blood loss

He began to read the last case that had taken place in Massachusetts. The body was that of a male in his fifties. He was found on a lake shore just north of Amesbury, close to the New Hampshire border. The wounds on the neck were similar to the latest victims, but there had been no attempt to conceal the body. It had been discovered by two fishermen in a boat not more than a day after the time of death. It just didn't fit the same M.O. but he began to read the M.E.'s report anyway.

Lead Detective: John Palmer	Date 7/7/ 2021
Name	Joseph Baylin
Age	52
Height	5' 11"
Weight	185 lbs.
Hair	Grey
Eyes	Brown
Cause of Death	Exsanguination

Don rested his head in his palms and massaged his temples with his fingers. Frustrated, he thought, *Maybe none of these murders has anything to do with Jane Doe at all. It's even less likely that they're connected to the Reardon case. Still, I've got nothing else. Even if they're not related there's nothing wrong with following up on every clue. If nothing else, maybe I can help solve some other cases.*

Murders were solved all the time by being thorough and chasing down leads. He would ask Erika to send the information to the Haverhill M.E. for comparison of the knife wounds.

Don opened the dossier from New Hampshire and read the description of the victim.

Lead Detective: Kevin Frazier	Date 7/4/ 2021 TOD
	Not Determined
Name	Unknown
Age	Est. 25yrs -30yrs
Height	5' 7"
Weight Est.	130 lbs.
Eyes	N/D
Hair	N/D
Ethnicity	Caucasian
C.O.D.	UD. Probable blood loss

This report described the body of a woman who was yet to be identified. The body was found by a group of hikers on July 4 in the White Mountain National Forest off of Route 302 near Bartlett. It was summer and by the time the body was found there wasn't much left of her. Her eye and hair color could not be determined but DNA tests showed she was definitely Caucasian and probably of Italian-Irish descent. The TOD was determined to be June 5, give or take a week. In spite of the extreme decomposition the deep gash could clearly be seen in the remaining tissue of her neck. After several weeks the leads had dried up and the investigation was put on the back burner. The M.E. handling the case was in Concord. Don added it to his list of information to be exchanged with Erika's office in Boston. He opened the next envelope and read the report.

Lead Detective:	Date 9/22/2021
Michael Behan	
Name	Patricia Nelson
Age	26
Height	5' 5"
Weight	125 lbs.
Eyes	Brown
Hair	Blond
Ethnicity	Caucasian
C.O.D	Exsanguination

The M.E.'s report described a 26-year-old girl from Danbury. Her name was Patricia Nelson. She had been found in a local park behind some maintenance facilities. The body was found approximately 30 hours after the murder by one of the park workers. Don looked at the photographs of the body. She had been placed behind several barrels of chemical detergents but no real attempt had been made to hide the body. She was dressed in Levi blue jeans and a sweater. She had been stabbed twice in the abdomen. Her throat had also been cut and her head was twisted to the side at a grotesque angle. It always bothered Don to look at these pictures. It was the hardest part of the job. It was evident from the amount of blood that the murder had taken place where the body was found. The date of the murder was September 21, only a couple of weeks earlier. Patricia had recently moved from her parents' home and was living with a group of friends in a rented house. She held a job at a restaurant where she was both a waitress and occasional bartender. Her parents, housemates and coworkers had all been interviewed for many hours. Several park workers had also been interrogated but no arrests had been made. A former boyfriend had been questioned but he had an alibi and he was not considered a suspect. She was well known in the area by many local residents as well as patrons of the restaurant. Patricia was not upper class. Nor was she fashionably dressed like Jane Doe. The case was high profile in the Connecticut papers for the past weeks. In that time there had been very little progress. Other than the M.O and the age of the victim there were no obvious similarities.

It's a long shot but it's worth pursuing, thought Don.

He wrote down the name and telephone number of the lead detective:

Michael Behan (203) 589- 7786

Don decided to speak with him later. Once again, he called the M.E.'s office in Danbury and got the wheels rolling for an information exchange with Erika. He put the folder in a separate pile. He continued to examine the dossiers from Vermont, Rhode Island and Maine. After several hours he had eliminated most of them as having possible relevance. There were only three that he put aside for further investigation. No obvious motivation could be determined in the other cases.

Letting out a sigh, he began with the six murders in New York.

Three of the folders were packaged together. He read the cover statement on the package.

Buffalo, N.Y.

The case concerned three victims that had been murdered at the same time. He opened the first one and began to read the M.E.'s report. Something stirred in his mind. The case sounded familiar to him. Three college students had been murdered in a small town near Buffalo. Apparently, they had all been killed during the night in a house that they shared off campus.

Lead Detective: Paul Arnold	Date 5/28/2021
Name	Leslie Anne Parks
Age	21
Height	5' 6"
Weight	120 lbs.
Hair	Dark brown
Eyes	Hazel
Ethnicity	Caucasian (White)
Distinguishing marks	Tattoo - left shoulder - Mermaid
Occupation	Student (SUNY Buffalo)
C.O.D.	Exsanguination

He began to read the description of the crime scene. All three were found in their beds with their throats cut. According to the M.E. the bodies had been discovered by a friend less than 12 hours after they were killed. That put the time of the murders at about three o'clock in the morning. Don looked at the photographs of the first victim, Leslie Anne Parks. The picture showed the body of a girl about twenty years old. Her throat had been cut right down to the bone. She had almost been decapitated. Her T shirt, panties and the bed sheets were soaked with blood. Her eyes were fixed and staring upward toward the ceiling. The report characterized the weapon as a hunting knife of about 12 inches in length. It also stated that the murderer was almost definitely right-handed. No determination of height could be made since the victims were all lying down when they were killed.

Don now recalled reading about the murders back in May. The names sounded familiar to him. It was in all the papers but none of them mentioned exactly how they had been killed.

He took out the file of the second victim. Her name was Angela Manzo.

Name	Angela Manzo
Age	22
Height	5' 9"
Weight	140 lbs.
Hair	Blond
Eyes	Brown
Ethnicity	Caucasian (white)
Distinguishing marks	Tattoo – hip –Snake and Eagle
Occupation	Student (SUNY Buffalo)
C.O.D.	Exsanguination

The description of the crime scene was similar to the first except that it took place in a different room. He looked at the photo of the body. The photo showed the victim on her back with her eyes fixed, staring at the ceiling just like the first girl. Again, her throat had been cut. Her head was pulled back so it showed how deep the knife had cut. The photos showed blood spray on the walls. The body, her clothing and the bed sheets were soaked red with blood.

Don began to read the profiles of the two victims. Both girls were from well-to-do families. They were both Juniors at SUNY in Buffalo and were apparently best friends. Neither girl was employed. Family members, friends and students had all been interviewed. None of them could shed any light on a possible motive. There was no indication of drug dealing or any other illegal activities. The case was at a dead end.

Don opened the file of the third victim, Frank Levick. He read the first page describing the victim.

Name	Frank Levick
Age	25
Height	6' 2"
Weight	185 lbs.
Hair	Brown
Eyes	Brown
Ethnicity	Caucasian (White)
Distinguishing marks	Birthmark left shoulder
Occupation	Student (SUNY Buffalo)
C.O.D.	Exsanguination

In this case the body was found lying face down on the bed. The head was turned to the side with the eyes staring blankly toward the door. Again, the bed was soaked in blood.

Don began to read the investigators report. Multiple sets of fingerprints had been lifted from various objects at the scene. Most had been identified as belonging to friends of the victims. Some were still filed as unknown. There were no witnesses who had reported seeing anything suspicious the night of the murders. Forensic tests indicated that a large amount of blood had been washed away in the shower stall. The clothes dryer also showed traces of blood. Evidently the murderer had taken some time to get cleaned up. Both the shower and the dryer had been wiped clean of any fingerprints.

Don continued to read further. All three victims had gone to a night club called The Light House the evening before the murders. Surveillance footage showed the three of them ordering drinks at the bar. Most of the patrons had been identified and interviewed. Some, however, remained unidentified. Efforts to locate them had been unsuccessful. A security camera at the front entrance had taken photographs of everyone entering the nightclub. Still unidentified was a male who entered wearing his motorcycle helmet. A clear image of his face could not be made from the security camera footage. A second person of interest was a girl who entered wearing a cowboy hat. A clear picture of her face was also not revealed to the camera.

Patrons at the bar had been shown the pictures of both of them and it was determined that they were not regulars. Actually, nobody could recall seeing either of them before. Pictures of both of them had been sent to law enforcement throughout the northeast and Canada.

Don was thinking that this was also a long shot. Buffalo was hundreds of miles from Boston. Again, the only similarities were the M.O. and the age of the victims. The odds of there being a connection was remote. Still, he wrote down the name and number of the lead detective.

Paul Arnold (878) 569- 2243.

Don took out another folder and began to read.

Albany N.Y.

Lead Detective: Dave Connelly	Date 6/3/ 2021
Name	George Weston
Age	23
Height	6'1"
Weight	180 lbs.
Eyes	Blue
Hair	Blond
Distinguishing marks	none
Occupation	Student SUNY Albany
C.O.D.	Exsanguination

The report described the body of a male victim found off State Road 157 near the Thompsons Lake Camping Area. The body was identified as a college student from SUNY Albany named George Weston, age 23, who had been reported missing two days earlier. There had been no attempt to hide body. The M.E. determined that the murder had occurred on the first day of June, 2021. The cause of death had been determined to be a deep cut to the throat. Don looked at the pictures of the body. He determined that there was enough similarity to this wound and the one found on the current victim to merit further investigation. Don continued to read. There were no suspects, motives or witnesses. His friends on campus had been interviewed but no one could shed light on what might have happened. The investigation had run cold. After a month of investigation by the local police and the Albany Police Department the murder had been categorized as a probable robbery and put on hold. Don looked again at the photographs. He decided to put this case on the list.

Don was beginning to tire and his eyes were red from poring over all the reports. There were only two more to go in New York. Exhausted, he pushed on and began to read.

Muttontown, N.Y

Lead Detective: Bill Snyder	**Date 9/18/ 2021**
Name	**Paula Carter.**
Age	**29**
Height	**5' 5".**
Weight	**135 lbs.**
Hair	**Brown .**
Eyes B	**rown.**
Ethnicity	**Caucasian (White).**
Distinguishing marks	**None.**
Occupation	**Professor Hofstra University.**
C.O.D.	**Exsanguination.**

This report described the body of a woman who had been identified as Paula Carter. She was found in Muttontown nature preserve in Nassau County, Long Island. She had been reported missing two weeks earlier by relatives and friends of her family. Her husband, James Carter, had also been reported missing and was currently being sought for questioning as a person of interest. Both of them worked as college professors at Hofstra University in Hempstead, NY. They were supposed to be going on vacation but never showed up at their destination. No one at the university could offer any useful information. The cause of death was listed as exsanguination due to a deep cut to the throat. Don looked at the photos. The fact that there was an attempt to hide the body and that the husband was missing drew Don's attention. Maybe this was somehow related to the Reardon case.

Don put it on his high priority list.

Don called the M.E. in Nassau county and again left instructions to contact Erika in Boston.

He looked at the last folder from New York. This case involved a murder in Islip Long Island. The victim most likely was assassinated by MS 13. Don was somewhat relieved that he could set this one aside.

He rested his head in his hands for a moment. He pressed a knuckle from each of his index fingers into his eyes squeezed them shut. He kept them shut for a minute and then blinked repeatedly. He raised his arms over his head leaned back and stretched out. He let out a sigh and took a much-deserved break.

Don decided to call Erica back and talk to her personally again. He called the number and Erica answered.

"Hi Erika. You're gonna kill me but I have a special request," pleaded Don. "I've sent you the coroner's report and pictures of several murders and one multiple murder that occurred last May in Buffalo. There are detailed photos of the neck wounds. In most cases they were taken within hours of the murders. I would like you to contact the M.E.s in each case and get their opinion about the weapon used. I know I'm asking a lot, but this could be really important. The bodies are piling up."

Erica could sense the urgency in his voice and sympathized. "Okay. I'll jump on it right now. I can probably give you a pretty good idea before the end of the day."

"Thanks a million, Erica. I really appreciate it."

"Okay, but don't interrupt me again. I'll call you," she stated adamantly.

"You have my word," promised Don.

He sat back and thought about what else he could do until Erica completed her examination.

There were now seven additional bodies that might somehow be connected to his case. However, unless a definite correlation was made, he would have to focus on the Reardon case. This was still his priority even if there was a serial killer on the loose, and that was still to be determined.

Don considered all of the cases he had set aside. The murder of Paula Carter seemed to be the logical place to start. Don began to think about the fact that the victim had her throat cut and there was an effort to conceal the body. The similarity to the current Jane Doe in the morgue was too much for Don to ignore. Also, the fact that her husband was missing added to his suspicions. Don wanted to jump in his car and drive to Long Island to begin his own investigation. He hated sitting around waiting when he had an idea in his head but he knew he would have to wait for Jack's approval.

If Erika couldn't make a reasonable case for a establishing a similarity between the murder weapons that wasn't going to happen. He would have to start at square one all over again.

Don looked up Detective Snyder's number and punched it into his cell. The phone began to ring. Once, twice then a third time. The call went to voicemail. Don decided to hang up and try again later. He didn't want to leave a message. He wanted to speak with the detective directly.

Frustrated, he looked up Detective Behan's number in Danbury. The Patricia Nelson case was still active and Danbury was on the way to Long Island. Don thought about how to approach the detective. He wondered what type of man Detective Behan might be. He thought carefully about what to say. Not all law enforcement agencies were eager to cooperate with the FBI. He decided to take a humble approach and dialed the number and waited.

"Detective Behan." Don heard the voice come over the phone.

"Hello Detective Behan. I'm Detective Corlino. I understand that you're the lead detective in the Patricia Nelson case."

"That would be correct, Detective. How can I help you?"

"I'm currently investigating the murder of a young woman in the Boston area and your case has come to my attention. There are similarities in the two cases. They were both in their mid-twenties. Also, the M.O. of the murder was somewhat similar. I was thinking that you might be able to help us with our case."

Don thought it might be better if he didn't mention that he was FBI at this time.

"Oh, from Boston—I know a Detective Ray Carrol in the 8th precinct up in Boston. Do you by any chance know him, Detective?"

"No. Sorry. The name doesn't ring a bell." Don thought about it and realized it would be better just to come clean. Nothing was worse than compromising trust from the beginning.

"Actually, Detective, I'm with the FBI."

There were a few moments of silence.

"FBI. Really? Why are you guys involved in this, Detective?" There was a hint of apprehension in Behan's voice.

"It's complicated. I'm actually investigating the disappearance of a married couple. The Reardon case. Maybe you've heard of it."

"I read something about it in the papers. Some rich, important banker and his wife, right?"

"Yeah. That's right."

"So how does the Nelson girl tie into your case?"

"She probably doesn't but I've run out of leads and I'm grasping at straws," admitted Don. He told Behan about the two unidentified bodies in the morgue and began to explain his theory.

"Interesting, Detective Corlino, but there was no attempt to hide the body in this case. The only thing in common is that a knife was used. Besides, one of your two unidentified victims was male."

"That's true, Detective Behan, but there are very few cases in which the victim's throat was cut all the way to the bone. It suggests anger or hatred. The cases probably aren't connected but I'd hate to think that they are and that we missed it. I'm probably on my way to Long Island and I'd like to stop by and ask the witnesses a few questions if you don't mind."

"Okay, Detective. It's your gas and your time. I don't have a problem with it but I don't know what you expect to find."

"I just want to establish if there's any connection between her and Boston. Maybe one of her friends might know something. I'm not suggesting that you weren't thorough in your investigation. You would have no reason to tie Boston into this. By the way, you can call me Don."

"Okay, Don. You can call me Mike. Should I expect you tomorrow?"

"I'm not sure yet. I'll give you a call if I'm coming. Good luck with your investigation."

"Same to you, Don. Until tomorrow then."

Don hung up and decided to try Detective Snyder again. He punched in the number (516) 965-3971. He waited again as the phone began to ring.

"Snyder here," came the voice over the phone.

"Hello Detective Snyder. This is Detective Corlino from the FBI in Boston. I understand that you are the lead detective in the Paula Carter case."

"That's right. How can I help you, Detective?"

"I'm investigating the disappearance and possible kidnapping of a bank executive and his wife here in Boston. The Reardons… You might have heard of it."

"Yes. It's been in the news. Do you suspect that our cases might be connected?"

"It's possible. The body of a young woman was found yesterday in a State Park in Milford just south of Boston. She had her throat cut just like Paula Carter. I'm waiting for the M.E. to verify whether the same weapon was used. Also, there was an effort to conceal the body. I understand your victim was found in a secluded area in Muttontown."

"That's correct, Detective. She was found some distance from one of the main trails through a nature preserve."

"Also, her husband is missing. You see where I'm going with this?"

"I do. Right now, we are not treating James Carter as a kidnap victim and the FBI hasn't been called in. He's wanted for questioning and considered a possible suspect. We've interviewed all of their friends. They were both professors at Hofstra University. We've also interviewed everyone who knew them at the University. They weren't notably rich and there was no ransom note or appeal for money. Friends said they were having a few domestic problems lately. We rejected the idea of a kidnapping pretty quickly. Do you have cause to suspect otherwise?"

"I have no evidence of that but I'd like to look into it. If the M.E. up here in Boston can make a connection between the murder weapons, I'm going to make a trip down to Long Island."

"So you think your Jane Doe might be connected to the Reardon case?"

"It's just a theory. I really don't know."

"Well, okay, Detective Corlino. Call me when you know more."

"I'll do that. So long for now."

Don returned to the task of reviewing the cases. He went through the four cases from New Jersey one by one. After an hour he determined that there was no obvious connection between any of them. He had gone as far as he could for the day. He put his feet up on his desk and waited for Erika's call.

CHAPTER 8

Boston PD Headquarters, 12:32 PM

McGowan and Morrow decided it would be a good idea to personally interview Peter Robertson. This was not only because he had a history of violence and contempt for the law but also because they had been at their desks for hours and they were dying for an excuse to stretch their legs. Morrow got Robertson's home address from the DMV as well as his phone number. He got up from his desk and gulped down the last of his coffee. Before they left the office, Morrow placed a fax to Enterprise as well as Avis requesting the identity of the people who rented the cars that were issued summonses. The other people on the list would have to wait till later. They also decided to personally pick up the surveillance tapes in Milton. After that they would call it a day and get some much-needed rest.

Eddie and Rob headed for their car. Eddie got behind the wheel and Rob entered the address into the GPS: 14 Lowell Road, Milton.

If Robertson was involved with this in some way a personal appearance by the police might spook him and trip him up. It was worth a shot.

They arrived at Lowell Road and knocked on the door. A woman about 30 years old peered out from the window and yelled to them, "What's your business here?"

"Police. We'd like to talk to Mr. Robertson and ask a few questions, ma'am."

"Oh shit! What's the asshole done now?" came the reply from behind the door.

"Nothing we know for sure, ma'am. We'd just like to check out a couple of things," Eddie assured her.

"Well, he's not here. He's probably down at Duncan's hanging out with his loser friends. That's a bar about a mile and a half from here on Canton Avenue."

"Maybe you could help us," offered Eddie. "Is Peter your husband?"

"Yeah," she said rolling her eyes.

"We would like to know about a parking summons he was issued about a week ago on Blue Hill River Road." Eddie informed her.

"We just want to ask him what he was doing there at ten o'clock last Saturday night. That's a remote area and we just want to get an explanation."

"Oh. I can tell you that. The idiot ran out of gas on his way back from the bar. He called me on his cell to come and pick him up. I had to drive him back the next morning with a can of gas," she explained.

Eddie and Rob looked at each other. It was all too believable.

"Okay. I guess that explains it," said Eddie. "Did you see anything unusual while you were out there?"

"No. Not really. I was just pissed off. Same shit different day."

"Okay, ma'am. Thank you very much. We think you have been honest with us," said Eddie.

Eddie and Rob went back to their car and drove down the block.

"Do you think we should bother going to Duncan's?" asked Eddie.

"Why not? We've got to be thorough. A lot of cases were cracked by perseverance."

Rob was known for that. Jimmy Dugan, their boss, nicknamed him "Thorough Morrow."

Eddie and Rob drove down Canton Avenue looking for Duncan's.

"Put it in the GPS," said Eddie. "Why screw around?"

After a few minutes they found it. The two detectives walked into the bar, trying to look casual.

They walked up to the bar and asked the bartender, "Can you tell us where we can find Peter Robertson?"

"Who's asking?" came the reply.

"We're detectives from the Hyde Park Precinct in Boston," said Eddie. "We just want to ask a couple of questions about last Saturday night."

At that time a man at the end of the bar stood up and began to walk toward the door.

"Peter," yelled Rob "You're not in any trouble. We just want to know if you saw anything on the road last Saturday night."

Peter continued walking and staggered into the door. Eddie and Rob had no trouble catching up to him.

"Peter, we just want to ask you some questions."

Peter pushed Rob away and said, "I wasn't drunk if that's what you want to know. You guys just don't give up, do you?"

"Look," said Rob, "we just want to know if you saw anything while you were out last Saturday night. We want to know if you saw a girl wearing blue jeans and a black shirt. She may have been with a guy."

"Naw. I didn't see nothing," slurred Peter. "Why can't you guys just leave me alone?"

"Did you leave the bar alone last Saturday or were you with a girl?" asked Eddie.

"No. I was alone," coughed Peter.

That got a chuckle from the bartender. "Yeah. I can swear to that," he said.

Eddie said to the bartender, "Maybe you should think about not overserving your customers. Maybe we should put an undercover in here."

The bartender shut his mouth and began to clean some glasses.

Eddie and Rob figured they were chasing the wrong lead and headed for the door.

"Well, what now?" asked Rob.

"We go collect those surveillance tapes from the local stores. We can get a couple of rookie cops to look at them back at the precinct. We should also drive down all the roads adjacent to the reservation and look for possible clues. You never know what might turn up."

The two detectives collected tapes from four different gas stations, a 7-11 convenience store, a sporting goods store, and the two restaurants that Sarah had told them about. They then took a slow cruise down Blue Hill River Road, stopping several times over the next two hours in places where there seemed to be easy access to the reservation. They walked along searching through the bushes and the side of the road for any hint of a clue. It was starting to get dark when Rob reached down and picked up a plastic card.

"Hey Eddie," he called out. "I got something here."

Eddie walked over and looked at the white laminated card. He read it out loud. "Elizabeth Hayes: Turner Free Library: 2 North Main St. Randolph, Mass. 02368."

"It's a library card. I wonder how it got out here," Rob thought out loud.

"Well Okay. Let's check it out when we get back to headquarters," said Eddie. Then we will call it a day and get somebody to look at these tapes.

· · · · ·

It was six o'clock and Mike was starting to wrap things up for the day. Mike didn't like Mondays. Who does? There was always something that didn't go right over the weekend that needed fixing. This week was no exception. He was the man in charge and would have to stay late.

Donna poked her head into his office and said, "Goodnight, Mike." Diane was right behind her and gave him a big smile. "Later, Mike. Safe home."

"Goodnight, girls. See you in the morning."

Mike worked for a while longer and left the office just after 6:15.

He hopped into his car, turned out of the parking lot onto Allen Street, and headed back toward Route 90. He got on the highway and started to drive west toward home. Mike checked his side-view mirror and eased the car over to the middle lane. He began to daydream about Brittany and his daughters and how much he loved them. He hadn't gone more than a mile when a black Harley motorcycle dropped into his rearview mirror. The bike raced up behind him and was right on his bumper. It moved aggressively back and forth behind him, revving the throttle. It stayed on his tail for about half mile and then suddenly pulled up on the left side of Mike's Subaru. The bike met his pace for a few moments. The rider was wearing a thick black leather jacket and a helmet with a tinted face guard. Mike could not see his face. The rider stared over at Mike. He then pulled in front of him, zigzagging back and forth erratically. Mike hit the brakes and began to pull toward the right shoulder. The Harley slowed down, then sped up and pulled up even on his right side.

What the hell is this about? Mike thought to himself. *Did I cut him off or something?*

Mike looked out the passenger window and mouthed the words, "I'm sorry," trying to apologize.

The bike then fell back behind the car, then raced up on the driver's side again. The rider gave Mike another long glare. It then roared off at ninety miles an hour and was soon out of sight. Mike was a little rattled for a couple of minutes but soon began to relax. He didn't think more of it, and it slipped from his mind. Traffic was good and he was home by seven o'clock.

Jamie and Roni greeted him at the door and they both gave him a big hug.

"Hi Daddy," they both chimed in unison.

"Hi little angels," he replied, picking each one up in his arms.

"Hi honey," called Brit from the kitchen.

Mike walked into the kitchen with the two girls still in his arms and planted a kiss firmly on her cheek.

"What's for dinner?" asked Mike. "Did you make us something special?"

Brit was true to her word and had made Beef Stroganoff from scratch. It was a bit high in calories but it was delicious.

They all sat down for dinner and began to talk about the highlights of their day.

Brit suggested, "Why don't we drive to Lake Placid on Friday for the Columbus Day weekend?"

Mike leaned over and whispered in Brittany's ear.

Brittany smiled and said, "Yeah, sure."

"I've got a better idea," Mike announced. "What do you say we all play hooky and drive up Thursday night? We can make it a four-day weekend. We can take Kardashian with us."

"Yay," screamed Jamie. "I'm more than okay with that."

"Me too," said Roni, jumping up from the table with a big smile on her face. She gave her daddy a big hug.

Things were looking really good. Mike didn't think he could ever be happier.

After dinner the girls did their homework and Brit got behind the computer to finish her work.

They all watched some TV for a couple of hours and went off to bed.

Another day had come to an end.

• • • • •

It was well after 7 PM when Eddie and Rob returned to police headquarters.

Eddie walked over to Jimmy Dugan's office with the surveillance tapes they had collected from the local stores. Dugan had decided to stay late and was still at his desk.

"I need to have someone look at these tapes, Jimmy. Can you get a couple of regulars to get on it ASAP? Explain to them what we're looking for and what to do."

"You got it, Eddie. There's a couple of rookie cops here now. I'll volunteer them right away."

Eddie chuckled and said, "Thanks, Jimmy."

He walked over to his desk and got the address and phone number for Elizabeth Hayes in Randolph.

He dialed the number and patiently waited as the phone began to ring.

"Hello," came the voice of a man over the phone.

"Hello," said Eddie. "I'm a detective with the Boston Police Department. I'm calling because we found a library card in Milton with the name Elizabeth Hayes on it. I'd like to ask a few questions if she's home."

"Honey, there's a cop on the phone that wants to talk to you," came the voice again.

After a few moments Eddie heard a curious but somewhat apprehensive voice of a girl say, "Hello. How can I help you?"

"Hello. Are you Elizabeth Hayes?" inquired Eddie.

"Yes. That's me," she replied.

"We found a library card that belongs to you on the side of a road in Milton. We would just like to know how it got there," explained Eddie.

"Oh! You didn't by any chance find the rest of my stuff, did you?" she pleaded hopefully. "My car was broken into about two weeks ago while I was hiking in the preserve."

Eddie said, "No ma'am. Sorry about that, but that explains things. Thanks for your cooperation."

Eddie hung up the phone and said to Rob, "Another dead end. We'll pick it up again tomorrow. Let's go home and get a good night's sleep."

"Want to hit Zan's on the way home?" asked Rob, hoping for a yes.

"Not tonight," answered Eddie. "I'm beat. You young guys just don't ever run out of energy." He got up from his desk and said, "You gonna walk me out?"

"No. I'm just going to take care of some loose ends and check on those faxes we requested from Avis and Enterprise and make a few more phone calls. I'll see you bright and early," said Rob.

"Don't stay to long at Zan's," laughed Eddie. "We need you sharp in the morning."

He walked out of the office, got in his car and drove home.

•　•　•　•　•

It was six o'clock in the evening when Don's cell phone rang. It was Erika.

"Yes, Erika. What have you got for me?" Don was ready to hang on every word.

"I compared the photos and microscopic close-ups of the vertebrae of Leslie Anne Parks, the girl in the Buffalo murders, with our Jane Doe. I chose to look at her first because she was the thinnest of the three. The cut went all the way to the bone and left marks on the vertebrae just like my girl in the morgue here. Get ready for this, Don. I can give you a ninety-five percent probability that the same type of knife was the murder weapon. I also found similarities to the wounds on Paula Carter and Patricia Nelson. I haven't had time to look at the other victims yet, but I thought you would want to know right away. I also had a chance to look at the soft tissue damage. It certainly looks like the same kind of knife was used," Erika concluded. "I'm going to have the lab run an Atomic Absorption Spectroscopy Analysis for metal fragments. I'll compare John Doe and Jane Doe for traces of Molybdenum, Vanadium, Titanium, and other compounds. I'm sure those tests were run on the other victims. I'll call again when I know more."

"Thanks a million, Erika. You're the best. I may be out of town for a while."

He hung up the phone and quickly called Jack Sullivan. Don drummed his fingers on his desk waiting for him to answer.

"Jack Sullivan."

"Hi, Jack. Listen, I've got cause to believe that there are several murders in the New England area that may be related to our case. I want you to authorize a trip to Long Island. I'll be using my own car."

"Are you sure about this?"

"I can't be sure they're connected but it seems like our best shot at making progress. We're stuck right now."

"Remember that you're working on the Reardon kidnapping and not Jane Doe. How long are you going to be gone?"

"Not more than a couple of days at most. I just want to ask some questions and get some info from the witnesses. It shouldn't take long.

If there's a reason to pursue it any further, I'll know pretty quickly. Has Tommy come up with anything in Chicago?"

"No. Nothing, really. He should be coming back to Boston in the next couple of days."

"Well, if something important comes up while I'm gone, I'm sure he can handle it."

"Okay, Don. I'll trust your instincts."

"Thank you, Jack. I'll keep you posted."

Don hung up and hit the speed dial for McGowan. It went to voicemail.

"Eddie! It's Don. It looks like we may have a serial killer on our hands. I'm not sure, but Erika just informed me that the same type of knife was used in our Jane Doe case as the one used in Danbury, Long Island and a triple homicide in SUNY Buffalo last May. I'll fill you in with the details when I know more. I'm sending the report to your precinct. You can check with Erika for more info. I'm about to take a little road trip out to Long Island. You and Rob be careful out there."

Don then called George Barnett over to his desk and brought him up to speed.

"Tell Tommy what's going on when he gets here. Also tell him where I went and what I'm doing. Also tell Greg what's going on," said Don. "And tell him thanks."

"You got it, Don. I'll get on it right now."

Don called his girlfriend, Cheryl. "Hi, honey. It's me."

"Hi, Don. What's up? I hope we're still on for dinner," she asked with a note of apprehension in her voice. She was used to Don breaking dates at the last minute. It was frustrating, but she was willing to put up with it. She truly loved Don. She was willing to spend some lonely days without him and learned to cherish the times when she could be with him.

"I'm sorry," he apologized, "but something really important came up. I'm going to Long Island tonight. I can't say when I'll be back. I promise that I'll make it up to you. I'll treat you to the best dinner you ever had and we'll make love for ten hours straight."

Cheryl laughed and said, "Promises, promises."

"If I crack this case, I'm sure I'll have a lot of free time for a while. You've been a real sport. I'm lucky to have a girl like you, Cheryl."

"You just remember that." After a few seconds of silence, she said, "I love you, Don. Be careful."

"I will," he assured her and mimicked a kiss over the phone. "I'll call you tomorrow."

Don then quickly dialed Detective Snyder in Nassau County.

Bill answered and Don said, "It's Don. I'm on my way."

"Understood, Don."

CHAPTER 9

Tuesday Morning, Oct. 5
Long Island

The blast of an angry car horn on the street below kicked Don out of his dream and into the real world. He raised his head slightly and began to take in the unfamiliar surroundings. Slowly his brain processed where he was. He recalled checking in to the Holiday Inn in East Meadow at about 1:30 AM, courtesy of the FBI. He looked at his watch. It was 6:54 AM. It was too early to call Detective Snyder. Don got himself out of bed, showered, dressed and got ready, hoping that the day would be productive. The hotel was less than a mile from the M.E.'s office at Nassau County Medical Center. He would definitely pay a visit to the M.E. before he left.

He decided to grab some breakfast at a greasy spoon on Hempstead Turnpike across from the Medical Center. Don ordered bacon and scrambled eggs along with a cup of coffee. He picked up copies of the complimentary newspapers. First, he leafed through the *New York Post*. It was one of the main NYC papers. It was mostly known for its sports coverage and conservative politics. After reading the headlines and the baseball scores he picked up a copy of *Newsday*, a local Long Island paper. On page 21 he came across a brief article referring to the Carter case. It basically stated that there was no further progress on the murder and that James Carter was still being sought by law enforcement.

• • • • •

Eddie awoke at 7:30 AM and hit the kill switch on the alarm. He reached over to the night table and picked up his iPhone. He checked his email first and then his voice mail. He listened to Don's message.

He decided to return the call immediately. Don picked up and Eddie said, "I got your message just now. When are you going to Long Island?"

"Already there," came the reply. "I drove down last night. Got to my hotel about one-thirty this morning. I'm a little groggy right now."

"Sorry to wake you so early. I just wanted to let you know I got your message. I'll tell Rob as soon as he walks in. That was good detective work you did. I assume the whole FBI is on nationwide alert."

"Yes, it is, Eddie. I also got a message from Greg at missing persons last night. He came across another murder of a college student in Youngstown, Ohio last April. Same M.O. We could have been on this case as early as last May if we had tied those two together. We still don't know yet if the Ohio murder is related, but it seems possible. Both murders involved college students. Maybe our Jane Doe was a college student. Probably a good idea to check it out. How're things going on your end?"

"We haven't come up with anything here yet. We're still going over the surveillance tapes. Nothing turned up on the state cameras. We collected the tapes from local stores in the area yesterday. My guys had a chance to look at them last night and wrote down some plate numbers. We're starting on them now. I'll keep you posted if something does turn up."

"Okay," said Don. "I'll do the same for you."

"Good hunting," said Eddie and hung up the phone.

Eddie got himself ready for work. His wife Lisa had gotten up earlier and made him coffee.

"Good morning," she greeted him.

"Good morning sweetheart," he echoed.

"Anything special you and Rob have planned for the day?" she asked.

She had gotten used to the idea that her husband was a cop, but it still made her nervous. Eddie knew that and tried to keep her in the dark when he had a dangerous assignment. Now that he knew they were investigating a possible serial killer, he did his best to downplay it.

"Not really. We're probably going to spend the day at the office. Real boring stuff."

Lisa was relieved to hear that.

Eddie finished his coffee, kissed Lisa on the cheek and headed out the door.

• • • • •

Don looked at his watch. It was 8:00 AM. He called Detective Snyder.

"Snyder here."

"Good morning, Detective. It's Detective Corlino. We talked yesterday." "Yeah. Hi Don. Let's drop the formalities. Call me Bill." "Okay. Good with me." "So how would you like to start the day, Don? What's most important to you?"

"I'd like to start with the Medical Examiner's office. I just have a couple of questions. I'd like to be on a first name basis with whoever is handling this case just in case we find out our cases are the same."

"His name is Ben Ornstein. I've worked with him before. He's kind of eccentric but he's good at what he does."

"How do you mean eccentric?"

"You'll see. All of these M.E.s are a little quirky."

"I guess they are," agreed Don. "I could never do that job. The pictures are bad enough."

"I hear ya. So where do we go after that?"

"I'd like to pay a visit to Hofstra University and talk to the profs Carter knew at work."

"No problem there. Hofstra's just down Hempstead Turnpike from NCMC. About a ten-minute drive.

"After that I'd like to interview people who knew them socially. Not everyone. Just their best friends."

"I can set that up for later this afternoon. There's only three or four people you need to talk to. I've already interviewed them and I can give you a synopsis of what they said."

"That would be fine. I'm only trying to find out if there's any connection between the Carters and Boston. After that I'd like to briefly visit Muttontown Nature Preserve and get an idea of the crime scene."

"Do you really need to go there? I've got plenty of pictures."

"I want to get an idea of how difficult it is to get out there and how much effort was made to hide the body. I just need to feel the crime scene, if you know what I mean."

"Actually, I do, Don. Okay. We should be able to get all that in. Where are you now?"

"I'm right across from NCMC. I'm at the Gold Star Diner."

"Okay, I'll meet you there in an hour."

• • • • •

Eddie walked through the doors of police headquarters and made his way to his desk. Rob had not yet arrived. It was not unusual for Rob to arrive late, and Eddie could picture him sitting at Zan's Bar until late in the evening.

A new list of 156 plate numbers had been left on his desk with a note from the two cops he had assigned to look at the tapes. It read Sept. 25 complete. Could not read all the plate numbers. The two officers had been very busy. It was a very time-consuming task, even with fast forward. He imagined the two officers gulping down coffee hour after hour and talking up a storm to fight off the boredom.

Eddie decided to pick up where they left off the day before and began to enter the plate numbers into the computer. After about fifteen minutes Rob arrived and took his place at his desk.

"Sorry I'm late," he said to Eddie.

"I've got some news from Don," said Eddie. "He called last night. Apparently, his hunch might be right. We may be tracking a serial killer. There's a connection between Jane Doe, a girl on Long Island, another one in Connecticut, and three college students that were murdered in Buffalo last May. There might also be one in New Hampshire and now another one in Youngstown, Ohio. Erika compared one of the Buffalo victims with Jane Doe and said there's a ninety-five percent certainty that the same type of weapon was used in both murders. Don is in Long Island right now."

"Wow," said Rob. "They're probably going to assign a team of detectives to this case now."

"And the FBI will now be officially involved," sighed Eddie. "Don seems to be someone we can work with but you know how territorial some of these FBI guys can get."

"In all fairness a lot of Boston PD is no different," admitted Rob. "But you're right, Don seems to be a professional. He just wants to catch the bad guys."

Rob began to help Eddie enter plate numbers into the computer. When they finished, they again crossed the data with known felons. This time two names came up.

"Got something," said Eddie. "Sex offender with two arrests for indecent exposure and improper touching of a minor. He's also been arrested for aggravated assault on a nineteen-year-old girl. Name is David Ulrich. He has an address right here in Boston."

"Well, there's one we should definitely check out," agreed Rob.

"Let's finish going through this list and we'll pay Mr. Ulrich a visit."

They had almost finished when Eddie said, "Got another one. Abdul Nasir. Busted for conspiracy to commit fraud and check fraud."

"Nice Jewish boy from Brooklyn," said Rob sarcastically.

"Oh, hello! There's also a connection with this guy to the Marathon bombings. It says here that he is a known acquaintance of some of Dzhokhar Tsarnaev's friends, including his wife."

"Where did we get his plate number from?"

"He was at a 7-11 on Route 28 near the Preserve on September 25 at 1:22 AM."

"Interesting," said Rob. "Does it mention if he was with a girl in blue jeans?"

"No. The guys looking at the tape weren't asked to do that. They just wrote down plate numbers. I think we should look at that tape and find out," suggested Eddie.

"That would be a very good idea. We should also check with Don and see what the FBI has on him."

Eddie wrote down Nasir's address:

68 Reservoir Ave

Newton, Massachusetts

"Why does Newton ring a bell?" said Eddie.

"That's where we busted that drug ring a couple of years ago. Remember?"

"Oh yeah. That's right. Those Albanians. Those guys were insane."

"They don't get much crazier," agreed Rob.

"Well, let's hope we don't have to deal with those guys again."

A few minutes later Eddie called Don.

"Detective Corlino," he answered.

"It's Eddie. I just wanted to bring you into the loop about one of the plate numbers we're checking out. There's a guy named Abdul Nasir. Apparently, the FBI was looking into him after the Marathon bombings some years ago. Is there anything you can tell me about it?"

"Yes. I remember the name. We had a tail on him for several months. The wife of the older Tsarnaev brother was an acquaintance of his, but we stopped looking into him as a suspect some years ago. Do you have any reason to be suspicious?"

"We checked the police records and he was arrested for check fraud. That's about all."

"I'll have FBI records send you the file on him right away, Eddie. It should be there in an hour or so."

"Okay, Don. Thanks. Good hunting."

"You too, Eddie."

Eddie retrieved the surveillance tape Nasir had been tagged in and fast forwarded it to 1:20 AM.

The tape showed a Mercedes SUV pull up and took note of the plate. It was Nasir's. They watched the tape and watched Abdul get out and walk into the store. Two minutes later he walked back out and got in his car. There was no sign of a girl or any other passengers in the SUV.

"Oh well. Gotta be thorough. He could have killed her before going to 7-11," argued Rob.

"Very true," admitted Eddie.

They got back on the computer and crossed the list with misdemeanor arrests. This time a slew of names popped up. Rob again got the address and phone number for each one. They had a busy day ahead of them.

"Well, we might as well begin with our two felons," said Eddie.

"Yup. We should definitely pay Mr. Ulrich a visit," suggested Rob.

"Okay. Then we'll drop by and check on Mr. Nasir. The rest of the names can wait until later."

Eddie and Rob got in their car and headed out. The two detectives followed the GPS instructions and headed for David Ulrich's house in North Boston. The address was listed as 50 Beekman Street, an apartment building in the Fitchburg district. The neighborhood was a rundown slum with untied garbage bags strewn across the sidewalk. It seemed that there had been no attempt by the local residents to improve the quality of the neighborhood. Ulrich's apartment was listed as 214. The two detectives trotted up the stairs and walked down the hallway looking for the number. They found the apartment and Eddie knocked loudly on the door.

"Who's there?" came a startled voice from inside.

"Police. We want to ask a few questions."

"Just a minute. I'll be right there. I'm not dressed."

Eddie and Rob could hear noises of someone closing drawers and hurrying around inside.

"Let's go," said Rob. "We haven't got all day."

Eventually the door opened and a disheveled, fat, balding man of about forty-five years of age appeared. He smelled of beer even though it was only nine o'clock in the morning.

He allowed the detectives in and nervously said, "How can I help you?"

"We'd just like to ask a few questions," said Eddie. "What were you doing in Milton last Sunday night a week ago?"

Meanwhile Rob was looking around the apartment. He spotted a magazine on the floor, sticking out from underneath a small table where Ulrich was standing. He walked over to try and get a better look. Ulrich tried to push it farther under the table with his foot. Before he could Rob saw pictures of some young naked girls in the magazine. They looked about twelve years old. Rob pushed Ulrich away and grabbed the magazine.

"So, what do we have here? Let's see." Rob held the magazine in front of Ulrich. "Like little girls, huh?" he said with disgust as he pushed the magazine in Ulrich's face.

"Look. It's not my fault. I can't help what I am," stammered Ulrich. "You don't understand."

"Maybe you can't," said Rob. "So why were you in Milton?"

"I was just driving through on my way back from Brockton. I was visiting my friend, Billy Palmer. You can check it out. I'll give you his number. I was there all day Sunday," insisted Ulrich.

He walked over to his desk and began to flip frantically through his phonebook. "Here's the number. Call him. You'll see. What's this about, anyway?"

"Where did you guys go? Can anyone else verify your story?" asked Rob.

"We were at the park the whole afternoon. I swear," said Ulrich.

"Yeah. Probably scoping out twelve-year-old girls together," said Rob, throwing the magazine at him.

Ulrich started to cry and fell back on his couch. "I'm not a bad person," he said, trying to hold back tears. "I really love kids."

Eddie looked at the pathetic lump on the couch and thought about how difficult it had been for him to reach the clearing where Jane Doe had been murdered.

"C'mon, Rob," said Eddie. "This isn't our guy. We'll check on his alibi just in case."

The profile didn't fit. The nineteen-year-old that he had assaulted probably looked like a twelve- or thirteen-year-old girl. That was his type. In any case they would follow up on it.

"It's a crime to own child pornography," shouted Rob, leaning over to get in Ulrich's face. "Get rid of all this shit. We're going to come back around to make sure you did."

Rob stormed out the door with Eddie in tow.

Don continued to read the paper and occasionally glanced out the window. The traffic on Hempstead Turnpike had grown from a small stream of cars that morning to a massive torrent in just over an hour. He had always pictured Long Island as a bucolic rural suburb. Once East Meadow was exactly that but now it resembled a small city. He watched a Chevy Tahoe turn into the parking lot and pull into a spot in front. A grizzled-looking man wearing a blue sports jacket emerged from the car. He stood about five-ten, give or take a couple of inches, and appeared to be in his mid-fifties.

That's gotta be him, thought Don. He watched as the man walked in the front door and began to look around. Don raised his hand and called out to get his attention.

He walked over and asked, "Don, I assume? Nice to meet you."

"You too, Bill. You want to grab a cup of coffee or something?"

"No. I'm good. I called Ben and let him know we were on our way. He's expecting us about now. If we're gonna get done with everything today we should get started."

"All right. I'm good with that."

"The M.E. is right across the road. We can just walk it."

"Sounds good. Let's go."

"Learn anything new since we last talked?" asked Bill.

"Missing persons sent a case file to my office yesterday. It was about the murder of a college student in Youngstown, Ohio. Same M.O. That makes five unsolved cases in which college students were the victims."

"That's definitely something to consider, but Paula Carter wasn't a student. She was a professor."

"That's true but she was tied to a university, I'm not drawing any conclusions. I'm just playing out a theory. It's very possible that none of these cases are connected."

They walked to the crosswalk, hit the signal button and waited for the light. The cars and delivery trucks rushed by at 60 mph even though it was a 40 mph zone. The light changed and they both hurried across the six-lane turnpike.

"The M.E. is in the basement of building Q on the other side. I've been there a thousand times. We can just cut through the main building."

"You're the boss. I'm following you."

In a few minutes they entered the Medical Examiner's office.

The door swung open and Bill said "Hi Ben. I brought a friend today. This is Detective Corlino from Boston. He's with the FBI."

Don observed a fragile man in his late sixties who looked very much like Albert Einstein. His clothes were clean but looked like they hadn't been ironed since they first left the store. His stark white hair stuck out in all directions and looked like the explosion of a mattress factory.

Dr. Ornstein looked up from his work and greeted them. "Oh, hi. How do you do? I'm just completing some work on this liver I've got here. Fascinating really. Just fascinating. But it's a lot to go into right now. Bill tells me that you're here because of the Paula Carter case."

Dr. Ornstein extended his hand and then took it back, realizing his gloves were covered with liver tissue.

"Oh. Pardon me. I forget sometimes."

He took off his gloves and extended his hand once more. This time Don accepted the offer.

"Hello Dr. Ornstein. It's a pleasure to meet you. I know you're busy and I won't take up much of your time. I thought I'd like to meet you personally in case my case is connected to yours."

"That's always good. I just spoke with your M.E., Erika Koenig, up in Boston. Sounds like a smart woman. Rare species around here. Let me tell you." He shook his head and rolled his eyes. "She filled me in about the Jane Doe she examined and the other cases you believe are tied in. Very interesting. Dead bodies talk to each other all the time. They just need someone to translate."

Ornstein let out a slight chuckle and turned to watch Don's reaction. He continued to smile as if he were keeping a special secret and then let out a not-so-subtle laugh.

Don looked at Bill, who gave him a nod.

"Doctor, what I'd like to ask you is about your impressions of the victim. I mean, did you get any kind of vibes from her? Sometimes you can tell something about the last moments of someone's life by the look in their eyes or the expression on their face. Like did she look surprised, scared or remorseful? Anything you can tell me would help. I'd also like your opinion about the angle of the knife and how tall the assailant might have been. That kind of thing. How deep was the wound? What was the mindset of the man who did this?"

"Well, the body was already a couple of weeks old. My best take is that she had a look of fear but also resignation of the inevitable. Like she knew it was coming. Do you follow?" Ornstein gave him a look as though he had a special knowledge of the dead.

"Somewhat. Please continue."

"I'd say that whoever did this had to be very strong but not a giant. Maybe five-foot-nine or eight. Maybe even shorter."

"And what would you say about the mental state of the person who did this?"

"That's hard to say, but anger is possible. Decisiveness is an absolute. There were no signs of hesitation. Whoever did this meant business. They knew they were going to kill."

"Okay, Doctor. Thank you very much. You've been very helpful. If I think of anything else, I'll give you a call."

He looked at Bill and implied that he had gotten what he came for.

"You're very welcome, Detective. Don't hesitate to call if you need something."

Bill and Don left the M.E. and returned to the diner.

"Why don't you leave your car at the Holiday Inn and I'll do the driving. I know exactly where we need to go," suggested Bill.

"Sounds like a plan," agreed Don.

After dropping off the car they drove down Hempstead Turnpike to Hofstra University.

"I've already told the concerned parties we were coming this morning. I'll call again and let them know we're on our way. We've agreed to meet in the Science Faculty room."

They pulled into the campus, parked in front of the science building and made their way to the faculty room. Several professors and adjuncts were waiting for them, and Bill introduced them to Don.

"I know you've all been interviewed before," said Don. "I just have a few additional questions. You all knew James and Paula quite well and I'm sorry for your loss. I'm still hopeful that we'll find James alive."

Don actually had his doubts about that.

"Let's begin with their relationship with each other. Who would like to give an opinion?"

There was a moment or two of silence and one of the professors in the group spoke.

"We've already been through this with Detective Snyder," he complained. "We're all still grieving. I don't understand why you can't get the information from him."

"Please, Dr. Benjamin. I know this isn't easy, but Detective Corlino might catch something that we missed before. We all have our own interpretation of what witnesses tell us. Also, it's better to hear things firsthand."

"They weren't talking to each other. A few months ago, they had a pretty good fight. I overheard James arguing with her on the phone. He seemed rather angry with her. He didn't know I was there," explained Dr. Benjamin. "Cathy seems to think that they ironed things out since then."

"Which one of you is Cathy?"

"I'm Professor Catherine Maturo," said a pretty brunette who looked to be about 40 years old. "It's true they weren't talking for a while, but I thought they got past that. They were okay again, or at least it seemed that way."

"The truth is it shocked all of us. We knew they had some problems to work out but nobody expected this. I just don't know what to think," offered another professor in the group.

Don and Bill looked at each other, unable to draw any conclusions.

"Thank you for your honesty and cooperation," said Don. "I know you're all still upset."

He collected his thoughts and continued.

"What I would really like to know is if either of them had a connection to Boston or if they knew any colleagues from that area."

Almost immediately several of them spoke up and said, "Yes."

"James was just up there about half a year ago attending a conference," said Professor Benjamin.

"What was it about?" asked Don.

Bill suddenly seemed to take an interest and listened intently.

"James was a chemistry professor. He was an expert on explosives. He gave a lecture about homemade devices to the Boston Police Department. You know, all the fallout from the Marathon terrorist bullshit. He was instructing them about what to look out for. You would be surprised what you can cook up with stuff that you can buy in Home Depot and drug stores. Real MacGyver stuff."

Don was hanging on every word. "Go on. What else can you tell me about that? I want to know all the places he's lectured and who his contacts were."

Bill began taking notes.

"He posted some things on the Internet about a year ago,"

Don turned his attention to the young girl who had spoken up. She seemed nervous about voicing an opinion and shied away when Don looked at her. She looked to be in her early 20s.

"What's your name?"

"My name is Emily Foster."

"Are you a professor here?" asked Don

"No. I was his T.A.," she answered in a timid, hesitant voice.

Don recognized her reluctance to speak and gave her an encouraging look.

"Please continue, Emily. Just tell me as much as you can."

"It was a bit controversial," she added. "Not everyone thought he should make that information public. I mean... He didn't explain how to make a bomb but he did make it known what chemicals to use. I guess he just wanted people to be aware and put out some red flags. Actually, making the explosives isn't that easy. You need special lab equipment."

"Can you give me that website?" appealed Don. "This could be important."

"I've got it right here," she said. She jotted it down and gave it to Don. She then went to the computer and punched up a file of all the places Professor Carter had lectured in the past two years.

"Here ya go. That's a list of all the places he lectured and all his contacts."

"Thank you all very much. You have been a tremendous help," Don told them in a sincere tone.

The two detectives headed back to the car.

"I'm impressed, Don. We never looked back that long ago into James's history. We had no idea he had a connection to terrorist activities. If this pans out, I owe you."

"We don't know anything yet. It's all just speculation. We might be on the wrong horse traveling in the wrong direction but we've got nothing else. Let's just go with it for now."

"I'll have my guys start looking in that direction right away. Terrorists are popping up everywhere these days. and they're not all foreigners. Long Island has had its share of jihadists and you know how they feel about cutting off heads."

"So next stop is the Burkes' house in Carle Place. They were the Carters' best friends. Only Joan is home. Her husband Ted is at work. She's expecting us. Their other friends are only a mile farther in Westbury. They're both on the way to Muttontown. We should be done before rush hour. Maybe you can beat it out of here before four o'clock."

"I think I'm gonna stay at the Holiday Inn one more night. Matter of fact, I slept pretty good last night. Nice comfortable pillows. Nice comforter. Best sleep I've had in some time. All courtesy of the EFF BEE EYE."

They both chuckled.

"Take whatever you can get. You're never gonna get rich doing this," lamented Bill.

"I'll drive back in the morning. I want to stop in Danbury on my way. I should get there early in the morning. I've got some interest there as well."

In twenty minutes, they were in front of the Burkes' house. Joan, who had been expecting them, came out to greet them.

"Hello Detective Snyder."

"Hi Joan. This is Detective Corlino, who I told you about. He'd like to ask you some questions."

Don introduced himself and began to ask about Boston.

Joan racked her brain and tried to think of anything that would help.

"I know he traveled a lot. I remember he went to Boston about six months ago. I don't know much about the specifics."

Don could see that she was still deeply anguished by the dark events of the past week. Still, he had to ask her about what she thought in regard to James's emotional state. There was nothing to arouse any suspicions and he decided there was nothing more he could learn from her. He thanked her and they left for the Dunlops' house in Westbury. After several minutes of questions Don decided he had nothing further to gain in this avenue.

"Thank you sincerely, Mrs. Dunlop. You've been a great help."

"Let's go." He motioned to Bill.

Bill looked at his watch. It was just after one o'clock.

"Do you want to stop for lunch before we go to the nature preserve?"

"Sure. Do you know a good place?

"Yes, I do. It's right here in Westbury. Angelino's, best Italian in Nassau County."

"I could go for Italian. All this running around is making me hungry."

Don and Bill sat in the restaurant and tried to make sense out of what they had learned. After an hour of deliberation, they had a good idea of how to continue.

Don was still leaning toward the theory that James and Paula were both victims and that he was most likely dead. Bill agreed that was likely but was still holding on to the possibility that James was the perp and that he was on the lam or had killed himself as well.

"Let's review what we've got," suggested Don. "I'm considering seven different cases here. Some of them seem to have a lot in common. I'm going to divide them into two groups for the moment. The first group is the Reardon case, the Carter case and the two unidentified bodies in the morgue in Boston. What they have in common is the murder weapon and the concealment of the bodies in a wooded area. That suggests a certain pattern and method."

"I'm with you so far, Don. Still, there's a lot of gaps to fill in, like how the Reardons would be connected to the Carters."

"Yeah, I know but we've gotta make some leaps in logic. In the end we will be either right or wrong. Let's just assume things for now. The other group of cases are the students. Youngstown, the three in Buffalo and one in Albany. There's also the girl who was found in the woods in New Hampshire. She wasn't a student because we cross-checked the DNA with every missing student in the nation. The only things that they have in common are the murder weapon and that they were college students."

"Maybe we've got two different serial killers," suggested Bill.

"Very possible," agreed Don.

CHAPTER 10

Tuesday Afternoon, 11:30 AM
North Boston

Eddie and Rob left Ulrich's place, climbed back in the car and headed south on 93.

"You know, it just occurred to me," said Rob. "Who likes beheadings? Jihad types, right? Our boy Abdul sounds like he could be of that persuasion."

"I'll have to admit, it did cross my mind," said Eddie. "But, let's not jump to any conclusions. We don't want to be accused of profiling. You know the political climate here in Boston."

"Right," said Rob. "What a backasswards world."

The detectives arrived at the address. It was a nice-looking Cape in a decent neighborhood.

They cruised past the house and took note of the Mercedes SUV in the driveway.

"There's our boy," said Rob. "I really would like to ask a few questions."

"Let's take Don's advice and wait. We might find out a lot more if we just stake the place out. Let's see who comes to visit."

"How about we ask the neighbors what they know?" suggested Rob, eager to jump right in.

"Couldn't hurt," agreed Eddie. "But be careful not to tip our hand."

They decided to go to the house next door. Eddie rang the bell and a girl in her early twenties answered the door.

"Hello," said Eddie, showing his badge. "We're detectives from the Boston Police Department. Could we ask you for a few minutes of your time?"

The girl looked at Rob and was immediately enamored. "Sure. C'mon in. Can I get you something to drink?"

By this time the two detectives were strung out on coffee. Truth was, what they really wanted was a double bourbon or a few cold beers.

"No ma'am, but thank you," said Eddie. "How about you, Rob?"

"I'm good right now, thanks."

"We'd like to ask you about the man living next door, Mr. Abdul Nasir. Are you familiar with him?" asked Eddie.

"You mean the Saudi guy? Yeah. I've seen him on campus over at Boston College. Everyone knows him as the Sheik. He's kind of a weirdo, if you ask me."

"Why is that?" Eddie persisted.

"I don't know. He acts real paranoid sometimes and there are all kinds of people showing up here at all hours of the day and night. The guy gives me the creeps. So do his friends."

"How do you mean?" asked Rob.

"I don't know. Most of them are Middle Eastern. Not that that's bad, but they all act like they're hiding something. Then there's this white girl that stares at me if I look in her direction. I think she's on drugs or something. I wouldn't be surprised if they were all on crack."

"I'm sorry. I should have asked you your name," apologized Eddie.

"I'm Joanie," said the red-headed Irish-looking girl. Her eyes had remained fixed on Rob, even though Eddie was asking the questions.

"Do you recall seeing a girl with dark hair, blue jeans and a black shirt anytime in the last couple of weeks?" asked Eddie.

"I don't know about the blue jeans or black shirt but there's a girl with dark hair that's here sometimes."

"When did you see her last?"

"Just yesterday," replied Joanie. "She's the one that stares at me."

Eddie and Rob looked at each other. It couldn't be their Jane Doe.

"Well, thanks, Joanie," said Eddie. "You've been very helpful. This is my card. Please call us if you see anything suspicious."

"I sure will. Do you have a card, too?" she said, looking at Rob.

Rob smiled and handed her his card.

The detectives returned to their car with Eddie behind the wheel and thought about what to do.

"Our girl Joanie might be right. These guys don't sound too kosher," said Rob. "I don't think they're going to answer the door for the likes of us anyway. It could be they're running a drug operation. Maybe we should just hang out down the block and stake the place out for a while."

Eddie agreed and they drove about fifty yards down the block and just waited to see who might show up. After about an hour a tall figure with dark hair emerged from the house and went to his Mercedes SUV.

"Let's follow him and see where he goes," said Rob.

"I'm on the same page."

The two detectives waited until the Mercedes was another fifty yards down the block before they pulled out. They watched as it made a left turn and then raced to the corner so they wouldn't lose sight of it. They spotted the SUV and followed at a distance down Homer Street in the direction of Boston. After a few miles, it took a right turn and again they raced to catch up. As soon as they rounded the corner, they spotted their quarry. This time the SUV had pulled up to the curb about 30 yards away.

"Oh shit," said Rob.

"No worries. I'll just cruise by."

Rob watched as "The Sheik" exited his car with a small package and headed for the house across the street. Eddie took a good look at the house as they cruised by just as he was approaching the front door. Rob also kept his eye on the house and spotted a figure in the upstairs window behind a partially open curtain. He got lower in his seat to get a better look. The curtain closed just as they were rolling past the house. Eddie took note of the number on the front door. They continued down the block and turned the corner.

"Let's turn around and stake it out for a while," said Rob.

"Right with ya."

The two detectives turned the car around and parked just down the street.

"Beacon Street," noted Eddie.

Again, the two of them began to watch the house from afar.

"That was a little strange. I mean the guy in the upstairs window. It was like he was expecting someone," remarked Rob.

"I agree. I definitely plan on mentioning it to Dugan."

● ● ● ● ●

Don and Bill Snyder continued to speculate and try to make sense of it all. After a very satisfying lunch they got back in the car and headed for Muttontown. They drove north on Route 106 toward Oyster Bay. This part of Long Island was beautiful. There were lots of trees on either side of the road and very few buildings. It was a lot more like Don had pictured it. Soon they were in Muttontown and Bill pulled into the nature preserve. The two detectives got out of the car and Don looked up at the towering trees.

"Well, this is it. The trail to the crime scene is this way."

The two of them set off into the woods.

"Is this the only way to get there?" asked Don.

"No. There are two horse trails that come in from the stables near Route 106 and one trail that comes in from Brookville Road. The entrance we came in on is on Northern Boulevard. That's the way most visitors would enter the preserve, but it's the farthest from where the body was found."

"Which would be closest to the crime scene?"

"The one on Brookville Road is only a hundred yards away, maybe a little less, but you can't park there. It's just for horses and pedestrians."

"I'd like to go there as well."

"It's still early. We've got time."

They took several different trails and after ten minutes they came to a cement wall. It seemed to be part of an abandoned courtyard. There were four walls that enclosed a small area.

Bill said, "A Russian big shot bought this whole area in 1910. He wanted to build a palace here but the war came and he lost all his money. This is all that's left of what they built. A lot of people come out this way to look at it. That's probably why the body was discovered."

"Do a lot of people know about this place?" asked Don.

"A lot of the locals do. I mean people from Oyster Bay. I don't think too many people outside Nassau County know about it. This is where we leave the trail. The brush gets a little thick from here on but it's only about 40 yards this way." They followed the cement wall and then turned off into the brush. "Right here, Don. This is where they found her."

Bill took a picture of the crime scene from his pocket and showed it to Don. It showed Paula Carter's body propped up against a tree. Her head hung at a grotesque angle and the gash in her throat was clearly visible.

"See here? This is that tree," he said, pointing. "Right here is where the body was."

Don looked at the picture and then on the ground where the grass seemed to be matted down. He couldn't detect any obvious signs of a struggle.

She must not have put up much of a fight. Don thought.

There was always a strange vibe when he visited the scene of a murder. It was like someone or something was trying to reach out to him.

"Do you think it's possible someone could have come in through that Brookville entrance with the intention of murdering her and hiding the body without having known that courtyard was here?"

"I suppose that's possible," reasoned Bill.

"It reminds me of how our Jane Doe was found. A bunch of kids had a hideout deep in the woods. The body would never have been found if it wasn't for them. Can we walk over to that gate on Brookville Road?" asked Don.

"I suppose so if you think it's necessary. But I've gotta warn you, there's a lot of ticks in the brush. Better check yourself out good when we get back to the car."

"No one said this was gonna be easy."

The two of them made their way toward the cyclone fence that surrounded the preserve. They struggled through what Don estimated to be about a hundred yards of brush until they reached the road. They then made their way along the fence for another twenty yards.

"The gate is right here," said Bill.

Don walked through the gate and checked out the road that formed the southern boundary of the preserve. He noted that there was absolutely no place where someone could park a car on the side of the road. Brookville and Muttontown were very wealthy neighborhoods that frowned on casual visitors. "It would have been difficult for someone to go unnoticed if they had come through this way. It would have taken a least a half hour for someone to force Mrs. Carter out here, do the murder and then make it back to the gate. Whoever did it wouldn't have taken the chance of leaving their car in the road and having it reported to the police."

"Good point," agreed Bill.

"Still, if they came in the way we did they would have seen the courtyard. Not exactly an ideal place to hide a body."

"Also true. So what's your theory?"

"Maybe whoever did this had an accomplice. They could have driven around while the murder was being committed and picked up their partner later."

"If that's true, it's unlikely that Carter murdered his wife. On the other hand, if Carter was kidnapped for his expertise in explosives, why involve his wife?" questioned Bill.

"Maybe they needed her for leverage to make James do their bidding or maybe she just got in the way. There's still a lot of possibilities."

Don took some mental notes and looked back at the woods they had just trekked through. "Is there an easier way back to the car?" he asked hopefully.

"We can walk the road back to Route 106 and get back that way," suggested Bill. "We'll pick up the horse trail and cut through."

"Sounds good. I think we're done here."

A half hour later they were back at the car.

"Run your fingers through your hair and check yourself for ticks. I'm not kidding. I had one on me last time I was out there. Nasty little shits," cursed Bill.

"I'll take a good shower tonight at the hotel."

"Is there anything else you want to get done today?" offered Bill.

"I think we're good. I can't think of anything right now. We should check with each other every day and share information. The FBI has a lot of sophisticated technology and a lot of data on their computers. I can give you a number to call in Boston if you need any info. I can also give you the names of two detectives up there who are working on our Jane Doe. Eddie McGowan and Rob Morrow. I'll give you their numbers as well."

"I appreciate that, Don. I've always wondered why law enforcement agencies weren't always on the same page."

"Same here, Bill. We're all out to get the bad guys. Right?"

Bill drove back to East Meadow and pulled into the Holiday Inn.

"I think we've had a productive day. I'm going to have to look at this case from the terrorism angle now," said Bill. "You've definitely been a big help."

"So have you, Bill. Thanks for everything today and good luck."

Bill drove away and Don walked into the hotel and headed for his room. It was just after four o'clock. He decided to call Eddie.

"Hi Don. What's up?"

"I'm down on Long Island investigating the disappearance of a chemistry professor who has an expertise in homemade explosives. His name is James Carter. His wife, Paula, was found murdered in a secluded area here in Nassau County. Sound familiar?"

"Interesting."

"I just thought I'd give you a heads up about a connection to a possible terrorist plot. I'm working with a Detective Snyder here on Long Island. We're looking at every angle right now. Of course, it might not have anything to do with terrorism. For all I know these cases are totally unrelated."

Eddie jotted down the names.

"What have you got so far?" Don asked

"We're still tracking down those parking violations and going through the traffic tapes. Mostly dead ends."

"Okay. I'll check back later with you guys. Call me if something turns up."

• • • • •

Mike was busy going over the latest updates to the Danson & Lawrence software. After an exhausting morning of last-minute adjustments, it was finally ready. He sat back in his chair, put his feet up on his desk, and shut his eyes.

Just at that moment Donna walked in and said, "Sleeping on the job, are we?"

"That's it. No lunch for you. One year," Mike joked.

"Just teasing, Mike. I know how hard you work."

"See if Diane wants to go out to lunch again. I just finished the Danson thing and I feel like celebrating."

"Oh, Mike. You're too nice."

"Nothing's too good for my girls. I should add a free lunch as part of the job benefits."

She put a large manila envelope on Mike's desk and said, "Thanks, Mike. I'll tell Diane. By the way these just arrived from Lexington Finance."

Mike and Brittany had woken up early that morning, as usual. Brit had gotten Jamie and Roni ready for school and seen the two of them off on the bus. She was at work in her own office and decided to give Mike a call.

"Hi lover," she whispered seductively over the phone.

"Who's this? Are you from the escort service? I told them next week!" Mike teased.

Brittany played along and said in her sexiest voice, "But you're entitled to a freebie. You're a preferred customer."

"Free! Well, come right over then."

Brittany laughed and asked, "Do you know when you'll be home tonight?"

"Probably at six-thirty. Maybe seven I'll let you know if I'll be late."

"Okay. See you tonight."

Mike took Diane and Donna to lunch. He returned to his office and began to pore through the document Donna had left on his desk. It was a request for a software modification for an important client. He spent the rest of the afternoon planning out solutions.

• • • • •

Eddie and Rob sat back and continued their stakeout. They talked about everything from Led Zeppelin to Eddie's case of poison ivy that he had probably picked up in the woods in Milton. Nothing further happened. Eddie looked at his watch. It was almost five o'clock.

"Let's call it a day and go back to the office," said Eddie. "We can check it out again tomorrow. Besides, I gotta piss. All that coffee."

They returned to the office and figured how they should proceed.

"Let's see if Sarah has any more info about surveillance tapes," said Rob.

"Good. I'll see if Dugan is in his office. We need to fill him in."

Rob walked over to Sarah's desk.

"Anything new, angel face?"

"You're such a schmooze, Rob. I'm on to you." Sarah looked up from her computer with a smile. "Don't ever change," she added.

Rob smiled and let out a knowing chuckle.

"I had two cops pick up some more tapes from local stores over in Milton. Those poor rookie cops are probably just getting to them now. That's about it."

"Okay, thanks, Sarah. Maybe you would like to join me and Eddie for a couple of drinks on us one of these days."

"Eddie already tried to bribe me with dinner yesterday. It's really not necessary, but thanks for asking."

"Okay. But let us know if you change your mind."

Rob walked over to the two cops who were looking at the tapes. From their expressions, it was clear that they were mental. They looked like they were hypnotized and about to throw up.

"How's it going, guys?"

"This is what we've got so far, detective," said one officer with a sour look on his face.

He handed Rob a list of plate numbers about a mile long.

"Okay, thanks, guys. Why don't you take a break? You can pick it up again tomorrow."

The two officers exchanged a look of total disgust and resignation.

Rob walked over to Jimmy Dugan's office, where Eddie was already filling him in on Abdul Nasir.

"We don't know if this guy has anything to do with Jane Doe, let alone the Reardon case. All we know is that his car was in Milton late at night at the time the murder could have occurred," explained Eddie.

"So where are you gonna take this? What do you want to do about it?" asked Dugan.

"We'd like to stake the place out. There are some suspicious things going on there. We spoke to one of his neighbors and she said there were all kinds of people coming and going at all times of day and night," Eddie continued.

Dugan just nodded and listened.

"On campus he's known as 'The Sheik.' Boston College is right nearby," added Rob. "We followed him from his house to another house on Beacon Street. There was a guy in an upstairs window hiding behind a curtain like he was a lookout and expecting someone. Nasir has a felony on his record for check forgery. It might be worth looking into."

"Okay, I'll give you guys some time to follow up on it, but if nothing comes of it by next week, I'm gonna have to pull the plug."

"Understood, Jimmy. I think we might be able to get something."

The two detectives walked back to their desks and began to discuss what they had learned. After half an hour Eddie looked at his watch. It was now seven o'clock.

"Want to hit Zan's?" asked Rob.

"Sure," said Eddie. "Why not?"

They called it a day and headed for Zan's Bar.

· · · · ·

At five o'clock Mike had had enough. He said good evening to Donna and Diane and left the office. He arrived home at six. He gave a big hug and a kiss to Brit, Jamie and Roni and looked forward to a nice, relaxing evening with the family. Another enjoyable but otherwise uneventful day had come to an end.

· · · · ·

Don figured he would shower that evening and skip it in the morning. He spent the next couple of hours focused on compiling facts and working out his best agenda. When he was done, he sat on the bed and called Eddie McGowan. It was 7:30 PM.

'Hi Don. What's up on your end?"

"I'm heading for Danbury to check out the girl that was murdered here a couple of weeks ago. After that, I don't know."

"Nothing special to add here either. Rob and I are heading for Zan's. We're gonna pick it up again tomorrow morning."

"Okay, Eddie. You and Rob be safe out there. I'll call you and keep you posted."

"Good hunting, Don."

Don got back to thinking about the facts and tried to make sense of it. Maybe they did have two separate cases going on. He lay back on the down pillows and comforter and let sleep take him.

• • • • •

It was 8 PM. Eddie had just gotten to Zan's. He met Rob in the parking lot and the two of them went inside and walked straight over to the bar and took a seat.

"Hi Zan," Rob called out.

"Hey, lover boy. Will you guys be having the usual?"

"Same for me, Zan," said Eddie.

"Same for me, too," said Rob

Zan opened a Becks for Rob and poured Eddie a bourbon.

"You boys arrest anyone today?" Zan asked, trying to start a conversation.

"No, but we had to shoot a couple of people for driving too slowly on the way over here," said Rob with a serious expression.

"Wise ass," she said. "So what are you guys working on?" she persisted.

"Top secret," said Rob. "We could tell you but then we'd have to kill you."

It was an old joke. Everyone over twenty had heard it by now, but Zan laughed anyway.

"So what are your thoughts so far, Rob?" asked Eddie, taking a sip of bourbon.

Rob thought for a moment and said, "We've got a couple of leads. Abdul Nasir, for one. We've got Erica and the crime lab still working on an ID for Jane Doe. There's also a possible murder of another student in Youngstown. What if our Jane Doe turns out to be a student as well? Nasir lives near Boston College. Our witness, Joanie, said Abdul is known on campus. I wonder if he's actually a student. We should check that out tomorrow."

"Agreed," said Eddie. "We should also find out how long he's been living there. Jimmy is going to assign a few more detectives to the case. We can let them chase license plates."

Alexandra saw the detectives speaking quietly to each other and nonchalantly started moving closer to them as she pretended to be wiping down the bar. The detectives noticed and stopped talking. They looked at Zan and then began paying attention to their drinks.

Alexandra looked up and smiled. "Can't get one past you guys, can I?"

"We are detectives after all, Zan," said Eddie.

"C'mon. I'm just curious. I want to know about what you guys do all day."

"You can read about it in the paper when we're finished," said Rob.

Zan went back to serving customers and socializing and the detectives resumed their conversation.

"Eddie, I think we should first see if the Sheik's Mercedes is at his house. Then we can stake out the house on Beacon Street again. Something's wrong over there. I don't know if it's connected to our case, but something smells lousy."

"I agree," said Eddie. "We really don't have much else to follow up on right now.

Eddie finished his drink and ordered another bourbon. The sweet, warm toxin was beginning to have its effect. He felt as good as he had all day. Rob ordered his third Becks. They spent the next hour talking to Zan.

At 9:30 Eddie looked at his watch and said, "Time to go home."

Rob said, "I'm gonna stick around for one more."

"See you in the morning. Don't stay too long."

"Don't worry," said Zan from the other end of the bar. "I'll throw him out before eleven o'clock. Promise!"

Eddie sighed and walked out the door.

CHAPTER 11

Wednesday, Oct. 6, 5:00 AM

It was five o'clock Wednesday morning and Don was already on the Whitestone Bridge heading north to the Bronx. The morning rush hour had not yet choked the city arteries and with any luck he would be in Danbury in an hour. He would have time to catch breakfast and read the paper before he called Detective Behan. Don continued to cruise north on the Hutchinson River Parkway and then turned north on 684. It was still dark out and he had the road to himself. He put the address for the Danbury police headquarters into his GPS and put the car in cruise control. He sat back, relaxed and let himself drift back into his obsession. The Jane Doe murder and the perceived similarities to the Paula Carter murder pulled at his thoughts like a magnet. He began to reconstruct his theory from the start. If the Reardons were in fact kidnapped why was there no attempt to extort money? If they had been murdered why was there no evidence? Why were there no bodies? Was there a connection between the disappearance of the Reardons and the Carters? Were the two bodies in the morgue somehow connected to this case? Was there a legitimate reason to tie in the other murders based solely on the weapon? Don's mind was reeling. Was there anything solid or was he just grasping for anything to go on? He began to have doubts.

Don turned off of 684 at the Danbury exit and made his way to Main Street. He started looking for an open diner and found one on Franklin Street, around the corner from the police station. He looked at his watch. It was seven o'clock and he wondered if it was too early to call Behan. *I'll wait fifteen minutes and give him a try*, he thought. *He's got to be awake by then.* He was eager to get started. There was a lot he wanted get done today. He had almost blown off the murder of Patricia Nelson. It didn't fit in with any of the other murders. She wasn't a student. No attempt had been made to hide the body and it was unlikely she had any ties to terrorist activities. The only common elements were her age and the type of weapon used, but there were lots of people with Vanadium steel knives these days. They were top of the line but expensive.

Don looked at his watch. It was 7:10 AM. He decided to risk pissing off Behan. He called the number.

Behan picked up on the first ring.

"Detective Behan."

"Hi Mike. It's Don Corlino from Boston. We spoke the other day."

"Oh yes. Hi Detective. Are you still planning on coming down to Danbury?"

"I'm here now. I'm at a diner around the corner from the station. When can we meet?"

"Come right over. I'm at my desk working on the Nelson case right now. I've been coming in early all week. Murders like this don't happen very often in Danbury and I'm under some pressure. I've been here since six o'clock."

Don let his eyes roll and let out a sigh. "I'll be there in five."

"Okay, Don."

Don paid his check and rushed over to the station. He greeted the officer at the front desk and flashed his badge.

"Hi. I'm Detective Corlino. I'm here to see Detective Behan."

The officer buzzed him in. "He's expecting you. Go right ahead."

Don walked into the central office, where several detectives were seated at their desks. He looked around and saw one of them motion to him.

"Over here, Detective." Don walked over and shook his hand. "Detective Behan. Take a seat please."

Don obliged and was about to speak but Behan beat him to it. "What is it that you think you can find out here in Danbury?"

Don thought about it and said, "Probably nothing. I just drove down to Long Island chasing another lead and Danbury was on the way back. I have to agree that there isn't much to tie my case to yours other than the type of weapon used."

"So what do you want to do? Is there anything you want to ask the M.E.?"

"No, I've got all I need there. I'd like to talk to some of her friends and co-workers. What I want to know is if she had any connection to the Boston area. Maybe her parents know something."

"Oh please, don't interview them unless it's absolutely necessary. Her mother was hysterical when I talked to her. It's not something I want to do again."

"So where should we begin?" asked Don.

"The Copper Pot. It's the restaurant where she worked. A lot of her friends hang out there at night. Her co-workers might also be able to tell you something, but it doesn't open till one o'clock for lunch."

Don thought about it. He really didn't want to stay the whole day. The other cases were his main interest. The possible connection to terrorism made the Carter case his first priority. He also wanted to follow up on the Buffalo murders since the new information about Youngstown came in. More than ever, he believed there was a serial killer on the loose, but working on two separate cases was difficult. He weighed his options and reminded himself that the Reardon case was his priority.

"Who was her best friend here in Danbury?" asked Don.

"A girl named Samantha Begg. They shared a house with a couple of other friends. It's only about five or ten minutes from here."

"Would they be available now?"

"They should be. You know kids these days. They sleep until noon."

A tall blond man of about 40 years old walked over to Behan's desk.

"This is my partner, Detective Carl Edelman. Carl, this is Detective Corlino that I told you about yesterday."

"Good morning, Don. So...you're with the FBI, I understand."

"That's right."

"And you think that the Nelson case is connected to a murder and possibly a kidnapping in Boston. What leads you to believe that?"

"In the last six months there have been an unusually high number of murders in the New England area in which the wounds were similar and the same type of knife was used. Patricia Nelson was one of them. As a matter of fact, that's the only thing that drew my attention to this case. It may not pan out. Miss Nelson was first stabbed twice in the abdomen. Whoever did this cut her throat to finish her off and make sure. That's not the case with the other homicides. I'd still like to check it out."

"Detective Corlino would like..."

"Call me Don. Please."

"Don would like to interview some of Miss Nelson's friends. Would you mind running him over to that house on Deer Hill Road, Carl?"

"If it's not going to take too long, I can drive you over there and drop you back here," offered Carl.

"That would be great. Thanks. This probably won't take more than an hour or two," Don assured him. "Will you be here when we get back, Mike?"

"I should be. If I'm not here and you need me, I won't be far away. You've got my number."

"If I don't see you later, I want to thank you for helping me out."

"No problem. Let me call Samantha Begg and let her know you're coming. Hold on a minute and let me make sure that she's home." He dialed the number and waited. "Hello Samantha. This is Detective Behan. I want to send Detective Edelman to your house with another detective from Boston who wants to ask a couple of questions. It won't take long. Is that okay?"

Don watched Behan as he talked on the phone.

"Good, good. They will be there in about 10 or 15 minutes. Are any of the others there? Okay fine. Thanks Samantha."

Behan looked at Don and said, "All of her friends are there right now. You should be able to get everything you want."

"Thanks Mike. I'll either call or see you before I go."

The two detectives headed out toward the house Patricia had shared with her friends. In ten minutes, they were there. Detective Edelman knocked on the door and Samantha answered it.

"Come in, Detective," she said.

They walked inside and found four other young people waiting for them in the living room.

"You all know me. We've talked earlier this week," said Detective Edelman. "This is Detective Corlino from Boston. He's with the FBI. He would like to ask you all a few questions."

The four housemates all looked to be in their early twenties and seemed somewhat nervous. One boy looked up surprised at the mention of the FBI.

"This is Ricky, Jen, Freddie and Donna," Samantha said, pointing at them as she introduced them.

"I would just like to ask a few questions about Miss Nelson's social life, if you don't mind."

"Sure. Anything we can do to help," said Samantha.

"Can any of you tell me if Miss Nelson had any friends or relatives from the Boston area? Also, I would like to know if she visited there in the past few months."

"Nobody I know, and I was probably her best friend," said Samantha. "Any of you guys hear of anything about Boston?"

They all thought for a moment and looked at each other.

"I can't think of anyone," said Jen. They all shook their heads in agreement.

"What can you tell me about the people she worked with? Did she ever mention any problems she was having with anyone?"

"No. She never mentioned anything like that. That was our favorite place. We all hung out there. She knew everyone. The Copper Pot is the most popular place in Danbury on weekends," said Rick. "Why's the FBI getting involved in this?"

"Just being thorough and checking out a connection to another murder," explained Don. "What about boyfriends? Do you know of anyone she might have been involved with?"

"There was her boyfriend Duncan, but she broke up with him about a month ago," said Samantha.

Detective Edelman interrupted, "We spoke to him already. He's got an airtight alibi. He was visiting relatives in Pittsburgh for the whole week of the murder. There's about fifty witnesses. We ruled him out as a suspect."

"Did they break up on good terms?" Don continued.

"I'd say so," said Samantha.

After a moment Rick, who had asked about the FBI, spoke up and said, "I'm not so sure about that, Sam."

"What do you mean?" said Samantha, somewhat surprised.

Rick seemed reluctant to speak up but continued, "I think Duncan was getting a little tired of her asking him favors all the time."

"Did you know Duncan well?" asked Don.

"Yeah. I'd say so. We were all friends. We met him about a year ago at the Pot. He's a nice guy. He would never do anything to hurt Patty. I'm just saying he was starting to feel like he was being used."

"You didn't mention this when we talked before," said Detective Edelman.

"Well, it was nothing really. I just didn't want to make Patty look bad. I mean she's dead and she was my friend," explained Rick, taking a slightly defensive tone. "Besides, you said he was in Pittsburgh when it happened."

Samantha seemed to be upset with this latest news. "You never told me that, Rick. I would have liked to know."

Rick looked a little guilty but didn't say anything more.

Don had a way of making people relax and open up to his questions. It was one of the qualities that made him a good detective.

"Anybody have any further thoughts about that? Did any of you see a change in her behavior?"

"Lately I noticed that she was flirting with a lot of guys. She was starting to get a bit of a reputation," said Jen.

"How so?" persisted Don.

"Well, she wasn't exactly rolling in money. None of us are. She was getting in the habit of getting guys to buy her drinks. She would flirt with them and then move on to another guy. She was getting pretty good at it. I tried to talk to her, but she just laughed and batted her eyes at me. It was starting to worry me a little."

"When did you first notice her change in behavior?"

"I'd say about two months ago. She started making comments about making something of herself and being stuck in a dead-end job. She said she was tired of struggling to make ends meet and that she could do better," said Freddie.

"What do the rest of you think about her state of mind the last couple of months?" asked Don.

"I never thought it was a big deal. I thought it was her trying to build a little confidence in herself. She was a good-looking girl but if you ask me, she was a little insecure. Ya know? Girls like it when guys pay attention to them and do things for them. We joked about it once in a while," explained Jen.

"What about guys at the Copper Pot? Anyone she was taking an interest in."

"Patty was a very popular girl. Lots of guys were falling all over themselves. It made me kind of jealous. It's a good thing I've got Freddie here," said Jen. She leaned over and kissed him on the cheek.

Samantha rolled her eyes and gave her a disapproving look.

"Do any of you know if she was seeing anyone in particular? Was she seeing anyone on a steady basis?"

"If she was, she kept it a secret from us," said Samantha.

"How far is the Copper Pot from here?" asked Don.

"It's about a mile... mile and a half," said Rick.

"How did Patricia get to work?"

"I have a car," explained Rick. "I would give her a ride back and forth when I could. Otherwise, she'd take her bicycle. She often did that when the weather was nice."

"Would that take her past the park where she was found?" asked Don.

"Not directly. The park is about two blocks over from the road she would take," continued Rick.

"What about when the weather wasn't nice?"

"Sometimes she took an Uber. She said she might be getting a car soon," said Samantha.

"You said she didn't have a great deal of money. Did she mention anything about where she was getting the car?"

"Some guy she knew. She didn't say who," said Samantha.

"About what time do you guys go to the Copper Pot? I'd like to go there and ask a few questions."

"The action doesn't start until after ten o'clock. It's just the dinner crowd until then," said Jen. "Really boring."

"Can I expect a lot of people she knew to be there tonight?"

"It's Wednesday. A lot of the regulars will probably be there. It's better than Monday or Tuesday," said Freddie.

"Yeah. Tuesday's like the Losers Club meeting," Jen chimed in.

Samantha gave her another look.

"Can you all do me a favor? I'd like the five of you to show up there tonight. I need you to point out people who knew her."

"Sure. I think we can all do that. Everybody cool with that?" Rick asked, looking at the others.

"So I can count on you all to be there at ten o'clock."

"I guess so," said Samantha.

"Thank you very much for your cooperation and I'm sorry for your loss."

Samantha gave him a faint smile and said, "Thanks."

The two detectives left and got back to the car.

"I thought you were eager to get out of here," said Detective Edelman.

"I am, but I just want to check something out first."

"What's on your mind?"

"This business about her getting favors from guys. I want to know who she was getting close to."

"None of them ever mentioned that when Behan and I interviewed them," said Edelman, sounding a bit annoyed.

"They were just protecting the memory of their friend. I think Samantha and Rick really cared about her."

"So what do you plan on doing for the rest of the day? You don't have to be at the Copper Pot for..." Carl looked at his watch. "...ten and a half hours."

"I'd like to pay a quick visit to her former boyfriend."

"Duncan Smith? We interviewed him for hours and like I said, he's got a rock-solid alibi."

"I'm not interested in him as a suspect, but he might know something."

"You don't think this case has anything to do with yours anymore. Do you?"

"Probably not, but if you don't mind, I'd like to spend today and tomorrow here in Danbury."

"It's fine with me, Detective. I'm sure it would be fine with Behan too. As long as you keep us up to speed with what you're doing I'm willing to work with you."

"I was hoping you would see it that way. Would you mind going with me to talk to Smith?"

"Not at all. I'll tell my partner where we're going."

$$\bullet \ \bullet \ \bullet \ \bullet \ \bullet$$

Eddie had arrived at work at eight o'clock and checked on the progress the two officers had made overnight. The two unfortunate officers looked like they needed hospitalization.

"Can you please have someone else assigned to this tomorrow?" pleaded one of them.

"I'll tell Dugan to get someone else," promised Eddie.

He once again returned to his desk to enter plate numbers into the computer. Rob showed up half an hour later.

"Good morning, Eddie."

"Good morning, Rob. Did you behave yourself last night?"

"Of course. Don't I always?"

Rob checked his inbox and began looking through the new info. "Got the names from Avis and Enterprise here:"

George Lincoln from Roslyn, NY

Michelle Dennis from Rochester, NY

George Martinson from Mesa, Arizona

"Got the numbers too. Let me make some phone calls."

"I'll check the numbers of the people we couldn't reach last time," sighed Eddie.

Half an hour later they took a break and looked at each other.

"Anything?" asked Eddie.

"Mr. Lincoln said he was hiking with his family and lost track of the time. The summons was issued at quarter after five. Just fifteen minutes after the no parking zone went into effect. Martinson claims he was gathering firewood for his house. Sounds believable. I called Michelle Dennis but it just goes to voicemail. Any luck on your end?"

"No. Nothing yet."

Eddie picked up one of the parking summonses and checked it against the list of unanswered calls. "Whoa. Got something."

"What is it?"

"One of the registrations on our original list doesn't fit the description of the car. The registration says it's a blue 2012 Honda Accord but the summons says it's a green 1997 Subaru Outback."

"What's the name?" asked Rob, picking up his ears.

"Adam Roach."

"Roach! Well, that's gotta be our guy," said Rob, giving Eddie a half-serious look. "What's the time and date of the summons?"

"Nine thirty PM on Sept 24. We definitely gotta check this one out," said Eddie. "Wanna do it this afternoon?"

"Sure. It's at least a misdemeanor if nothing else. Is the address local?"

"It's in Dedham on Washington Street. Not too far."

"Let me call Michelle Dennis again. I'm gonna leave a message on voicemail for her. I just want to tie up all the loose ends."

Again, the call went to voicemail. Rob explained who he was and what it was about. He left his number and called Enterprise again.

"Enterprise. How can I help you?"

"I'm Detective Robert Morrow with the Boston Police Department. We are trying to track down a girl who rented a car from you. Her car was ticketed in Milford. The Traffic Summons Department requested a name from the plate number we have. Her name is Michelle Dennis. I want to find out more about her information."

"Do you have an official number I can call you back on? I have to verify that you are actually the police, you understand?"

"Yes, of course. It's 617-343-5600. Just tell the operator to forward the call to Detective Morrow."

Rob went back to his list and waited for a reply.

Eddie and Rob continued making phone calls for the next half hour.

Rob's desk phone rang and he picked up. "Detective Morrow."

"Yes, Detective. This is Enterprise. You wanted information about Michelle Dennis."

"That's right."

"All I can tell you is that she rented the car in person on September 20. She returned the keys to the drop box sometime on the morning of the 26. Sorry I can't be of more help."

"Okay. Thank you very much." Rob hung up and turned to Eddie. "Eddie. Get this. Michelle didn't drop the car off in person. She left the keys in the drop box early on the 26."

"Interesting. She's not answering her phone?"

"That's right."

"You said you have an address for her in Rochester? Maybe we should call the Rochester Police Department and have them cruise by her place?"

"Good idea. We should probably check the computer and see if she has any arrests on her record."

"Okay. You call Rochester and I'll check the computer."

Eddie punched in the information. Rob figured it would be better to wait for the results before he called.

"What have we here? There's a Michelle Dennis with an arrest for prostitution in Rochester. Let's find out if that's our girl."

Rob punched in the number.

"Rochester Police Department. Sergeant Price speaking. How can I help you?

"I'm Detective Morrow with the Boston Police. I'm trying to track down a girl named Michelle Dennis. She doesn't pick up her phone, and we have concerns she may have been the victim of foul play. She rented a car from Enterprise and gave her address as 34 Monroe Street in Rochester. We would like to have you send a patrol car over there and see if she's there."

"Sure, Detective. Let me transfer you to Sergeant Karobkin. He can help you out."

Rob waited and explained his request to the sergeant.

"No problem. We can send a patrol car by. Anything else?"

"Yes, Sergeant. Our computer shows an arrest record for a Michelle Dennis. We're not sure if it's the same girl. We'd like to corroborate the information."

"Okay, Detective. I'll get on it immediately. Let me call you back in half an hour."

"Very good. Thank you, Sergeant."

Eddie and Rob continued the drudgery of entering plate numbers into the computer. After an hour they had a list of five new names to check out.

The phone rang and Rob picked up. "Detective Morrow."

"Yes, Detective. This is Sergeant Karobkin. First, we checked on the arrest record you requested. The address you gave us does confirm she's the girl who was arrested; however, we have a new address for her now. It's 54 Verona Street. We had a patrol car go by and knock on the door, but there was no answer. We'll try again later."

"Okay. Thank you again, Sergeant."

"What did you find out?" asked Eddie.

"She's the same girl who got arrested. Maybe she ran into the wrong guy this time. She might be our Jane Doe."

"If that's true, the guy took a lot of trouble to return the car."

"That's true. It doesn't really add up. Maybe we should call Don and let him know, in any case. It could be important."

"Couldn't hurt," agreed Eddie.

Rob called and Don picked up. "Hi Rob. What's up?"

"We followed up on one of our leads and we have reason to believe we might be on to something. One of the summonses we looked into was a rental from Enterprise. The car was rented by a girl by the name of Michelle Dennis. It was parked in the preserve on Unquity Road on September 25. She didn't return the car in person, and she has a record for prostitution. We're pursuing the possibility that she's our Jane Doe. The Rochester Police are looking into it. We have an address for her as 54 Verona Street in Rochester, New York."

Don wrote down the name and address on a piece of paper and put it in his pocket.

"Good work, guys. Keep me posted. I'm still in Danbury. I spoke with the detectives here and interviewed some of the victim's friends. I want to track down one more lead before I leave."

"Okay, Don. We'll be in touch."

CHAPTER 12

Wednesday, 11:30 AM

Don's spirits were somewhat lifted when he received the call from Rob about the possible I.D. of Jane Doe. *Eddie and Rob did some excellent work,* he thought to himself. He wanted to get back to Boston and follow up on Michelle Dennis as well as the terrorism angle. But he also wanted to follow his instincts about the murder of Patricia Nelson before he left. He let Carl know of his plans.

Detective Edelman got on his cell phone and called Duncan Smith.

"Hi Duncan. It's Detective Edelman. Are you busy right now?"

Don listened to the conversation.

"Good. I'm on my way over with an FBI detective from Boston. He'd like to ask some questions. Yeah. The FBI. That's right. We'll be there in 10 minutes."

Don took out his own phone and said, "I've gotta make a couple of quick calls myself. It won't take long."

"Knock yourself out."

Don pulled out the list of James Carter's contacts that his T.A. had given him earlier. He found the number for Captain Christopher Wyatt, the head of the Joint Terrorist Task Force in Boston, and punched in the number.

"Captain Wyatt," the voice came over the phone.

"Hello Captain Wyatt. This is Detective Corlino. I'm with the FBI in Boston."

"Hello Detective. How can I help you?"

"I would like to know if you remember a chemistry professor by the name of James Carter. He was a guest lecturer at one of your seminars about six months ago."

"James Carter? Yes, I do, Detective. Interesting guy. He's the expert on homemade explosives, right?

"That's right. Did you know him well?"

"That sounds ominous. No, I only knew him professionally. What's happened?

"His wife Paula was found murdered on Long Island. Right now, he's missing. That's all we know."

"I'm sorry to hear that. Why are you interested in his appearance at our seminar?"

"I'm investigating the disappearance of Kevin Reardon and his wife Jennifer. I'm sure you've heard of them. It's been in the news."

"Yes. That bank executive and his wife. And you think these cases are somehow related?"

"Possibly. There's another case that may be related. A girl was found murdered in Milton a few days ago. She had her throat cut. There are a lot of similarities to the Paula Carter murder. What I want to know about is the people he may have had contact with in Boston, either socially or professionally."

"It was six months ago so my memory of him isn't that clear. I think he visited some professors at Boston University. That's about all I can remember right now. I'll ask around. Maybe one of my team will remember something. Is there anything else I can do for you?"

"Yes, Captain Wyatt. I would like to give you the numbers of two detectives who work out of the E-18 precinct in Hyde Park. Their names are Eddie McGowan and Robert Morrow. Maybe you've heard of them."

"The name Morrow rings a bell. He was the detective who was honored by the Mayor some time ago but I don't know them personally."

"I also want to give you the number of Erika Koenig. She's the M.E. at Boston University."

"Erika. Yes, I know Erika. I've had a chance to work with her in the past. I have her number."

"Good. She can fill you in on the details of a murder that took place recently in Milton. If you hear of anything that might be of value, please pass the information on to her and Detective McGowan. I'll give you the numbers now."

"Okay Detective. I'll do that."

Don texted him the numbers and thanked him. He then called Jack Sullivan.

"Hi Jack. I'm still in Danbury. I'd like to stay here for a little while longer. I think I may be on to something."

"Okay, Don. Just remember that your priority is the Reardon case. I don't want you getting sidetracked."

"I've made some progress there. Yesterday I uncovered a possible link to terrorist activities concerning the Carter disappearance and his wife's murder on Long Island. I'm gonna have McGowan follow up on it."

"Very well. I trust your instincts. Do what you think is best. Remember, I've got a lot of people barking at me."

"Thanks Jack. I appreciate it."

Detective Edelman looked over at Don and said, "Well, you lead an exciting life. We get about one murder a year here in Danbury and that's usually a drug-related incident. We have our share of MS13 types. A murder like this might happen once every twenty years. We've got six detectives working on it day and night. That's practically everyone. I hate to admit it but every detective in the department wants to be the dog that finds the bone. You know what I mean?"

"I've seen that everywhere. If you solve a case you get promoted. More money. More status. I can't say that I blame them."

"I appreciate you trying to help out on this case, Don. We followed up on several leads and did a lot of interrogations but we're no closer to a suspect. You've had a lot of experience. What do you think is our best shot?"

"Rick and Jen said that her behavior had changed in the last two months. They felt that she was trying to get ahead by using her looks and taking advantage of guys. I think we should play up that angle. Maybe Duncan can shed some light on that."

"Okay. I'll let you ask the questions."

They pulled up in front of house and Duncan was waiting for them in front.

"Come in please," he said. "I understand you're with the FBI."

"Yes I am. I'm Detective Corlino," Don said, offering his hand.

"Why is the FBI taking an interest in this?" Duncan asked.

"I'm following up on the possibility that Patricia's murder may be connected to another murder that occurred in Boston a few weeks ago. I know you're still in shock about this, but I'm going to have to ask you some difficult questions. Are you okay with that?"

"I guess so. I want this guy caught more than anyone."

"How long were you seeing Miss Nelson?"

"A little more than a year. We first met at the Copper Pot back in April a year and a half ago. We started going out that summer."

"Would you say your relationship with her was a happy one? I mean, did you fight a lot or was it peaceful?"

"Until a few months ago everything was great. We were always laughing. We were like best friends."

"What do you think changed?"

"I really don't know. I thought about that a lot before we broke up. Patty just started complaining about having to share a house and never having any money. I got the feeling she wanted something more. She said she was almost 27 years old and her life was going nowhere. She could get really testy sometimes."

"This is going to be hard but I have to ask the question. Do you think she might have been seeing someone else?"

Duncan winced at the question. "I don't know, Detective. I thought she might be, but I didn't want to believe that. I still don't know for sure."

"Did she ever talk about moving out of her place or moving to another city?"

"No. Nothing like that."

"Can you think of anyone in her life that might have been able to help her financially? Like a rich local kid? Maybe she mentioned an older guy she met?"

Duncan stared at the ground and began to think. After some time, he regretfully shook his head and had to say no.

"What about getting a car? Did she ever mention wanting to buy a car?"

"Yeah, she did. All the time. She was tired of being dependent on other people. I think she felt trapped. I went with her a couple of times to look at some cars for sale around town but they were either too expensive or just plain shit. Oh, sorry. I mean they sucked. You know what I mean?"

"Yeah, Duncan. I remember when I was your age. It's tough to get ahead. Is there anything you can think of that she might have done to make extra money? Is there anyone she might have gone to? Did she take a special interest in any of the people who were trying to sell a car?"

Again, Duncan shook his head.

"Can you think of any of her friends who might have suggested where she could get a car?" Don persisted.

Duncan looked at Don and said, "Nobody we knew well, but there might have been someone. A friend of mine, Jeff, said he knew a guy who was thinking of buying a Jeep or an Outback and might want to unload his old ride for the right price. That was a couple of months ago. Patty was asking Jeff about it. I never met him. His name is Eric or something."

"Did Patricia know Jeff well?"

"Sure, we hung out at my house all the time. Jeff also hangs out at the Pot. I guess you could say we were all friends. Samantha, Rick, Jen, Freddie, Donna—they all knew Jeff."

Detective Edelman interrupted, "We talked to Jeff. His last name is Bergman. He didn't seem to think he had anything that could help us solve this. Right now, he's not high on our list of suspects."

"Jeff would never do anything like this. If you met him, you'd know that. He's just not the type," said Duncan.

"This friend of Jeff's—did he ever go to the Copper Pot?"

"No. Only Jeff knows him. I think he's from Brewster over in New York. You could ask Jeff."

"Could you call Jeff and ask him for a phone number? Also, could you ask Jeff to come to the Copper Pot tonight? I'd like you to be there as well."

"Sure. We usually all go there on Wednesday." Duncan picked up the phone and called his friend Jeff. "Yo, Jeff. I'm sitting here talking to a detective from the FBI. He wants you to come to the Pot tonight. He wants to talk to you. Everyone is going to be there."

"Get his friend's phone number, too," Don reminded him.

"Yeah, Jeff. Listen, you remember that friend of yours who was thinking of selling his car? I think his name was Eric or Eddie or something."

Duncan picked up a pencil and jotted down the name.

"Eddie Lubin. L-U-B-I-N. Got it. And his phone and address?"

Duncan looked up and said, "He said he doesn't know his phone number or address offhand."

"Can I get Jeff's number?"

"Sure. It's 445-8323."

"Thank you, Duncan. If you think of anything that might help us, please call Detective Edelman and let him know. No matter how insignificant it might be. We want to know about anybody who recently came into her life. Especially an older guy or someone with money."

Don stood up and said, "Detective, I think we're done here for now. We will see you later tonight, Duncan. You have been very helpful, and I am very sorry for your loss."

"Thank you, Detective. Please catch this guy soon, all right?"

The two detectives went back to their car and drove back toward police headquarters.

"Well, what now, Detective?"

"How about we grab some lunch? After that I'd like to make some phone calls. We'll see what turns up."

"I really appreciate your help, Detective. We've been working on this case for more than a week and we don't have a main suspect. So do you think this Eddie guy is involved?"

"Just following up on a hunch. If it doesn't pan out, I'm leaving tomorrow. My boss wants me to focus on another assignment." Don took out his wallet and handed Edelman his card. "This is where you can reach me. I can get information from the FBI database. If you need a favor, call me. Do you know a good lunch spot?"

"Yeah, I know just the place."

The two detectives ordered lunch and Don made a phone call to Jeff Bergman.

"Hello, Jeff. This is Detective Corlino from the FBI in Boston. I spoke to your friend Duncan this morning. I would like to ask you about your friend Eddie Lubin."

"Sure. He's not really my friend. I hardly know him."

"Just tell me everything you can about him."

"I only met him a couple of times. He was a friend of my older brother some time ago. He's like 38 years old or something. He lives over in Brewster. That's like 20 miles from here."

"Do you know if he was interested in hunting?"

"Yeah. My brother was. I think that's how they knew each other."

"I understand he was selling a car some time ago. Is that right?"

"Yeah. It was a 99 Honda Prelude. Real nice ride. Everybody loves those cars."

"Did your friend, Patricia, ever go to look at the car?"

"No. I gave her his number but he wanted like three grand for it. She could never afford that and it was all the way in Brewster."

"I see. Is there anything else you can tell me about Eddie?"

"Not really. If you really want to know you could ask my brother."

"Thank you very much, Jeff. I will talk to you again at the Copper Pot."

Don hung up and dialed another number.

"Who you calling?" asked Tom.

"FBI database."

Don punched a sequence of keys on his phone including an FBI access code and a search request. A moment later he received a text message with a phone number.

"One more phone call."

Don called the FBI computer database in Boston and said, "This is Detective Don Corlino, security code Alpha – 7222157 – Omega. I need the records of a sale of a 99 Honda Prelude by owner Edward Lubin of Brewster, NY. I also need the plate number and his current address. STAT, please. Call me back as soon as you can."

The detectives continued with their lunch and waited for the call.

A few minutes later the phone rang and Don answered, "Corlino."

"Yes, Detective," a woman's voice came over the phone. "You requested an address and a record of sale for a car?"

"That's right."

"No record of sale on that Prelude. Original owner Edward Lubin. Plate number FLB 2885, address 59 Crestwood Road, Brewster NY, according to NY State MVB."

"Thank you very much. I don't know your name."

"Jennifer," came the reply.

"Thanks, Jennifer. Love ya. Have a wonderful day."

Carl looked over at Don, expecting an explanation or what was going to be the next move.

Don continued eating his lunch and asked Carl, "How long does it take to get to Brewster?"

"Not long. Less than half an hour at this time of day."

"Feel like taking a ride out to Brewster this afternoon?" asked Don.

Carl looked at Don, this time visibly intrigued. "Okay. I'm down," he said.

Carl was getting excited at the thought of maybe cracking the case. They finished their lunch and Don stopped at his car to pick up a few extra magazines of ammo. A few minutes later they were headed down Route 84 toward Brewster. Carl kept his foot to the metal and they were there in twenty minutes. The GPS located 59 Crestwood Road and soon they were approaching the house.

They turned onto Crestwood Road and the GPS announced that they were 50 yards from their destination.

"There's that Prelude," said Carl, his voice filled with excitement.

Don took out his Sig Sauer P228 and checked that it was loaded.

"That's a nice piece," said Carl. "I want one. Top of the line."

"I guess you have a Glock 22. Make sure it's loaded. You may need it."

Don picked up his phone and punched in a number.

"Who you calling now?"

"Eddie Lubin."

"What?!"

"Hello Eddie. My name is Duncan. A friend of mine told me that you're looking to sell a 99 Prelude."

There was a long silence and a voice replied, "Who..who is this?"

"A friend of yours gave me your number and said you had a 99 Prelude you might be looking to sell. I've been looking through the papers but I can't find one. I was hoping yours is still available."

There was another moment of silence and a hesitant voice came over the phone. "No. No. I'm not looking to sell. Sorry."

"Oh. That's too bad. Well, thank you anyway. Goodbye."

"Yeah, goodbye."

Carl looked at Don with a curious gleam in his eye. "So? You really think you got something?"

"I'm not sure. I was just trying to spook him a little to see how he reacted. The guilty get nervous."

They pulled up just down the road from the Prelude.

"Just put the car in park and let's see what happens," Don said. "Remember, we're not sure of anything yet so take it easy."

The detectives waited patiently for about twenty minutes. Don talked casually about his girlfriend, Cheryl, and the fact that she was getting impatient waiting for a marriage proposal.

Carl just looked at him, trying to figure out if Don was for real.

He continued talking and asked Carl, "So do you have a wife and kids?"

"Yeah. My wife Marge and two sons. Eric and Peter."

"Any vacation plans coming up?" continued Don.

Carl bit his lower lip and tried to keep his mind on the conversation.

At that moment a man who looked to be in his late 30s emerged from the garage carrying what looked like camping gear. He began walking toward the Prelude.

"Let's go, Carl. Remember, stay cool and let me do the talking."

The two detectives got out of the car and walked toward Eddie.

"Planning a trip Mr. Lubin?" Don called out to him.

Eddie looked at the two men, who were obviously detectives.

"What do you guys want?" said Eddie nervously.

"We just want to ask you a couple of questions, Eddie."

"About what?"

"About a friend of yours."

"Who would that be?"

"About someone who was interested in buying your car, Eddie."

Eddie was now visibly starting to sweat. "I'm not selling my car. What the hell?"

"Do you by any chance know a guy named Jeff Bergman?"

Eddie looked like he was about to puke.

"What about a girl named Patty?"

At that point Eddie dropped his gear and bolted back toward the garage.

"Stop. FBI," Don yelled.

Eddie continued to retreat into his house.

"Time to call for backup and sit on the house," said Don.

Carl was a little unsure about what to do. He had never been in a situation like this.

"Just be cool. We can wait it out until we get a warrant."

At that moment a window in the front of the house opened and Eddie appeared with a rifle.

"Cover," yelled Don as loudly as he could.

Carl and Don ran behind the Prelude and kept their heads down.

"The police are on their way, Eddie," Don shouted out. "Just give it up. Nowhere to run."

They could hear Eddie cursing through the open window. "Shit. Shit. Fuckin' shit. God damn motherfuckers. I'll blow your fuckin' heads off."

"Take it easy, Eddie," implored Don. "No one needs to get hurt. Just be cool."

Eddie continued to panic and curse. Then there were a few moments of silence, followed by the sound of a window breaking in the back of the house.

"He's running," said Don. "Get to your car radio and call for backup. Explain the situation. Suspect on the run, armed and dangerous. Give our exact location. I'll go around the side of the house. You just stay put and keep your weapon handy."

Don ran to the garage and carefully made his way around the right side of the house. He could still hear Eddie cursing. He heard him as he jumped from the rear window and landed in the courtyard behind the house. Don got to the courtyard just in time to catch a glimpse of Eddie as he disappeared around the far corner. Eddie had ditched the rifle but was now carrying a semi-automatic pistol. He was heading back toward the front of the house. Don figured he was trying to get to his Prelude and make a run for it. Don raced back the way he had come toward the front of the house.

"Carl, he's coming around the other side. He's going for his car."

Carl had his Glock ready and took a position in the street behind Eddie's car.

Don got to the corner of the house and motioned to Carl where Eddie was.

Both detectives held their ground, figuring time was on their side. A few moments went by and then the sound of sirens could be heard in the distance.

"Drop the weapon and come out with your hands up," pleaded Don. "Don't make things worse."

The world was closing in on Eddie. Like a crazed animal caught in a trap, he suddenly broke toward his car, cursing and firing his pistol at Edelman. He continued toward the street, trying to get an angle on him for a better shot.

Don didn't hesitate. He fired one shot, hitting Eddie in the lower back. Carl fired twice and hit Eddie in the left shoulder. Eddie went down instantly, screaming in pain and cursing at them.

"Don't move Eddie," demanded Don.

He ran to where Eddie was lying on the front lawn and took the pistol. In seconds he had him in cuffs. Carl also ran over, keeping his Glock trained on the now-helpless Eddie Lubin.

"Oh fuck. I'm shot. You fuckin' assholes. You shot me."

Don had Lubin on his stomach with his hands cuffed behind him and frisked him for other weapons. He found a 10-inch hunting knife in a sheath that was strapped to his belt under his jacket.

"Interesting, Eddie. What's this?"

"Fuck you, asshole," was Eddie's only comeback.

Don took out his cell phone and called 911.

"What's your emergency?"

"FBI detective Don Corlino. I've just shot a murder suspect. Send an ambulance to 59 Crestwood Road in Brewster."

"Could you spell your name, Detective?"

"C-O-R-L-I-N-O. Corlino," he repeated.

"Ambulance is on the way. ETA about five minutes."

"Thank you," said Don. "I'll stay on the line."

He began to read Lubin his rights.

Lubin cursed, "I did everything for that cunt. Took her places, bought her shit. She wanted me to give her my Lude. I kept telling her no. Then she said she was gonna dump me and go back to her boyfriend. Fuckin' bitch."

"I advise you to remain silent, Mr. Lubin."

Carl Edelman was still in shock. He had never fired his weapon other than on the firing range. He sat on the grass, took some deep breaths and began to take in what had just happened.

"First shoot?" Don asked him.

"Yeah. I guess we'll have to fill out lots of reports."

"I'd like you to write all the details for the police report. You and Behan are the lead detectives. You can write it any way you like. Make sure you give Behan part of the credit. I really can't afford to get involved too much. I've gotta get back to my kidnapping case. I'm sure I'll be busy most of the rest of today answering questions to the Brewster and Danbury Police."

"I'll do my best to have them make it quick."

"I'm also gonna have to question Mr. Lubin tomorrow. You should be there with me when I do that."

The sirens were now just down the block.

Don said, "Tonight I would like you to go to the Copper Pot. Duncan and the others should hear it from you and not the papers."

"Good idea, Don."

After a few minutes the Brewster police arrived and took Eddie Lubin into custody. He was loaded into the ambulance and brought to the hospital. The two detectives spent the rest of the afternoon filling out the reports. Detective Edelman tried to keep the smile from his face and felt somewhat embarrassed when he noticed Don looking at him.

"You earned this, Detective. You put your life on the line to bring Eddie Lubin to justice."

"Thank you, Don, but I know it was really you that cracked the case."

"Enjoy the moment, Carl."

• • • • •

Eddie and Rob worked out of their office until after five o'clock.

"Let me check with Rochester again," said Rob. He called Sergeant Karobkin. "Good afternoon, Sergeant. Morrow here again. Anything new?"

"I'm afraid not. We paid another visit to her Verona Street address. Still nobody home. We even went by her old address to inquire about her. Nothing there either."

"Okay. Thanks. Would you call me just before you get off tonight? Let me know where we stand."

"Sure, detective. No problem."

Frustrated, Rob said, "What do you say we pay a little visit to our friend Mr. Roach?"

"Sounds good. I'm getting a little stir crazy."

"Okay. Let's roll. Make sure you've got your Glock handy."

"Always do."

They drove to Dedham and found Washington Street. Rob looked at addresses as Eddie cruised slowly down the street. It was still raining and the fading sunlight glistened off the pavement.

"There's our blue Accord," said Rob. "The correct plates are on it now."

Eddie brought the Tahoe to a stop in front of the house.

"How do you suppose the plates wound up on the wrong car?"

"We're not gonna find out sitting here," said Eddie. "Keep your guard up."

They got out and walked to the front door. Eddie rang the bell. The two detectives waited for half a minute and rang the bell again. Again, they waited.

"His car is here. Maybe he's asleep."

"I'll go around back and see if he's on the porch or something," said Rob.

"Mr. Roach," Eddie called out. "Anybody home?"

Rob disappeared around the side of the house as Eddie tried the bell again.

After a minute Rob was back. "Found our green Subaru in a garage in the back. No plates on it. So what now?"

Eddie pounded on the door again. "Mr. Roach. You home?"

A muffled voice came from inside. "Who is it?"

"Boston Police, Mr. Roach. We'd like to ask you a couple of questions."

"Just a minute. I'll be right there."

The door opened and an elderly man stood before them with a blank stare. "Yes. What is it you want?"

"Is that your Honda Accord out front, Mr. Roach?" asked Eddie.

"Yes, it is. What's the problem?"

"Have you had cause to be in the Blue Hills Reservation in Milford in the past few weeks, Mr. Roach?" asked Eddie.

"Blue Hills? No. No, I haven't," he said, rubbing the sleep from his eyes and trying to clear his mind. "Forgive me. You woke me up."

"A summons was written to a car with your license plates on Saturday evening September 24 on Unquity Road in Milford."

"That's not possible," said Roach. "I haven't driven in over six months. I don't even have the keys. My daughter took them away last spring. She didn't want me driving anymore. The car doesn't even start. We've been trying to sell it for the last month."

"Actually, Mr. Roach, the summons was issued to a 1967 green Subaru Outback. Can you explain that?" said Eddie.

He waited for a reaction, not tipping his hand that they had already seen the Subaru in the garage.

"Oh shit!"

"What is it, Mr. Roach?"

"My grandson, Dennis, keeps his car here in the garage in back. It's a green Outback. It's not registered. He's trying to make enough money to get it on the road and I let him keep it here."

"Where is your grandson now?" asked Rob.

"Probably out with his friends. Who knows?"

"Is there a way we can reach him?"

"That's not easy. You might ask my daughter."

"Can we get her number from you?"

"Sure, but I'm a little curious. Why are a couple of Boston detectives bothering to check out the wrong plates being on a car? Did anything happen?"

"We're not sure of anything yet, Mr. Roach, said Eddie. "We would just like to ask a few questions. By the way, how old is your grandson?"

"He'll be 26 later this month."

"Okay. We think you've been honest with us, Mr. Roach," continued Eddie. "Can you get that phone number for us?"

"Sure. It's 986- 222-1578. That's about the only thing I can still remember off the top of my head."

"Thank you very much for your cooperation. We'll be in touch," said Rob.

Eddie and Rob walked back to their car and were about to leave when an old rusted Toyota pickup truck came racing down the street and screeched to a halt in front of the house. A boy jumped from the passenger seat and ran toward the house.

Eddie and Rob both jumped from the Tahoe and Rob called out, "Dennis. Stop, Dennis. Boston P.D."

The Toyota hit the gas and sped off down the road. Dennis took off on foot and began to run down the block. Eddie got the plate number of the pickup and Rob went after Dennis on foot.

Mr. Roach came back outside and yelled to his grandson, "Dennis, come back. Come back."

Eddie could never have caught up with a young man in his twenties but Rob had no trouble running him down. He caught up with him and tackled him on a neighbor's front lawn before he had gone fifty yards.

Rob pulled him to his feet and said, "What's the problem? Got someplace you need to go? Why don't we go back and have a talk with your grandfather?"

Rob grabbed him by the arm and pulled him back to where Eddie was waiting in front of the house.

"Look what I found," said Rob.

"Dennis, what's going on here? What have you gotten yourself into?"

"We'll ask the questions, Mr. Roach," said Eddie, cutting him off.

"Can you tell us what you were doing on Unquity Road in Milford Saturday evening a week and a half ago?"

"I don't know what you're talking about," said Dennis, not looking up at the detectives.

"Come on. You're gonna try and tell us that's not your Outback in the garage? We know you switched plates with your grandfather's car. You were issued a parking summons," Rob pressured him.

Dennis just looked at the ground and said nothing.

"Look. We can do this here or downtown at police headquarters. We just want an explanation," offered Eddie.

"Was anybody with you or were you out there by yourself?" asked Rob.

Dennis just kept his mouth shut and turned away.

"Okay. Let's go downtown. Put your hands behind your back," said Rob, taking out a pair of cuffs.

"Wait," said Mr. Roach. "Dennis, just tell them why you were there. I'll help you out if you're in trouble. What do you think he's done, detectives? Dennis isn't a bad kid. Let me try and talk to him."

"We're investigating a homicide. We need some answers. Now," said Eddie.

"Homicide? I don't know anything about a homicide. All right. I'll tell you. My friends and I were growing some weed out there. We planted it last spring and it was ready to harvest. We needed a car to bring it back. It's in the garage right now. I'll show you."

Dennis led the detectives and his grandfather behind the house to the garage. He lifted the hatch on the Outback and pulled away a tarp. There were about thirty or forty large marijuana plants.

"I was just trying to get enough money to get the car registered so I could help out my mom," pleaded Dennis.

Eddie and Rob just looked at each other.

"Zan's?" said Rob.

"Why not?"

"Don't smoke it all tonight," said Rob as the two of them walked away.

· · · · ·

At around seven PM Detectives Corlino and Edelman had finished with most of the paperwork on the Eddie Lubin shooting.

"I'll finish up tomorrow, Don. I know you're eager to get going," said Carl.

"I'm staying until tomorrow. I want a chance to interview Eddie. Also, I'd like to talk to Patty's friends. They should hear it from us rather than the paper."

"Good idea, Don."

They drove back to Danbury and went to the Copper Pot. They both had a couple of drinks before Duncan, Samantha and the others showed up.

Don and Carl explained what had happened earlier that afternoon and that a suspect was now in custody. Don tried as tactfully as possible to tell Duncan about what had happened and added that Patty was probably murdered because she wanted to break it off with Eddie. Jeff was inconsolable about the fact that he was responsible for introducing Patty to Eddie Lubin. The detectives said good night and went off in search of another drinking establishment.

Don made reservations at the local Best Western and made plans to meet with Carl the following morning for breakfast. They agreed to drive back to Brewster and interview Eddie at the hospital.

Before he hit the sack, Don called Cheryl. "Hi sweetheart. What's up with you?"

"Hi Don. Where are you?"

"In Connecticut right now. I might be back in Boston tomorrow."

"You are going to take me out? Right?"

"Of course. I promise. You are my reason for living."

"Yeah. Right. Just get home safe. Okay?"

"Promise you. I'll see you soon. Kiss-kiss."

"Love you."

"Ditto."

About ten minutes later he got another call from Rob.

"Hi Rob. Where do we stand?"

"Eddie and I are at Zan's. We're talking things over. I just checked with Rochester again. They're having trouble finding out anything new about Michelle. Nobody's answering the door at the address we have. I'm gonna try again tomorrow."

"Okay, Rob. Thanks. I'll probably be back in Boston tomorrow."

"Very good, Don. Talk to you then."

Don sat for a while, contemplating a strategy. He was still torn between which move to make. He could follow up on the terrorism angle in Boston, or dig deeper into the student murders. He weighed the benefits of each. Rochester was on the way to Buffalo. Maybe he would have better luck than the Rochester Police in tracking down someone who could tell them more about Michelle. After an hour of arguing with himself, he hit the bed and enjoyed a well-deserved sleep.

· · · · ·

Mike and Brittany had both left work an hour early. Brittany was busy packing suitcases for their trip the next day. Jamie and Roni were holding hands, looking at each other and dancing in circles. They were like two kids on Christmas Eve, dreaming about the presents under the tree.

"No more school till Tuesday. No more school till Tuesday," they chanted.

Mike and Brittany could hear them from upstairs.

"I know exactly how they feel," said Mike.

"I could use a break, too," admitted Brittany.

Mike gave her a big kiss and said, "You earned it, honey."

Jamie, Roni and Mike watched TV for a couple of hours while Brittany prepared a late dinner. Soon afterward they were headed for bed.

CHAPTER 13

Thursday, Oct. 7, 7:30 AM

Don awoke to his alarm at 7:30 the next morning. He got himself dressed, checked out of the Best Western and made his way to the diner he had eaten the morning before. He had agreed to meet Carl at 8AM but he had not yet arrived. He picked up a copy of the local paper and smiled. The news of Eddie's arrest had already hit the papers. A picture of Detectives Edelman and Behan together appeared on the front page. They were old photos taken some time ago. There was no picture of him but the story of how Eddie was caught did mention his name. Don kept reading and smiled to himself. After a few minutes Detective Edelman walked in with Behan at his side. They spotted Don and walked over to his table.

"Good morning, Detective," said Behan, offering his hand. "I'll have to say I'm impressed. It took you less than a day. I just want to say thank you on behalf of the citizens of Danbury. Especially Mrs. Nelson. I spoke with Patty's parents last night as soon as I heard. She's still distraught but at least now she knows what happened.

"Glad I could help. Carl was a superstar. I'm sure you read the report."

"I did. Carl also told me that you told him to embellish the truth on our behalf. In fact, the report gave credit to the entire Danbury Police Department. We all thank you for that."

"It's your town, Detective Behan. It just sounded better that way. Take a seat and join me for breakfast."

"So what's your next move? Are you going back to Boston?" asked Carl.

"Actually, I've got two detectives working on the case there. There's not a lot I can do for the moment. I want to continue tracking down leads concerning our Jane Doe in the morgue. I'm not sure my boss will give me the latitude, but I want to take a road trip up to Buffalo. There was a triple homicide a few months ago in which a similar weapon was used. Just like in your case."

"Do me a favor, Don. Let us know about your progress. I'd really like to know how things work out," said Behan sincerely.

"I'll do that." Don looked at his watch. "I should probably call my boss now. If you guys will excuse me for a minute—if the waitress comes order me two over easy, bacon, home fries and rye toast."

Don excused himself and called Jack Sullivan.

"Hi Jack. It's Don. I'm finished here in Danbury. I'd like to…"

Jack cut him off and said, "I heard. Took you less than 24 hours. That's pretty good. Even for you. I'm guessing you called to ask about the other case you mentioned."

"You guessed right, Jack."

"Okay, Don. I trust your judgment. If there's anyone I've got working for me who can crack this case, it's you. Try to get me something I can tell them. The Mayor is getting antsy."

"I'll try my best, Jack. I've got to go back to Brewster this morning with another detective to question Eddie Lubin. I hope I can find out what

I need to know in Buffalo in less than a week. McGowan and Morrow are working on some leads up in Boston."

"Okay, Don. I'll check on their progress from time to time. If anything breaks, I'll let you know. Keep me posted."

"Will do. Later."

Don returned to the table and sat down. "Well, I'm off to Buffalo for a while."

"That's great," said Carl. "You really think it's going to lead to something?"

"This case is more than four months old," said Don. "Clues aren't going to come so easily and I don't think witnesses are going to be of much help at this point." Don realized his social gaffe and immediately regretted saying it.

Carl noticed but just smiled and took it in stride.

Don said, "I just gotta make one quick call and we can ride out to Brewster." He took out his phone and dialed detective Arnold in Buffalo. "Hello Detective Arnold, I'm on my way to Buffalo. I should be there by Friday morning."

Behan and Edelman listened to one side of the conversation and a lot of "uh huhs."

After a few minutes Don said, "Okay if my plans change, I'll keep you posted."

The three of them finished breakfast and Don suggested to Carl that they get under way. Behan offered to pay the check, stood up and once again thanked Don for his help.

"I'll meet you over in Brewster," said Don. "Putman Medical Center, right?"

"You got it."

0

Half an hour later the two detectives were in the parking lot of the medical center. They walked to main floor reception and showed their credentials.

"We would like to talk to the doctor in charge and ask about the condition of our suspect."

The receptionist called the officer in charge of watching Eddie Lubin as well as the attending physician.

"Hello detectives. I heard you're the ones who arrested our perp. Nice job," said the officer.

"Thanks," said Don. "What's the condition of our suspect?"

"I'll call the doctor. He's in the ICU checking on him right now. All I know is he's still pretty out of it. He curses a lot for someone with that much dope in him."

"Yeah. Just a few anger issues," Carl chimed in.

The doctor exited the ICU and greeted them. "How can I help you, detectives?"

"What's his condition?" asked Don.

"He's going to be all right. None of the major organs were seriously damaged, but you did fracture his hip. He's going to be in some pain for at least a couple of weeks."

"I can't say that my day is ruined knowing that. Is he capable of answering any questions?" pressed Don.

"I can lighten the morphine drip. He'd be lucid in a couple of hours but I don't know how much you would be able to get out of him. Besides I hear he lawyered up."

Don turned to Carl and said, "Carl, I really don't have time for all this now. I'm gonna leave you to ask some questions. It's highly unlikely that Eddie Lubin is tied to my Jane Doe in Boston, but just to be thorough, ask a couple of questions and find out where he was for the past few weeks. Talk to Duncan's friend Jeff. Find his brother and question him about Eddie. See if he's got friends in Boston."

"Okay, Don. I'll do that. I guess you're on your way then."

"Yeah, I've only got a few days before I'm called back to the fort."

"Good luck, Don, and thanks again."

"You too."

Don made his way back to his car and set out for Rochester.

· · · · ·

Eddie was sitting at his desk entering plate numbers into the computer when Rob came in.

"Good morning, Rob." He handed a stack of papers to him and said, "It's either this or Beacon Street. Make up your mind."

"Good morning, Eddie. Give me some time to think about it."

Eddie's phone rang and made up Rob's mind for him. "It's Don," said Eddie.

"Hi Eddie."

"Yeah, Don. What's up?"

"I'm in Brewster. I'm heading up to Buffalo to check out those students who were murdered. I'm going to stop in Rochester on the way. Maybe I can find out something new."

"Rob and I are split between tracking down new leads and staking out that house on Beacon Street."

"I mentioned to you the other day that there might be a tie to terrorism. I called Captain Wyatt of the JTTF. I want you and Rob to touch base with him and share information. His office should be in my building or close to it."

"Yeah. We can do that. Rob would be thrilled with a change of scenery. Frankly, so would I."

"Okay then. I'll be in touch again soon. Later."

"Good hunting, Don," Eddie said, "Get ready to be happy. Don wants us to drop in on the JTTF and talk to Captain Wyatt. Have you ever worked with them?"

"No, I haven't."

"Me either. It might be interesting to find out what it's about."

"At this point I'm getting a little tired of sitting in a car rereading the same paper."

"Let's call Captain Wyatt and see if he can meet with us."

"Sounds like a plan," agreed Rob.

"Let's tell Jimmy to put those poor bastards back on the plate numbers."

Half an hour later they were sitting in Wyatt's office.

"Good morning, detectives. Don Corlino brought me up to speed on the case you're working on. I understand you're following Abdul Nasir. We know of him as an acquaintance of some people who knew Dzhokhar Tsarnaev. I'm sure you're familiar with the name."

"Yes, Captain. The Marathon bombing was traumatic for everyone. Neither of us worked on that case, but I'm sure he's still known to most of the cops in Boston. It's been a few years, but it's hard to forget."

"I can give you the names of some people we're watching." Wyatt handed a list of names and addresses to Eddie. "We have both FBI agents and regular Boston PD following them from time to time. Most of them are men but there's also a couple of women on the list. We've made a couple of arrests. Mostly credit card fraud, check forgery and drug dealing. That kind of thing. We did make an arrest for armed robbery recently. I'm sure you understand that we're spread pretty thin these days. We just don't have enough personnel to address everything."

"I can attest to that," said Rob. "There's so much that gets under the radar."

"Just so you know, we have people watching Nasir from time to time. I'm aware there's probably illegal activities going on in that Beacon Street house. Probably drug trafficking. So far, we haven't been able to tie in anything to terrorist activities. That's our priority. We suspect they're trying to raise money, but we don't know for what. You guys are looking at this from another angle. We've considered the idea that the Reardon disappearance might be linked to terrorism, but we don't have much to go on."

"We don't know much either," admitted Eddie. "We're just going on a hunch. Detective Corlino thinks there might be a connection. I'll have to say he has good instincts. He solved a murder in Danbury yesterday. It took him less than a day."

"He seemed pretty sharp when I talked to him a couple of days ago. I understand he's looking into several murders he feels might be related."

"Yes. That's how we got onto this track. We were originally assigned to a Jane Doe found in Milton. We've been tracking down plate numbers from surveillance cameras. That's how we got Nasir's plate. His Mercedes was in a 7-11 parking lot late at night near the preserve where she was found. That was September 25. M.E estimates that as the T.O.D."

"All right, detectives. Keep me up with any developments and I'll do the same for you."

Eddie and Rob stood up and shook hands with Captain Wyatt.

"Will do. Good hunting," said Eddie.

They left the JTTF and thought about what to do.

"Let's at least give Nasir a drive-by. We can decide what to do after that," said Rob.

"I'm down with that. Maybe we can convince Jimmy to assign a couple of plainclothes cops to stake it out."

"Good idea."

The two detectives set out for Beacon Street.

• • • • •

Mike and Brittany woke up early, filled with excitement about their planned escape to Lake Placid. The girls were already downstairs playing with Kardashian, who could sense that today was special.

Mike sat up in bed, stretched his arms with a satisfying growl, and gave Brittany a big hug and a kiss. "Love you," he whispered in her ear.

A smile instantly crossed her lips. "Of course, you do," she teased.

Mike got out of bed and started for the bathroom. Brittany jumped up and rushed up behind him. "Me first," she said, playfully pushing him aside.

"Hey," exclaimed Mike.

Brittany just laughed and shut the door behind her, smiling impishly.

Mike decided to get revenge and started knocking on the door. "Brittany... Brittany...Brittany..." he kept repeating.

He could hear Brittany laughing to herself behind the door. After a minute or two she opened the door just a crack. "Yes. Can I help you?" she said, peering through with a big smile on her face.

Mike began to push the door open and Brittany resisted. He pushed a bit harder and she began to relent. Eventually she surrendered and Mike was inside.

He put his hands around Brittany's waist and looked passionately in her eyes. "You can't resist me. Don't even try."

Brittany held his gaze and said, "You're right."

She kissed him full on the mouth and they stood that way for several moments.

"Wanna shower together?" he suggested.

"Why not?"

They both jumped in and let the warm water caress them. Life was perfect.

Downstairs the girls were setting the table for breakfast. Kardashian was trying her best to get in the way, feeling somewhat left out.

"Let's surprise Mom and Dad with breakfast," suggested Jamie.

"Yeah. Let's make pancakes."

"Okay. Good idea. I'll start mixing up some batter. I've done it before with Mom."

Meanwhile Mike and Brittany had finished their shower and had begun to get dressed. They had already packed two suitcases and loaded them into the car the night before. They wanted to get to the mountains early so they could do some hiking that day.

"Have we thought of everything?" asked Mike.

"I'm pretty sure we're good. I called Mrs. Avery yesterday and asked her to keep an eye on the house. I can't think of anything else."

"Okay. Then I guess we're good to go."

They could hear Jamie and Roni downstairs. Kardashian let out an occasional bark. "Let's get the girls ready. We'll make a quick breakfast and we're outta here."

Mike and Brittany walked down the stairs and into the kitchen.

"Surprise!" Jamie and Roni sang out in perfect harmony.

The table was set for four. A large platter of pancakes was stacked in the middle. There was also a plate of bacon accompanying it. A glass of freshly squeezed orange juice was placed at each setting.

"Oh look, honey. Somebody must have snuck into the house and made us all breakfast," teased Mike.

"Oh Daddy," sighed Jamie.

"It was me and Jamie. We did it," said Roni in protest.

Mike got on one knee and gave them both a big hug.

Brittany just smiled and watched them with amusement.

Kardashian ran in circles, wagging her tail furiously, barking at them all.

They all sat down at the table and helped themselves to what turned out to be a delicious helping of pancakes, bacon and syrup. The left-over bacon mysteriously disappeared from the table.

After breakfast they quickly washed and dried the dishes. Brittany got the girls ready and Mike locked up the house and secretly slipped Kardashian half of a "Doggie Downer." They all piled into the car and they were off.

Two hours later they were in Lake Placid. Mike pulled into the Maple Leaf Inn and Brittany checked them in. Mike brought the two suitcases inside.

"It's a little late to climb a mountain. How about a nice walk around Mirror Lake?" Mike suggested to them. "They have plaques in the sidewalk commemorating all 46 high peaks in the Adirondacks."

Mike had climbed them all. Most of them more than once.

"What does komemerade mean?" asked Roni.

"Commemorate. C-OM-M-E-M-O-R-A-T-E," Mike spelled it out. "It means to honor."

"Why would someone honor a mountain?" she asked.

"Most of them are named after people who accomplished important things," Mike explained. Children never stopped asking questions. "How about we walk around twice? That's about three miles. That should work up an appetite for lunch."

Also, Kardashian could probably use some sobering up, thought Mike.

"Jamie, get Kardashian's leash. I'll take the backpack and bring some water bottles," said Brittany.

"I'll carry it," offered Mike.

"Don't be silly. I need the exercise. Do you want me to get fat?"

That got a chuckle from Jamie and Roni.

Brittany looked at them with her eyes crossed and stuck out her tongue. That got an outright guffaw from both of them.

"Let's get going then," said Mike.

They all piled into the car and parked in front of the Black Bear. It was on the shore overlooking Mirror Lake.

"We can get lunch here after our hike," said Mike.

The four of them began their walk with Jamie in tow behind Kardashian. They came to the first plaque. It was for Mt. Marcy: 5,344 feet it stated.

"Marcy is the highest mountain in N.Y. State," said Mike.

"Oh. Can we climb that one?" asked Jamie.

"That's a long hike," said Mike. "I think we should start with something a little easier."

Roni was still very young and Mike didn't want to spoil her love for hiking by giving her something to difficult.

"How about Cascade Mountain?" suggested Mike. "The trail starts right at the road. It's about a two-hour hike to the top. You can see the entire Great Range from up there. It's definitely the best view for the least amount of effort. We can pack some sandwiches and picnic on top."

"I checked the weather," said Brittany. "It's supposed to be a beautiful day. Almost no chance of rain and about 65 degrees."

"Well, that's settled, then. We can wake up around seven and get an early start."

They continued to walk around the lake, stopping to look at each plaque. Mike had a story to tell about each one. After about two hours they were back at the restaurant.

"Ready for lap two?" asked Mike, making sure Roni was up to it.

"Sure, I wanna hear more stories," said Jamie.

Even Brittany was eager to hear about Mike's adventures.

They set out again and after another two hours they were back. They left Kardashian in the car and enjoyed a well-deserved lunch.

"What do you say we go around again? Only this time we'll go in the opposite direction," suggested Mike.

"Okay, but let's rest up a little in those nice-looking Adirondack chairs we saw down the street. They look really comfortable and it's such a beautiful view from over there," said Brittany.

"Good idea," said Mike.

They each picked out a chair, although Roni's was much too big for her. It was comical watching her try to get comfortable.

"Come sit on my lap, Roni," said Mike.

"Is that the restaurant we passed on the other side of the lake?" asked Brittany.

"Yes. It's called The View. They have a deck for outside dining. We can have dinner there tonight if you like," suggested Mike.

"Fantastic. I really love this place, Mike. What a great idea to take a couple of days off."

Brittany looked out over the lake. She could see Whiteface Mountain in all its glory in the distance.

The fall foliage was really kicking in. It was hard to imagine anything more beautiful.

CHAPTER 14

Thursday Afternoon, Oct. 7, 12:30 PM

Don had left Brewster that afternoon and was on I-87 heading for Albany. If the traffic was light on I-90 he could be in Rochester before four o'clock. The highway sailed by and as always Don began to think about the case again. Michelle Dennis was still a loose end. There was a possibility that she might be Jane Doe. He began to go over the facts again. The picture on her license revealed she had dark hair. There was significant decomposition before the kids had found the body in Blue Hills Reservation and that made a positive I.D. difficult. So far, they could not rule her out as a possibility. The license indicated a height of 5' 7"—approximately the same as Jane Doe. Her rental car was ticketed in the Blue Hills Reservation. Michelle had not personally returned the car to Enterprise. Someone had left the keys in the drop box. It was unlikely but still possible that she had been the victim of a rape or robbery. If someone she knew had murdered her, they had gone through a lot of trouble to make sure she was not found right away. That also meant they would not want to draw attention by having a rental car in her name go missing. There was also the fact that she wasn't answering her cell phone, but that could have other explanations. Most likely Michelle was not relevant, but Rochester was on the way. In a few short hours they could eliminate her as a victim or possible suspect. He had her Rochester address from the license she had shown at Enterprise. With any luck he could find her at home or maybe her neighbors would be of help. Her license indicated that her last address was on Verona Street near Jones Square Park. He punched the address into the GPS and continued cruising down I-90. His mind went back to thinking about his obsession.

• • • • •

Meanwhile, back in Boston Rob and Eddie were staking out the Beacon Street. house. A number of suspicious-looking vehicles had come and gone. They took note of each one and filmed them from down the block. At four o'clock, Rob said, "My legs are cramping up. Want to call it a day?"

"Good with me," agreed Eddie.

"Zan's?"

"I was hoping you say that. Let's go."

• • • • •

It was about quarter past four o'clock when Don reached Lyell Avenue. Even in the afternoon there were a couple of girls already hanging out on the street corner. Their reason for being there was not hard to figure out. It was sunny and relatively warm for an October day in Rochester. Warm enough for the girls to be showing some skin. *Not a great section of town,* Don thought to himself. Michelle had a prior arrest for solicitation. The pieces seemed to fit. The GPS told him to make a left on Verona Street and that his destination was 50 yards ahead on the right. He pulled up to the curb, walked up to the door and rang the bell. Eddie McGowan had put in a request to the Rochester Police to pay a visit and check up on Michelle, but there had been no one home. After several attempts they gave it a low priority. Don waited for several minutes and tried to look through the window for any sign of life.

Might as well walk up to the corner and ask a few questions, thought Don. He headed back to Lyell Avenue and casually walked around, looking at a couple of girls who smiled and winked at him. Don thought to himself that they were actually rather attractive for street girls. One was a tall white brunette. She wore a tight yellow mini-skirt with a matching top. The other girl appeared to be Hispanic. She was a bit shorter but she had a figure that was a definite plus in this business. Don knew that if they tagged him as a cop, they were not likely to be cooperative. He also figured that Michelle never used her real name while conducting business. If he showed them a photocopy of Michelle's license, they might get suspicious. He carefully folded the edges so that only her picture showed. Don weighed his options and figured his best chance was to start a friendly conversation and turn on the charm. He feigned shyness, slowly walking in their direction, hesitating several times. He would quickly look away and avoid eye contact when they looked at him. The girls began to smile and whisper to each other.

Finally, he approached them and said, "What are you gorgeous ladies doing on this beautiful day?"

"Oh, I like this guy," said the brunette.

"Yeah. He's cute," offered the other girl. "So what's a handsome stud like you doin' on this beautiful day?"

"I got a thing for hot-lookin' girls with bad intent."

The girls both laughed.

"Well, we sure got that," said the brunette. "So have you made up your mind?"

"Excuse me?"

"Have you decided which one of us you want to do bad things with?"

"Give me a couple of minutes. I'm workin' up an appetite. Maybe both of you."

Again, they laughed and smiled seductively at Don.

"A threesome. What do you think, Gloria?" said the blond haired girl, smiling at her friend.

"Sounds like fun. I'll give it a go."

"Do you girls have a place around here?" asked Don.

"There's a motel just down the block," said the brunette. "How many hours you gonna need? The rooms are $25 an hour. Then of course, there's our commission."

Don thought that was an original way of putting it.

"So... we've never seen you here before. Are you from Rochester?" said Gloria.

"I used to live around here a few years ago. I figured I would cruise by and see if I could find an old friend. Do either of you know a girl named Michelle?" Don took out the photo and showed it to them.

"She's a friend of mine," he continued. "I have her phone number. I tried to call several times but I got no answer. I was on my way to Buffalo and figured I'd give it a shot. I know she still lived in the neighborhood a year ago. She was in the same trade as you girls. I was a customer of hers."

Gloria sighed and began to think he wasn't interested in getting laid after all. There was an unwritten code about not giving information about each other to strangers... especially cops.

"Are you a cop or something?" said Gloria. "Come on, Jill. Let's go."

Don realized he wasn't going to get anything with deception. These girls were streetwise and not likely to fall for his act. "No, wait. Please. Okay, I'll be straight with you. I'm with the FBI in Boston."

Don showed the girls his FBI identification. "She's not in any trouble. We're just worried about her. She may have been the victim of foul play and we would like to find out one way or the other. If you know anything, please help us out."

Jill and Gloria looked at each other. Both seemed to have a lot of reservations.

"Please. Anything you can tell me about her could help."

Jill seemed to soften in her attitude and looked at Don sympathetically. "He's not a vice cop, Gloria. I don't think the FBI is gonna run a sting on us."

"Yeah. That's Mickey," said Gloria. "We were wondering what happened to her. Last time we saw her was back in May. We didn't think much of it. She's taken off with guys before. Last winter she went to Florida for two months with this guy she met. I think she was hoping to find a guy who would take care of her. I don't think she liked working the street, but she always wound up back here."

"Did she ever dress in fancy jeans and expensive clothes?" asked Don.

"She had some nice stuff when she was working. You know how it is? Nothing over the top expensive," said Gloria.

"What was she like? How would you describe her personality?"

"She was kinda shy for a pretty girl. Like she had some esteem issues. People liked her. She was sweet," said Jill.

"Like a lost puppy," added Gloria.

"Do you know if she had any friends in Boston? Maybe she met someone from Boston last July."

The girls looked at each other, searching for a nod of recognition. After a moment or two they both shook their heads.

"Sorry, Detective. We don't remember Mickey ever mentioning Boston."

"Her license gives her address right here on Verona. Do either of you know if she lived there with anyone?"

Again, the two girls looked at each other, wondering if they were doing the right thing for Michelle. But Don had a way breaking down walls.

"Maxine lives there. It's her house. She lets Mickey stay there sometimes. I'm sure she will be able to tell you more than we can," said Gloria.

"She kinda took her in and looked after her. Maxine is a bit of a loner. They were friends."

Jill looked at her watch and said, "If it's a normal day she's probably at the Cock's Inn."

Don started to ask Gloria more about Maxine and then did a double-take at Jill with a puzzled look.

The girls both laughed out loud.

"It's a bar two blocks down Lyell on the right." Jill pointed in the direction.

"She's about 45 years old and she's got reddish hair."

"Thanks, girls. The FBI thanks you. And Michelle thanks you. Stay out of trouble, girls."

Don began to walk down the street.

Jill called out after him, "If you change your mind about that threesome, we'll be here all day."

Don laughed and pointed his finger at Jill. She gave him a smile that could melt a glacier.

As he walked toward the bar Don thought about what to ask Maxine. *Will she be cooperative?* He figured an honest, direct approach was probably best. It seemed that Jill and Gloria liked Michelle and were sympathetic to his questioning. If he expressed concern for Michelle's safety, Maxine would probably be willing to help. He walked into the bar and immediately noticed a middle-aged redhead sitting at the bar. She had a half-finished drink in front of her. He took a seat two stools away from her and ordered a beer from the bartender.

He smiled at Maxine and said, "Pretty warm for this time of year, hey?"

"Yeah, global warming for sure."

Don was glad to see that she was still fairly sober and able to answer questions.

"I like it. We should be burning more fossil fuels."

Maxine smiled and said, "Yeah. That works for me too."

Don figured he better not bullshit too long and took a more direct approach. He took the picture of Michelle from his jacket and put it on the bar in front of Maxine.

"I'm with the FBI, Maxine. I was told you might be able to tell us about this girl."

"Oh shit." Maxine let out a long sigh and took a large gulp from her Jack and soda. "What the hell has she gotten herself into?"

"She's hasn't broken any laws that we know of. We're just trying to locate her. We have a phone number but she doesn't pick up. We're a little worried about her."

"Me too. I've tried to call her a bunch of times in the last few months. It just goes to voicemail. I reported her missing to the Rochester Police. They said they would look into it, but I think when they found out she had a prior for prostitution they just blew it off. How did she get on your radar?"

"She rented a car in Boston. She got a parking ticket near a crime scene. We just want to ask her if she saw anything."

"What kind of crime scene?"

Don thought for a moment and figured there was no delicate way to put it. "The body of a girl was found in a wooded area south of Boston. We're trying to determine if it could be Michelle. Do you know if she knew anybody from the Boston area?"

"Oh God."

"Look, we really don't know if it's her. The car was returned to the rental company so we're not sure of anything. I heard she stayed at your house sometimes. Is that right?"

"Yeah. I told her she was welcome to crash there as long as she didn't bring home any johns."

"Did she leave any personal items there? Like a hairbrush… toothbrush… lipstick. Anything we could use to get a DNA sample? It might be the only way to find out."

"Yeah. She left some stuff there. I'm sure there's a hairbrush in the upstairs bathroom. We could walk over there. Wouldn't take a minute."

"Okay. Let's go."

Maxine chugged what was left of her drink. Don offered to pay her tab and left his beer on the bar. They walked out together and headed back toward Verona Street.

On the way the girls saw them and Jill called out, "Hey Max."

"So that's how you found me."

"They just wanted to help Michelle," Don defended them.

"Yeah. I guess so."

They reached Maxine's house and she escorted him inside. "The house is a bit of a mess," apologized Maxine with a nervous chuckle.

"You should see my place," offered Don, trying to make her feel better.

"Come on upstairs. I'll show you her bathroom."

"Just a second. Do you have any large Zip-loc plastic bags in your kitchen?"

"Yes, I do. I'll get you some."

She came back from the kitchen and they walked up the stairs into the bathroom. Maxine pointed out Michelle's hairbrush and a toothbrush. Don placed them in separate plastic bags. He looked in the medicine cabinet and found a ChapStick.

"Is this Michelle's?" he asked.

"I'm sure it is."

He placed it in another bag and said, "I'm sure this will be enough."

Maxine started to choke up and said, "She's dead, isn't she?"

"We don't know that," he tried to reassure her.

"If Michelle could answer she would pick up," insisted Maxine, starting to fear the worst.

"We don't know that either. She might have just lost her phone somewhere."

It wasn't enough to convince her and the tears began to flow.

"Give me your phone number. I'm going to FedEx these things to the lab in Boston first thing in the morning. We should know one way or the other in a couple of days. I'll call you as soon as we know. Would you like to come back to the bar? The drinks are on me."

"Okay, Detective. That's nice of you."

"You've been of enormous help. Actually, the drinks are courtesy of the FBI."

They left Maxine's house and Don stopped at his car to drop off the Zip-loc bags. They walked back to the bar and Don ordered a Jack and soda for her and a beer for himself. He put a hundred on the bar and said, "The lady drinks for free tonight."

Don took a seat next to Maxine at the bar and tried his best to make her feel better.

"She always let me know if she was going somewhere," said Maxine. "She wouldn't just take off without telling me."

Don didn't want to give her false hope. He had serious doubts about her wellbeing himself. On the other hand, he didn't want to crush all hope either. He thought about what to say.

"All we can do now is hope."

After a couple of beers Don said he had to keep moving toward Buffalo and should get back on the road.

Maxine gave him a hug and said, "Please let me know the minute you find out."

"I will," promised Don.

He walked out the door and headed back toward his car. The sky had begun to grow darker and Don could see storm clouds beginning to form in the west. In a few minutes he was back on I-90.

He headed west toward Buffalo and the rain began to come down hard. Once again, his mind went to his private island. Solving puzzles and thinking critically wasn't even his own choice. He was drawn to it. An hour and a half later he pulled up to a Best Western near FBI headquarters. It was only 8:30 in the evening and after checking in, he decided to knock down a couple of beers in the bar. By 10:30 he was fast asleep.

• • • • •

Up in Lake Placid Mike, Brittany and the kids had finished their third lap around the lake. Mike drove back to their cabin at the motel and they freshened up. They all relaxed and decided to play a game of Monopoly. Mike and Roni were the first to go. Jamie finally won when Brittany landed on Boardwalk with two hotels.

Later that evening they went to The View and enjoyed a delicious steak dinner.

CHAPTER 15

Friday, Oct. 8, 9:00 AM
FBI Headquarters, Buffalo

Don drove his car down Elmwood Avenue toward FBI headquarters. He had agreed to meet with Detective Arnold at nine o'clock AM. It was now ten minutes to nine. The sky was leaden and it looked like it was going to pour again at any second. He could see FBI Plaza in the distance and figured it would take him at least another ten minutes to make his way through traffic and get there. Raindrops were already beginning to fall and Don turned on his headlights and windshield wipers. It was becoming very dark out even though it was after daybreak and the sun had already risen. By the time he got to the parking lot the rain was starting to come down more steadily. Don parked as close to the front door as he could. He had slept as long as possible so he would be well-rested for the long day ahead. He was already late and he didn't want to keep Detective Arnold waiting. Don looked at his watch. It was five minutes after nine.

"Shit!" he said out loud.

He wanted to get the hairbrush and other articles to the DNA lab as soon as possible. He took his jacket off and wrapped it around the Zip-loc bags and found a newspaper to cover his head. He opened his door, climbed out, slammed the door shut and made a mad dash for the entrance. Right on cue the skies opened up and it began to pour buckets. It didn't take more than fifteen seconds to cover the distance but by the time he got there he was soaked right down to his underwear.

"Shit, shit, shit," he repeated as he ran inside.

The pretty blonde at the reception desk noticed and looked up. "Can I help you?" she said looking somewhat startled at the drenched figure in front of her.

"I'm Detective Corlino from the Boston field office. I'm supposed to meet with Detective Arnold. Is he here yet?"

"Yes. That's him over there on the bench," she said with a smile. "You look like a drowned cat," she added, looking sympathetic. "There's a hand drier in the men's room. That might help some."

"Thanks," said Don and walked over to meet the detective.

Paul saw him coming and rose to greet him.

Detective Arnold was a tall solidly built man about 6'4" tall. He was certainly an intimidating figure. He put out his hand and said, "Detective Paul Arnold. I take it you're Detective Corlino."

"That's right," said Don. "Please forgive my appearance. I got caught in the rain."

"I see that. You take that kind of thing for granted here in Buffalo with the lake right next to us. You should see it snow in the winter."

"I've heard stories," said Don, raising his eyebrows. "Give me a second. I've got some urgent things to take care of."

Don walked back to the receptionist and said, "Excuse me. Who can arrange to send these items to the FBI headquarters in Boston?"

"I'll take care of it," she replied.

"Make FedEx priority, please. I want the results of a DNA test ASAP."

"We have a DNA lab right here in Buffalo," she offered.

"Thanks, but this is a hot case in Boston. They'll give it top priority. I want it run today."

"Okay, Detective. I'm on it."

"Do you have a pen and paper?" Don asked.

The receptionist obliged with a pretty smile and handed him a notepad and a pen.

Don wrote a note stating: *TOP PRIORITY: CARE OF JACK SULLIVAN: MICHELLE DENNIS DNA*

He then got on his phone and called Jack directly.

"HI Don. What's the latest?"

"I'm at FBI headquarters in Buffalo. I'm sending you a package via FedEx. It should get there this afternoon. It's a hair sample of a girl who may be our Jane Doe. Her name is Michelle Dennis. Please make sure it gets run today. Even if they have to work all night. Then arrange for a cross with our victim. I need those results ASAP."

"Okay, Don. You know this can take anywhere from 24 – 72 hours."

"Yeah. There should be more than enough hairs in that brush. It shouldn't take very long to replicate enough DNA strands."

"Okay, Don. Keep me posted. I'll let you know as soon as possible if it's a match."

"So long, Jack."

Don walked over to Detective Arnold and said, "I'm just gonna run over to the men's room and dry out as best I can. I'll be back in a few minutes."

"Take your time. My boss told me to spend the whole day with you and help you with the investigation. This town is still pretty uneasy about what happened here last May. It certainly doesn't help that we never caught the guy," explained Paul.

Don went to the men's room, removed his shirt and held it under the drier. He hung it on a hook and then took off his T-shirt and tried his best to wring out the excess water.

No point in trying to dry the pants. They will just have to dry out by themselves, he thought to himself.

After about fifteen minutes he put his T-shirt and shirt back on and thought, *That will have to do.* He returned to the lobby and resumed his talk with Paul.

"I would like to interview the girl who found the bodies as well as the neighbors," Don began. "I would also like to interview witnesses at the nightclub where they were partying the evening before. After that I would like to go to your office and watch the videotape from the nightclub."

"Sure," said Paul. "No problem. But I don't think we're gonna find anything new. My interview with the witnesses was pretty thorough and it's been almost five months. Also, I gave the surveillance tapes from the night club to the FBI last May. They have them on file upstairs in the computer room. They weren't able to identify our suspect with face recognition software."

"I don't doubt that you did a thorough job, but I would like to see the murder house myself. I have a sixth sense about these things. Don't ask me how. I just feel things sometimes. How long will it take to get there?" asked Don.

"Not long. About half an hour. It's on Ashford Street in the Brighton area. But most of the people I interviewed were students. There are two major campuses close by. They may be at class now."

"Of course," said Don. "I'd still like to go there and check it out."

"I have the names and phone numbers of everyone here on my phone. Why don't you drive and I'll start calling them now? I'll ask them if they are available."

The two detectives headed for the door. It was still pouring out. Paul took a collapsible umbrella from his coat.

Don said, "Just a sec. Let me see if someone can spare an umbrella." He walked over to the receptionist and pleaded his case.

"You clean up pretty good," she laughed. "Of course, Detective. I'll lend you mine."

"Thanks, but I can't promise I'll be back before you leave."

"That's okay. If worst comes to worst, I'll steal someone else's," she joked. "You won't arrest me, will you?"

Don laughed and said, "Thanks again. I owe you one. What's your name?"

"Janice," she replied, smiling sweetly as she handed him the umbrella.

Paul said goodbye to Janice and the two detectives departed and headed for Brighton.

Don and Paul pulled up in front of the house on Ashford Street. The air was cool and damp and there was still a light rain falling. They exited the car and began walking toward the house. Maybe it was only because he knew what had happened there, but Don immediately felt a chill throughout his body.

My clothes are still wet, he told himself.

"We can go right in," said Paul. "No one lives here right now. It's still considered a crime scene. Besides, nobody wants to rent this place."

Paul had the key to the house. He unlocked the door and the two detectives walked in. Don stood by the door for a few moments and slowly began to move farther into the house.

"The ground floor has a living room, a kitchen, a dining room and a bathroom. Nothing on this floor has been changed since the forensic team was first called to the scene. The bedrooms are upstairs. That's where the murders took place. We don't think any of these rooms were relevant to the murders," said Paul.

Don looked around the living room and began to take mental notes. "You say nothing at all has been changed downstairs in any way?"

"That's right, detective."

Don noticed that one of the windows in the living room was just barely open. "Was the front door locked when the police first answered the call?"

"No. The door was unlocked. Their friend, Kathy Legosi, who discovered the bodies, knocked on the door for several minutes. She knew where the hidden key was. When there was no answer, she let herself in. She went upstairs and found Leslie dead. She didn't go into the other rooms. The 911 operator said she was gasping for air and had difficulty explaining the situation. It took several minutes to calm her down enough to get an address."

"Okay let's go upstairs," said Don.

As Don climbed the stairs, he felt an eerie awareness that the murderer had almost certainly come up this way.

Paul directed Don to a room at the top of the stairs. "This is where Leslie Anne Parks was murdered," said Paul.

The bed sheets and mattress had been removed and taken to the crime lab. Blood spray was still evident on the wall beside the bed. On the floor were streaks of dried blood that had now turned brown. Don recalled the photos of the dead girl staring at the ceiling with her throat cut. It sent more chills rippling through his body.

"Looks like our perp cleaned up in here somewhat before they left," said Don. "Probably left some footprints they had to cover up."

"All three rooms show the same thing," said Paul. "Whoever did this took some time before he left. He felt very comfortable." He showed Don the next room. "This is where Angela Manzo was murdered."

There was blood on the wall in this room too.

Don began to pick up vibes from the murder scene. It was like he could sense the mindset of the murderer. He could sense anger, yet there was also something that suggested passion and excitement, as if the killer took pleasure in his actions.

They moved on to the last room.

"This is where our male victim, Frank Levick, was murdered. We think he might have been waking up when it happened. Probably happened really fast. From the position of the body, it looks like he made an attempt to get up. There's no blood spray on the wall, so it seems he was on his stomach. The murderer probably straddled him and then cut his throat right away. Almost all the blood went downwards into the pillow and mattress. He probably struggled for a few seconds before he died. By the way, I don't know if you read in the report. All three of them were legally drunk. They also had traces of cocaine in their blood. The girls weren't so bad but he had a BAC of 0.15 He probably couldn't have done a great job fighting off his attacker."

Again, Don started picking up vibes. In this room he sensed more anger and rage. It was as if the murderer had wanted him to wake up so that he would know what was going on before he died.

Next Paul showed him the bathroom and shower, where the killer evidently had cleaned up. The crime lab techs had used Luminol in the sink and shower. They determined that large amounts of blood had been washed away. There had also been a great deal of blood on the floor. Brown streaks of blood were evident in the hallway between the murder rooms and the bathroom.

"The murderer probably used a towel from the bathroom to wipe out the footprints," explained Paul. "Whoever it was evidently washed their clothing in the laundry downstairs. There's evidence of blood in the washing machine. We found the blood-soaked towel here in the hallway."

The two of them trotted down the stairs to check out laundry room.

Don looked inside the washing machine. He couldn't see anything unusual.

He walked over to the drier and asked, "Did the crime lab examine the lint in the filter?"

"Yes, they did, but it hadn't been cleaned in some time. There were fibers from so many different types of cloth it was virtually impossible to isolate them all. Some of them matched clothing from the girls' closets upstairs. We matched some of the fibers to a pair of blue jeans that belonged to Leslie Anne Parks. There were also some probable matches to some other clothing. We couldn't connect anything to a particular fiber of clothing that didn't belong."

"Okay," said Don. "I guess that wraps it up."

"Let's go next door and talk to our witness. I've set up a time for 12 PM with Carrie Sommers. She's the only neighbor that's really going to help us here. She knew the two girls, although not well. But she does recall some things from that day."

The detectives went next door and Don introduced himself. "I'm Detective Corlino. I'm with the FBI in Boston."

"I'm Carrie Sommers, Detective. Nice to meet you."

"I have a few questions I'd like to ask you, Carrie."

"Of course, Detective. Anything I can do to help. I'm still not completely over this."

He began to ask questions about what she could recall.

"At what time did you last see the girls?" began Don.

"It was in the early evening between 6 and 7PM."

"Did you speak with them?"

"Yes. They were planning to go out to The Lighthouse. It's a real popular place with students these days."

"How did the girls seem to you? Did they act any different than usual?"

"No. They seemed really happy and eager to party. They've always seemed a little on the wild side to me."

"How do you mean?"

"Oh, you know. They weren't exactly shy or timid. It seemed to me that they were the kind to experiment and try a lot of things."

"What makes you say that?" persisted Don.

"Well, I think they might have been kinda into each other. Ya know?"

"Please continue," urged Don.

"Well... One time I saw them making out on the back porch. I think they were drunk. When they saw me, they asked me if I wanted to join them for a beer. Then they started giggling and smiling. They kept looking over at me and whispering to each other. It was a little embarrassing."

Paul had not heard that before. Don had a way of coaxing facts out of witnesses.

Don continued to ask questions. "Do you recall anything else from that day? Anything that comes to mind. Even if it seems insignificant."

"Well, like I told Detective Arnold, I may have heard a motorcycle early the next morning. Maybe five or six AM. I'm not sure if I heard the bike starting up or if it just drove by. I was still half asleep."

Carrie shuddered when she thought that the murders had already occurred at that time. Don noticed it.

"Okay," said Don. "You've been very helpful, Carrie. Thank you very much."

"Yes. Thanks again," added Paul.

"Detective?"

"Yes."

"Can I ask you why the FBI is looking into this?"

"It's just something we're following up on, Carrie. We just want to cover all our bases."

The two detectives said goodbye and walked out the door.

"Do you want to interview the Legosi girl now?" asked Paul.

"Yes. I would like to learn more about their social lives and other friends."

"We asked all those questions back in May. Apparently, the girls had lots of different boyfriends over the past year. They were rather attractive and wild at heart. You know how college girls of that age are."

"Yes. Indeed, I do," sighed Don.

Ten minutes later they pulled up to Kathy Legosi's apartment. Paul rang the bell and Kathy appeared at the door.

"This is Detective Corlino. He's with the FBI. He would like to ask a few questions."

"Okay. Come on in."

"This won't take long," Don assured her. "I just need to know a couple of things."

"Please sit down, Detectives. I really want to see this guy caught. I'll do anything I can to help."

"Let me begin by asking you if any one of them had any friends or relatives in the Boston area?"

"Yes. Frank has a sister who goes to school there. Her name is Samantha Levik. She goes to Boston College."

"When did you last speak to her?"

"She came to the funeral back in May. That was the only time I ever met her or spoke to her."

Don wrote the name down. "Was Frank close with his sister?"

"Not that I know of. He never really talked about her."

"Can you think of any other ties any of them could have had to Boston?"

Kathy thought for a moment and shook her head.

"What can you tell me about Leslie and Angela? Did they have any current boyfriends?"

"I told Detective Arnold all I know about that. I gave them a list of about ten guys that they knew in the past year."

"We interviewed all of them, Don. They all have airtight alibis," insisted Detective Arnold.

"Okay. I'm going to ask you something a little personal now, Kathy."

Kathy looked at Don with some apprehension.

"Did either Leslie or Angela ever come on to you? I mean did they suggest something unusual?"

Kathy looked at the ground, unsure how to answer.

"No. They never tried to get me into anything weird like a threesome, if that's what you mean. But there was one time Angela got really drunk and kissed me full on the mouth. I figured it was just the alcohol and laughed it off."

"Did either of them have a lot of girl friends?" persisted Don.

"No. I was pretty much the only one. They had lots of guy friends, though."

"Can you think of anything else you can tell me about Leslie, Angela or Frank? Like a change in their behavior in the months before this happened."

"No. I've already told Detective Arnold everything I could think of."

"Okay, Kathy. Thank you very much for your cooperation. You've been very helpful."

Don stood up and said, "If we need you in the future, we'll let you know."

The detectives walked out, thanking her again, and headed for their car.

"Where to now?" asked Paul.

"Why don't we grab some lunch? We're not supposed to meet Rick at the Lighthouse until two o'clock."

• • • • •

Eddie took his seat at his desk and checked his inbox. There was another list of plate numbers and another note: Sept 24 complete. There was a list of another 214 plate numbers.

Oh joy, thought Eddie to himself.

Jimmy Dugan walked over to Eddie's desk with two police officers.

"Good morning, Eddie," said Jimmy. "I've assigned two more officers to the Jane Doe case. Get them up to speed and give them something to work on. They're gonna have to start somewhere."

"Okay, Jimmy. I'll do that." Eddie smiled and handed the two detectives the list of plate numbers. "You can start by entering these in the computer and checking with the DMV. Cross the list with known felons," Eddie continued.

He went through the entire routine.

One of the officers rolled his eyes and muttered something inaudible. The other calmly accepted his fate.

It was 7:16 when Rob walked in. "Ready to roll?" he asked.

"Ready as ever," replied Eddie.

Stakeouts could be dull but it was better than entering numbers into a computer.

The two of them left the Hyde Park precinct headquarters and walked to Eddie's car. The sun was just beginning to rise but the humidity made it feel warm outside.

Eddie and Rob stopped at a 7-11 for coffee and a couple of newspapers and drove to Beacon Street. They were going to take turns reading the paper and watching the house.

"Don't read too fast, Rob," said Eddie. "It's going to be a long day."

"I've taken up doing crossword puzzles, Eddie. Didn't I tell you? Great way to pass the time." He turned to Eddie and gave him a big shit-eating grin. Eddie shook his head.

At 8:40 Rob took over and Eddie began to read the paper.

The storm that had hit Buffalo the night before was closing in on Boston. The sky became dark and rain drops began to hit the windshield. Soon it was coming down hard.

After about ten minutes a dark blue van pulled up in front of the house.

Rob said, "Got something here, Eddie."

Eddie stopped reading and looked down the block.

He took out a video camera, rolled down his window and started filming.

Three Middle Eastern-looking men climbed out of the van. They covered their heads with their jackets and ran toward the house. They got to the door opened it and went inside.

"You get all of that? That should be enough to get a warrant," said Rob facetiously. "I guess we can go home now."

"Well, at least we got another plate number to work with," said Eddie, trying to put a positive spin on things.

The detectives sat back and resumed taking turns watching the house.

"What's a five-letter word for boredom?" asked Rob. "Second letter is an N. Forth letter is a U."

"Ennui," replied Eddie.

"How do you spell that?"

"E – N - N – U – I," Eddie spelled out.

"Yeah. That fits," said Rob. "How'd you get so smart?"

"Born that way. Just comes natural."

They continued with their stakeout. Nothing interesting happened for the next few hours.

It was almost twelve o'clock.

"Wanna break for lunch? We can go to Charlie's," suggested Rob.

"That's like twenty minutes away," objected Eddie.

"C'mon. Nothing is going to happen here for the next couple of hours."

Eddie knew Rob wanted to visit Meriam. It was no secret.

"Sure. Why not?" Eddie relented.

Eddie started the black Chevy Tahoe and got underway.

Rob looked up at the second story window as they rolled slowly past the house.

Traffic was heavy and it took them almost half an hour to get to Charlie's. They parked as close as they could and ran to the luncheonette.

They took their usual seats and Rob craned his neck, looking for Meriam.

After a minute she appeared from the kitchen with her arm supporting a tray of burgers.

"Hi guys. I'll be right with you," she said, smiling at Rob.

"How do you do it? What's your secret with women?" asked Eddie.

"Born that way. Just comes natural."

Eddie nodded his head, knowing he deserved that.

Meriam finished unloading her tray and came over to take their order. "How are you guys doing today?" she asked.

"Much better now that we're here with you, Meriam," said Rob.

"You are such a charmer, said Meriam with her patented coy demeanor.

Eddie just sat back and took it all in. He had never learned to flirt the way these two had. He relied more on the sympathy of women and his honest good intentions.

"What can I get you guys today?" she asked.

"What do you suggest?" said Eddie.

"We have a great special today. Tuna noodle casserole. Everyone is giving it a thumbs up. On a rainy day it really hits the spot."

"Sounds good," said Eddie, handing the menu back to Meriam.

"Make that two," said Rob.

"Anything to drink?"

"No thanks. We're gonna stop for coffee at 7-11. We're on a stakeout today," explained Rob.

Meriam disappeared into the kitchen and the detectives again began to think and talk about what they could do.

Soon Meriam arrived with their orders and began to flirt with Rob as she put the plates in front of them. "So what's the stakeout about?" she asked Rob with curious eyes.

"Real James Bond stuff. They don't just send anybody on these stakeouts," he said, trying to impress her.

"Sounds exciting."

"Oh yeah," said Eddie, looking at his watch. "I can't wait to get back."

Rob gave a chuckle and Meriam caught on.

"You guys," she said, walking away.

They finished with lunch, paid the check, and headed for the door.

When they reached it, Rob said, "Just a second, Eddie."

He hurried back over to Meriam. Eddie watched from afar as Rob began to talk to her.

He saw Meriam smile and nod her head. Rob took out his phone and began to punch some keys.

He walked back over to Eddie and said, "Let's go."

They returned to the car, got in, and Eddie started to drive. Rob had a smile stuck on his face.

"What was that all about?" asked Eddie.

"I've got a date tomorrow night, big guy."

Rob gave him a friendly punch in the shoulder.

• • • • •

Brittany woke up early and got Jamie and Roni ready for their hike in the mountains. Mike got his backpack from the car and went through his checklist. There was a headlamp for each of them, two lighters, a couple of survival knives, a roll of duct tape, tie wraps, a first aid kit and an aluminum foil blanket. It was unlikely they would need any of those things but Mike knew enough not to get caught in a bad situation. On their way they stopped at Subway and bought sandwiches to take with them. Roni made sure they had some bacon for Kardashian.

Soon they arrived at the trail head and they began their hike up Cascade Mountain. The trail was less than two miles but it was quite steep at some points. Mike had to help Roni and Jamie climb up a challenging rock face. Even Brittany had some trouble with it. Roni groaned with the effort, but came up smiling at the top.

"That was neat, Daddy. This is so cool!"

It was eleven o'clock when they reached the summit. The top of the mountain was a flat granite outcropping. There were no trees and a refreshing mild breeze made for a pleasant afternoon. The four of them stood there and took in the panoramic view all around them.

Mike pointed south and said, "That's the Great Range over there. From left to right you can see Lower and Upper Wolf Jaws, then Armstrong,

Gothics, Saddleback, and Basin. Marcy is hidden just behind Basin." Mike knew every inch of the Adirondacks. Every mountain looked as if it were on fire, with red and yellow leaves showing off their gift to nature.

"It's so beautiful, Mike. I don't think I could ever be any happier."

Roni and Jamie were running around on the top of the mountain with Kardashian psychotically chasing after them.

"Be careful, girls. Don't get to close to the edge," warned Brittany.

"Okay, Mom, we'll be careful," yelled Jamie.

Mike and Brittany walked over to the north side of the mountain, which fell off steeply to the Cascade Lakes far below. The bright sunshine reflected off the water and made them appear like two sparkling sapphires set in a silver bracelet.

"I could live up here," said Brittany.

"Maybe one day we can get a vacation house in town."

"I like that big wooden one on the lake. You know. The one that looks like a log cabin."

"Oh yeah. What do you suppose that costs?" said Mike, knowing it was way out of their price range.

"Oh. Come on. For my birthday. Please. Pretty please," she joked with a pouting face.

"Okay. I'll just quit my job and take up robbing banks."

"Whatever you think is necessary, honey."

Mike grabbed her around the waist and began to tickle her. Brittany let out a short yelp and struggled to break free. She laughed and ran back toward the top of the mountain. Mike chased after her. Jamie and Roni just looked on with amusement, not sure what to make of it. They looked at each other and just shook their heads.

After an hour they broke out the sandwiches and a couple of bottles of apple juice.

"What do you think?" asked Mike. "Porter Mountain is just over there. It's one of the forty-six high peaks. It won't take more than half an hour to get there. If we want to climb all of them some day we might as well climb that one now. If you climb them all you can be a member of the Forty-sixers Club."

"Ooooh. I want to be a member," cried Roni.

"Me too," said Jamie eagerly.

"Well, it's settled then. Right after lunch we'll get up there."

"How are you feeling, girls? Do your legs feel tired?" asked Brittany.

"I feel great," said Roni quickly.

"I'm fine," said Jamie.

They all finished lunch while Kardashian gobbled down about a quarter pound of bacon, which Roni fed her one piece at a time. They set out for Porter and reached the summit. They stayed for about fifteen minutes and a half hour later they were back on Cascade. They stayed for one last look at the magnificent view and then began their descent down the mountain.

CHAPTER 16

Friday afternoon

Don and Paul left Kathy's apartment and headed for the Lighthouse. The rain had lightened up a bit but it was still damp and nasty out. It was only two o'clock PM and the nightclub was not due to open for another five hours. Paul had arranged for the owner to come down and talk to Don. Don also wanted to look around the club for himself. Paul grabbed his cell and dialed the number for Rick Feinberg.

"We're here," said Paul.

"Just walk right in. The door's open," he said.

Rick was sitting at the bar waiting for them. "I'd offer you guys a drink but I know you're on the job."

"Yeah. We've still got a lot of things to do today," said Don. "But thanks."

Don introduced himself and began, "I understand you knew the murder victims."

"Yes. Yes, I did. The girls were regulars here," explained Rick.

"What can you tell me about them?"

"I never talked much to Frank, but I knew the girls pretty well," reflected Rick. "They were here a lot more often than he was. Leslie and Angela were here almost every night. Real party animals. And not bad to look at, if you know what I mean. They had guys hittin' on them all the time. They were good for business."

"I see," said Don. "Can you recall what they were doing that night and who they were with?"

"Yes. Like I told Detective Arnold, they were partying with a lot of people early in the evening. Later on, they started hanging out with this big motorcycle guy. You know the type: about 250 pounds, big muscles, tattoos, big mouth. They all started getting drunk. I was a little concerned. Later in the evening this real pretty girl joined them. The security tape at the front door shows that they all left at closing, about one o'clock AM."

"How do you know for sure he was riding a motorcycle?" asked Don.

"He brought his helmet inside with him. Carried it around the bar with him."

"Do you know if they left together?" asked Don.

"The tape doesn't show that," said Paul. "We don't know if they might have met up later. What the tape does show is the motorcycle guy left first. He turned to the right when he left the club. It shows Leslie, Angela and Frank leaving together about a minute later. They also turned to the right. The other girl left about half a minute after that and turned left toward the river."

"Do you recall them talking to anyone else?" asked Don.

"Like I said before, early in the evening they were talking to lots of people. A lot of them are regulars from the University. They all know each other. The motorcycle guy and the other chick I've never seen before."

"Okay," said Don. "Thanks a lot. Mind if I just look around for a while?"

"Help yourself. I'm staying here now till we open anyway."

Don walked around the club, taking notice of the dance floor, the tables, the glass mirrors and the stage. There was a large disco ball suspended from the ceiling.

After ten minutes he walked over to Paul. "I think I've seen enough here," said Don. "Do you have recordings of the interviews of the witnesses?"

"Yes, we do. We interviewed about fifty people who were here that night. They really couldn't tell us much. We were never able to track down the two people they were partying with. The surveillance tape from inside doesn't really show a good picture of either of them. Ironically, it's got great photos of Leslie, Angela and Frank. The camera was over the bar. It was there to keep the customers and bartenders honest," explained Paul. "The girl never went up to the bar. The guy had his back to the camera when he ordered drinks. Some luck, huh? We had a sketch artist work with Rick and some of the patrons. We put together a decent drawing of the guy. The girl was wearing a cowboy hat. It was dark and she sat at the table the whole night. I'm afraid the only ones who got a good look at her were our victims and the motorcycle guy. I've got the drawings back at the office. We posted them on all the Buffalo TV stations for over a week last May. We also aired the security camera footage from the front door, but that also doesn't show a clear photo. We got nothing from the public that checked out. I sent the sketches and the security film to the FBI at that time. I'm sure there's a nationwide FBI alert circulating on them after the recent developments this weekend."

"Yes, there is. I printed out the sketches for myself before I left last night," said Don.

"I think Motorcycle Man is our guy," said Paul. Paul and his fellow detectives had given the suspect the moniker 'Motorcycle Man.' "He's been the main target of our investigation since this happened. Remember? Carrie Sommers says she heard a motorcycle early that morning."

"It could be," said Don.

"You would figure the guy would come forward, when he heard about it on the news. Unless he was guilty. Right?"

Don had to agree. It was a strong argument.

"Let's go back to FBI headquarters," said Don. "I want to look at those security tapes in slow motion."

They headed back to FBI Plaza. It was still drizzling and it was considerably colder out.

Don's pants had still not completely dried out.

The detectives walked in the door. Janice was still at the reception desk. Don walked up to her and handed the umbrella back to her. "I had to get back here and save you from a life of crime," said Don.

Janice laughed and gave him a big smile. "Thanks, Detective. I appreciate your integrity and dedication."

Don asked her, "Where can I get on a high-definition screen and download a video from our database?"

Janice called over an agent who was standing nearby and said, "Could you escort these two detectives to room 312? They need to use the high-def scroll."

"Sure thing, Janice. Right this way, gentlemen."

Inside the room they found a technician seated in front of a large screen. He was scrolling through a video of a bank surveillance tape. He was an expert on the use of the state-of-the-art crime analysis equipment.

The two detectives showed their badges.

"Can I help you, detectives?"

"We would like you to download a surveillance tape that was submitted to the FBI last May. I need to check it out in high-def and in slow motion," said Don.

"That I can do. Do you have the reference number? If not, I can do a search by date submitted and location."

"I've got it here in my phone," said Paul. "Just a second. He took out his cell and went to notes.

Paul gave him the number. After a few minutes they had it on screen.

"What's your name?" asked Don.

He always liked to know the name of the people he was working with. It was more personable and pleasant that way.

"Harold Jaffy at your service, Detective."

They began with the front door footage. The camera was placed about five feet above the front door. It was not the optimum location for identifying faces. They were able to pinpoint the arrival of Motorcycle Man at 9:32 PM. Unfortunately, he was still wearing his helmet at the time. He took off the helmet as he entered the establishment, but his face was partially blocked by an awning until he was directly beneath the camera. After that he had his face turned downward and to the side, making a positive ID difficult. They had no better luck with 'Cowgirl' as they had nicknamed her. They put her arrival at 10:06 PM. She was wearing her hat and the camera did not provide a good shot of her face.

"We've looked at all these tapes before," said Paul. "We had the FBI look at it, too."

"That was last May," said Harold. "We upgraded our system with highly sophisticated software last month. It's already broken some cold cases. Face recognition is a useful tool but you need a good picture. We've got something better now. A lot can be determined from the simple motion of a human body. It's amazing how different every human being is. All you need is a few hundred frames and you can get a pretty close match to another film strip. There's a unique ratio between someone's stride, arm length, height, shoulder breadth and other factors. The software is capable of making thousands of critical measurements."

They ran the video segments through the computer. The software was able to identify signature body movements of both Motorcycle man and Cowgirl.

"Okay, if you can give me some idea of where I should start looking, I'll have the computer do a cross analysis," said Harold. "The more we can refine our search the better chance we'll have."

"Give a priority to night clubs and biker bars in the area and restrict it to May. Also run any tapes that involve the arrest of motorcyclists," suggested Don.

Harold went to work on locating and entering the most promising surveillance tapes.

After a brief search he had a list of about two hundred tapes. He entered the first one and the computer sprang into action.

"This is going to take forever," said Don.

"It's okay. Computers don't get bored," said Harold. "We can let it run all night. I'll just keep feeding it more tapes."

Don and Paul began looking at the tape from the Lighthouse night club. They started viewing the footage from the bar camera beginning at 9:32. They isolated the footage of Leslie, Angela, Frank and Motorcycle Man. Then they began to go over the video in slow motion. It was slow, tedious work.

Don kept an eye out for any sign of a cowboy hat.

Then at mark 12:45 AM the camera picked up the image of a girl reflected in a mirror by the side of the bar.

"Hold it! Hold it," said Don. "Back it up just a little, Harold. Right there! Stop!"

There was a partial image of 'Cowgirl.'

"Blow that up. Get a hard copy photo. Isolate that segment and run a face recognition with our database."

Harold again entered the image into the computer and began the face recognition software. "Well, that's as much as we can do for now," he said. "We just have to kick back and wait for the computer to do its thing. Either of you guys play chess? How about poker?"

• • • • •

Eddie and Rob drove back to their Beacon Street stakeout.

"At least we don't have to walk around outside today," said Rob, trying to put a positive spin on things.

"Don't jinx us. You'll make the weather gods angry and we'll wind up walking in the Milford woods again."

"I thought you liked nature."

"Only when it's nice to me."

Rob took out the crossword puzzle from the Tribune and began to read the clues. Eddie looked down the road and kept an eye on the house. At about three o'clock the sky turned the color of dark gray slate. The rain, which had been a slow drizzle, became a persistent shower.

Rob was having trouble seeing the clues in the darkness. He tossed the paper aside and said, "I give up."

"I guess you'll have to keep me company now," said Eddie with the mandatory shit-eating grin.

Rob knew he deserved that and let out a chuckle.

The two detectives fell into a conversation about the Patriots' chances without Tom Brady in the upcoming game against the Jets. Time passed slowly for the next hour and a half. They talked about everything mundane in their lives, including Eddie's crabgrass problem and Rob's tyrannical fifth grade teacher who gave him detention just for looking out the window and not paying attention.

It was still raining hard when the same blue van that had been there earlier rolled down the street and came to a stop in front of the house. Again, the three men ran for the front door with their jackets over their heads.

"That looks suspicious. Why are they running? Why are they hiding their faces?" said Rob sarcastically.

"I know. I know. We've got no choice. We can't tip our hand by questioning them directly. We just have to be patient. The more film we can get of people coming to visit the house the better. If we can identify any of them as known felons or connect them to terrorist activity, we might get a judge to issue a search warrant."

Rob thought a direct approach might work better.

Eddie and Rob resigned themselves to their fate and continued to watch. About half an hour later the three men ran back to their car and drove away.

"Well, that's all the excitement I can stand in one day. It's almost five o'clock. What do you say we hit Zan's?"

"Sounds good to me," said Eddie. "Let's stop back at the office first. I want to check on our two officers going over the tapes."

They drove back to precinct headquarters and got the new list of names to check out.

"Anything special that hits you between the eyes?" asked Eddie.

"Not really."

Half an hour later they were sitting at the bar talking to Zan.

Mike and Brittany and the girls had completed their hike back down the mountain. On the way home they stopped at a Stewarts convenience store for some ice cream. Jamie and Roni got pistachio cones. Mike got chocolate chip. Brittany got a cup of hot tea.

"Where should we go for dinner?" asked Mike.

"I could go to The View again," said Brittany. "That steak was delicious. The rest of the menu looked great, too."

"Sounds good to me," Mike agreed.

They got back to the cabin and showered up. An hour later they were at the restaurant watching the sunset over Mirror Lake.

It was a day they would all treasure in their memories forever.

After dinner they went back to the motel and fell fast asleep almost immediately.

• • • • •

Don and Paul stayed at the video lab for another two hours. The computer had come up with a few hits but nothing with a high percentage match. It was now eight o'clock.

"Do you work tomorrow, Harold?" asked Don.

"No. It's my day off. But I'll leave instructions with Pete. He takes over at twelve o'clock. He works till eight. I'm sure he wouldn't mind a little overtime. I'll tell him to expect you at what? Nine o'clock?"

"What do you say, Paul?"

"I can be here at nine. No problem."

The two detectives left and Don went back to his hotel room. He was exhausted. He took his gun from his shoulder holster and laid it on the dresser. He took off his shoulder holster, hung it on door and began to get undressed. He took his cell phone from his jacket pocket and placed it on the night table by his bedside. His pants were still wet. He took out his wallet from his pants pocket and placed it on the dresser. A small piece of paper was stuck to it. It was soaked through and through from the rain that morning. Don fell into the bed, hit the lights and was asleep within seconds.

CHAPTER 17

Saturday Morning, Oct. 9, 8:30 AM
Buffalo

Don had left instructions for a wakeup call at eight o'clock with the receptionist at his hotel. The phone rang and he forced himself out of bed. He was still trying to make up for lost sleep. He jumped in the shower and then got himself dressed. He made a mental list of what he wanted to get done that day. He put on his shoulder holster and threw his wallet into the right front pocket of his pants. They were now dry. He noticed the wet piece of paper on the dresser and tried to remember what it was. It was still too wet to try and unfold it so he put it in his shirt pocket. He holstered his gun, put on his jacket and headed out.

This time he arrived early, at 8:45. The sun was shining and the sky was bright blue. Maybe it was a good omen. Don walked in and greeted Janice.

"Is Detective Arnold here yet?"

"He just called. He said he would be here in a half hour."

"I'm gonna run up to 312 and check on the results from our search. Please tell Paul I'll be upstairs," he said, walking away.

"I'll do that, Detective. Good hunting."

Don stopped and turned around. He looked at Janice and said, "Funny. I know someone else who says that."

"You guys have a tough job. I just want you to know that I know that."

"Thanks," said Don with a smile and went to take the elevator upstairs. He walked in to room 312. There was a different technician on duty. Don introduced himself and said, "Did Harold leave any messages for me?"

"No, but he explained to me what you guys were looking for. He gave me instructions last night before he left. The computer spit out a 'strong maybe' on Mr. Motorcycle. Apparently there was a big fight in a biker bar in Tonawanda last April. The video shows a guy with the same walking motion as the video from the nightclub. Also, he's carrying what could be the same helmet in his hand. He was hitting some guy in the head with it. Cops arrested a bunch of them. Here's the list of names. We don't know which name goes with Mr. Motorcycle. The mugshots should be coming in from Tonawanda PD any minute."

"That's great news," beamed Don. "You gotta love technology. What's your name, by the way?"

"Just call me Pete," he said.

Pete put the video of the bar fight on one of the TV screens. He began to scroll through it and froze the video on a frame that clearly showed the suspect's face.

"That's our guy," said Pete. "Computer gives it better than 85%."

Don looked carefully at the face on the screen. The long, blond unkempt hair and the shoulders definitely bore a strong resemblance to the man in the video from the nightclub.

"That could be the same guy," he said. "We just need a name to go with it."

Paul Arnold walked through the door. "Any good news?" he asked.

"We have a possible ID for Mr. Motorcycle," Don informed Paul.

"That's great. That's the best news I've heard in a long time. How did you come up with that?"

"The computer has been comparing videos all night. Probably went through several hundred surveillance tapes by now. We put a priority on any tapes that involved motorcycles. We call the program *Miss Google Eyes*. It can discern between the slightest differences in the motion of a human body," explained Pete. "It's a hundred times better than the old software. That would never have picked it up. It's also ten times faster. We're really putting a dent in our backlog of cold cases."

"Harold was explaining that yesterday. Quite impressive," said Don.

Both Harold and Pete took pride in their work. They were always eager to try out the latest software.

Pete heard the sound of the FAX machine in the corner and went over to check it out.

"Here're the mugshots from Tonawanda."

Don let Paul look at the pictures first while he looked over his shoulder. There were eight pictures to look at. Paul began to look carefully at each one.

"That's him," said Paul, comparing one of the mugshots to the face on the screen.

"Absolutely," said Don.

They both looked at the mugshot. Together they said the name out loud. "Brian Dawson."

"Do they have an address to go with that name?" asked Don.

"I'll find out for you right now," said Pete. He put the name Brian Dawson into the computer.

The computer spit back: Last known address 18 Dunn Avenue, Tonawanda, N.Y.

"What do you say we take a drive up there?" said Paul. "We could be there in less than an hour."

"Sounds like a great idea," said Don. "Before we do that let's put out a nationwide APB. But, remember this guy is only a person of interest. Make sure everyone knows we only want him for questioning right now."

Paul was eager to get moving. He was convinced they had the right man.

"Let me first call the FBI in Boston," said Don. "I want to send this photo to my guy in the crime lab. I also want to send these tape segments over and have them crossed with local surveillance tapes over there."

He called Greg Phillips' number and again got voicemail with the familiar John Waite tune.

Greg picked up and said, "Yes, Godfather. How can I honor you today?"

"Greg, do you have the new software that can ID people by their body movements?" he asked.

"Yes, we do. All the FBI crime labs got the new software last month. That program is great, but we still need to know where to look. The more we can refine our search the better the odds of getting a match. If we can limit the search to a few hundred tapes or less we can usually get a hit if our guy is in them at all."

"I'm going to send you a couple of tape segments, a mugshot and a couple of other photos. We're looking for a guy named Brian Dawson. I would like you to compare them with as many surveillance tapes as possible from the Milton area soon as you can. I know I'm asking a lot, Greg, but this is really important."

"It's okay, Don. I've got clearance from Jack yesterday to give you anything you want ASAP. You're the priority case right now."

"Thanks, Greg. Call me as soon as you know anything."

The two detectives thanked Pete and headed back downstairs.

Don stopped at the reception desk to talk to Janice on the way out. "Paul and I are going on a little road trip. When do you get off?" he asked.

"I get out of here at five o'clock," she answered.

"If we're back before five o'clock maybe we can all have some dinner together. It's on me," said Don.

"Sure. I'm okay with that."

"Later," said Don as the two detectives walked out the door.

Don and Paul got to the car, punched the address into the GPS and headed toward Tonawanda. An hour later they were there. They found Dunn Avenue and located number 18. There were several motorcycles parked in the yard in front.

"Got your gun ready?" asked Don.

"Yup. I'm set."

They walked up to the front door and knocked. A heavyset girl about forty years of age opened the door. "Yeah. Who are you guys? What do you want here?"

"I'm Detective Corlino. I'm with the FBI," said Don, showing his badge. "This is Detective Arnold from the Buffalo police department."

"Ricky, it's the cops," she yelled into the house.

They heard a commotion in the back of the house. Then there was the sound of a toilet flushing. Don tried to see past the girl, who was still blocking the front door. He looked farther into the house. He could see just enough to see Brian and two other large men race out the back door. They almost took it off the hinges as they barreled through into the back yard.

Don tried to get past the girl but she wasn't budging an inch. He ran around the side of the house and got there just in time to see Brian and the other two men climb awkwardly over a fence in the backyard.

He raced back to the front of the house

"Let's try to head them off with the car." said Don. "You drive." He flipped the keys to Paul.

They ran back to the car and raced to the corner.

"Turned right," said Don. "Keep your gun handy, Paul. Maybe we can spot Brian on one of these side streets."

They cruised down the block and Don looked down each cross street when they came to an intersection. Don looked at the Google map on his phone and tried to figure out where he might try to go.

"Turn right here, Paul. Step on it."

Paul hit the gas and the car quickly made it to the next intersection. Don saw one of bikers run across the street and disappear into a back yard. It wasn't Brian. Apparently the three of them had split up.

"Go up to the next street. Quick."

Paul hit the gas once more and the car lurched forward. Don looked up and down the block. Nothing.

"Turn left. Go."

They continued to make rights and lefts, hoping to spot Brian. Paul made another left and Don caught sight of him. Brian was running down the side street a few hundred feet down the block.

"There he is. Turn right."

Paul turned and sped down the block. They caught up to Brian and Paul stopped the car. Don jumped out and identified himself.

Brian was out of breath and gasping for air. He continued to run in a pathetic attempt to get away.

"Hold it," ordered Don as he approached Brian. "We just want to ask you some questions."

Brian turned and took a wild swing at Don.

Don neatly ducked the punch and Brian fell clumsily to the ground.

"Now I'm going to have to arrest you," said Don.

"What for? I haven't done anything."

"You just assaulted a federal agent. Maybe you should just do as you're told."

Paul was now out of the car and had his gun trained on Brian.

"Don't move," demanded Paul.

Don grabbed Brian by his hair and pushed his face onto the sidewalk. He pulled one of his arms behind his back and put the cuffs on him.

"You have the right to remain silent. Anything you say can and will be used against you in a court of law. You have the right to an attorney..."

"Blah, blah, blah. I know my rights," blubbered Brian.

Don yanked him up to his feet and opened the rear door of their vehicle. He pushed Brian's head down and got him into the backseat as he continued to read him his rights. The two detectives got back into the car.

Don turned around to look at Brian and said, "Why don't they ever learn, Paul?"

"Beats me. Back to FBI headquarters?"

"Yup."

• • • • •

Saturday morning 8 AM

Eddie was already at his desk when Rob walked in. He sat down at his own desk and said, "Good morning, Eddie."

"Morning, Rob. Ready for another thrilling day on Beacon Street?"

"Honestly Eddie, can't we just work out of the office today? We've still got some loose ends to take care of. We could have a couple of other guys do the stakeout."

Eddie looked at Rob, smiled and thought to himself about Rob's upcoming date. *Probably got a little case of nerves.*

"Why not? I'll tell Jimmy to put some guys on it. Where do you want to start?"

"We've got some more names from the surveillance cameras. Jimmy had those guys working all night. We can make some more phone calls. Also, there's still that Dennis girl."

"Right. The DNA Lab is still working on those things Don sent them. They said they'd call as soon as they got something."

"We could try to get a warrant to search her credit card statements."

"That would take some time and a little more to go on. Why don't we wait to see if she's our victim?"

Rob let out a sigh and said, "Okay. Let's have some of those names."

Eddie shook his head, smiling, and gave Rob a list of half the names. He kept the other half for himself. There were no felony arrests on either list but there were several misdemeanors.

The two of them picked up their phones and began to make calls.

• • • • •

Saturday Morning 8 AM

Mike woke up, yawned and looked over to Brittany. They were sleeping in separate beds since they were all sharing the same room. Brittany was still fast asleep and snoring quietly.

How cute is that? thought Mike. He didn't have the heart to wake her and just watched her sleep. *Maybe I should get my phone and make a video.*

The moment was lost when Jamie got out of bed and headed for the bathroom, waking up sleeping beauty.

She looked over at Mike and said, "Good morning, sweetheart."

"Good morning. Did you sleep well?"

"Like a rock. I feel like I just went to sleep a minute ago. Ooooh. I feel my legs. I'm a little sore."

"We'll take it easy today, honey. We can do something else. Maybe we can drive up to the top of Whiteface?"

Mike walked over to the window and pulled back the shade. The beautiful sunny weather had yielded to gray, leaden clouds. "Uh oh. It looks like it might rain."

"Well, that rules out Whiteface. I'm not up to playing another game of Monopoly. What can we do?"

"I noticed that new adventure movie is playing at the theater here in town. It's about the two little kids and their dog. They get stranded in a cabin in the woods and they have to make it back to civilization. What's it called again?"

"'The incredible journey home' or something like that."

"Do you think you can manage to sit through it?" Mike asked, looking sympathetic.

"Just feed me enough popcorn and I'll be okay."

"Want to go to IHOP for breakfast?"

"Sure. Let me take a shower and get the girls ready. Oooooh," said Brittany as she tried to stand up.

"It'll get better. Just keep moving and stretch out a little."

Jamie got out of the bathroom and looked out the window. "It's starting to rain, Daddy."

"We're gonna see a movie this afternoon. It's the one about the boy, his little sister and their dog."

"Oh, cool. That sounds great."

"How are your legs feeling?"

"Just fine, Daddy. I feel great."

Brittany looked at her with a bit of envy. Kids seemed to be indestructible.

The conversation woke up Roni and she jumped out of bed. "Are we going hiking again?" she asked eagerly.

"Not today sweetheart. It's raining," said Brittany. "We're going to the movies after lunch."

"Cool. Can we get popcorn?"

Brittany smiled and said, "I think you inherited that gene from me."

"What's a jeene?"

"You got yourself into that one, Brit. You can explain it while I take a shower."

When Mike got out of the bathroom, she was still trying to explain it to Roni.

After breakfast they took a drive to Saranac Lake and passed the time looking at the fall leaves glisten in the rain. The road was a beautiful tapestry of red, orange and gold. When they got back, they grabbed lunch and caught the two o'clock matinee at the Palace Theater.

They all got a big helping of buttered popcorn and sat back to enjoy the movie.

Halfway through Mike turned to his wife and said, "How we doing, honey?"

"Not bad. This movie is actually pretty good. I'm enjoying it."

The dog in the movie was a yellow lab just like Kardashian. He was busy fighting off a huge bear that was coming after the little girl.

"I'll bet Kardashian would do that, too," said Roni.

"You bet she would!" said Brittany, shoveling another handful of popcorn into her mouth.

Jamie and Roni shouted out encouraging words to the dog in the movie.

"Get em, Kardashian!" cried Roni.

The family sitting a few of rows in front of them all turned around with puzzled expressions.

Mike and Brittany just looked at each other and laughed.

After the movie was over, they went outside. The rain had let up and the sun was beginning to make a comeback.

"One more walk around the lake," suggested Mike. "It'll help make your legs feel better, honey."

"I guess so. Let's pick up the dog first. I'm sure she's going crazy wondering why we left her behind."

"Fine. Then we can get some dinner and just relax in the cabin tonight."

"Sounds like a plan," said Brittany.

CHAPTER 18

Saturday, Oct. 9, 11:30 AM

Eddie and Rob were still at work three hours later and still had nothing special to show for it.

"Why don't we call it a day?" said Eddie, thinking that Rob could use a little time off before his date with Meriam.

"You know what? I'd just as soon work another hour or two. Why don't we order a pizza and split it with Sarah?"

"Okay, it's on me."

• • • • •

Don and Paul had arrived back at FBI headquarters. They pulled Brian out of the car and brought him into interrogation. They had Brian sitting in a chair with the mandatory overhead light on him and began asking questions.

Don began with, "There're a lot of nice-looking girls over in Brighton aren't there, Brian?"

Brian looked up at Don with a puzzled stare. "What are you talking about?"

"We were just wondering if you spent a lot of time there. You know, maybe hitting the club scene now and then."

Brian started to fidget nervously. "I thought you guys were narcs. What's going on here?"

Don let Paul take the lead. It was his case, after all. "We are, Brian. We're trying to take down a major drug cartel and your name came up. Seems there's a major distribution hub right here in Buffalo," said Paul, trying to rattle Brian. "We've been following you for some time now. What do you have to say for yourself?"

"You guys are crazy! Just cuz I got busted for coke don't mean I'm some big deal. I did my time for that and I've kept myself clean. I swear."

"Yeah, right. What was all that this morning? Last time I heard that many toilets flush was when I was smoking in the boy's room and the principal walked in."

Don smiled at Paul's attempt at humor.

"Why did you guys run? If you had nothing to hide, why not just talk to us?"

"I swear. I'm not a bigtime dealer. Ricky ran out the door and I panicked. I just took off."

"We busted a couple of girls for cocaine. We showed them some pictures and they IDed you as the guy who sold it to them. We're just curious about who sold it to you and how many clubs you go to."

"I don't go to fuckin' clubs and I don't sell fuckin' cocaine. And why do you have my fuckin' picture?"

"Come on, Brian. We've got you on fuckin' tape," said Paul.

Don almost let out a laugh but stifled it.

Brian was getting visibly nervous now. He was starting to put two and two together.

"Look! Why am I here?" he demanded, still trying to feign ignorance.

"What about the Lighthouse, Brian? Ever been there?"

"I don't know. What's the Lighthouse?"

"Brian! We have you on tape being there the night of May 8 last spring."

Now Brian got outright defensive. "Look! I might have sold them some coke but I had nothing to do with that crazy shit."

"So you know what we're talking about?" said Paul.

"Of course. The whole fuckin' country heard about it, but I didn't have anything to do with it."

"Why didn't you come forward? You must have known we'd be looking for you."

"Are you kidding? Every time I deal with cops I get fucked."

"Yeah. So it seems. Your record says you've been locked up six times in the last five years. All for fighting or drugs."

"Yeah, but murder's just not my thing, ya know?"

"So start telling us everything you know," demanded Paul. "Did you ever meet them before that night? Did you go home with them?"

"No. We just talked and had a few drinks. I went home alone."

Don looked at the grotesque mess that was sitting before him. Unless it was for the cocaine, he couldn't imagine two good-looking young girls inviting him back to their place.

"What can you tell us about the girl with the cowboy hat?" asked Don.

"Not much. Real looker, that one."

"Did she buy any cocaine from you?"

"No! None of them did."

Paul glared at Brian.

"Come on, Brian. We have you on tape snorting up at your table. All of you."

Paul was lying but it worked.

"Okay, but I didn't sell them any."

Don and Paul looked at each other.

"Start telling the truth, Brian. You gave them some coke. You wanted to go home with them. They turned you down and they laughed at you. Then you followed them home and murdered them all. Didn't you?" yelled Paul with his face just inches from Brian's.

"No! No! No! I didn't do anything. I swear. I didn't do it."

"Come on, Brian. Did you murder the girl with the cowboy hat too?"

"No. I didn't do anything," he repeated. "I didn't kill anyone."

Don jumped in and played good cop. "Wait a minute, Detective. Give him a little time. I'm sure he can explain everything."

Brian looked somewhat relieved.

"So tell us more about that night. Were any of your friends there?"

"No. It was just me. Someone told me about the place. It was the only time I was ever there."

"Who is someone?" Paul was still in his face.

"I dunno. Some guy I met in a bar."

"Tell us more about the other people you met there. What about the girl with the cowboy hat?"

"I don't know. I swear I would tell you if I knew anything."

"Did she tell you her name?" Paul was in his face again.

Brian looked to Don for help.

"What was her name?"

"I don't remember. April, I think. Something like that. She said she was from Toronto or something."

"What else can you tell us? Think hard or you're doing more time."

"She said she was on her way to Florida. She asked me if I knew a decent motel in the area. I told her I wasn't from around there, but maybe the girls could help her. That's all. I swear."

Don looked at Paul and said, "Let's step outside for a second."

The two detectives stepped back into the main office.

"I know you're going to be disappointed but I don't think this is our guy," Don said.

"Why don't you think so?"

"Whoever committed these murders is very smart. It took a lot to get away clean with three murders. This guy is one cucumber away from a tossed salad."

"I guess you're right. He's no Einstein. So where do we go from here?"

"Let's just keep pushing him for more information about Leslie, Angela and Frank Levick. Somebody knows something. There are always hidden clues."

It was now quarter past two. Don knew that his time was not unlimited. Jack would be getting pressure from the mayor and that meant he would be getting pressure from Jack.

Don felt his phone vibrate in his pocket. He answered it. "Corlino."

"Hello, Detective. This is Deborah Earns from the DNA lab in Boston. I have a note here to contact you ASAP about the results of a DNA cross with a Jane Doe in the Medical Examiner's Office."

"Yes. What can you tell me, Deborah?"

"That test came back as negative. The hair samples don't match Jane Doe."

Don didn't know how to feel. "Thank you, Deborah. I appreciate your effort."

"You're welcome, Detective. Do you need anything else?"

"No. Not right now, but I'll probably be talking to you again."

"Very well. Goodbye then."

"Anything important?" asked Paul.

"Just another dead end, but you've got to keep looking."

"So what now?"

"You can only hold Brian for twenty-four hours. We don't have anything solid on him. Just keep asking him about that night and keep up the pressure. I'm gonna run up to the video lab and have them send a copy of the Lighthouse tape to the Boston lab and other FBI headquarters around the country. We can use that Ms. Google technology. Maybe we'll get lucky with Cowgirl. Maybe she can tell us something. The problem is we have no idea where to look."

"So I guess you're gonna head back to Boston."

"My boss is hot on another case and we don't know if these murders have anything to do with it. The trail is getting colder every day. It's 2:30 right now. If I leave now, I can make Rochester by four o'clock. I have some news to give someone. Then I got a stop in Albany tomorrow and its back to Boston."

"Well, good luck, Detective. Thanks for your help. If I can get anything more out of the tossed salad, I'll let you know."

Don laughed and said, "Good luck, Paul. It's been good working with you."

"You too, Don."

Don went to the reception area and said goodbye to Janice, apologized for skipping out on dinner, and thanked her again for the umbrella.

Janice smiled and said, "Come visit us again, Detective, and next time bring a raincoat and an umbrella."

"I'll do that, Janice."

Don took out his phone and called Eddie.

"McGowan here."

"Hi Eddie. It's Don. I called to let you know the results were negative for Michelle Dennis. She's not our vic."

"Okay, thanks Don. Any other news?"

"Yeah. That suspect with the motorcycle probably isn't our guy. I'm giving up here and heading for Albany to check out the murder of a college student there named George Weston. I've got to call Detective Connelly and let him know I'm coming tomorrow. If nothing pans out there, I'm heading back for Boston. I'll probably be back by Monday. Tuesday at the latest."

"Okay, Don. Good hunting."

"Funny, the receptionist at FBI headquarters in Buffalo says the same thing. Good hunting to you, too. Eddie."

See you soon, Don."

Don called Detective Connelly.

"Hello. Detective Connelly speaking."

"Hello, Detective. This is Don Corlino from the FBI in Boston. We spoke a few days ago about the Weston murder. I know tomorrow is Sunday, but if you could spare a couple of hours, it would be greatly appreciated. Maybe we could meet for an early lunch or something. My treat."

"Okay Don. I think that would be fine. We haven't gotten anywhere with the case since June. I could use any new input. There's a good spot called Pete's Place just off Route 20 near the university. Say one o'clock?"

"Sounds great. I'll see you then."

An hour later Don walked into The Cock's Inn in Rochester. Maxine was sitting at the bar. He took a seat next to her and said, "I have some good news, Maxine."

Maxine looked up with a hopeful look in her eyes and said, "Oh. Hello, Detective.

"Michelle is not our victim."

Maxine broke into tears and threw her arms around Don. "Oh! Thank God! Thank you, Detective."

"Can I buy you a drink?" offered Don.

"Oh, yes. You're too nice," Maxine managed to get out through the tears.

Hearing that Michelle was not the victim in the nature preserve was a relief; however, there were still unanswered questions. Don still had two missing people and a Jane Doe.

After a couple of drinks Don left a slightly drunk Maxine and headed for Albany.

Meanwhile Eddie and Rob finished up for the day and agreed to pick it up again on Monday morning. Rob was still feeling the nerves. Eddie wished him luck and headed home.

CHAPTER 19

Saturday, Oct. 9, 4 PM

Rob left the office just after four o'clock and got home half an hour later. He called Meriam and she answered the phone.

"Hi, Rob."

Her voice melted Rob's heart in an instant. He could picture her smiling in her coy, flirtatious way and was momentarily lost for words. "Hi Meriam. I'm home getting ready for tonight. I just wanted to ask you if you like Italian," he finally managed to get out.

Meriam picked up on his nervous tone and chuckled softly. "Sure, I love Italian."

"Okay. Dress casual. I know this really great place in Bay Village. They have the best hot bread and the best lasagna I've ever had."

"Mmmmm. Sounds delicious. Lasagna is my favorite."

"It's set then. I'll pick you up around seven o'clock. How do I get to your place?"

"Do you know the Franklin Park Zoo in Roxbury?"

"Oh, you live in the zoo?"

"Yes. I have my very own cage," joked Meriam. "I'm right next to the tigers. Grrrr."

Rob laughed. "Does your cage have an address?"

"I'm on Ruthven Street. It's the yellow house on the corner with Elm Hill Avenue. It's a block from the zoo."

"All right. I'll see you soon, pussycat."

"Can't wait. Bye." She whispered another soft growl into the phone and hung up.

Rob smiled. He couldn't contain his excitement. For the next minute he walked around his apartment talking to himself. "Yes. Yes. Yes," he repeated while clenching his fist.

He took a shower and got dressed. An hour later he was outside Meriam's house. The butterflies were beginning to flutter around in his stomach as he knocked on the door.

Meriam came to the door with a big smile and said, "Hi Rob."

She was dressed in light blue jeans and a tight-fitting white Eddie Bauer T shirt. She had a dark green leather jacket on over the T that concealed just enough to make it respectable.

Rob's eyes almost popped out. "You look stunning," he said.

Meriam smiled and batted her eyes seductively. "Thanks Rob. You're looking pretty good yourself."

Rob walked her to the car and opened the passenger side door of his Mercedes coupe. Meriam slid into the seat with the grace of a jungle cat. It was as if her every movement was by design.

Rob had to keep himself from ogling her and being too obvious. He walked around the back of the car, climbed inside and took his seat behind the wheel.

"So how did you find out about this place?" asked Meriam.

"Some of the other detectives in our precinct go there. They know all the good places in town. I've been getting tips from them for years."

"I guess an investigator would know best."

Rob put the Mercedes in gear and set out for Bay Village.

"How was your stakeout last Thursday?" Meriam asked, trying to start up some conversation.

"Not too exciting. These things often drag on for days without anything going on. But you never know. Sometimes all hell can break loose in the blink of an eye."

Meriam was impressed. She regarded him with awe and respect. The conversation continued and twenty minutes later they arrived at the restaurant.

Rob gave his name to the hostess and explained that he had reservations for the evening. She escorted them to a table and notified the waiter. A minute later the waiter appeared and asked them if they cared for a beverage before they ordered.

"Do you like Sauvignon Blanc or would you prefer something else?" asked Rob.

"Oh, I love Sauvignon Blanc. You seem to know me already, Detective," said Meriam, suggesting a slight vulnerability with her eyes.

"I'd like to get to know you even better."

Meriam continued smiling coyly. "Would you, now."

The two of them continued to flirt and a few minutes later the wine arrived, along with a basket of warm bread and butter. The waiter decanted the wine and waited for approval. Rob gave the nod and he filled both of their glasses.

"I'll return in a few minutes to take your order," said the waiter.

Rob raised his glass and saluted Meriam. "To a beautiful girl and a lovely evening."

"To a handsome hunk and good company," returned Meriam.

The waiter returned and asked if they had made up their minds.

"I'll have the Lasagna Bolognese," said Rob.

"Same for me," said Meriam.

"Could we also get the figs with bacon and chili sauce?"

"Of course, sir."

"You've gotta try these, Meriam. They're delicious."

"I'll try anything. I'm an adventurous girl." She looked at Rob with a slightly naughty look in her eyes. The wine was starting to do its job.

The evening continued and they continued their light banter.

Rob looked across the table and said, "Did you ever consider becoming a model?"

Meriam smiled. "Funny that you ask. I just went to New York a few weeks ago to see if I could get into that very thing. They took a couple of pictures of me in different swimsuits. I had a lot of fun."

"Wow. A swimsuit model."

"They said they wanted me to do some more photos for jeans and other stuff."

"What other stuff?"

"Well, various undergarments," Meriam smiled, pretending to blush.

Rob continued to listen intently.

"I might actually be in a TV commercial very soon."

"A movie star! Wow. I'm on a date with a movie star."

"Actually, that's my secret dream. I've always liked pretending I was someone else. I like trying to create different characters and personalities."

Rob thought about how she flirted with the patrons at Charlie's and figured she was a natural.

The appetizers arrived and Rob offered one to Meriam. She took a tiny bite and savored the taste for a moment. She licked her lips and said, "Mmmm. These are fantastic, Rob. You're right. I want the recipe."

She ate the rest of the appetizer, still looking at Rob, and licked her lips.

Rob took one and chomped it down in one bite. He lifted his glass again and said, "Here's to Hollywood."

Meriam took her glass, met his and said, "Here's to tough film noir detectives."

They continued to enjoy their wine and figs. Rob was thrilled at how well the evening was going. After a while the lasagna arrived and they enjoyed dinner with some excellent homemade bread and butter.

The wine was gone and Rob said, "How about one more for the road?"

Meriam said, "Sure. Why not?"

Rob ordered another glass of wine for each of them.

This time Meriam offered the toast and said, "To a very delightful evening."

"Absolutely."

They continued to flirt and learn about each other. After half hour Rob paid the check.

Meriam was starting to feel a little giddy.

They left the restaurant and Rob drove back to Meriam's house. Rob walked her to the front door. The tension between them was electric.

Meriam stood on the doorstep, looking into his eyes. She knew what was on his mind.

They both stood there for a few moments.

"Thank you for a wonderful evening," she said, smiling sweetly. She pressed her lips against his and slipped her tongue into his mouth.

For a moment Rob thought he was going to fall down. After what seemed like an eternity, their lips parted. They stood there for a few more moments with their arms around each other.

"Call me soon," she whispered in his ear.

"Count on it," he said.

Rob walked back to his car. He looked back toward Meriam, who was still standing on the porch. He blew her a kiss and got in his car. As Rob drove back home, Meriam didn't leave his mind for one second.

CHAPTER 20

Sunday, Oct 10, 7:30 AM

Don had driven from Rochester and arrived in Albany late Saturday evening. He had booked a room at another Best Western and awoke early Sunday. His meeting with Detective Connelly was set for 12:30 that afternoon. He decided to have a light breakfast of a corn muffin and coffee. He once again began to think about the pieces of the puzzle. Brian had turned out to be a dead end.

He was beginning to doubt if that case had anything to do with the Reardons. Still, there were no other leads. He thought about the fact that some cases were solved by investigating the flimsiest of leads. The unsolved murder of George Weston could not be ignored.

• • • • •

Brittany woke up before the rest of her family and walked to the window. Her legs were feeling better. She opened the curtain and looked outside. The early morning sky promised another day of beautiful weather. She looked at Mike and the girls and thought, *Let 'em sleep a little longer.* She took a shower and toweled off. When she walked back into the bedroom everyone was wide awake.

"So what's the plan for today, Mike?" she asked.

"Jamie and Roni want to hike up Algonquin Peak. It's the second highest mountain in the state. It's over 5,000 feet, but the trail starts at the Adirondack Lodge. We can drive there and that's over 2,000 feet up, so it's not that tough. It's a beautiful day and the view from the top is just as nice as Cascade. How are your legs feeling?"

"I'm still a little sore but I think I can handle it."

"It's probably about the same amount of time to the top as the other day," Mike assured her.

"I'll be fine. I just want to make sure the girls are okay."

"I'll bet I could do it twice in one day," bragged Roni.

Brittany smiled and said, "I don't doubt it."

It was good to see that she was so healthy and that her lungs were in such good shape. Apparently, she had no lingering effects from her bout with pneumonia as a young child. Brittany and Mike were both grateful for that. It was one of the reasons they encouraged the girls to love hiking in the woods.

They got themselves ready and had breakfast at the Golden Eagle in town. Once again, they stopped to pick up sandwiches at Subway and the compulsory bacon strips for Kardashian. By ten o'clock they were on their way into the woods. The trail was level for about a mile before it began to rise steeply up a rock outcropping. They took their time, stopping several times to take in the beauty of the streams, waterfalls and pools which were adorned with the neon lights of recently fallen leaves. It was one o'clock when they reached the summit. Once again Mike pointed out the different mountains.

"That's Iroquois Peak over there, said Mike, pointing southwest. "It only takes an hour to get there and back. It's the eighth highest of the forty-six. Anyone want to give it a shot?"

Roni and Jamie were immediately on board.

"Maybe I'll just wait for you guys here," said Brittany.

"Come on, Mom. Don't you want to be a Forty-sixer?" complained Roni, sounding disappointed.

"Yeah. Come on, Mom. Be a Forty-sixer," Jamie chimed in.

They both started to chant, "Forty-six, forty-six, forty-six."

Mike looked at Brittany sympathetically but the girls continued their chant.

He had to laugh when she finally agreed to come. "I'm sorry, honey. I'll make it up to you."

"Yes, you will," she said, giving him a playful jab in the arm.

They made the round trip and soon they were on the way back down the mountain. Once again, they stopped for ice cream on their way back to the cabin and had dinner at The View that evening.

Another beautiful day had come to an end.

Brittany didn't wake up until nine o'clock the following morning.

• • • • •

Don arrived at the diner fifteen minutes early and read a copy of the New York Post he had picked up at a 7-11. At 12:30 sharp a dark-haired man about six feet tall came through the front door. He began to look around the diner.

That's got to be him, thought Don. He motioned him to join him at the table.

"Detective Corlino, I presume. Dave Connelly," he said, extending his hand.

"Yes. Call me Don."

Dave took his seat and said, "The rib-eye is really good here, but nothing will disappoint."

"Sounds good to me," said Don, putting the menu aside. "So what can you tell me about your victim?"

"My partner and I interviewed almost a hundred people. Most of them were students from the state university. I don't want to paint a dark picture of someone I didn't know personally, but let's just say he got mixed reviews at best."

"What do you mean?"

"He had a few friends on campus. A couple of them spoke well of him, but for the most part he was not well liked."

"Continue."

"There were a few girls we talked to that absolutely hated his guts. One or two suggested that he sexually assaulted them. I'm pretty sure he raped one of them. She didn't want to talk about it, but I got the message."

"Did any of them file a complaint with the university?"

"Yeah. But you know how things are. They try to downplay and suppress that kind of thing. Some world, hey?"

"So what else can you tell me?"

"One of the girls we talked to said our boy roughed her up once. She dumped him after that and one of her other guy friends beat the shit out of him. We talked to him but he has an airtight alibi for the entire day. That was June 1. That's when the M.E. says it happened. He was seen on campus all day. He attended two classes for the mini-semester. Those are three-credit courses given in a couple of weeks. He was marked present for both of them. That would have put him on campus from nine o'clock A.M. until four o'clock P.M."

"So what else?"

"Apparently, he had a history of slapping girls around. A real scum-bag. Let's just say there were a lot of people who didn't rue his demise."

"Did he have a girlfriend when he was murdered?"

"We asked that. Nobody really knew anything for sure. One of his friends said that he mentioned a new girlfriend. We followed up on that but we could never track her down. If he did have a girl, she probably wasn't a student there."

The waitress came and took their orders.

Don wondered if sticking around and asking questions was going to bear any fruit. Detective Connelly had been thorough in his investigation. It seemed likely that George Weston's death came about due to his own bad behavior. In any case the trail was now cold and it was unlikely he could find out anything new. Boston was calling him home.

"I guess I've learned what I came to find out," said Don. "I'm heading back to Boston this afternoon."

"Sorry I couldn't help you more, Detective."

"If you find out anything you think might be important call me. Here's my card."

The two detectives finished their lunch and wished each other good luck.

By two o'clock Don was back on I-90 heading for Boston. He took in all the information he had learned and the wheels began to turn again. He thought about Michelle Dennis. From the description he had gotten from Maxine and the two hookers it was unlikely that she was involved in any of this. Still, she was missing and that was nagging at him. What could have happened to her? Maxine said Michelle hadn't given her any indication she was just going to take off. She had turned out not to be Jane Doe. How did she wind up in Boston? Who was she with?

Don decided to call Eddie. He punched the name into his phone.

"Hi Don. Anything new?"

"Not really. I just wanted to know if you made any progress locating Michelle Dennis."

"Not yet. We really don't have enough to get a warrant for her credit card info. If she were officially listed as a missing person, we could get a judge to sign off on one. I'm sure you could pull some strings."

"She's been known to take off before, Eddie. Her friend reported her as missing a year ago. She turned up a few months later."

"That doesn't make it easy, but see what you can do."

"We don't have too many other things to go on right now. How's that tie-in to terrorist activity going?"

"We're still staking out those guys on Beacon Street, but nothing yet."

"All right. I'll talk to missing persons tomorrow. That's about all I can think of. Oh, wait. Did you check with Boston College and the other major universities about possible missing students?"

"Yes. We check with them every day for an update. Nothing so far."

"Well, I guess that's about it then."

"Talk to you tomorrow, Don."

"Okay, Eddie. Later." *One more call to make,* thought Don. He punched Cheryl's number and waited.

"Hi, honey. Where are you?"

"I'm on my way back to Boston. I'm just outside Albany on I-90. I'm gonna stop by my place first and put on some fresh clothes. You okay with tonight? We can go out for some dinner and drinks."

"Of course. It's been a week since I last saw you. I can't wait. Don't speed but get here as soon as you can."

"I'll be there around seven o'clock."

"Okay, honey. See you then."

As soon as Don hung up the phone he was back on the job. He began to think about the pieces of the puzzle from the start. For the next two hours his mind went over all that he had learned from detectives, medical examiners and witnesses. He thought about the possible tie-in to terrorism. He thought about the college students who were all murdered with the same type of weapon. He thought about every detail over and over. How these things might fit together was unclear. He still felt in his gut that there was a chance these murders were connected to the Reardon case. Even if it turned out not to be, there was still plenty of evidence that they were related to Jane Doe back in the morgue in Boston. He began to believe with some certainty that Jane Doe was a college student. Probably a graduate student. Erica estimated her age to be somewhere in her late twenties. From the way she was dressed she was going to be missed by someone sooner or later. It had been about two weeks since the estimated time of death. Why had no one reported her missing?

It was just after five o'clock when Don pulled up to his apartment. He took his small travel case from his car, brought it inside and went through his shirt pockets. He found the small piece of paper that had been soaked by the rain in Buffalo. He tried to remember what it was. He placed it on the dresser and dumped his clothes into the hamper. He took a quick shower put on a fresh pair of pants and a clean shirt. Half an hour later he was knocking on Cheryl's door.

Cheryl opened the door, threw her arms around Don and planted a big kiss on his lips.

"Well, you really did miss me."

"I always miss you when you're away. I worry about you. You know that."

"There's really nothing to worry about. You watch too much TV." Don always downplayed the danger of his job.

Cheryl secretly knew that wasn't true, but tried to convince herself that everything would always be OK.

Don gave her a reassuring hug and returned the kiss. "So, what are you in the mood for?"

"I could go for a nice, juicy steak and a bottle of red."

Don quickly agreed even though he had steak for lunch that afternoon. "How about Anthony's Steak House?"

"You know what a girl likes. Lead the way."

They drove to Anthony's and were immediately seated by the hostess, who remembered them. The waiter took their order and they began to talk. As usual Cheryl began to hint about making a commitment. She joked about time flying by and that another birthday was just around the corner.

Don knew where she was going and tried to change the subject. "Have you thought about what you want to be for Halloween? We are invited to your friend Suzie's party again this year, right?"

"Yes, of course." Cheryl sighed and decided she would be better off letting it go and just enjoy the evening.

They continued to talk about mundane things and soon their food arrived. Don and Cheryl enjoyed a very delicious dinner and shared the wine. When they finished dinner, they ordered a second bottle of wine to go.

Later that evening they sat on the couch together and watched High Sierra with Humphrey Bogart on the television. Cheryl loved old movies. Bogie was her favorite. By the end of the movie, they were both a little buzzed.

The two of them found their way to the upstairs to the bedroom. Cheryl lay on the bed and looked seductively at Don. Don took off his shirt and flexed a mock he-man pose.

Cheryl laughed and said, "Come here, Adonis," motioning with her hand.

Don straddled her body and began to undo the buttons on her shirt. Cheryl began to purr softly as he worked his way down to her belt. He undid the buckle and slowly pulled the zipper down. She lifted her hips slightly and made it easier for him as he pulled her pants below her knees.

Cheryl undid his buckle and returned the favor.

Don moved his hand slowly up her outer thigh, then gently brought his fingertips across her stomach and continued to her arching chest. She drew a deep breath as her heart began to beat faster with no will of its own. Soon they were both naked and wrestling each other into a fevered passion.

Half an hour later they lay beside each other, breathless, their skin moist and their bodies aching with pleasure. Don whispered softly in Cheryl's ear and soon they were asleep in each other's arms.

CHAPTER 21

Monday, Oct. 11, 7 AM

Don called Jack Sullivan early that morning to plead his case for following up on the student murders. "Good morning, Jack. Sorry to wake you so early."

"Good morning, Don. That's okay. What's on your mind?"

"I was just wondering if Tommy was still in Chicago."

"Yes, he is. He's supposed to fly back this afternoon. Why? What do you have in mind?"

"What I'd like is for Tommy to fly to Youngstown. There was a student who was murdered there last April with the same M.O. as the other students I'm investigating."

"Yes. I was filled in on it."

"I wasn't far from there when I was in Buffalo. At the time I was a lot less sure about my theory. I wanted to follow up on James Carter and the terrorism angle, so I didn't bother going there. Since then, I've become more convinced that all these murders are connected. The more I think about it, they're connected to Jane Doe as well. Tommy can rent a car and interview the lead detective. I don't know his name. You'll have to call Greg Phillips and have him get in touch with Tommy. Tell him to get as much information as possible from the victim's friends about who he was hanging out with."

"I can do that. I'll call Tommy now and tell him to book a flight to Youngstown."

"Good. I'll check with you later today and see where we stand."

"Sounds good, Don. Later."

Don got himself ready for work and headed over to FBI headquarters. Captain Wyatt's office and the Joint Terrorism Task Force were located in the same building. The JTTF was a coalition of members of the Boston Police Department as well as FBI agents. Although Don had worked with members of the JTTF before he had never met Captain Wyatt. At eight o'clock he decided it wasn't too early to call.

"Captain Wyatt, JTTF. How can I help you?"

"Hello, Captain. This is Detective Don Corlino. We spoke a few days ago about James Carter."

"Yes, Don. I remember. Detectives Morrow and McGowan have been in touch with me. We met last Thursday here in my office. They're staking out a house here in Boston."

"That's right. They seem to think there are some illegal activities going on, but they don't know exactly what yet."

"So where do you want to start?"

"I'm over in the building next to yours. If you have time I'd like to come by now."

"Sure. I'll be right here."

Don walked over to the JTTF and found Captain Wyatt's office and knocked on the door.

Captain Wyatt greeted him and offered him a seat.

"How can I help you, Detective Corlino?"

"I'd like a list of all the people James knew here in Boston, professionally as well as casually."

"I don't know much about his personal life but you can ask at Boston University. He lectured there several times."

"Yes. His T.A. at Hofstra mentioned that. What I'd like to find out is if he had much contact with local members of the police department who might have been working with the JTTF. For instance, anyone who attended the lecture he gave here about explosives. That might lead to something."

"I can ask Detective Wilson. He was in charge of coordinating the lectures we were giving at that time. I'm sure he still has a list of all the attendees. You might want to check with the Head of the Chemistry Department at B.U. I'm sure he knew James. Is there anything else I can help you with?"

"Well, I just wanted to meet you in person. I'd like to know a little about any active cases you're currently investigating. Now that there's a possible terrorist link to my case, I'd like you to give me a heads-up on anything to do with bank fraud or extortion. After all, Reardon is a high-profile banker."

"Got ya. I'll keep you informed if I learn of anything suspicious."

"Thanks. I've worked with some of your guys before. It's good to finally meet you. Talk later."

They shook hands and Don walked out toward his car.

• • • • •

Rob walked into the police station just after nine o'clock and walked over to his desk. Eddie was already there, as usual.

"Good morning, Rob. How was your big date with Meriam?"

Rob looked as if he was on some very good medication. He had a big lysergic smile on his face the way infatuated lovers often do.

Oh God, thought Eddie. *What am in for today?*

"You think Meriam is an attractive girl when she's just working at Charlie's, right?"

"Sure," agreed Eddie without a moment of thought.

"Well, you should have seen her out of that uniform."

Eddie raised an eyebrow and gave Rob a questioning look.

Rob immediately realized his meaning could be misinterpreted. "I mean you should see her all dressed up. Wow! She is smokin'."

"I can imagine," Eddie said sheepishly.

"I can't wait to see her again. I think she really likes me."

"That's really nice, Rob. I'm happy for you."

"Thanks, Eddie. So what's the plan for today?"

"Well, we have a choice. We can stake out Beacon Street again or track down more of these plate numbers. What do you think?"

"Why don't we call Don and see where he is now?"

"Good idea."

Eddie punched in Don's number.

"Corlino."

"Hi Don. Eddie here. Just thought I'd check with you to see where we stand."

"Nothing solid right now. I tried to find out what I could about Michelle Dennis. So far that's just a dead end. I'm going to turn my attention to James Carter and work on the terrorist angle. It seems a logical way to go. When I found out he lectured here in Boston about homemade explosives it got my attention. If you couple that with the way his wife was murdered, we can't ignore it. I just talked to Captain Wyatt and got some leads. What are you guys focusing on?"

"We're staking out a house here on Beacon Street. We have some reason to watch Nasir. He's a known felon and his car was in Milford late at night September 24. Everything else is leading nowhere. What about the other murders you were investigating? By the way, congrats on solving the Nelson murder. Jack Sullivan called and told us."

"Thanks, Eddie. I'm not giving up on the angle that these college student murders are connected. They may not have anything to do with the Reardons, but it's something we have to consider. My partner Tommy Brown is still out in Chicago. I asked my boss to have him check out the Youngstown murder back in April. Any word yet about missing students?"

"Nothing so far. We keep checking with all the colleges. What about Michelle Dennis? We got the word she's not our Jane Doe."

"That's right. Unfortunately, we don't have enough to get a warrant for her credit card records. I spoke with a girl named Maxine up in Rochester, but she doesn't know anything. Apparently, Michelle was very secretive about her past. I think she might have had something to hide. Maxine told me she was on the shy side. That's a little strange for a girl in her profession."

"Well, it looks like we're still pretty much in the dark."

"I can't help thinking I'm close to something. It's right there swimming around in the back of my mind."

"I know the feeling, Don. Good hunting."

"I'll let you know as soon as anything new pops up. Later, Eddie."

Rob looked over at Eddie and said, "Anything?"

"Nothing to jump up and down about. Don's talked with Captain Wyatt from the terrorist task force. He's also having his partner follow up on the Youngstown murder."

Rob thought about his options about chasing down new plate numbers or staking out Beacon Street. Neither seemed an attractive way to spend the day.

"Why don't we try to find out more about Michelle Dennis? I know we don't have enough to get a warrant for her credit card info, but maybe we can do an end run," suggested Rob. "Don said Greg Phillips in missing persons would help us out. He can get access to addresses, phone numbers, license plates almost anything. The FBI has all kinds of information that could help us.

"Sounds reasonable. We're running out of promising leads," agreed Eddie.

"Let me Google her name first. Maybe we can find out a little more about Michelle."

"Check out Facebook as well."

Rob entered Michelle Dennis, Rochester into a Facebook search. Sure enough, a plethora of information appeared, including where she was born and where she went to high school.

"Says here she was born in Buffalo. She went to Riverside High School. She belonged to a group called *Save the Lakes*. I guess that's an environmental organization. It also lists a couple of her friends. Let me google some of them. Maybe we'll get lucky. I'll try Allison Simonetti, Buffalo...Bingo. I got an Alice Simonetti. Let me check her *About* info." Rob hit the necessary points on the touch screen and the information appeared. "It says here she also went to Riverside. She still lives in Buffalo."

Rob jotted down the name.

"I just don't understand why people put all this personal information out there for everyone to see," said Eddie.

"I know. It's like walking around naked in a grocery store."

Eddie let out a chuckle.

"Let's try Adrian Raimo, Buffalo."

Again, they got a name. Rob looked at her info and said, "We've got a gold mine here. She also went to Riverside and still lives in Buffalo."

Rob wrote down the name.

"I've got a Maxine Glover."

"That's probably her friend in Rochester. Don said he spoke to her. I'm sure she would have told Don if she knew anything."

"Apparently Michelle didn't have too many friends on Facebook," said Rob. "I've got a girl named Gloria Rivera. That's about it."

"Let's call Greg and see if we can get addresses and phone numbers for her Buffalo friends. Maybe they can help us track her down."

Eddie called the Missing Persons Bureau of the FBI.

"Missing Persons. Greg Phillips. How can I help you?"

"Hi Greg. This is Detective McGowan of the Boston Police Department. We're working with Detective Corlino on a Jane Doe case. I know he's been in touch with you about it. He told us you might be able to help us out."

"Don Corleone. Of course. What can I do for you?"

Eddie chuckled.

"We would like to get the phone numbers of two girls in Buffalo who might be able to give us some information on a missing girl. Her name is Michelle Dennis."

"Yes, Don mentioned her name, but she hasn't been officially declared missing yet. Don told me she's taken off before and the Rochester police are reluctant to follow up on it."

"That's right. That's why we could use your help. Their names are Allison Simonetti and Adrian Raimo. Both of them are twenty-six years old, and both went to Riverside High School in Buffalo."

"Should be a piece of cake. If they haven't moved in the past few months or changed their phone numbers, I should be able to get them in less than an hour."

"That would be great. Thanks a million, Greg."

"Why don't we stay here in the office for a while? We've got a list of possibilities from the tapes. We can make some more phone calls while we're waiting for Greg's call," suggested Eddie.

"Good with me."

The two of them started making calls. Half an hour later Greg returned their call. "I've got those numbers and addresses for you, Eddie."

"That was quick."

"Anything for Don Corleone. Adrian Raimo, 44 Albert Street, Buffalo, N.Y. 14207, (716) 824-5611. And I've got Allison Simonetti, 10 Crowley Avenue. Buffalo 14207, (716) 965- 8844. Anything else I can do for you?"

"No. Not right now. This will help a lot. We just want to tie up this loose end if we can. Thanks a lot, Greg."

"Not a problem. Anything I can do to help."

"I'll call you if I think of anything else. Thanks again."

"Should we tell them we're with the Boston P.D.?"

"They may not be cooperative if we do. You know how friends try to protect each other. Why don't we try a different approach? Just tell them you're her friend first and see how far you get."

"Let's try Allison Simonetti first." Rob called the number.

"Hello."

"Hello Allison. My name is Rob. I'm a friend of Michelle Dennis and I'm trying to get in touch with her. She's not answering her phone. I was wondering if you know where she is?"

"Mickey? I haven't heard from her in a couple of months. She's not answering my texts. She hasn't posted anything on Facebook either. I hope she's okay. How did you get my name?"

"She mentioned that you were high school friends together with a girl named Adrian."

"Yeah, Adrian Raimo. We were all friends. I still know Adrian but neither of us has seen Michelle in a couple of years. Not since she moved to Rochester. She said she was working in a supermarket there or something. She was supposed to go to Florida with some guy last year, but I don't think she ever did."

Rob felt a stab of sorrow and empathy for Michelle. The world was a cold, confusing place for some people.

"How did you get my number? It's not listed," said Allison, becoming a little suspicious.

Rob thought for a moment and said, "Actually I'm her boss at the supermarket. She wrote down your name as an emergency contact."

"Me? Not Adrian?"

"Yeah. She listed Adrian also. I just called her, but she didn't answer."

"Oh. Okay."

Allison was starting to buy it.

"Do you know if her parents still live in Buffalo?"

"Her parents got divorced a long time ago. Mr. Dennis moved away like twenty years ago. She lived with her mother here in Buffalo. I'm pretty sure she still lives here."

"Do you have an address or phone number?"

"She lives over on Ross Avenue. I forgot which number. I don't know what her phone number is. Mrs. Dennis changed her name back to her maiden name after the divorce. I think it's Mrs. Jefferson or something like that."

Rob wrote it down. "Last time I talked to her she said something about Boston. Do you know anyone she might have known there?"

"No, I'm sorry. I don't."

"Okay. Thanks Allison. I'll have her call you if she comes back."

"You're welcome, goodbye."

Rob called Adrian.

"Hello."

"Hi Adrian. I'm a friend of Michelle Dennis in Rochester. She works for me and she hasn't showed up for a few days. She has you as her emergency contact person. I was wondering if you've heard from her."

"Mickey? No, I haven't. I got a text from her a few months ago. That's about it."

"She mentioned something about going to Boston for the weekend. Do you know if she knew anyone there?"

'No. She never mentioned anyone from Boston."

"She listed her mother as a contact as well, but I can't read it. I think it says Mrs. Jefferson or something."

"That's Jeffries. She lives over on Ross Avenue. She's still there."

"Okay, thanks, Adrian. Have a nice day."

"You, too."

"You know I have an idea," said Rob, standing up and putting his palms on his desk.

"What's that?" said Eddie.

"Why don't we have Sarah call Michelle Dennis's credit card company and inquire about possible fraudulent charges? We don't have to be too specific. If we can get an idea of where she uses the card, we might be able to track her down."

"Sounds a bit unethical. We can't call from here, of course."

"I know an old pay phone in the railroad station. It's one of the few still around. Let's see if we can bribe Sarah. This time she'll have to accept our offer about drinks and dinner."

The two of them marched over to Sarah's office and put on their best smiles.

Sarah looked up and did a double-take. "Okay guys. I give up. What's your angle this time?"

"No angle, sweetheart. We just came over to tell you how much we appreciate your dedication and appreciation for how hard our job is," said Rob with feigned sincerity.

"Really. It's true," concurred Eddie.

"Okay then. How can I help you?"

"We need someone with a sweet, convincing, angelic voice to make a little phone call for us," said Rob.

Sarah looked at them with a wry smile and said, "Okay, who am I calling?"

"Just Visa. You want to check on your charges. Your name is Michelle Dennis and you suspect your boyfriend has been using your card for the last few days. You just want the charges listed for the last two weeks. Tell them you rented a car from Enterprise back on September 20 and you want to verify all the activity after that."

"Aren't they going to ask me some questions about my mother's maiden name or something?"

"Just try to sound convincing. The last four digits on the card are 1525," persisted Rob.

"Okay, give me the number."

"Oh, we're just gonna make a short trip to the railroad station and use the pay phone."

"Come on, guys. What are you getting me involved with?"

"Don't worry. They'll never know it was you. Just think—you would be an instrument of law and order and a crusader for justice," pleaded Rob. "Besides, then you could feel justified in accepting our hospitality and joining us for dinner."

Eddie just stood there watching Rob in action.

"Okay, okay. Let me get my coat."

The three of them went down to the station and Rob coached her again about what to say. He gave her a slip of paper with Michelle's name, age, address and mother's maiden name on it.

Eddie put a couple of quarters in the slot and dialed the number for Visa Customer Service.

The representative answered the phone. "Hello, Visa Customer Service."

"Hello, my name is Michelle Dennis. I'd like to check on some of the charges made on my card."

"Can you give me your card number?"

"No. I don't have the card with me. My boyfriend has it. That's what I want to ask about. I think he might be buying himself a few presents, if you know what I'm talking about? I remember the last four digits are 1525."

"I'm going to have to ask you some questions first, ma'am. What's your current address?"

"It's 54 Verona Street, Rochester, New York, zip code 14608," said Sarah confidently.

"What's your mother's maiden name?"

"Jeffries."

"All right. How can I help you?"

"I just want to know about any expensive purchases in the last couple of weeks. I'm a little worried."

"You can report your card stolen and I can put a hold on the card or cancel it if you want."

"No. I don't want to go through all that hassle. Can you just tell me if there are any large items?"

"Maybe, you can tell me where you used the card. Then I can give you an idea."

"I rented a car from Enterprise back on September 20."

"Yes. I see that. There's also the purchase from an Apple store for $1,456.58."

"Oh, that's right. That was me, too," said Sarah immediately. She went on a fishing expedition. "I used the card at a 7-11 in Milton a couple of times. Do you see those?"

"I see some 7-11 charges, but they're not in Milton. I have several charges to a 7-11 on Chestnut Hill Avenue in Boston."

"That's right. I was staying near there for a few days. So there's nothing else over twenty-five dollars in the past few weeks?"

"Just a gas station in Boston for $145.50. That's a Shell station also on Chestnut Hill Avenue."

"Yes, that's right. I made that buy. What day was that again?

"September 22. There's nothing else in the past few weeks."

"Okay. That's a relief. Thank you so much."

"By the way, ma'am—just a reminder. You didn't make your minimum payment for August or September. You should take care of that or we're going to have to freeze your card."

"Oh. Okay, thank you. I'll take care of it."

Sarah hung up the phone and relayed the info to Rob and Eddie.

"Fantastic, Sarah. You did great," Rob commended her. "You definitely have to join us at Zan's really soon."

"Absolutely," agreed Eddie.

"Okay. You win. Let me know when."

They walked back to the police station and Rob thanked Sarah one more time.

"So what do you think, Eddie? Do we stake out Beacon Street or should we scope out the 7-11 on Chestnut Hill Avenue?"

"We have a picture of Michelle. Why don't we ask the guys who work there if they have seen her lately? If nothing pans out, we go back to Beacon Street. We'll get those two rookies to keep looking up plate numbers and crossing them."

Rob smiled, thinking about the expression he had seen on their faces a few days ago.

Eddie walked over to Dugan's office and filled him in on the situation.

"Okay. How's Corlino doing on his end?" he asked.

"He still thinks there's a good chance those five murdered students are related. He just doesn't know how yet. We're still working the angle that they could be related to our Jane Doe. We're not sure if it's related to the Reardon disappearance."

"All right, you and Rob keep working on the Jane Doe side of it. Maybe we'll get lucky."

"I'll keep you up to date as soon as we find out anything."

• • • • •

Meanwhile Jamie and Roni had gotten up early and were outside the cabin playing with Kardashian. Mike got up half an hour later. He let Brittany sleep for another half hour and then softly whispered in her ear.

"Good morning, honey."

Brittany just moaned and said, "Give me a few more minutes."

"Okay, sweetheart. It's another beautiful day. We can drive the car up to the top of Whiteface and then head home. We'll take it nice and easy. I promise I'll make it up to you for making you go all the way to Iroquois Peak."

"You better buy me that house on Mirror Lake," groaned Brittany with a note of justification.

Mike just laughed and said, "I'll look into it right away."

He let her sleep a little while longer and then he began to pack up their stuff. Brittany got up and made sure the girls were ready for the day.

"Why don't we skip breakfast and just drive up to Whiteface? They have a nice place on top of the mountain. We can have an early lunch there and beat the traffic home," said Mike.

"Good thinking. I hate sitting in traffic," agreed Brittany.

They drove up to the top of the mountain and Mike once again gave his complimentary geography lesson.

"That's Mirror Lake down there on the left."

"Wow," said Jamie.

"That's Algonquin Peak way over there. That's where we were on Sunday," said Mike, pointing southwest.

"Oh, neat," exclaimed Roni impressed with their accomplishment. "Can we do it again this afternoon?"

"Oh God! No!" cried Brittany.

Mike just laughed and said, "You girls did great. In four days, you knocked off four mountains. Five if you count this one. That's pretty good for anybody. Only forty-one more to go. Of course, we should climb this one for real one day."

"When can we do some more, Daddy?"

Mike looked at Brittany with a question in his eyes.

"Maybe Thanksgiving if it's nice weather," said Brittany, eager to be on board.

"Cool," said Roni.

"But, if it's snowing, I want to go skiing," she quickly added.

"Yeah. Me too," agreed Roni.

• • • • •

After Don had left Captain Wyatt's office he returned to his car and punched Boston University into the GPS and arrived at the campus twenty minutes later. Don walked up to a Chinese girl and asked for directions to the Chemistry Department. She walked with him part of the way and then pointed to a large building in the distance. Don thanked her and then made his way there. He read the directory and found the office for the Department Head. He read the name on the door: ARTHUR MADDOX, Ph.D.

Don knocked on the door and a distinguished-looking man answered.

"Yes. Can I help you?"

Don showed his FBI credentials and said, "Pleasure to meet you, Doctor Maddox. My name is Don Corlino. I'm with the FBI. I'm sorry I didn't call first, but I had to come here anyway. I'd like to ask you a few questions."

Dr. Maddox looked a bit surprised and intrigued that the FBI had come knocking on his door. "Yes. Yes. Come in please, detective. How can I help you?"

"I'm currently investigating the disappearance of a banker and his wife here in the Boston area. You might have read about it. Their name is Reardon."

"Yes. I've read about it. Very strange."

"I'm also investigating the disappearance of someone you might know, who may or may not be connected to this case."

Dr. Maddox was now very attentive and hanging on every word.

"Do you remember a professor from Hofstra University on Long Island named James Carter?"

"Yes, I do. He lectured here at the university a few months ago. What's happened?"

"We don't know exactly. Did you ever meet his wife, Paula Carter?"

"No. I do remember him mentioning that he was married."

"She was found murdered in a nature preserve not too far from the university."

Dr. Maddox gasped and said, "My God."

"What I'd like to know is if he had any personal friends from the university or if he worked closely with one of your other chemistry professors."

"Yes. Professor Kallart was interested in his work. As I remember he was an expert on homemade explosives."

"That's right, Doctor."

"Both Professor Kallart and I had some apprehensions about the website he put up. He was making it public about what readily available products could be used to make a bomb."

"Many of his colleagues at Hofstra had similar concerns," agreed Don.

"He reassured us that without special knowledge and equipment, there were no real concerns. The idea was just to raise a red flag and give a heads-up to police and FBI."

"I can see the point," said Don. "There was very little regulation over ammonium nitrate until Terry Nichols blew up the Federal Building in Oklahoma City. Now it's monitored very closely. It's almost impossible to get dynamite these days. It's not so easy to make a bomb anymore."

"That is somewhat of a relief. Still, I hear about all these IEDs over in Syria and Afghanistan."

"They have a pretty sophisticated underground network over there. It's not as easy as it sounds. The Tsarnaev brothers had help with the explosives when they planted the Marathon bomb."

"I guess you're right, Detective. It's a scary world these days."

"Can you tell me where I can find Professor Kallart?"

"He should be here now. He has a class from…" Maddox looked at his watch, "…nine until eleven. He should be getting out in fifteen minutes.

Room 245. If you want, I'll have someone go there and tell him to come to my office."

"That would be great."

Maddox called his assistant over and asked her to relay the message.

"So how do you think Professor Carter's disappearance is tied in with Mr. Reardon?"

"There was an attempt to conceal Paula Carter's body. Her throat was cut. Whoever did it didn't want her to be found. We have a Jane Doe in the morgue who was murdered under similar circumstances. I know that's not much to go on, but the fact is that there was no ransom note for the Reardons, and there are no dead bodies. At this point I don't know what to think, but I suspect the worst."

"Like I said, it's a scary world, Detective."

"Agreed," said Don with a solemn look in his eyes.

Professor Kallart appeared a few minutes later. "Yes, Arthur. What is it?"

"George, this is Detective Corlino with the FBI. Detective, this is George Kallart."

The two men shook hands.

"George, I'm afraid I have some disturbing news to tell you," continued Dr. Maddox.

"Oh? What's going on?"

"You remember James Carter from Hofstra, right?"

"Yes. What's happened?"

"James has gone missing. What's more is that his wife Paula has been murdered," Maddox explained.

"Oh my God. That's awful!"

"Detective Corlino would like to ask you some questions if that's all right."

"Of course, Detective. What do you need to know?"

"First of all, do you know if James knew anybody in Boston personally?"

"Not that he mentioned. I can't say with certainty, but he was here and gone pretty quickly. He got here from Long Island and gave a lecture that same day. He spent some time with me that afternoon and caught a plane back to Long Island that evening. I don't think he had time to visit anyone else. He did mention that he gave another lecture to the JTTF a few weeks before."

"Yes, I met with them this morning. What can you tell me about the special procedures that were necessary to make the explosives?"

Kallart looked at Dr. Maddox for a moment and then said, "The final product he was talking about is very similar to nitroglycerin. Most of the actual reagents can easily be found in drug stores and hardware stores. All you need is any one of a variety of skin lotions you can get almost anywhere. You also need nitric acid. You could also use sodium nitrate, potassium nitrate or ammonium nitrate, but of course those things are regulated. Nitric acid is not. Understand, with this compound you wouldn't need that much of it. The problem is that it's highly unstable during its synthesis. Even afterwards it's extremely dangerous to handle. It has to be kept at very low temperatures while it's being made. I'm talking like minus forty degrees Celsius."

"Forgive me, Professor. What temperature is that in Fahrenheit? I only got a C in chem."

Maddox and Kallart chuckled.

"Funny, but minus forty Celsius is exactly the same as minus forty Fahrenheit. It's where the two lines intersect on the graph."

"I see. So in other words, very cold," said Don.

"That's right. What's more is that the temperature has to be very carefully monitored during the entire process. If the temperature goes above minus thirty, BOOM, the whole building will be leveled. If it goes below minus fifty, BOOM, the whole building will be leveled. Bit of a paradox."

"I get the idea," said Don.

"The final product is a liquid. As I said, it's like nitroglycerin. It has to be stabilized by pouring it into sawdust while it's still at minus forty. Dynamite is made the same way but nitro is a lot more stable. This stuff is like nitro on steroids. You need a special additive to make it stable. It's really more like C4 plastic explosives."

"Sounds like pretty dangerous stuff," agreed Don.

"Even I was shocked when I saw the demonstration. All you would need is a few pounds to level this building. That's why James was so concerned. If it fell into the wrong hands, they could do a lot of damage."

"Is there anything else I should know?"

"Yes. C4 needs a primer to set it off. All this stuff needs is a good jolt. If you dropped it from a roof top, BOOM. You could also put a bullet in it. Same result."

Don stood up and said, "Well, I guess that's about all I need. If you can think of anything else, please give me a call at this number." Don handed each of them a card.

"Of course, Detective. We'll do whatever we can."

Don said goodbye and headed back for his car. On the way he called Greg Phillips at Missing Persons.

"Yes, Godfather. How may I serve you today?"

"Hi Greg. Have you talked with Tommy yet?"

"Yes, Don Vito. I gave him all the info he needs. The name of the victim is Randolph Fletcher. Went by the name of Randy. He's described here as White Caucasian, 23 years old. The lead detective is Neil Jefferson. The date of the murder is believed to be April 14."

Don stopped him. "What do you mean *believed to be?*"

"He was found in his dorm room during the Easter break. The M.E. couldn't pin it down exactly."

Plenty of time for the perp to put some distance between himself and the crime scene, thought Don.

The instant he had that thought, something buzzed like static in his brain, but only for a brief second. Something was bugging him. He just couldn't put his finger on it.

"Anything else I can do for you for you, Godfather?"

"Not right now. Thanks Greg. I promise Cheryl and I will have you over for dinner sometime soon."

"Dinner with the family. I am honored. Will Sonny and Michael be there?"

Don just groaned and pushed the end call button.

CHAPTER 22

Monday, Oct. 11, 12:30 PM

Rob made several copies of Michelle's license picture and the two detectives got into the Tahoe and headed out for the Chestnut Hill 7-11.

In twenty minutes, they were there. Eddie identified himself to the clerk as a police officer. He took out the picture from Michelle's license and said, "Have you seen this girl in the last couple of weeks?"

The clerk looked carefully at the picture and said, "No, officer. It does not look familiar."

"Are there any other people here at the moment who we could ask?"

"Nadeem," he yelled to the back of the store.

A young man appeared from the stock room and Eddie showed him the picture.

"Have you seen this girl?"

"No, sir I do not recognize her."

Rob and Eddie looked at each other with some disappointment.

"When do your shifts change here?" asked Eddie.

"We have three shifts. We work from eight in the morning until four in the afternoon. Then my cousins Ajish and Jalaj come in and work until midnight. Kaushal works until I show up again."

"Can you show them this picture? If they recognize her, please have them call me at this number."

"Of course. What has she done?"

"Nothing that we know of. We'd just like to ask her some questions. She's very hard to get hold of. By the way, can you give me your name?"

"My name is Suresh."

"Suresh, I assume you have surveillance tapes for the past few weeks," said Eddie.

"Yes, we do. We keep them for ninety days just in case we need them."

"Could you please let us have those tapes? We need everything you have going back to the beginning of July."

"Of course, they are in the office. Nadeem, watch the register."

A few minutes later Suresh returned with a box of tapes.

"Thank you very much. We'll get these back to you as soon as we can."

Rob picked up a copy of the Globe and another paper. They both poured themselves a large cup of coffee and Rob put a ten on the counter. "My treat this time, Eddie."

Eddie and Rob thanked the clerk once more and walked back to their car.

"Let's check out that Shell station. I'm not looking forward to sitting in the car again all day," suggested Rob.

"Might as well. It's still early," Eddie agreed.

They located the Shell station just down the street and pulled up to the Quickie Mart.

"The 7-11 and this gas station are really close to each other. It's almost certain that Michelle spent some time in this neighborhood. She probably lived close by," suggested Eddie.

"I agree. I think we should ask around at other shops in the area. You never know."

"This is also very close to Boston College and not far from Beacon Street. Do you think that's just a coincidence or are we on to something?" Eddie added.

"Maybe she was staying with someone she knew at the college."

"There are almost 15,000 students there. It would be real long shot to find someone who knew her. She didn't go to school there. We know that."

Rob walked up to the clerk at the register and handed him the picture of Michelle's license.

"We're with Boston PD. Have you seen this girl in the last couple of weeks?"

The attendant looked carefully at the picture and said, "Sorry. Can't say that I have."

"Anybody else work here?"

"There's a mechanic who works here, but he won't be in until twelve o'clock today. He usually works from eight until five, but he took this morning off."

"How long do you keep your surveillance tapes?" asked Eddie.

"Thirty days, Detective, but we don't keep them here. They're in the central office. I'll have to put in a request."

Rob let out a big sigh and looked at Eddie. "Beacon Street?"

"I guess so."

"Thanks for your time. We might be back later," said Rob.

"Always willing to help you guys. Best of luck."

The two detectives paid a visit to a few more local stores and then reluctantly made their way over to Beacon Street. They made a point of cruising past the Sheik's house on the way.

• • • • •

Don spent the next few hours at his office going over the list Captain Wyatt had given him. He tried to establish as many connections between them as he could. He took special note of anyone who had ties to the local universities.

• • • • •

It was now almost four o'clock and there hadn't been too much action at Beacon Street.

"What do you say we knock off at five and call it a day?" said Rob.

"Good with me."

"Zan's?"

"Good with me."

• • • • •

Mike, Brittany and the girls ate lunch and drove back down the mountain. Soon they were headed back down 87 south toward Albany. Brittany tried go get some more sleep, but finally gave up on the idea.

Mike thought of a way to pass the time.

"Girls, who did the penguins invite over for Thanksgiving?" asked Mike.

Jamie and Roni thought about it for a minute. "We give up. Who, Daddy?"

"Antarctica."

"Oh, Daddy. That's so silly," said Jamie.

Roni just smiled and said, "Tell another one.

"Why do eggs hate riddles?"

Again, the girls thought about it.

"The answer cracks them up."

That got a groan from Brittany.

"Did you hear about the kidnapping at school?"

They all waited eagerly for the answer.

"They woke him up."

That got a groan from all three of them.

Mike cracked dad jokes all the way back, getting an occasional groan from Brittany.

Roni couldn't get the smile off her face. Soon they were back home.

They all agreed the past few days were the most fun they had had in a while.

• • • • •

Don decided to check with Eddie and Rob on their progress and called Eddie's number.

Eddie picked up. "Hi Don."

"Anything new, Eddie?"

"We got some info on Michelle."

"Yeah, Greg told me you guys had him look up a couple of names and addresses."

"We were able to get her mother's maiden name. We called Visa and got some of her credit card purchases. It seems she spends a lot of time around Chestnut Hill Avenue. That's a couple of blocks from Boston University, by the way. We went down there this morning and asked around. Nobody recognized her. She made an expensive purchase from an Apple store as well."

"Interesting."

"Would you like to meet Rob and me at Zan's tonight? It's a little place over in Hyde Park."

"That sounds like an excellent idea. We can talk business face to face."

"Say about six o'clock?"

"Perfect. I'll meet you there."

When Don arrived Eddie and Rob were seated at the bar. Don walked over to them.

"Hi guys, I guess this is your regular place."

"You guessed right," said Rob. "Zan, come over here a minute. I want you to meet someone."

Zan trotted over and reached her hand across the bar. "Hi. My name is Zan. I'm the owner here."

"Hi. Pleased to meet you. I'm Detective Corlino. Call me Don."

"Are you with Boston PD, too?"

"Don is with the FBI, Zan. He's working with us on a case," explained Eddie

"Ooooh, FBI," said Zan. "What are we having tonight?"

"I'll just have a beer. Make it a Becks. I'll have what Rob's having."

"Don't drink all my beer now," warned Rob.

"Stop it, Rob. Ignore him. There's plenty."

The three detectives sat by themselves at the end of the bar and began to discuss the day's events.

"So do you still think Michelle is related to this case, Don?" asked Eddie.

"It's hard to say. I don't think she ever had anything to do with college campuses in the past. From what I could gather, she doesn't fit the profile of our other victims. It's a little curious that she doesn't answer her phone, but you say she made a purchase at an Apple Store a few days ago. Maybe she lost it and just now got around to replacing it."

"Sounds reasonable," said Eddie. "But if she did, she's got a new phone number. Why would she do that?"

"Maybe she wanted to leave her past behind her so she could get a new start," said Rob.

"So why is she hanging out around Boston University?"

"She could be turning tricks there," said Eddie with a resigned look on his face. "I've seen this all before. Some girls try to start over, but before you know it, they're right back in the same old rut." Both detectives nodded their heads in agreement.

Zan was wiping down the bar and surreptitiously moving in their direction. Rob smiled and kicked Eddie's foot. He made a motion with his eyes toward Zan. They all stopped talking.

Zan tried to act innocent and said, "Gotta keep the bar clean, fellas." She drifted back toward the other end of the bar.

"She's always trying to eavesdrop on our conversations," explained Rob.

Don smiled and glanced in Zan's direction.

"So what do you recommend for us tomorrow?" asked Eddie. "Do we stake out Beacon Street or try to locate Michelle?"

"I would say it's probably a good idea to split your time between the two," said Don. "You said you went down this morning to check out the places she used her credit card. Why don't you check them in the afternoon? Show her picture around. Maybe you'll get lucky. I've got a list of names from Wyatt I'm going to work on tomorrow."

"That's what we had in mind. If she's still hanging out around there, sooner or later somebody is bound to recognize her."

"Next round is on me gentlemen," said Don.

"Line 'em up," said Rob.

Zan brought them another round of drinks. "Can't you even give me a little clue? I promise I won't tell anyone. I swear," she said, putting on her sweetest smile.

"We promise to tell you all about it one day," said Eddie.

The three of them continued their conversation for the next half hour, and Eddie bought the next round.

"Next one's on the house," offered Zan.

Don seemed reluctant at first but finally agreed to stay.

"Let's all get in touch tomorrow afternoon," suggested Don.

"Okay. How about we meet here at six?" said Eddie.

"I'm good with that, unless something comes up," said Don.

Eddie and Don left after the next drink. Rob had one more with Zan.

CHAPTER 23

Tuesday Morning, Oct. 12, 9 AM

Don arrived at his office and once again began going over the list Captain Wyatt had given him. He googled the addresses of the suspects to see where in Boston they were located. He jotted down all of those that were close to universities as a priority. An hour later he looked at his watch. It was 9 AM.

It's 8 AM in Chicago. Tommy's awake by now I'm sure, thought Don.

He called Tom 's number.

"Yeah, Don."

"What have we got so far?"

"I spoke with Detective Jefferson yesterday. We're going to talk with some of Randy's friends here on campus today. He interviewed all of them six months ago, but no one seemed to have any relevant information. It was Easter vacation and almost all of the students were home for the holidays."

"See if you can find out who was on campus at the time. Maybe you can jog a few memories."

"I'm way ahead of you, Don. Apparently, there were a lot of foreign students on campus who were here the entire vacation. I want to talk to them."

"Good idea, Tommy. Call me if you find out anything."

"Will do. Later."

Don checked the criminal records of the names he had written down and refined his list to five suspects. Three of them were busted for drug trafficking, one was arrested for check forgery, and one was arrested for aggravated assault with a deadly weapon. A hunting knife.

All of them had been paroled and were now free to live their lives.

He called Captain Wyatt.

"Yes, Don. What can I do for you?"

"I know you're short-handed, Captain, but I was hoping you could spare the manpower to tail a few suspects.

"How many are we talking about?"

"I've got a list of five priorities." Don explained why he had put them on the top of the list.

"Okay, Don. If you really think the Reardons' disappearance is somehow tied in to terrorism, I'll play along for now. But understand, I can't spare them indefinitely. Let's say two weeks and if nothing comes up, I'll have to pull the plug."

"Understood, Captain. Thank you."

"I'll give you the names and phone numbers of the agents I assign to each suspect. That way you can get any new info straight from them."

"Very good, Captain. Thanks again."

Don sat back at his desk and thought about his next move.

George Barnett walked over and said, "Where do we stand with the Reardon thing right now?"

"I'm still tracking down some leads on the Jane Doe angle, but I can't say I've got anything solid."

"I'll let Jack know. I don't have to tell you the climate around here. The mayor doesn't care about excuses. He wants results. I sympathize with all you guys."

• • • • •

Just like almost every other morning, Eddie was at his desk when Rob walked in. He had a look of decisiveness about him as he took his place across from Eddie.

"Good morning, Rob."

"Good morning, Eddie. Anything of value on those 7-11 tapes?"

"They're still going over them. They're concentrating on the days that Michelle's card was used. The problem is we don't know the time of day she made the purchase. It's a lot to go through. There are a couple of girls who came in that resemble her license picture but we couldn't make a positive ID. We made a couple of still photos from the tape and wrote down the time of day. Maybe we can have Greg Phillips run them through the face recognition program." Eddie threw several pictures on Rob's desk.

"I was thinking last night about how we should use our time today. I know Michelle Dennis isn't our Jane Doe, but I trust Don's intuition. I really think our time is better spent trying to locate her. There are some things that just don't add up. One way or another, I'd like to tie up loose ends."

Eddie wasn't sure if Rob was actually convinced of that or if he was just fed up and frustrated with the Beacon Street stakeout. "I'm okay with that. Unless we actually witness Nasir do something illegal, we're probably not gonna get anywhere. So I guess you want to go back to Chestnut Hill Avenue."

"If she's still in the area, we're bound to run into her sooner or later."

"All right. Let's do that. But before we go, we really should have Jimmy assign a couple of different cops to go over those tapes. I'm starting to worry about those guys."

Rob smiled and said, "You're right."

Eddie went to Dugan's office and explained what they were going to follow up on and pleaded the case for the two unfortunate cops. Even Dugan had to smile and agreed to find two other victims. Eddie and Rob set out for Chestnut Hill Avenue.

"Let's stop at the Shell station again and see if they have those tapes," suggested Eddie.

Rob spotted the mechanic, who was working on a car up on one of the lifts. His shirt and hands were black with oil and a gray smudge was streaked across his forehead. Oil was pouring from the pan into a capture barrel.

Rob walked over to him and identified himself. "Boston PD. Can you tell us if you've seen this girl?" He handed him the picture.

He looked at the photo and read the description on the license. "Five feet, seven inches. Dark brown hair. Green eyes. There was a girl who came in a few weeks ago who sort of matches that description, but I don't think this is her. It looks a little bit like her, but no. I know license pictures aren't always flattering. I mean, people gain and lose weight. Sometimes they're just having a bad hair day when they get their picture taken. Ya know? The girl who came in here was a real hottie. I mean, you wouldn't forget her easily. She wanted some work done on her motorcycle. A big Harley. The engine was running rough and kept stalling out. I replaced the spark plugs. She also had her brakes done. I remember looking forward to her picking it up again."

"Do you know how she paid for the work?" asked Rob.

"You would have to check inside. I don't deal with that end of things. Sorry."

"Okay. Thank you very much. If you do see a girl who looks like the license picture, please give us a call." Rob handed him a card.

"Sure thing, detective."

Rob and Eddie went inside and greeted the attendant they had spoken to the previous day. "Do you have the surveillance tapes of the register and gas pumps we asked for yesterday?"

"Yes, I do, detectives." He handed over several tapes. "From September 1 up until yesterday."

"Call us if you remember anything."

Eddie and Rob thanked him and were on their way.

"Want to check out some more local places?" said Rob.

"I guess so. Then we can grab some lunch and drop these tapes off at headquarters."

"The day she used the card at the Shell station was September 22. I'd like to do a fast forward of the tape and see if we can ID her," said Rob. "Maybe we'll get lucky. We can send any pictures we get over to the FBI."

"Why don't we call Don and tell him what we've got?" said Eddie.

"Good idea."

"Yes, Rob. What's up?"

"We have a bunch of tapes from a 7-11 and a gas station near Boston College. We made some still photos from the tape. We'd like to run Michelle's license picture through the facial recognition software at the FBI and compare them. What do you think?"

"I'll tell you what. Why don't you make a copy of the tape and send that as well? They have some amazing software these days. It can compare and identify people based on the movement of their bodies. I've seen it work when I was up in Buffalo. I'll talk to the guys in our video department."

"Okay, Don. We'll get on that right away. I'll give you a call later on. Maybe we can hit Zan's again tonight."

Don chuckled and said, "Sure. Why not?"

• • • • •

Mike had left for work and Brittany had put the girls on the bus for school. She got dressed for work headed for the office. On the way she stopped at the 7-11 for coffee. It was a routine for her as well as Mike.

"Good morning, Raj," she smiled as she walked in the door.

"Good morning, Mrs. Davis," he replied. "Glorious day, isn't it?"

"Yes, it is. My favorite time of year."

"Mine too," he agreed. "There is no place like New York in October."

Mike and Brittany both liked Raj. He was always friendly and good natured. Sometimes Mike would imitate Raj at the dinner table. Jamie and Roni would giggle and Brittany would admonish him.

"Mike, that's so politically incorrect."

The girls would encourage him. "Do it again, daddy."

All Brittany could do was shake her head and smile. Brittany got her coffee and paid at the register.

"So long, Raj. Probably see you again tomorrow."

"Always a pleasure." he said as she walked out the door.

It took about a half hour to get to her job at Diamond Marketing Strategies. She didn't mind the drive to work. It relaxed her. She arrived at work, said good morning to everyone and took her place at her desk. Brittany was easy to get along with and very popular at work. She had a reputation as a problem solver and often helped out her fellow employees. She had made an appointment with one of her most important clients for eleven o'clock that morning. It wasn't going to take more than an hour at most. After that she planned to go to lunch with her best friend at work, Anne. She had originally planned to go straight home after that, but that morning she got a call from a special client she had taken under her wing.

Mrs. Cooper was a sweet old lady who had considerable talent as an artist. She had drawn a number of sketches with a Christmas holiday theme. She wanted to print thousands of cards and sell them in sets of twenty cards each. However, she did not have the slightest idea of how to market her merchandise. It was not an important account and not going to bring in a great deal of money, but Brittany had a soft spot in her heart for her. She had made an appointment to meet her at two o'clock.

Brittany made several more calls to clients. At 12:30 she walked over to Anne's desk.

"Ready to go, Anne?"

"Yup. Where do you want to go?"

"How about TGIF?" suggested Brittany.

"Sounds good. You driving?"

"Sure. No problem."

It was always nice to see her friend Anne. Brittany felt she could always count on her.

They talked over lunch and returned to the office. It was now 1:45 PM and they found Mrs. Cooper waiting for them.

"Anne, this is Mrs. Cooper. She's trying to market her Christmas cards. I'm going to help her set up a web site."

"Good morning, Anne. It's nice to meet you," said Mrs. Cooper in a soft, mousy voice.

"Nice to meet you, too," said Anne smiling affectionately. "I'll let you two get started."

Brittany spent the next hour explaining all the tricks about how to get the most out of her website. When they were done, Mrs. Cooper stood up and said, "Thank you so much. You're such a dear."

"No problem. If there's anything else you need help with, don't hesitate to call," said Brittany, smiling broadly. She walked with her to the elevator and once again said goodbye.

Mrs. Cooper thanked her repeatedly as the elevator doors closed.

Anne met Brittany back at her desk and said, "Where did you find her? She's adorable."

"She just called us out of the blue asking for advice about her cards. She sounded so sweet and innocent I couldn't turn her away."

Brittany tied up a few loose ends, said goodbye to Anne and left for the day. She arrived home, picked up the girls from Mrs. Avery's house and began to prepare dinner. Mike arrived home an hour later. Jamie and Roni were waiting and ran to meet him.

"How are my little angels today?" he asked, giving each of them a hug.

"I won the Spelling Bee at school," said Roni.

"That's my girl," said Mike.

Mike walked into the kitchen gave Brittany a hug and said, "How was your day, sweetheart?"

"Nothing special, honey. Just a day like any other. How was yours?"

"Actually, it was a bit strange. Remember I mentioned to you that the CFO of one of our clients went missing a few weeks ago? The firm is called Lexington Finance in Boston. I'm the one who designed the original software for them."

"Yes. I remember you mentioning something about it."

"The guy's name is Reardon. It was in the news. I never met him personally, but I've worked closely with their computer department and some of their top financial executives. No one knows what happened to him. His wife is missing, too."

"That's a little creepy. How long have they been one of your clients?"

"About two years. I got a call from the main office in New York this morning. They want to know more details about that software."

"Don't they have people down there who can handle it?"

"Yes, but I'm the expert. Nobody can do what I do," said Mike, wearing a silly smirk.

Brittany rolled her eyes.

"I just got a request for a software upgrade from Lexington Finance yesterday morning. I guess that's why they finally brought me into the loop."

"It's a bit odd that they wouldn't let you know sooner."

"Who knows how corporate America thinks?"

Mike ran upstairs and changed into more comfortable clothes and they all sat down at the table. Brittany continued making dinner, her mind now a bit distracted. Later that evening Jamie and Roni did their homework while Mike and Brittany watched TV.

At ten o'clock they were all in bed. Mike soon fell fast asleep. Brittany lay awake for another hour staring at the ceiling thinking about what Mike had just told her about the disappearance of the Reardons and the mysterious request for the software change.

CHAPTER 24

Tuesday Evening, 6 PM

Don had arranged to meet Eddie and Rob at Zan's at six o'clock. He walked in and took a seat at the end of the bar, where the two detectives were already nursing their first drink.

"Good evening, gentlemen. I see you've gotten the jump on me."

Zan walked over and said, "You're becoming a regular here, detective," placing a Becks in front of him. "I'm gonna have to give you an 'I love Zan's' T-shirt."

"Good advertising. You're gonna be a millionaire before you know it."

The three detectives sat at the bar and once again discussed what they had learned and what their best options were.

"My priority is still the Reardon disappearance," said Don. "I should probably work with the JTTF and make my boss happy. That angle is probably more likely to get results. You guys have a little more latitude. I know you were asked to work with me on this, but your priority is Jane Doe. We don't know for sure if these cases are related at all. I think you should probably focus on figuring out Jane Doe's identity."

"We're still putting most of our efforts in that direction. We follow up on anything that has possible ties to Milton and the Blue Hills Reservation. We're still getting plate numbers and checking with the universities. Remember, Nasir does fit into both circles of our Venn Diagram," said Eddie.

"That's true. I'm hoping that my partner, Tom Brown, can give me some useful information. He's still out in Youngstown. He's supposed to call me if he finds out anything."

"So what's the plan?" said Rob.

"Remember that the FBI has an arsenal of information on virtually everyone in the country. Don't hesitate to call me or Greg. Sooner or later, somebody is going to report our Jane Doe missing. She wasn't a nobody."

The three of them continued going over the facts, trying to come up with a new angle. Half an hour later, they were satisfied they had covered everything.

"Who's ready for another drink?" said Rob. "My turn to buy."

Zan set up another round and floated back and forth, flirting with the guys in the bar. When they had finished their drinks Eddie and Don decided to call it a night.

Rob decided to have one more. He wound up having two. He talked with Zan for another hour and figured it was time to go. Meanwhile, Eddie went home and had dinner with his wife. He watched some TV and retired for the evening.

Don also returned home. He pulled some leftovers out of the fridge, threw them in the microwave and turned on the TV. He sat in his easy chair eating dinner and then dozed off watching reruns of *Law & Order*. It was ten o'clock when Don's phone rang. It was a familiar ring tone: "Bad, Bad Leroy Brown."

"Hi Tommy. What's up?"

"Hi Don. I got some information for you on Randy Fletcher."

"Go ahead. Shoot."

"I interviewed all the same people that Detective Jefferson did, but got nowhere. I did eventually find someone he'd missed."

"Go on."

"There were some Korean students who were here at the beginning of the Easter vacation. The campus was almost empty at the time. They all went to a seminar in Columbus a few days later. They weren't around when the murder supposedly happened but one of them did remember Randy when we showed him his picture. His name is Jung Man."

"You're kidding!"

"No. You can't make this shit up. They were still in Columbus when Detective Jefferson interviewed all of Randy's friends."

"So what did you find out?"

"He said he remembers Randy walking around campus with a black-haired white girl."

"Was it just the two of them or were there other people?"

"Just the two of them. We asked Jung if he could give a more detailed description of her. He doesn't speak English very well. All he said was, 'Wowwwie.'"

"Anything else you can tell me?"

"Detective Jefferson is going to follow up on locating that girl. That's about it for now."

"Okay, Tommy. Are you coming back soon?"

"Yup. Should catch up with you tomorrow."

"See you then."

Don picked up the plates he had used for dinner, walked over to the kitchen and placed them in the sink. On his way back to the living room he noticed the crumpled paper he had left on the dresser a few days earlier. He picked it up and began to unfold it, trying to remember what it was. Then it came to him. It was the address for Michelle Dennis that Eddie had given him a week earlier. The buzzing in his ear began again.

Don sat back in his easy chair. What had been lurking in a gray cloak and hidden from his determined eye began to emerge from the shadows. In a flash all the pieces snapped together like a bear trap.

With a sudden sense of urgency Don called Eddie McGowan.

• • • • •

Rob had left Zan's at eight o'clock. He had planned on going home, but had a sudden change of heart. Much the same as Don, he too obsessed with puzzles from time to time. This one was no different. He decided to pay a visit to the Chestnut Street 7-11 and ask a few more questions. It was for this determination that Jimmy Dugan had given him the nickname *Thorough Morrow.*

Rob walked into the 7-11 and identified himself to the clerk at the counter.

"Yes. Suresh told me you might stop by. My name is Ajish. He showed me the picture of the girl you were asking about. I cannot say for sure if she has been here or not. There are so many different girls who come in. There are many students from the college with dark hair who look somewhat like the picture."

Rob asked Jalaj, the other worker, who pretty much gave him the same answer. Unwilling to give up he began to question people as they came in the door.

"Have you seen this girl?" he asked hopefully with each new customer. After an hour he was no closer to an answer.

Maybe she's left the area, he began to think. *The card was used several times in August and September, but the last known purchase was more than a week ago.*

Rob continued to ask customers about the photograph as they walked in paying particular attention to people who appeared to be in their twenties and thirties. A dark-haired girl who somewhat resembled the picture walked in.

"Have you seen this girl?" he asked. "Her name is Michelle Dennis."

She looked carefully at the photo but eventually said "No. I'm sorry. She doesn't look familiar."

It was now just after nine thirty. Feeling tired and frustrated, Rob thought about calling it quits and going home for the evening. *I'll give it until ten o'clock,* he thought.

At a quarter to ten a black Harley motorcycle pulled up in the parking lot. Rob could see clearly that the rider was a girl. Her tight blue jeans accentuated her very shapely hips. A black sequined leather jacket complemented the rest of her outfit. She took off her helmet, revealing a wave of long, flowing black hair. Rob was immediately impressed. He remembered what the mechanic had said about the girl who had brought in her Harley, and that Michelle's credit card had been used at that Shell station. With renewed enthusiasm he approached the girl.

"Good evening, miss. I'm a detective with the Boston Police Department. Can you tell me if you have seen this girl?" He showed her Michelle's picture

She looked at the photograph and immediately said, "No."

"Could you take a closer look, please?" persisted Rob. "Her name is Michelle. We've been trying to locate her for the past week. Are you sure you don't recognize her?"

"No. I don't," she said adamantly.

Rob thought that was a bit curt. The girl hastily gathered up two bottles of Pepsi, some potato chips, a Payday peanut bar and a copy of the Globe. She shot a furtive glance at Rob, which wasn't lost on him. She put some money on the counter and headed for the door.

Rob, with obvious intent, stood in her way and said, "Could you just look at this picture one more time? You barely gave it any thought."

This time she took the picture from Rob's hand and stared at it for a moment.

"No. I'm sorry," she said, somewhat annoyed, handing it back to him. "I don't recognize her."

She sidestepped Rob and walked out the door.

Rob caught a vibe from her impatience and reluctance to cooperate.

He watched her closely as she got back on her Harley and began to drive off.

He waited until she was far enough down the road and then quickly ran to his car.

It had begun to get cooler outside and there was a dampness in the air. A light mist hovered just above the road.

The Harley cruised slowly down Chestnut Hill Avenue. Rob pulled out of the parking lot and began to follow her at a distance. She drove about a quarter mile made a left turn on Clinton Road. Rob waited until she was far enough ahead before he made the turn. He watched as the bike pulled up on the side of the road about sixty yards ahead. He pulled his car over and shut off his headlights.

The black-haired girl took off her helmet and pulled something from her jacket pocket.

Rob sat back and waited. She seemed to glance back toward him and then put what appeared to be a cell phone to her ear. After a couple of minutes, she put the phone in her pocket, put her helmet back on and pulled away from the curb.

Rob kept his lights off and began to follow her again. *Probably stopped to take a call*, he thought.

After a series of rights and lefts the Harley turned south on Jamaica Way. There were other cars sharing the road with them now and Rob turned his headlights back on. They continued traveling south through Jamaica Plain and headed down Morton Street.

We're heading into Mattapan, thought Rob. *My favorite place.*

Rob kept a distance behind the bike, being careful not to lose her. The Harley made a right turn off Morton and finally pulled up in front of a government housing complex.

Interesting. What's a beautiful girl like that want in a place like this?

Rob watched as she secured her helmet to the front wheel with a cable lock and got off her bike.

Can't be too careful in this neighborhood, he mused to himself.

He continued to watch as she took something from her saddlebag and tucked it inside her jacket. Rob watched her as she began to walk toward the housing project. When she had disappeared between the buildings, Rob jumped out of his car and ran down the block after her. He stopped briefly to take a picture of her license plate with his cell phone. While he had the phone out, he noticed that Eddie had messaged him.

It'll have to wait, he thought.

He continued his pursuit and caught sight of her through the mist just as she rounded the corner. Rob raced to where she had been and carefully peered around the side of the building. He could barely see her up ahead on the dimly lit walkway between the buildings.

Rob began to walk slowly behind her, keeping a safe distance between them.

She walked on and then turned right around another corner. Again, he ran to catch up to her. When he got to the point where he had last seen her, he looked to the right. It was a dead end. There was nothing but a dark closed off courtyard. She was gone.

Where did she go? He walked slowly into the courtyard. When he got to the end, he noticed a narrow opening between the buildings on the left. It was less than a foot wide and seemed to connect to an open area on the other side. Rob tried to squeeze through but immediately realized the futility. Evidently his quarry was quite familiar with the area.

Was this just a shortcut that she knew about? Did she know I was following her?

He ran back out of the courtyard and mentally estimated where the opening would lead to. He took a quick right, ran about twenty-five yards to the corner, and made another right. About twenty yards down there appeared to be another opening between the buildings.

Keeping close to the side of the building, he cautiously inched his way down toward it.

When he got there, he looked to the right.

An alleyway about three feet wide and fifty feet long seemed to lead back toward the courtyard where he had just been. A brick wall across the top restricted access to anything over four feet in height. He walked slowly through the damp air and made his way down the alleyway. When he reached the overhang he crouched down, ducked his head and came out on the other side. He raised his head and saw several dumpsters lined up against the wall in a small enclosed area.

It was the last thing Morrow would ever see.

CHAPTER 25

Wednesday, Oct. 13, 9:00 AM

Eddie had been at his desk since 8:30 that morning. He was eager to get the results of the tapes he had sent to the FBI video lab. If Don's theory was correct the 7-11 tapes could throw some light on what happened to Michelle Dennis. He decided to call Don.

"Yeah, Eddie. Anything new?"

"I'm curious about those tapes we sent to your lab. I just wanted to know where we are right now."

"I'm at the lab right now. I got Jack to give it top priority. We've got several tapes running concurrently, but it's still going to take some time. I'll let you know the minute we find anything."

"Okay, Don I'm waiting for Rob to come in. Then we'll go back to that 7-11 and poke around some more."

"Okay, Eddie. Later."

It was now just after nine. It was about the time he expected Rob to walk in. When Rob had still not showed up at 9:45 he decided to give him a call. After four rings it went to voicemail.

Maybe he stayed at Zan's too long last night, thought Eddie.

He tried again at ten o'clock. Again, he got voicemail.

Eddie decided to call Don again.

"Yeah, Eddie. What's going on?"

"Rob hasn't showed up yet. I tried to reach him, but it just goes to voicemail."

"Did you tell him about my theory that our suspect might be a girl?"

"I messaged him at about ten thirty last night. I assume he got the information."

"Do you know if he went straight home after he left Zan's?"

"I don't know anything right now. Zan doesn't get into her place until after eleven."

"You don't think he went looking for Michelle by himself last night?"

"I don't know. I'm not sure."

"Let me know the minute he comes in."

Eddie called the number for Zan's but got no answer. With deepening concern gnawing at his gut, he tried to focus on some of the other leads he had gotten from the Blue Hills Reservation. At eleven o'clock he tried calling Zan's again. This time she picked up.

"Zan's. How can I help you?"

"Hi Zan. It's Eddie McGowan."

"Oh, hi Eddie. What's up?"

"I was wondering what time Rob left your place last night. He hasn't showed up at work and he's not answering his calls."

"Oh my God. He left here at about eight o'clock. I hope he's all right."

"He didn't drink too much or anything like that?"

"No. He had like two more beers after you left. That was it."

"He didn't mention if he was going anywhere, did he?"

"No. As a matter of fact he said he was going home."

That gave Eddie a small sense of relief. "Okay. Thanks, Zan. I'll talk to you later."

Eddie walked over to Jimmy Dugan's office. "Good morning, Jimmy."

"Good morning, Eddie. What's up?"

"Rob hasn't showed up yet and he's not answering his phone. I'm gonna take a drive over to his place and check on him. If he comes in call me right away."

Jimmy looked up from his desk, appearing somewhat concerned. "It's not like him to be this late without calling. Let me know what you find out."

"I'll do that. Talk to you later."

Eddie jumped in his car and drove to Rob's place. His car was not in its usual parking spot. With every minute, Eddie was becoming increasingly concerned. He knocked on the door, but no one answered.

Maybe I should check out the Chestnut Hill 7-11 and see if they know something.

Eddie got back in his car and hurriedly drove toward Boston College and Chestnut Hill.

When he got to the 7-11, he rushed inside and found Suresh at the register. "Do you know if my partner was in here last night sometime after eight o'clock?"

"I wasn't here then, Detective. Kaushal was on duty from four o'clock until twelve."

"Could you call him? It's very important."

"I'm sure he's asleep now. He won't answer his phone, but I can run back the tape from last night."

"Yes. Let's do that."

Suresh rolled back the tape and put it on the monitor.

"Start at eight o'clock and fast forward through it, please."

Eddie watched as customers came and went, hoping he wouldn't see his partner come through the door. His heart sank when the tape showed Rob walk in at 8:32 PM.

Suresh continued to fast forward the tape and Eddie watched as Rob began questioning the customers. At 9:48 the tape showed a very pretty dark-haired girl come through the door.

"Right there. Slow down the tape, please."

The tape showed Rob approach her and begin to ask questions. He showed her what was almost certainly a picture of Michelle. At 9:50 the tape showed the girl pay at the register and head for the exit. Eddie watched as Rob seemed to block her path and again attempt to show her the picture. She indulged him for a brief moment and then walked out. A minute later Rob left the store.

"I'm gonna need this tape right now," he told Suresh.

"Of course, Detective. Anything you want."

Eddie called Don. "Don, I'm at the 7-11 in Chestnut Hill. Rob was here last night. I've got a tape that shows him talking to a girl who matches the description you gave to me. I think he followed her after she left."

"That's not good, Eddie."

"I've got the tape with me. Are you still at the video lab?"

"Yes. I'm here."

"I'm on my way."

• • • • •

Brittany had gone to her office that morning and was going over a few details with Anne concerning an account they had worked on together. At one o'clock they decided to break for lunch. They brought some photos of different clothing lines with them and made some final decisions about which ones to promote for their advertising campaign. After lunch they returned to the office.

· · · · ·

Eddie arrived at FBI headquarters at just after one o'clock. He identified himself and raced up to the video lab. Don greeted him with a solemn look. "Let's stay positive and hope for the best, Eddie."

"I hear you, Don. Here's the tape. Let's get started."

"At what time did our suspect walk into the store?"

"About a quarter to ten. She was only there for about two or three minutes."

"That should be enough for our program," said Don optimistically.

They fed the tape into the "Miss Google Eyes" program and compared it to the tape Don had recovered from the Lighthouse in Buffalo. Although that tape did not show a clear picture of the girl's face, it did show an unobstructed view of her as she walked across the bar.

Don and Eddie waited anxiously as the program did its thing. A few minutes later the computer spit out a result.

"This gives a better than 98% certainty that our unidentified witness in the Buffalo murders is the same person Rob questioned last night," said Don. "We gave her the name Cowgirl because of the hat."

"I can see how face recognition might not be helpful. You can barely see her face in the video," said Eddie.

"We still don't know who she is, but at least we know who we're looking for."

Don ran the 7-11 tape back to where a clear picture of the girl could be seen. He froze the tape at several points and made several still photos.

He called George Barnet. "George, it's Don. I'm sending you some photos of a suspect in our Jane Doe murder. Please send it to every office in the country. It's likely she's still in the Boston area, so put out an APB immediately."

"I'll do that, Don. Keep me posted. I'll let Jack know right away."

Eddie thought for a minute and said, "I just thought of something. There's a good possibility our suspect owns a motorcycle. Someone of her description got some work done at a Shell station in Chestnut Hill. If we're lucky we might be able to get a plate number and possibly a name. The tape is already here in the video lab."

"Let's get started then," said Don.

The two detectives fast forwarded each tape, looking specifically for a motorcycle to come into view. Three hours later Eddie identified the bike. "Bingo. Ohio license plate 82 MVR. Let's put out a nationwide APB."

"Call the Ohio State MVB and get a name for that registration," added Don.

Half an hour later they had a name: James Gordon.

"Who the hell is James Gordon and how the hell does he fit in to all of this?" Eddie said with some puzzlement and exasperation.

• • • • •

At three o'clock Anne decided to wrap things up and told Brittany she would be in the next day. "I'll see you tomorrow, Brit. Don't work too hard."

"Don't worry about me, Anne. I'll be out of here in half an hour."

Brittany decided to call Mrs. Cooper to see how things were going with her Christmas cards and the new website. After a few rings it went to voicemail.

She decided to call Mike. "Hi honey. What time do you expect to be home?"

"I'm probably going to work until six. I shouldn't be any later than seven."

"Okay, I'll have dinner ready around that time. Love you."

"Love you too, sweetheart."

Brittany tried Mrs. Cooper a second time. Again, it went to voice-mail and it gave her the usual options. This time she left a message asking her to return her call. She left her office at a quarter to five and began her drive home.

It was four thirty in the afternoon when Brittany pulled into her driveway, turned the engine off and walked in to her house. She put down her bag and took out her cell phone and dialed Mrs. Avery. "Hi Dawn. I just got home. I'm coming over to pick up the girls. Are they ready?"

"Yes, Brit. Rachel wants to know if she can come over to your house for a while. They want to play fetch with Kardashian."

"Not tonight, Dawn. I'm sorry. Roni's got some homework to catch up on and Jamie's got a math test tomorrow. Maybe later this week."

"Okay, Brit. See you in a minute."

Brittany strolled down the street punching numbers into her phone. First, she called Mike. There was no answer. *Probably busy with a client,* she thought. Then she tried to call Mrs. Cooper for the third time. Again, no answer. She continued to walk toward the Averys' house, focused on her cell phone. She took no notice of the blue van parked by the side of the road, although it was not familiar in the neighborhood. She walked up to the Averys' front porch and opened the front door.

"Dawn, I'm here."

Jamie, Roni and Rachel came running up to her and appealed to her one more time.

"Can Rachel come over? Just for half an hour. Please … Please … Please, Mom."

"Not tonight, girls. Mommy's tired and you girls have studying to do."

"Okay. Sorry, Rachel. We'll see you tomorrow."

"Thanks for looking after them, Dawn. I really appreciate it. Mike and I will have you guys over for dinner one of these days real soon."

"Thanks, Brit. I'd love that. I haven't seen Mike in months."

"How about next Friday night? I'll have to check with Mike but I don't think he's got any plans."

"Sounds like a date. I'll let you know."

Dawn and Rachel waved goodbye and went back inside while Brittany and the girls walked back toward their house.

"How was your day at school, girls? Anything special?"

"Not really," replied Jamie.

"How about you, Roni?"

"Kenny Taylor brought in this snake for show and tell. Some of the girls were screaming and making faces. They're so silly. I've seen a hundred garter snakes behind our house. Big deal."

Brittany laughed and said, "That's my nature girl. Takes a lot to scare you."

They walked past the blue van without much thought as to why it was there.

"Remember we went camping at that place in Pennsylvania and we saw all those rattlesnakes at the bottom of the cliff?" said Jamie.

"Now that was scary," said Brit.

They walked on and talked about the upcoming weekend. They did not notice the van slowly following behind them. Just as they reached their house the van sped up and came to a sudden stop next to them.

A girl Brittany did not recognize jumped from the van and stood in front of them. She was dressed in blue jeans cut-offs, sneakers, a baseball cap and a casual light blue Adidas sports shirt. She looked like a typical girl out for a jog. She pulled a large knife from the sheath tied to her belt and made sure Brittany saw it.

"Get in the van," she said quietly but with attitude. She did not want to draw attention. "Get in the van … now. All of you. Right now." She motioned toward the van with the knife.

Brittany was stunned and her heart began to race. *Is this really happening? Am I dreaming some terrible nightmare? Who is this girl? What does she want?*

A ray of sunlight caught the knife and the gleam of the polished metal flashed in Brittany's eyes. Terror gripped her in the pit of her stomach. Soon it filled her whole body and for a moment she was frozen. Then she looked at Jamie and Roni. Instinct took over. Her focus went from her own sense of self-preservation to protecting her little girls.

Brittany looked up and down the street for help, but it was deserted. If she had been alone, she might have made a run for it. She looked at Jamie and Roni and saw the fear in their eyes. She had no choice. "Do what the lady says, girls. Get in the van."

The girls looked at each other and then looked at their mom. Tears welled up in Roni's eyes. "Mommy," she pleaded, looking for a sign of reassurance.

Jamie put her arm around her and said, "C'mon Roni."

"It's going to be all right, girls," Brittany reassured them.

Reluctantly the three of them got into the back of the van.

The girl climbed in the front seat and ordered the driver, "Okay. Let's go."

The van took off down Birch Street and turned the corner onto Cedar Lane. A moment later it was out of sight.

Brittany tried to calm herself. Her heart was pounding.

The van reached the end of Cedar Lane and turned right onto Forest Park Drive.

Everything was surreal. What was going on? *Think… think… What can I do?* Her mind was racing.

Jamie and Roni were now in tears. "Mommy, what's going on?"

The black-haired girl turned around in her seat and stared at them. She still had the knife in her hand and held it up for Brittany to see. "Shut the hell up."

The van came to the end of Forest Park Drive. There was a red light. The van made a stop and then turned right onto State Route 50. They passed several familiar landmarks: the Sunoco station, Bank of America, and the 7-11.

Think, God damn it. Should I jump out and yell for help? she asked herself. *No, too dangerous. They would still have the girls. What would they do without me?*

Then it came to her. She took her best and only shot. If she only had time…She reached into her jacket pocket. She tried her best not to draw attention from the girl in the front seat. Brittany knew her cell phone like her own hand. She grasped it in her hand and pushed the "on" button.

If she took the phone from her pocket, they would notice and take it from her. Dialing 911 was not going to work. She tapped the phone icon. Brittany knew which options would come up. She had just called Mike and she hadn't cleared it.

She knew exactly where to touch the phone. She pushed the "recent calls" option.

Mike will pick up … she prayed to herself, holding her breath. *Come on. Come on. Please pick up.*

How many rings before voicemail would take it? How long before they would notice her hand in her pocket?

Please pick up… please… please.

Brittany calculated the time for five rings. Either Mike had picked up or voicemail was beginning its familiar options routine.

How long did that take? How long before Mike would know? How long would voice mail stay on? Brittany counted the seconds. *Now!* she thought.

She began to speak. "Where are you taking us? Who are you people? What do you want from us? Just let us go."

"Mommy," Jamie cried. "Why are they doing this?"

"I don't know, sweetheart. Just stay calm. I love you, girls."

Jamie took off her backpack and tried to reach inside for her cell phone.

"Give me that," demanded the girl and grabbed the backpack. "Take off your jacket and give it to me." With an icy stare, she looked Brittany dead in the eyes. "Right now. I'm not fucking around."

Brittany knew she had run out of time. She looked at the dashboard console and saw the Dodge logo.

"Get your hand out of your pocket. Fuck! Show me your hands."

At this point the driver, a man in his late twenties, turned around with a pistol in his hand.

"Blue Dodge van. South on route 50. A man and a woman. Late twenties," she managed to get out.

Brittany felt the crushing blow of the pistol to her temple and slipped into darkness.

THE NIGHT HAS GREEN EYES

PART II

Four Months Earlier

CHAPTER 26

Sunday, June 13
Four months earlier

Gillian eased her Harley down Route 302 through the lush green hills of Vermont, playfully negotiating each curve in the road. It was a beautiful spring day and she had chosen not to wear her leather jacket or her helmet. The sun warmed her face and arms and the wind stroked her long raven-black hair. When the road straightened, she let go of the handlebars and spread her arms like a bird in flight. She had no obligations or places to be.

She felt completely free.

Gillian could feel the Harley vibrate between her legs and wondered if she could get aroused without actually touching herself. She began to fantasize and let her mind fill with erotic thoughts.

Gillian was not at all shy. Nor was she afraid of consequences.

The Harley seemed to drive itself and Gillian let her mind wander back in time. She had been born Gillian Amber Sands but now rarely used her real name. Gillian grew up in Dubuque, Iowa with her parents and older sister Heather. Early on her parents realized that she was troubled.

She would sometimes steal money from her mother's pocketbook when she wanted something, and she had been caught shoplifting in local stores on two occasions. No charges were ever filed due to her age but her parents were well aware of her troubling behavior.

School was not going well either. Her teachers often complained that she was disruptive in class and often got into fights with her fellow classmates. She had once set fire to a garbage pail in the hallway and got suspended for a week. Her parents were at a loss to understand. Their other daughter, Heather, was a model student and had never been a problem. They had taken Gillian to a psychologist for counseling but it proved to be of little help. As time went on, they realized that they could no longer control her. When she was fourteen her parents sent her to a private school for troubled girls.

Gillian hated it.

When she was fifteen years old, she packed up some things in her backpack and hitchhiked her way to Miami. At first things were difficult. She had fallen in with some fellow runaways. Their names were Brian, Paul, Evelyn and Sarah. Each of them had a story to tell about their abusive parents or a tragic childhood experience. Gillian had no such story to tell. She was simply the product of her own pathology. They made ends meet by panhandling and shoplifting. Gillian was still just a skinny girl but she was very strong and had an inner rage. She would almost always prevail when she got in a fight… even with the boys. She soon had the respect of her companions, and she became their unofficial leader.

As the days passed, she became more and more streetwise. Gillian continued living this way for almost a year, until she had just turned sixteen. She managed to feed herself well and keep herself reasonably clean. Her shoplifting skills allowed her to acquire some nice clothes for herself and her friends. Each of them had two backpacks in which they carried their belongings. They would all move from place to place, and they managed to stay under the radar of the police. The weather in Miami was always warm and life outdoors was not that demanding. However, Gillian did not care for life on the streets and was determined to do something about it.

One Saturday morning she decided to hitch to Miami Beach. She had never been to the beach before. When she got there, she walked along the shore and took notice of all the beautiful girls in their swimsuits. She envied them.

Gillian walked across the street and strolled down the block, checking out the mannequins in the clothing store windows. Her eyes caught sight of a risqué black bikini. Immediately she knew what she wanted. She walked in, pretended to be making up her mind and managed to put it in her bag without being noticed. She left the store, walked down the street to a McDonald's, went to the lady's room and tried it on. She looked in the mirror and liked what she saw.

She walked back across the street and hit the beach. It was there that she met a college student from Miami University named Dave. She started up a conversation and they spent the afternoon on his beach blanket. Several hours passed and he eventually invited her back to his dorm room, where they smoked pot, drank wine and listened to music. Dave found her extremely attractive and asked her to stay the night. Gillian was thrilled at the thought of sleeping in a real bed for a change. She immediately said yes.

Later that evening Dave pulled her close to him and began to kiss her and softly stroke her arms and legs. He reached under her T-shirt and smoothly moved his hand up her stomach to her breasts. He could feel Gillian's heart beating faster as she began to draw deeper breaths with each caress.

He unbuckled her belt and slowly unzipped her Daisy Dukes.

Gillian's heart was now racing.

Dave reached into her shorts with both hands. He let one slip in behind her and let the other ease down in front. He coaxed her shorts down to her ankles and she eagerly kicked them off. She continued to encourage him, grabbing him around the waist.

Dave kept his hand firmly planted on her ass and pulled her toward him as he brought his other hand up between her thighs.

Gillian was on fire.

Dave unzipped his fly and took out what he had.

She began to kiss his chest and slowly worked her way down his body. When she reached his waist, she began to use her tongue. She found herself becoming ever more excited.

Dave threw her backwards on the bed and pinned her down. Gillian cried out in pleasure-pain as he pushed himself inside her. It was her first time. Dave continued to make love to her and felt her body shudder when she let go.

• • • • •

Gillian continued riding down Route 302, enjoying every curve the highway had to offer. She began to smile as she thought about her first real sexual experience. Dave had invited her to stay the night but she wound up staying for a month.

Dave had no complaints.

Gillian had a lot of natural talent. She did not look or act like a sixteen-year-old girl and it was easy to convince everyone that she was two years older. She was a strikingly beautiful girl.

The day after she met Dave, she paid a visit to her former companions and told them she had met someone special and she was going to live with him. She wished them all well took her backpack with her. They were sad to see her go.

She continued to live with Dave until the end of the semester in June when Dave told her he had to return to his home in Michigan. The dorm room was no longer available. She packed up her things and set out for Gainesville.

As time went on Gillian became more adept at persuading guys to accommodate her. College boys were easy. She realized that college campuses provided an excellent way to survive. It was definitely better than living on the streets. It wasn't long until she had found another place to stay. Gillian continued moving from one college to another. If there were too many questions or if the secret of her age was discovered, she simply moved on to another campus and another guy. She now had a definite routine. By the time she was seventeen she had learned to talk or fuck her way into getting anything she wanted. It was at Tulane that she met Jimmy.

Jimmy was an easy mark. He was not very good at meeting girls and was somewhat of a loner. With the promise of some special favors, she persuaded him to give her his Harley Davidson. It was an old bike and was only worth about a thousand dollars. Jimmy's parents were rich and were always trying to make him happy with new toys. He bought himself a brand new Harley.

Jimmy taught her how to ride and soon she felt comfortable on the bike. The two of them spent most of their time together. They took several road trips to New Orleans and the Gulf Shore. Gillian was in love with her new toy. In that time, she became an accomplished rider. She stayed with Jimmy for a few more weeks and gave him memories he would never forget. He had never met a girl like Gillian. Jimmy was the only one who actually knew her real name. She knew that she would eventually move on, but she actually enjoyed spending time with Jimmy.

When she left, it broke his heart.

It was now easier for Gillian to move around from place to place. She was now almost eighteen years old and she had filled out impressively. She was no longer a skinny teenager.

She left Tulane and decided to head north. Eventually she drifted to Ohio. It was here that she met a student named Mike Davis at Ohio State University. Mike was a computer science student. He was 19 years old and had an apartment off campus. They met in a bar near the university and they spent the night partying. Mike was immediately infatuated with her and invited her home. It wasn't long before Gillian had moved in.

Mike was only a sophomore at the time and had not yet begun to take his studies seriously. Every night their life consisted of wild bars and infamous frat parties. Gillian liked to enter wet T-shirt contests and show off what she had to offer.

One night they attended a party that was totally out of control. She climbed up on a table and began to move her hips and shoulders and smile seductively. By this time most of the guys were half-drunk. They doused her in beer and began to pull at her clothes. It made Gillian feel like a real slut.

She loved it.

She pulled off her soaking wet T-shirt and began to swing it over her head, her body glistening in the light, as she danced and moved her hips in a way very few girls could. This was met with loud applause and shouts of encouragement from the guys. Some of the girls liked it too.

Mike was not jealous and he didn't mind being seen with such a beautiful girl. Their lives went on this way for the next few weeks. After about a month their wild life had begun to affect his grades. One of his professors called him into his office and sat him down for a talk. He warned Mike that if his grades didn't improve, he would fail the course. That meant that he might flunk out of school. Ordinarily the prof would not have bothered, but he saw something special in Mike.

It was at about the same time that Mike met a girl in his economics class. They spent some time studying together in the library and were soon meeting regularly. They went on a date to a local restaurant and a movie. Her name was Brittany, and Mike was beginning to fall in love.

She changed his life.

A week later he had to tell Gillian that things had changed. He tried to tell her tactfully that she had to move out. He had found her exciting and fun but he knew that she was not good for him. Gillian was a wild child and a little too crazy for him. Besides, there were suspicions that she had been stealing money from some of the girls at the frat parties and people were beginning to talk.

In the morning Gillian packed her belongings, jumped on her Harley and drove away. She didn't let it show but she felt hurt. It was the first time that she had felt something special for a guy. She turned the bike east and headed for Pennsylvania.

· · · · ·

Gillian thought back about that day. She tried to understand why Mike had tossed her out. She knew about Brittany but was convinced that Mike still preferred her. After all, they were living together. Brittany was just a friend he studied with. It was almost ten years later but a nagging pain still lingered. No other man had ever touched her heart. She always felt a sense of betrayal. She had been really good to Mike.

Why did he leave me? she thought.

Gillian felt a slight stab of anger in her gut. She hit the throttle and let the bike fly down the road. She began to think about all the turns her life had taken since that day... about how her life had changed. She had once imagined that she would marry Mike and that she would spend the rest of her life with him. Everything was all fucked up. Life had betrayed her.

Gillian began to think again about the day she left Ohio. She had headed east and made her way to Penn State. It was there she met a student named Tony Bain in a bar off campus. He was a student at Penn State. She had used her charms effectively and convinced him to share his apartment. She was becoming a pro. She lived there for about a month and fell into a familiar routine. Life might have gone that way for some time except that fate intervened.

Gillian recalled the night she accompanied Tony to a bar in Harrisburg. Tony had gotten drunk early and decided to go back home.

She had decided to stay. It was there she met John and Lisa. John was an older man of about 35. Lisa was a pretty 28-year-old girl. It was Lisa who first spoke to her. She invited Gillian to join her at a table she was sharing with her friend. They introduced themselves and Gillian told them her name was Dana. They sat at the table and John bought a round of drinks for the three of them. Lisa seemed to have a sixth sense about Gillian. After a couple of drinks, she began to open up about her own life and hinted that she and John had a rather unusual means of making a living. This intrigued Gillian, who began to tell them more about her own life. With every drink the three of them got more and more cozy. Lisa explained to her that she and John never spent much time in one place.

"We're grifters," she had finally admitted.

Lisa began to elaborate. They had been running a scam that involved suckering college boys into fronting money to buy a large quantity of cocaine. The girl they had been working with got herself arrested for trying to cash a bad check. They needed a replacement for their con. Greedy, lustful boys were easy targets and Gillian would fit perfectly into their plans.

The scam would run like this:

Gillian would use her special talent to meet college guys and get them to trust her. After a few days she would introduce them to Lisa. Lisa would pose as the girlfriend of a dealer who had been arrested. She would claim that she desperately needed money and didn't have time or know where to unload the drugs.

Gillian would tell them that she had no money of her own. She would ask them if they could get a couple of friends to chip in and get two thousand dollars together to make the deal. She would tell them that she knew where she could sell it and turn a quick profit. They would then go to a remote area far off the beaten path and Lisa would then show them the cocaine she had in the trunk of her car. She would offer them a taste and Gillian and Lisa would also do a line to be more convincing. They would arrange to return to the same place when the mark came up with the money and make the exchange. When the deal went down, John would show up dressed as a cop. He would threaten to arrest them all but would generously offer to let them go if they gave him the money and the drugs. Gillian and Lisa would act scared and plead with the mark to cooperate. After the sting they would arrange to rendezvous and split the cash. Gillian jumped at the idea of making some real money and eagerly agreed to join in.

Gillian did not own a cell phone but agreed to call them when she had found a mark. A few days later she had a fish on the line. She gave Lisa a call. The deal was set up and all three of them played their parts perfectly. They were very convincing. The mark could not go to the police without implicating himself in a felony.

In a few months Gillian, John and Lisa managed to con about thirty thousand dollars. They were constantly on the move and never returned to the same place. She never saw Tony or Penn State again. Gillian found this life style exciting and became more and more willing to take chances. She actually opened a bank account. She considered herself a success. She liked the action.

· · · · ·

Gillian decided to take a break and pulled her Harley over into a convenience store and got a Pepsi. She decided to take a short walk in the wooded area near the side of the road to give her legs some exercise. She let the sun shine down on her face and breathed in the fresh mountain air. It was a relief to leave her past behind, if only for a moment. After a half hour she was back on the bike, heading for New Hampshire.

Her mind drifted back to that fateful day almost ten years earlier. She had continued to participate in the con with her two companions John and Lisa. She recalled how one day things had gone terribly wrong. The mark had suspected a scam and had put up a fight. He was not a small person. John had to stab him in the neck with a knife to fend him off. It was not a fatal wound, but he began to bleed profusely. Lisa screamed and was almost frantic. Gillian, however, had remained totally calm. She remembered watching intently and recalled the sudden rush she felt. It seemed to exhilarate her whole body. She felt an excitement inside her she had never felt before. Gillian was beginning to change.

John and Lisa decided it would be best to stay low and they decided to split up. Gillian made her way back to Florida and resumed her old ways, finding guys to shack up with. John and Lisa headed for California.

· · · · ·

The years went by and Gillian was now almost 27. With each passing day the pathology that was stalking her continued to progress. Bad chemicals were beginning to invade her brain. With every passing day Gillian became more prone to violence.

She had become a very dangerous girl.

Gillian had been involved in several violent altercations in the last few years, including several robberies, but somehow managed to avoid being arrested. She had become addicted to thrill-seeking and danger. With each new experience she became more emboldened. She loved the adrenalin rush that came with close calls.

· · · · ·

Gillian's mind snapped out of her daydream and she continued to glide through the mountain passes of Route 302. She could see the high peaks of the White Mountains in the distance. She had started her journey in Florida two months earlier. Until just recently, she had never been in any serious trouble—nothing she could do hard time for—but things had changed now.

She began to think about what had happened to her in the past few weeks. It had all begun in Youngstown at the State University of Ohio. Gillian had once again resorted to her familiar routine of finding guys who would put her up and do her favors. This time it was a student named

Randy. She had arrived on campus just as the Easter vacation had begun. The dorm was empty and Randy's roommate would be gone for the next ten days. He couldn't resist Gillian's advances and agreed to let her stay.

After two nights together, Gillian began to regret her choice. Randy wasn't exactly qualified to write the Kama Sutra. In addition to this, he had a few obnoxious habits. And he snored like a rhinoceros. When they awoke in the morning Gillian made up her mind to ditch him. Randy decided to take a shower and left Gillian in the room by herself. He had taken her out to dinner the previous night and made a point of trying to impress her with a large roll of hundred-dollar bills he kept in his pocket. Randy was not in the top five percent of his class academically. She didn't mean him any harm but couldn't resist the opportunity. She quickly got herself dressed and went through his pockets. Just as she found the money Randy came back in through the door.

Whether it was a matter of hurt pride or just righteous indignation, Gillian would never know. He grabbed her by the arm and screamed at her, *You bitch. You rotten little bitch.*

He tried to pin her against the wall but Gillian surprised him with her strength. She brought her knee up between his legs and for a moment he was stunned and fell to the floor. She made an attempt to get out the door but he grabbed her by the ankle and held on. He wasn't going to let go. Randy started screaming for help at the top of his lungs. She continued to try to break free but he was tenacious. Anger welled up in Gillian's mind. She wasn't going to let this impotent little prick take her down. For the past six years Gillian had always carried a hunting knife with her for protection. She swung around and took off her backpack, unzipped the side compartment and took out the knife. She stooped down, grabbed Randy by the hair, and with one vicious stroke cut his throat from ear to ear.

At first, she was shocked by what she had done. She picked up her backpack and was about to run out the door, but instead she hesitated. She turned and watched with fascination as Randy grabbed his throat. He had a look of terror in his eyes. Blood was pouring out onto the floor.

After a few seconds Randy stopped struggling but the blood continued to flow for almost a minute. Gillian felt an adrenalin rush. A strange feeling came over her. It was almost sexual in nature and she felt exhilarated. She watched for another minute as the blood began to pool up in the corner.

There was no one else in the dormitory. Gillian stopped in the washroom and cleaned the blood from her face and hands. She checked her hair and clothes and made sure that she removed every trace. When she was good to go, she left the campus and headed east toward Buffalo, New York.

Maybe Randy didn't deserve to die, she thought. *Oh well, there is nothing I can do about it now.*

Gillian remembered having those thoughts that day and how her life had changed since then. What was happening to her? It all seemed surreal. She was never a saint, but now she had become a different person. At first, she had a pang of guilt and remorse but now she felt completely detached.

The distinction between right and wrong was becoming cloudy.

CHAPTER 27

Sunday Afternoon, June 13

The road curved onward over hills and dips like an amusement park ride. Her mind went back to her younger days and she began to think about Mike Davis. She opened the throttle wide and let the Harley fly. Mike was still the only man that had ever meant anything to her.

When she reached Bretton Woods, she could see Mount Washington towering above the trees. Gillian slowed down and pulled her Harley into a convenience store parking lot. She noticed that the wind had blown the top buttons of her shirt open, revealing her breasts. She could see the clerk inside the store, who had heard her bike as she pulled in and now seemed to be quite interested in her arrival. He couldn't have been more than fifteen.

Let's have a little fun, she thought.

She smiled to herself and purposely left her shirt unbuttoned. As she dismounted her bike, she let her shirt fall loosely away from her body. Gillian took a quick look at the boy behind the counter whose eyes were now riveted on her. She walked into the store prepared a cup of coffee, picked up a newspaper and went to the register.

"What's your name, cutie?" she said, putting on her most seductive smile.

"Boo," he stammered. "Bobby... Bobby. What's yours?"

Gillian did all she could to stifle a laugh. "My name is Giselle. Can you tell me what mountain that is?" she said pointing upwards, making sure her left breast was completely visible to him.

"That's Mount Washington. I've climbed it several times. It's the highest mountain in the state. Over six thousand feet," he managed to get out. Bobby thought he was going to pass out on the spot.

"Is it hard?" said Gillian, leaning provocatively over the counter.

"What?"

"To get to the top. Is it hard?"

"Oh! It takes me and my friends about two and a half hours."

"Is it nice being on top?"

"Yeah. It's awesome. You should try it."

"Maybe I will," said Gillian, smiling impishly as she turned and walked out of the store.

Bobby never took his eyes off her.

Let's tease him a little more. This is too much fun, she mused.

Gillian walked back outside and took a seat on the bench in front of the store. It was just below the window at the end of the counter where Bobby was working. She had her back to him and she was sure he would try to get another sneak peek. She sipped her coffee and began to read the paper. It was a copy of the Boston Globe. The headline was about terrorism. The FBI was concerned about ISIS recruitment on the internet.

Interesting. I've never been to Boston. Maybe I should check it out. She began to think.

She continued to read further and her eyes caught a small article about three college students who had been brutally murdered about two weeks earlier in Brighton, New York. The article went on to say that the police had yet to identify any suspects. The left corner of her mouth began to turn upward and a satisfied smile curled across her lips.

Gillian let the afternoon sun warm and bathe her body. She closed her eyes and let her mind drift back in time. It was two weeks earlier when she first arrived at the SUNY Buffalo campus. It was May 27 and the spring semester was over. Just like in Youngstown, the campus was almost deserted and her odds of finding a place to stay here were not good. After looking around for a few hours she figured her best shot was to find out where the best watering holes were. She began to ask around. She noticed a pretty girl walking by who appeared to be a good person to ask.

"Excuse me. I'm new here and I'd like to get an idea of where the best party places are."

"Don't waste any time, do you?" she said with a laugh. "There are several places close by but my favorite is called the Lighthouse. It's about ten miles away over in Brighton. You take I-90 north. Then get off on 266 towards Tonawanda. It's right on the Niagara River."

"Are you going to be there tonight?" asked Gillian.

"Maybe. I don't know yet, but the place is always packed. You'll have a good time."

It was still too early for the nightclub and Gillian decided to check out Niagara Falls first. She remembered being awed by its power. There were still so many things in the world that she wanted to see. After spending the rest of the afternoon there she drove her Harley back toward Tonawanda. There were beautiful views of the Niagara river on her right. She took her time and stopped for dinner on the way.

It was just after ten o'clock when Gillian arrived at the Lighthouse. She took off her helmet, chained it to her bike and put on the cowboy hat she had purchased at the falls. After the bouncer checked her I.D., she walked straight to the lady's room and checked her look in the mirror.

She remembered thinking, *Watch out, guys.*

She left the lady's room and took a seat at a table in the corner. In less than a minute there was a group of three guys looking at her and talking amongst themselves. They continued to talk for several minutes and Gillian was beginning to wonder if they would ever have the balls to come over and start a conversation.

Eventually one of them came over to her and said, "Hi. My name is Frank. Can I join you?"

He seemed attractive enough to Gillian and she said, "Sure, grab a seat. My name is Celeste."

"That's a beautiful name to go with a beautiful face."

"Oh, thank you. That's sweet. Do you come here often?"

"Probably about three nights a week. I live pretty close by. I share a house with a couple of friends."

"Are those your roommates you were just talking to?"

"No. Actually I live with a couple of girls."

"Oh. A real lady's man."

"Not really. Say, can I get you something to drink?"

"Sure. How about a Jack and soda?"

"Comin' right up."

After a few minutes Frank returned with her drink and they continued to talk. Gillian began to work her charms and in less than ten minutes she had found out that he lived in a house nearby.

"I've never seen you here before, Celeste. Are you from around here?"

"No. Actually I just got to Buffalo today. I was heading east to New York and I figured I'd stop and see Niagara Falls. Do you know a decent motel where I could stay the night?"

"You could stay at my place," Frank offered smoothly.

"Oh great. That's really nice of you. That makes things simple."

Things were going according to plan.

Gillian watched as two girls who had been at the bar chatting with some guys walked over to their table. One was a blonde about five foot nine. She had a pretty face and was an attractive girl, although she was built rather solidly and looked like she would make a good middle linebacker.

The other was a brunette. She was a very pretty girl, about five foot six, with a more demure stature.

"Celeste, these are my housemates Angela and Leslie."

"Hi, Celeste. Nice to meet you," said Angela in a deep, sultry voice.

"Same here," said Leslie.

The three of them sat down and began to engage in small talk.

After a few drinks Angela said, "I've never seen you here before, Celeste. Are you from around here?"

"I just got finished telling Frank I'm heading east and stopped to see Niagara Falls."

"Where are you staying?"

"Frank just offered to let me stay the night if that's okay," said Gillian, looking at Frank for reassurance.

"Sure. That's fine," said Angela quickly. "We live just down the road."

"No problem," added Leslie. "That way I can have a couple more drinks."

They continued to talk and soon a large, oafish-looking man carrying a helmet in his hand walked over to them. He put a capful of white powder on table.

"Can I interest anyone in this?" he asked.

Angela looked up and said, "I'm assuming that's coke."

"Finest in town," he said, spreading a line on the table.

Gillian and her three companions all looked at each other.

"Why not?" said Angela.

They all smiled and agreed. Frank generously offered to buy an eight ball for the four of them. The man with the motorcycle helmet slipped a small packet to Frank and then put some more lines on the table. Frank rolled up a crisp twenty-dollar bill and looked carefully around the room. He snorted up a line and handed the bill to Gillian.

"Here you go, Celeste."

Gillian took her turn and handed the twenty to Leslie. When they had all had a blast, Frank suggested another round of drinks. Half an hour later they were all flying high.

Frank put out another four lines and suggested, "We'll save the rest for when we get home."

The coke was keeping them somewhat sober and making them talk more than they usually did. An hour later it was almost one o'clock and the club was about to close. The bartender announced last call.

"Hey, Celeste. I have a green Dodge Challenger parked around the corner. What are you driving?"

"I've got my Harley parked right outside. It's about twenty yards down the block."

"Ooooh. A biker chick. I like it," said Leslie.

"I'll swing around and you can follow us back to our place. It's about a quarter mile down Brighton Road. I'll get my car."

"Okay. Sounds good. See you out front."

Gillian left the club and jumped on her bike. Within a minute Frank appeared with his car and she followed him back to his house. The two of them went inside.

"Make yourself comfortable on the couch. I'll get us a couple of beers."

A few minutes later Angela and Leslie walked in and joined her in the living room. Frank came back from the kitchen carrying four bottles of Stella. He took a seat on the sofa with Gillian and pulled a glass top table toward him. He took out the packet of cocaine and put another four lines out.

"You first, Celeste. You're our special guest," said Frank.

They all did another line and continued to drink beer.

"So what do you plan on doing in New York, Celeste?" Angela asked her, trying to keep the conversation active.

"I've never been there. I just want to check it out. I've heard it's different from anywhere I've ever seen."

"I was there once. I went to the top of the Empire State Building. You gotta do that. It was so cool," said Leslie.

They kept drinking beer and Frank put out more lines. They were all getting very wired.

Leslie took her turn and handed the makeshift straw to Gillian. "Thanks, Leslie," she said.

"Call me Lez," she said with a smile.

Angela let out a soft chuckle. After a while Gillian started to notice that Leslie kept looking at her. Her eyes were becoming more intense with each minute. Angela looked back and forth from Gillian to Leslie, smiling as if she and her roommate had a special secret to share. Gillian was beginning to catch on.

Frank put out some more coke and said, "This is the last of it. One more line for each of us."

Frank did his first and gave the straw to Leslie. She moved closer to the table and did a line for herself. Gillian took her turn and offered the straw to Angela who got up from her chair and bent over the table. She snorted the last line.

Instead of returning to her own chair she sat down on the sofa next to Gillian. She lay back, relaxed and let the palms of her hands slide down the top of her thighs.

"I feel so good," she said.

Frank watched with amusement. She then put her hand casually on Gillian's thigh. Instinctively she pulled away and moved closer to Frank. Gillian wasn't gay but was always open to trying new things. Perhaps if they had approached her differently, she could have been persuaded to join in on their sexual adventure. However, Angela took her initial reaction as an unwillingness to participate. Angela gave Frank a nod.

He took Gillian by the shoulders and pinned her down on the sofa.

Angela grabbed her legs and held on while Gillian began to fight and kick.

"Get the fuck off of me," she yelled at Frank trying to free herself.

Frank was surprised at Gillian's strength. He had to put his full weight down on her shoulders with his knees as he held on to her arms.

Angela managed to finally get control of her legs. She eagerly unbuckled Gillian's belt and unzipped her jeans.

Frank pulled her T-shirt up above her breasts and ran his hand down to her stomach.

Together the two of them managed to get her jeans below her knees.

"Come on, Lez. Don't be shy. Join us," said Angela.

At first, she seemed reluctant to participate but after some further encouragement from Frank she decided to join in. She found Gillian irresistibly sexy and the coke had gotten her totally excited. Leslie got on her knees by the sofa and put her hand on Gillian's stomach and began to kiss her passionately up and down her body.

Gillian began to fight with everything she had.

"I'm sorry," said Leslie in a guilty voice, but she continued to have her way with Gillian's body.

Gillian began to arch and twist violently but her efforts were in vain against the three of them.

Angela forced her knees apart and brought her hand up slowly between her thighs. "Wow. What a body!" she said with a lascivious grin.

Gillian glared at her with the eyes of an angry snake.

Frank continued to pin her down painfully, with his knees still on her shoulders. He began to caress her breasts and then ran his hand all the way down to where Angela was already at play.

Gillian's struggles only heightened their excitement.

Angela unzipped Frank's pants and pulled out his already rock-hard cock. She gave it a couple of strokes and then undid her own jeans. She put her hand inside and got herself aroused.

"Hey, Leslie. Come have a taste of this," said Angela with an enthusiastic laugh.

Like a pack of hungry wolves, they all had a piece of Gillian.

Angela continued to caress her in her most sacred spot.

Through no choice of her own Gillian became aroused herself. Her body tensed and after one final moment of defiance she surrendered. Her body relaxed and her breathing slowed. "Get the fuck off me," she screamed at them again.

Frank took his knees off of her shoulders and the three of them let her get up.

Gillian quickly pulled up her pants and glared at them.

"We'd invite you to stay, but we only have three beds," said Frank sarcastically.

"That's not true, Frank. You can share mine, Celeste," said Leslie.

She was half serious and hoping she would say yes.

Gillian felt the rage well up inside her but knew it was hopeless to fight all three of them, and her knife was in the saddleback of her bike.

"I've really got to go to the bathroom. Can I just use yours?"

"Sure. Why not?" said Frank with a callous, unfeeling smirk.

Gillian went to the bathroom, threw some water on her face and looked in the mirror. The look in her eyes frightened even Gillian herself. She found the window and judged that she could get through it. She unlatched the lock, opened it slightly and walked back to the living room.

She walked past the three of them without as much as a glance and screamed, "Fuck you" as she went out the door.

It was now almost three o'clock in the morning. She got on her bike and drove down the block. When she was about a hundred yards away she pulled over, got off the bike and got her knife and a tiny Maglite out of the saddlebag. She made her way back toward house where she had just been raped. She watched from the bushes and watched the lights go out in the living room. A moment later the upstairs lights went on. She waited until all the lights were out again.

Another twenty minutes, she thought to herself.

She made her way around the back of the house, pushed the bathroom window open and with the skill of a ninja slipped inside. She turned on the Maglite to the dimmest setting and found the stairs. She took off her shoes and began to climb her way up. There was a soft creak as she hit one of the steps. She waited for a moment, listened and then continued to climb. Gillian got to the top of the stairs and saw an open door on the left. She looked in. She could see Leslie's dark hair on the pillow. She moved on to the next room. Angela seemed to be fast asleep. She continued down the hall and came to Frank's room. Her anger was beginning to peak. Frank was asleep on his stomach and snoring lightly. With one quick move she straddled his body, pulled his head back and cut his throat almost to his spine. Blood gushed out as she pushed his face into the pillow.

"It's too bad you can't scream with your throat cut. Isn't it?" she whispered in his ear.

She kept her knees pressed firmly down on his back. Gillian was hoping Frank was coherent enough to understand what was happening to him. In a few seconds he stopped struggling. She got off of him, lifted his head and looked in his terrified eyes. She smiled as she watched the last signs of life leave his body.

Gillian quietly made her way back down the hall and went into Angela's room. She was on her back with her long blond hair loosely draped about the pillows. She tiptoed up to the bed and stood over her. Angela's soft white neck was fully exposed. Gillian paused for a few seconds to savor the moment and then pulled the knife slowly across her throat. Angela's body began to twist in spasms as blood splashed over everything, including Gillian. The last thing Angela saw was a pair of cobra eyes glaring at her. It was a moment Gillian would treasure.

Apparently, the noise had woken Leslie, who called out, "What's going on?"

A few moments later Gillian walked slowly into her room, still carrying the Maglite. The dimly lit visage of Gillian, covered in blood, sent a bolt of terror through Leslie's body.

She sat up in bed and began to scream. She could see the gleam of the knife as it turned in the soft light. Gillian continued to walk slowly across the room and sat on the bed next to her. She whispered, "Shhhhhh. Still want to share your bed with me?"

Leslie's eyes were bulging out like two large marbles.

"I just want you to know, I think you're a very pretty girl, Leslie. If you had asked me nicely, I probably would have done anything you wanted. We could have had fun together."

She pushed her down on her back, straddled her body and placed her hand on Leslie's left breast. "Do you like that?" she whispered.

Leslie's heart was pounding. She struggled frantically to free herself but she wasn't strong enough. She looked up helplessly into Gillian's eyes and resigned herself to her fate.

Gillian brought her face closer to Leslie's, hesitated for a moment, looked her in the eyes and kissed her passionately on the lips. "I know this wasn't your fault. It was your friends who planned it all. I really don't blame you or hate you. But you have to understand that I can't let you live."

With those words Leslie's heart began to jackhammer in her chest.

Gillian drew her knife quickly across her throat. Blood began to gush out with each beat of her heart. Gillian kept her hand on Leslie's chest, pushing her down into the bed. It took almost half a minute before her heart beat for the last time. Leslie's eyes softened as the life left her body. They remained fixed on Gillian, who was looking down on her sympathetically. It was as if she had received redemption from her.

Gillian sat on the bed and just watched her with curiosity. *She's even more beautiful now,* she thought.

After a few minutes Gillian walked to the bathroom and climbed in the shower fully clothed. She let the warm water wash her clean. When she was done, she took off all her clothes, got a few towels, and pushed them down the hallway with her feet. She went to the basement and put her T-shirt and jeans in the dryer. Half an hour later she got dressed, walked upstairs and put on her shoes. She made sure the front door was locked and then climbed out the living room window. It was now 4:40 AM. By five o'clock she was on I-90 East.

· · · · ·

Gillian's mind snapped back to the present. She took another sip of coffee. She smiled and remembered Bobby. She let her head hang backwards to look in the window. Sure enough, there he was, looking down at her. He suddenly vanished from the window. She had to laugh.

Guys are all the same, she thought.

Gillian folded the newspaper, gulped down the last of her coffee and got back on her bike. She took a last look in the window and waved goodbye to Bobby, who waved back. She turned the Harley around in the parking lot and roared off down the road. Bobby raced outside, ran to the road and watched until she was out of sight. Bobby didn't sleep a wink that night. He spent the entire night in bed fantasizing about her.

CHAPTER 28

Gillian let her mind wander as she made her way east toward the Maine border. Route 302 was dotted with small, bucolic towns that were rich in American history. The sun was beginning to set when she noticed an old cemetery by the roadside. There was something about the humble simplicity of the gravestones that drew her attention. The grass had not been cut for some time and it partially obscured some of the names and dates. It seemed to Gillian as if no one was willing to wake the dead and chose instead to let them rest in peace. There were many graves with dates going back to the 1700s. She took notice of one in particular. The name Mary Taylor was fading on the ash-colored granite stone. Below it were the dates 1747- 1774.

Only twenty-seven years old, she thought. *I wonder what her life was like and why she died so young.*

She remained there for some time, just looking at the grave and wondering. Eventually, Gillian got back on her Harley and pulled away, looking back one more time at the haunting image. She was deep in thought as she rode through the beautiful countryside. She thought about what had happened to her in Brighton.

Frank and Angela deserved what they got, she thought. *Perhaps all three of them did. In any case I couldn't let Leslie live. I had to finish what I started.*

Gillian could justify what she had done up until the time she left Buffalo. What happened after that was not so easy. At that time, she had committed four murders in less than two months. Somehow it had changed her. The thought of killing was becoming more acceptable to her. There were times that she felt compassion and a sense of right and wrong. At other times she felt anger. Sometimes she felt nothing at all. Two separate and distinct sides of Gillian were beginning to emerge. One of them was going to prevail.

Gillian thought about the hours after she left Buffalo and the plans she had come up with.

For the past several years Gillian had a phony license that she had stolen from a girl at a frat party. Her name was Danielle Stewart. She kept it just in case she was pulled over by the cops. She also used it to get into bars and nightclubs. She never used that name when she was meeting new people, but she had used that license to get into the Lighthouse.

What if the bouncer remembers my name? She worried. *Sometimes guys make a point of remembering me. What if I get pulled over and the cops recognize the name? There were plenty of people who saw me with Frank and the others at the Lighthouse. Did anyone see me ride away on my bike? What about Youngstown? Would the police be able to tie all these things together? Could they track me down? I need to disappear and become somebody else. But how?*

Gillian began to think about it more seriously as she headed toward Rochester. Whether it was logical or not, it seemed to her that she needed to assume a new identity. She needed to find someone who looked like her and wouldn't be missed. The idea became more and more appealing to her.

Where can I find someone whose identity I could steal? A college coed would be missed right away. So would a waitress or a girl with a nine to five job. Maybe a streetwalker. Of course. The police wouldn't bother to look into the disappearance of a hooker. But I have to find the right one.

Gillian decided to pay a visit to Rochester University and get some information. She walked into the college library. She went straight to the computer room. First, she googled *remote wooded areas outside Rochester.* She got several hits. She got a pen and wrote down the name Corbett's Glen and took note of how to get there. It seemed the perfect place for her purpose. She then googled *where do prostitutes hang out in Rochester?* Instantly the computer spit out four different locations. Gillian wrote them down. Lyell Avenue, Hudson Avenue, Bay Street and Monroe Avenue. It was amazing what you could find out on Google. Gillian decided to try her luck on Monroe Avenue first. She parked her Harley and walked up and down the street, looking for girls with dark hair who were her approximate height. She struck up several conversations, pretending to be a working girl herself. Not one of them seemed to be a good choice. It appeared they all had close ties to the other girls in the neighborhood. Gillian was looking for a loner. She decided to move on to another hunting ground.

Gillian cruised down Lyell Avenue. There were several girls already on the street, although it was only three o'clock in the afternoon. They came in all different sizes and colors.

"Whatever you want, honey" was a phrase heard a hundred times a night. Gillian slowed her bike and began to look closely at one of the girls. She had dark brown hair. She wasn't as beautiful as Gillian, but she had a pretty face and a tight body. She seemed to be about 25 years old. Gillian rode another fifty yards and parked her Harley on the side of the road. She got off her bike and began to walk back nonchalantly in the direction of the girl she had just sized up. She stood for a moment, pretending to be interested in a display in a clothing store window. She continued to glance over and study her quarry like a leopard planning an attack. Gillian could sense that this girl was somehow different from the others. She waited a few more minutes and then walked over to her.

"Hi," said Gillian. "Want to try something different? I'll make it worth your time."

A smile came slowly to the girl's lips and she said sheepishly, "Well, what are we talking about?" She expected that she would be asked to do a threesome with her and a boyfriend or something like that. It wouldn't be the first time someone asked her. Gillian took note that the girl had green eyes like her own. They were also roughly the same height and weight.

"Oh, just some good, clean fun. Nothing too crazy. My name is Roxanne. You can call me Roxy." As usual Gillian never used her real name. "How about we share a beer and get to know each other? It's on me," said Gillian.

"They call me Star around here. That's not my real name, of course," the girl replied.

"Come on. How's that bar down the street? I'm buying and I'll tell you what I want."

"Okay. Let's go."

The two of them sat at the bar for over an hour as Gillian got her to loosen up. The walls came down and Star told Gillian her real name was Michelle. She had been working the streets for the last four years, after her mother had thrown her out. Her mother had caught her and her stepfather fooling around on the couch when she walked into the living room unexpectedly. She blamed it on Michelle and went crazy. Gillian told Michelle a story of half-truths about her life. She kept telling Michelle how pretty she was and that she was very attracted to her. She said that she had some bad experiences with men and was sick of them. She added that she had been curious about being with another girl but had never yet tried it. As the time went by, Gillian coaxed more and more personal information out of Michelle. She was way too trusting to be in her line of work. Michelle was quite impressed with Gillian. She was actually intrigued by her offer.

"Do you have a lot of friends in the area, Michelle?"

"Not really. I know this girl, Maxine, who lets me stay at her place sometimes. That's about it."

Gillian listened with increasing interest. "Say, it's getting late," said Gillian. Why don't we find a place where we can be alone?"

"I know a motel just down the road. It's twenty bucks an hour for a room."

"Ya know, I got a better idea. It's a beautiful evening and I love nature. I know just the spot where we can be alone. We can go there on my Harley."

"Ooooh. A cycle slut," said Michelle with a laugh.

"Gotta keep up appearances."

Michelle was beginning to like Gillian and was looking forward to their tryst. "Aren't you going to ask me what I charge?" asked Michelle, smiling flirtatiously.

"Okay. How much?"

"For you, how about two hundred for the rest of the day?"

"You've got a deal. Let's get out of here."

Gillian got on her Harley, kick started it and Michelle climbed on behind her. They set out for the Corbett's Glen nature preserve.

• • • • •

Gillian's mind snapped back to the present. The images of the graveyard were still haunting her. The sun had set and darkness was beginning to settle in. She turned the headlight on and continued riding east. She was still 30 miles from I-95. That would take her south toward Boston and New York.

Gillian began thinking about what she had done after she had left Buffalo. She thought about the moment Michelle had climbed on the back of her motorcycle and remembered thinking to herself, *Can I really go through with this? This girl hasn't done anything to me.*

The two sides of Gillian were at war. At the time it seemed perfectly logical to carry out her plan. The side of her that was normal, if there ever really was one, was losing out. She had no regrets about Frank and Angela. She actually enjoyed killing them, but this was different. In spite of her chosen profession, Michelle actually seemed like a decent person. The murders of Randy and Leslie weren't as easy to live with. Gillian continued to struggle with her conscience. The two different sides of her could not live in the same body. Ultimately, she had to kill the side that was nagging at her. It was at that moment that she lost herself. The old Gillian was completely gone. She opened the throttle and raced down the road, leaving her conscience behind in the darkness.

She began to think about Michelle again, this time in a different light. She thought about how she had persuaded her to walk down a dimly lit trail that led them deep into a remote part of the woods. They came to a spot where there was a large pile of stones by the side of a small pond. *Perfect*, she thought.

"It's just a little farther. You've got to see this place. It's so beautiful."

Michelle was like a deer in the headlights. She had no clue what was coming. Gillian came up behind her and put her arms around Michelle's waist.

"Time to give me what I want," she whispered in her ear.

Michelle smiled and said, "I'm all yours. Take anything you want."

Gillian pulled the knife from her jacket, grabbed Michelle's hair and coldly slit her throat. Blood began to flow in a torrent and quickly soaked Michelle's T-shirt. She never really understood what had happened to her.

Gillian felt Michelle's body go limp and let it slip through her arms to the ground. She watched her eyes as she lay there, looking up at her with a puzzled gaze.

"It's okay," she whispered. "I'm here for you."

Gillian watched as the last spark of life disappeared from Michelle's eyes. She walked over to the pond and rinsed her knife clean. She put it back in the sheath and stowed it in her jacket. After she had cleaned most of the blood from her arms, she picked up Michelle's handbag. She took out her wallet and checked her license picture.

Good enough, she thought.

Gillian put it in her pocket. She then took out her Visa and ATM cards and kept them as well. When she was satisfied there was no further identification, she tossed the bag aside. She then got Michelle's cell phone, went to settings and changed the password. She checked the call log and saw that most of the recent calls were from guys. Only their first name was given. There was Tom, Dave, Greg and Max. None of them had called in the last week.

Probably just clients, she thought. *I doubt they're going to cause any trouble.*

She went to Facebook and checked her home page. Only five friends followed her.

Sad, she thought. *She really was alone in the world.*

Gillian put the cell phone in her pocket. She then took Michelle's lifeless body by the armpits and dragged her over to a large pile of softball sized rocks by the river bed. She placed her in a small, shallow depression and began to pile the rocks on top of her. An hour later she was satisfied that she had done a good job in concealing the body. She looked down at her jeans and shoes and noticed that they were still covered in blood. It was a warm night and Gillian had plenty of time. She waded into the pond, stooped down and began to wash the blood away. When she was done, she walked back over to the grave she had just prepared for Michelle. She stood there and said a few final words for her.

"Thank you," she said out loud.

Michelle's body would never be found.

Gillian walked back along the trail to where she had parked her Harley and was soon on her way.

• • • • •

Once again Gillian's mind snapped back to the present. She saw a sign for a Stewarts convenience store and stopped to fill the Harley with gas. She got a cup of coffee, sat on a bench outside the store and thought about Bobby. She wondered if he had gotten her out of his mind by now.

Probably not, she thought. She chuckled to herself. It made her feel better.

• • • • •

It was less than two weeks earlier that Gillian was at the University of Albany campus. It was there that she met George Weston. He also rode a Harley, and they hit it off right away. At first, he seemed like a nice guy and Gillian felt she could trust him. They spent the night together and things were going well. The following morning, he suggested taking a ride out to Thompson Lake Camping Area out on State Road 157. Little did she know that George was hiding a dark, sinister side of himself. When they arrived at the camping area George's behavior began to change. He started dropping hints about his special desires. Gillian was not willing to play along and let him know it. George was not one to take no for an answer. He began to get rough with her and slapped her across the face. He had no idea of the buzz saw he was walking into. Gillian flew into a rage and kicked him square in the balls. This infuriated George. She saw it coming and turned away from him, concealing her actions. She quickly pulled her knife from her jacket and made an attempt to get away from him. Gillian didn't want to kill him but he ran after her and tried to take her down. She made what could only be described as a brilliant defensive move and somehow wound up on top of him. She stabbed him once in the side of the neck and then finished him off with a quick cut across the throat. She jumped up off of him and did her best to avoid the arterial spray. She really wanted to get away clean and quickly got back to her Harley. In minutes she was on her way. She figured it was a good idea to stop heading east and instead went to Route 87 and headed north for the Adirondacks.

What the hell is going on? she thought. She began to think about what happened in Buffalo and what had taken place just moments before. *Is it my own fault?* She started to believe it might be her life style and the way she dressed that was inviting trouble. Actually, it went much deeper than that.

• • • • •

Gillian finished her coffee and got back on her bike. She hit the throttle and the Harley roared down the road, leaving the past far behind.

CHAPTER 29

Sunday night June 14

Gillian continued riding through the Maine countryside. She had planned to make it all the way to Boston but the night air was beginning to cool. She was still 25 miles from I-95 when she felt the first raindrops on her face. Soon it was coming down steadily and the road was becoming slick. Gillian was getting tired and decided it would be better to stop and rest. She saw a large green and white sign by the side of the road. It said The Maple Leaf Motel. It had an inviting look about it and she decided to pull over. She walked into the office and checked in with her old license. She wasn't going to start using Michelle's for another week, just in case somebody had reported her missing. She got to her room, lay down on her bed, and drifted off into sleep.

Gillian awoke eight hours later. She went to the window and pulled back the curtain. The rain had washed the air clean and it promised to be beautiful day. She felt refreshed and optimistic about the future. It was a brand new day.

She walked outside and breathed in the cool, fresh morning air of the Maine woods and thought, *Why not spend some more time up here? There's no reason to rush off to the big city.*

It was only a quarter to eight and checkout time wasn't until eleven. She took a short trip to the convenience store down the road and got a cup of coffee and Monday's issue of the *Boston Globe*. She returned to the motel and sat in a chair in front of her room. She sipped her coffee and began to read the headlines. The top story was about the future of low-income housing in Boston. The gentrification of some neighborhoods which had provided affordable housing for many low-income families was becoming an election issue. The mayor was under fire for his policies, which seemed to cater to rich land developers. She read further about a bank executive who had started a hedge fund and was becoming a major player in urban development and Boston's future. His name was Kevin Reardon. There was a picture of him and his wife on the front page next to the article.

Must be nice to be rich, she thought. She read further and the article mentioned that he worked for Lexington Finance. She continued browsing through the paper taking an occasional sip of coffee.

Gillian was startled when Michelle's cell phone suddenly rang in her pocket. She was hoping that would never happen. *Oh shit,* she thought to herself. *Somebody's always got to be a pain in the ass.*

She had never owned a cell phone herself but was familiar with how they worked. She allowed the call to go to voicemail.

"Hi, Mickey. It's Maxine. I haven't seen you in over two weeks . Where are you? Give me a call, okay?"

Gillian thought about messaging her back and making up some kind of story but decided it might complicate things.

Better leave it alone, she thought.

Gillian started to play with the cell phone and looked at some of the icons. There was Facebook, the iTunes store, Music, the App store, Google and several others. She tapped the Google icon and the format came up.

What should I ask it? she mused. She thought for a few moments. *Mike. Let's find out about Mike,* she decided.

She tapped in Mike Davis. The name of an American author and a famous baseball player came up. She tried Mike Davis: Ohio State Alumni. The picture of a professor appeared. When that failed, she tried Mike Davis: computer science. A list of several people from all over the country came up. She began to read about each one. One by one she eliminated them as possibilities. She began to read about a successful software engineer who worked for a company named Affirmed Software. She read on. More information began to come up. He now lived in Forest Park, New York. He had a wife named Brittany.

Brittany. That was her name. She's the one who stole Mike away from me.

Gillian decided to google Affirmed Software. Google gave a New York City address as well as an upstate address in Albany. She googled Forest Park and saw that it was close to Albany.

That's got to be where he works, she thought.

It was amazing how quickly she was able to find out all about him. It had taken less than five minutes. She continued to read about Affirmed Software and tried to find out as much as she could. She tried Affirmed Software clients. To her surprise a long list appeared on the phone. She went down the list and came to one that sounded familiar. *Lexington Finance. Where had she heard that name?*

Her mind struggled to recall. *Of course, the article in the paper.*

She picked up the *Globe* and read the article again: *Kevin Reardon, Hedge Fund Manager and Bank Executive.*

The wheels began to turn in Gillian's mind. She tried googling Lexington Finance. A link to the webpage appeared. She accessed the site and a description of who Lexington was came up. They specialized in financing private real estate ventures in the northeast.

Gillian never had a formal education but she was very shrewd and very streetwise. Her intelligence was certainly not a handicap. She wasn't sure exactly what she had in mind but she decided to on a fishing expedition. Maybe she was just curious about Mike after all these years. It was Monday morning and only ten minutes to nine. Most engineers would not be at work yet. She decided to call Affirmed Software. She googled the phone number for the Albany office and dialed the number.

"Affirmed Software. Diane speaking. How can I help you?"

"Hello. I'm with Lexington Finance in Boston. We have an account with you. We seem to be having a problem accessing some of our clients' records. I would like to ask a few questions about the current software. Can I speak with one of your specialists?"

"Mr. Davis is the expert on that. He isn't in right now. He should be here any minute. Should I have him call you back?"

Bingo, thought Gillian. Whether it was fate or just dumb luck she wasn't sure, but it seemed to her that something was beckoning her to follow this road. "No. I'll call back later. It's not an emergency. Maybe we can figure it out on our end."

"Very well. Goodbye then."

Gillian sat back in her chair and began to think. After almost ten years, she still felt a spark for Mike. She began to wonder what her life would be like now if he hadn't cut her loose.

I don't think I would have ever left him. I know he cared about me. I wonder what would have happened if that bitch Brittany hadn't showed up?

The more she thought about it the angrier she got. The bad chemicals in her brain were on the march again. *I wonder what Mike is like now. I wonder if he's got kids. Is he still in love with Brittany?*

With every minute she was becoming more obsessed. She dug her nails into the chair and her eyes flared.

Her cell phone rang. It was Affirmed returning her call.

Caller I.D. Of course. I should be more careful. She let the call go to voicemail.

"Hello, Ms. Dennis. This is Mike Davis with Affirmed returning your call. I see that you're calling from a private number. I assume you're working from your home computer. If you have any problems, please don't hesitate to call. Goodbye."

Gillian was tempted to pick up the phone and talk to him but she thought it would be better if she weren't recorded. Besides, she wouldn't know what to say or how to answer his questions.

I'll message them later and tell them the problem has been resolved. That should take care of it. As long as they don't call Lexington Finance and start asking questions about who I am.

The sound of Mike's voice got Gillian even more wound up. It was like the past came rushing back into her life like waves crashing on the beach. She went back to voicemail and listened to his voice again. Even after ten years his voice still affected her in a way no other man's did.

Why did I give up so easily? I was young and insecure. I should have fought harder to keep him. If I could only go back to that time knowing what I know now. It wasn't fair. He should be with me.

Gillian pounded her fists on the chair and jumped up. A fever was building inside her. She began to pace in front of the motel. The peaceful thoughts she had that morning were now turning into a violent tempest. She thought about what to do. She was becoming more and more determined to set things straight. Her mind began to fill with all sorts of possibilities. Her whole life she had managed to stay one step ahead of the law. *Why should it ever be any different?*

Logical or not, she started to work on a plan to get back in his life. *Does Mike still love his wife? Probably. I'll have to deal with her.*

Gillian thought about whether she could actually get Mike to love her. Her thoughts were becoming more illogical and disconnected. At this point she wasn't sure if love was what she actually wanted. Maybe revenge and closure was what she was looking for. She began to think about ways she could complicate his life. *Maybe blackmail. If I had something on him, maybe I could become a part of his life.*

She began to devise a complicated and risky plan. *I won't be able to pull this off by myself,* she thought.

Just like poor Michelle, Gillian was a loner. She had gone from place to place and never bothered to maintain ties with the people she knew. She was quite capable of living her life as an island. She entertained herself very well. *How can I recruit someone to help me?*

Gillian continued to pace in front of the motel and looked at her Harley parked in front. Suddenly an old memory came rushing back to her. She remembered when she first got the bike and the trips she had taken to New Orleans.

Those were fun days. She thought about how easy it was to talk Jimmy into giving her the bike. A small taste was all it took. *Jimmy. I'll try Jimmy. I'll bet he's still ready to do anything I ask.*

Jimmy had given her his number. It was one of the few she bothered to keep. She got a small address book from her saddlebag and looked it up. She punched the number into the phone and hoped she would get an answer. It had been more than ten years since she had talked to him. The phone began to ring.

"Hello," she heard him say.

"Hi, Jimmy. Guess who?"

Jimmy looked at his phone. The caller ID said Michelle Dennis. Jimmy thought for a minute and said, "It says here your name is Michelle. Do I know you?"

"Don't you recognize my voice?"

Jimmy thought again and said, "Gill, Gillian. Is that you, Gillian?"

"Hi, Jimmy. Yeah, it's me," she said in her most sultry voice. "How are you?

"I'm doing okay. How are you? Where are you? Christ, I haven't heard from you in ages."

"You won't believe it. I'm still riding around on your old Harley. I'm up in Maine right now. I was sitting here just daydreaming. I was staring at my bike and I thought about you. I know, it's been about ten years."

"So what are your plans? I'm still living in Ohio. If you want to drop in let me know."

"Actually, I'm on my way to Boston. I should get there by tonight. I was thinking about New Orleans and all the fun we had. Remember cruising down Bourbon Street and the time we took the ferry to Algiers? That was so cool."

"How could I forget? It was the best time of my life. I mean that."

"So what are you doing these days?"

"Nothing much. Just bummin' around. You know."

"Do you still have your Harley?"

"Yup, I'll never stop riding my bike."

"Feel like taking a ride out to Boston? We could hang out and have some fun."

Jimmy felt like a ten-year-old boy whose long-lost puppy had just come home. "Sure. I'm not doing much right now. If I jump on the bike now, I can be there by tonight. It takes about ten hours."

Jimmy remembered what it was like to be with Gillian. No other girl had ever given him that kind of pleasure. He pictured her perfect body and her ivory skin. His mind began to swim with love and lust. *Is this real or am I dreaming?* he thought.

"Where are you staying in Boston?" he asked enthusiastically.

"I don't know yet. I've never been there before. Probably near Boston College. I'll call you when I know more." Gillian realized nothing had changed in ten years. She could probably get him to do anything she wanted.

"Okay. I'll call you when I get there. By the way, why does your caller ID say Michelle Dennis?"

"Long story. I'll tell you when you get here. Drive safe, Jimmy."

"Okay. Hope to see you tonight."

Jimmy ended the call and let out a yell that could be heard all the way from Cleveland to Cincinnati.

Gillian smiled and thought about how easy that had been. She looked at the call log in her phone and entered Affirmed Software into her contact list. With a satisfied grin she sent Mike a message which simply read: Problem has been resolved. Thank you, Mr. Davis.

Gillian took a shower before she left. She packed a few belongings and jumped on her Harley. She now had a definite plan. She raced down the last few miles of Route 302 and headed south toward Boston.

CHAPTER 30

Monday, June 15, 12:30 PM

Gillian cruised south down I-95 and began to think about how she was going to carry out her plan. She had to be careful not to push Jimmy too hard. He had never been a part of any of her dark past. It was going to take a little convincing with just the right bait. Gillian was sure she could get it done.

In addition, it was going to take at least a couple of months to work out all the details. She needed to set up a place that was out of the way. Someplace where no one would notice people coming or going and no one would ask questions. She was also going to need money. Lots of it. Still, with the proper patience and diligence it could work. She reached the city just after noon and made her way toward Boston College. As she rode down I-90 she began to make a plan.

I should get a motel for the two of us tonight. I'll feel Jimmy out and figure out where to go from there. If I can't get him to play along, I'm going have to try something else. Maybe a road trip to Cape Cod will bring back some nice memories of when we spent time riding together.

Gillian got a room at a Days Inn on I-90 and went to Boston College to wait for Jimmy. She walked around campus and before an hour had passed several guys had already hit on her. Ordinarily it would have been just what she wanted but now she had other priorities. Eventually she got to the student center and decided it was a good place to hang out and wait for Jimmy. As part of her usual routine, she bought a newspaper and a cup of coffee. She took a seat by the window and began to read. Again, the headlines were about foreign and domestic terrorists. She read about the JTTF and how the FBI had coordinated with local police departments to get ahead of the situation. As she sipped her coffee, she looked out the window. She noticed a poster on a lamppost that said,

IF YOU SEE SOMETHING,
SAY SOMETHING.

The Boston Marathon bombing was still fresh in the minds of many people. It gave Gillian another idea.

It was getting close to six o'clock and Gillian decided to take a walk around the Chestnut Hill Reservoir. She had been on her bike for most of the last four days. The walk would do her good. She got to the other side of the reservoir and started looking for a good place to get dinner. She found a café and took a seat with a nice view of the lake. She began to think about the public service poster she had seen earlier. Terrorism. It struck fear in the hearts of almost every Boston resident. It was an interesting angle she could incorporate into her already sinister plan.

She ordered dinner with a glass of wine and gazed out over the lake as she ate. She thought about Mike and what she was now willing to do. Hearing his voice again had triggered something inside her. She thought about Brittany and how she had come between her and Mike. She wondered what would have happened if she hadn't been in the picture. The anger inside her was beginning to smolder as she clenched her hand tighter around her wine glass. Gillian let the fire burn. It felt good to hate. Her eyes flared as her rage at Brittany now spilled over to Mike.

He didn't have to leave me. He had a choice. It was as much his fault as hers, she thought.

It had been more than ten years earlier. Whether her feelings for Mike were real or if it was just a way for her to focus her anger at life was lost on Gillian. Everything was cloudy in her mind. Logical or not, she began to hate Mike as well.

After dinner she used Michelle's credit card for the first time. There were apparently no issues. It gave her a sense of satisfaction that her plans were working out. She was gaining confidence in herself. It was now late evening and she decided to walk back through the reservoir to the campus. It was a warm spring night and she began to feel at peace again. Making plans seemed to help subdue her anger and sense of betrayal. At a quarter past nine her cell phone rang. It was Jimmy.

"Hi Jimmy. Where are you?"

"I'm at a rest stop just outside of Boston on I-90. Where are you?"

"I'm at Boston College by the student center. There are signs on I-90 that will take you right here. Then just ask for the student center. I'll be waiting outside."

"Be right there."

Jimmy had just spent the last ten hours fantasizing about Gillian's body. His mind was piqued. He got to the college, parked his bike and quickly found the student center. He began to look around and saw a girl with long black hair sitting on a stone block with her back to him. *That's got to be her,* he thought.

He walked up slowly behind her and said, "Guess who."

Gillian spun around with a big smile and threw her arms around him. "Jimmy," she yelled enthusiastically, planting a firm kiss on his lips.

Jimmy put his arms around her waist and lifted her off the ground. He playfully spun her around and said, "Hi beautiful."

They stood there for several moments and looked in each other's eyes.

"Jesus, you have gorgeous eyes," he said, unable to look away.

She could hypnotize men without even trying.

"What do you say we walk around the reservoir? It's a beautiful evening and we can catch up on lost time," she suggested.

"Show me the way."

The two of them walked around the reservoir, and Gillian laughed and joked about all the good times they had had together. Jimmy felt like he was in a mid-summer night's dream. He hadn't felt this good in a long time.

"So what have you been doing for the past ten years, Jimmy?"

"Oh, nothing special. I do a lot of riding mostly."

"Got a girlfriend?" she said, smiling at him with her eyes.

"Not really. There's a girl, Susie, I hang out with sometimes, but we're just friends. Mostly."

"Mostly?" Gillian laughed and gave him a playful nudge with her elbow.

"What do you do for a living?"

"I'm sort of self-employed. I do a lot of different stuff."

"So you don't have to go back to Ohio if you don't want?" she asked.

"No. I guess I don't."

Jimmy looked at her, wondering why she asked him that. He was hoping Gillian wanted to spend some serious time with him. Lord knows he wanted to spend time with her.

"So what made you call me out of the blue, Gee?" Gee was the pet name he had given her ten years earlier.

"To tell you the truth, I was feeling a little lost this morning, Jimmy. I was looking at my bike and I remembered how I got it. You were always good to me. I don't have any real friends. You're about the closest thing to a friend I've got."

"I'll always be there for you. If you're ever in trouble I'll be there."

"I know. Thank you, Jimmy. You're so good to me." She stood in front of him, buried her face in his shoulder, and pulled him close.

Jimmy's heart was beginning to slip away. Gillian could feel it.

"Where are you staying tonight?"

"I've got a room over at the Days Inn over on the highway. You must be tired. Why don't we go over there now? We can get a good night's rest and do something together tomorrow."

"My Harley's over by the student center. Let's ride to the motel together."

When Jimmy saw Gillian's bike he said, "There she is. I remember her well. God. That bike's over twenty years old. It was ten years old when I first got it."

"Still runs like a deer," said Gillian, defending her ride. Hop on. I'll take you to your bike."

Jimmy climbed on behind her and put his hands on her waist. She kick-started the bike and got under way. Gillian thought about the last passenger she had on her bike.

What would Jimmy do if he knew? What would he think of me? Would he still want me?

They got to Jimmy's bike and the two of them set out for the motel. Jimmy's mind was doing flips. The thought of spending the night with her after all these years was making him crazy. She was even more beautiful now that she was grown up. They arrived at the Days Inn. Gillian unlocked the door and walked in. Jimmy followed behind. She went to the mini-bar and found a couple of bottles of red wine and offered one to Jimmy. She sat on the bed and turned on the TV. Jimmy took a seat in the chair nearby, facing her.

"I've got a great idea. Let's take a road trip tomorrow. How about Cape Cod?" said Gillian enthusiastically.

"Sounds great. I've never been there. I've seen pictures, though. It looks really nice."

They continued to talk for the next hour and shared another bottle of red.

They finished their wine and Gillian said, "Let's get an early start tomorrow." She took off her jacket and got out of her jeans. She yawned and stretched her arms out over her head provocatively. She climbed in bed and got under the sheets.

Jimmy got undressed and climbed in next to her.

He snuggled up next to her and started to caress her shoulders and ran his hand down her hip.

"Oh, Jimmy, listen. Can we slow things down a little? I'm very confused. I just need a friend right now. Please don't be mad. I'm just not ready. I hope you understand."

"Of course. You sleep tight and we'll talk in the morning."

"Goodnight, Jimmy. I love you."

Gillian closed her eyes and turned away to conceal her smile. Things were going just fine.

Jimmy rolled over and moved to the other side of the bed. He thought he might actually die.

The next morning Gillian awoke and lay on her back, looking up at the ceiling. She made sure Jimmy was awake and she stretched out seductively, making sure he was watching. "Good morning, Jimmy."

"Morning, Gee."

"I'm gonna jump in the shower. If we're going to Cape Cod, we should get an early start."

"I'm good with that."

Gillian pulled her T-shirt up over her head, threw it on the bed and disappeared into the bathroom. Jimmy listened to the water splash and pictured Gillian's naked body becoming slippery and wet as she caressed herself with soap. It was almost too much to bear. He pictured himself in the shower helping her wash herself. He was beginning to get hard as he lay on the bed fantasizing. Every primitive instinct was telling him to jump up and join her. He remembered what she had said to him the night before and decided he better not. He really wanted things to work out between them. He could wait.

Gillian stepped out of the shower and walked back into the bedroom wearing just her panties. She finished drying herself and pulled her T-shirt back on over her head. Her hair was still wet and now the T-shirt had become wet. Her firm breasts were slightly visible underneath.

"Your turn," she said, smiling at Jimmy.

Jimmy got up and got himself ready for the day. He was a bit more modest than Gillian had been. They checked out of the motel and were soon on the road. They headed down Route 3 and decided to stop for breakfast in Plymouth. They found a nice place on the shore overlooking the bay. The waitress came and put placemats in front of them. There were all sorts of tourist attractions printed on them.

"Oh, the Mayflower. Let's go check out the Mayflower," said Gillian.

"Sure. Why not? We can go see Plymouth Rock, too."

"Wow. There's just so much I want to see in the world. Let's just take our time and move slowly."

Jimmy was eager to spend as much time with her as he could. He was already in love. He probably had been from the first day he met her. "We could spend all week here if you like. I'm not in a hurry."

"Great. Do you have to take care of anything back in Ohio? Are you renting an apartment or anything?"

"No. I live with my mom," he said, looking at Gillian with a lame expression on his face.

Gillian just laughed and said, "Good. You can party with me all summer."

Jimmy was thrilled to hear her say that. "I'll give her a call and tell her I won't be back for a while."

Everything's falling right into place, she thought.

After breakfast they paid a visit to the Mayflower.

"Just think about the people who came over on that ship," said Gillian. "It says a hundred and two people were on it. Look how small it is. That must have taken a lot of guts."

"Or a lot of desperation," Jimmy added.

It was another beautiful morning and the two of them walked around the harbor area. They visited Plymouth Rock and then climbed to the top of the Gurnett Lighthouse. They could see clear across the Bay from the top.

"This is awesome. I want to go over to the other side," said Gillian.

"We've got all week. Let's check out the whole cape."

"We could go see Nantucket, too."

"Okay. Do you think we'll be able to bring our bikes on the ferry?"

"Why not? Kinda reminds me of New Orleans and the ferry to Algiers."

"I miss those days, Gee."

After they visited the lighthouse, they got back on the road and headed south for Sandwich. They walked around through the town, looking at antique stores and glassware shops. They got to the town square and stopped to look at some of the historical buildings. There was a bronze plaque stating that Sandwich was the oldest town in Cape Cod. *Settled 1637* was etched in the stone beneath it. Gillian thought back to the cemetery she had seen in New Hampshire. She wondered if the girl who was buried there was a descendant of someone who came over on the Mayflower. It was a much smaller world back then. The image of the gravestone began to haunt her again.

"Let's find a motel and get some dinner," she said. "We can walk around some more afterwards."

"Good with me."

Vacancy was not that easy to find in Cape Cod in June. After searching for some time, they found a room, but it was pricey.

"My turn to pay," offered Jimmy.

"No. No. Let me," insisted Gillian.

"Oh! How did you get so rich, Gee?"

"I'll explain it to you over dinner, Jimmy."

That aroused his curiosity.

They found a cozy restaurant and ordered diner. Gillian insisted on a large bottle of wine. After she had downed a couple of glasses, she figured it was time to test the waters. *I need to know if he's going to play along or if he's going to run,* she thought.

"There's something I've got to tell you, Jimmy," she said, biting her lower lip. She cast her eyes downward at the table, trying to act remorseful. "After I left you in Tulane, I spent a lot of time moving from place to place. I met a lot of different kinds of people on the way."

Jimmy looked at her and just nodded and listened.

"I was in Pennsylvania and I fell in with some bad people. You've heard the word grifter, right?"

"Yeah, sure," Jimmy said, listening intently.

"I met this guy and his girlfriend at a bar. At first, they seemed really nice. We spent the night drinking and talking. When I look back on it now,

I feel so stupid. I was only eighteen years old, Jimmy. God they were good. They managed to talk me into being part of a scam. I was so stupid, Jimmy. I screwed up."

Jimmy took her hand and said, "It's okay, Gee. I've done some things myself I'm not proud of."

"That's not the end of the story. I spent months running the same scam with them. Their names were John and Lisa. He was like 35 years old. She was in her late twenties. It was my job to sucker college guys into falling for their story. We would set up a drug deal with a kilo of cocaine and make up a story about how Lisa had to unload it cheap. I was pretty good at finding the right guys. When the deal went down Johnny would show up dressed as a cop and we would just take all their money."

"So these guys were no saints either, Gee. It's funny. I'm proud of you. They deserved what they got. They were probably dealers themselves. Just let it go."

"That's not the end of it, Jimmy. One day something went wrong. The guy put up a fight. Johnny stabbed him in the neck. It was awful. There was blood everywhere. We took the money and we all split up. That was the last time I ever saw John and Lisa. I don't know for sure, but I think the guy probably died."

Jimmy was ready to forgive her anything. He wanted to be her knight in shining armor. "It wasn't your fault, Gee. You didn't mean for that to happen. Did you tell John and Lisa your real name?"

"No, they don't know. You're the only one I ever told my real name to."

That made Jimmy feel special. At that moment he would have jumped off the top of the Freedom Tower if she asked him to. "So, there's no way they can track you down, then."

"I suppose not. I've probably changed my name fifty times since then. That was over nine years ago. I never had a real job. I've been running scams and stealing from people for a long time."

Jimmy looked at her with sympathy and unconditional love. He was ready to forgive her anything she might have done in the past. "It's okay, Gee. Believe me. I meant it when I said I'd always be there for you?"

"Thanks, Jimmy. I believe you."

Gillian wasn't sure yet about how far she should push. She decided it was enough for the moment. The groundwork was being laid. It was probably better to spend another day or two with him first. They finished dinner and walked through town again, laughing and talking. Late that night they went back to their motel. They shared some more wine and hit the hay. Jimmy spent another frustrating night.

In the morning they continued their ride farther out onto the Cape and stopped at Orleans. They did some sightseeing and came upon a miniature golf course. The theme was a pirate ship with cannons and water hazards.

Gillian said, "I challenge you to a game," with a playful look in her eye.

Jimmy accepted. The two of them laughed and joked and teased each other when they missed. He watched her joy as she jumped in the air after she made a particularly difficult shot. Jimmy was falling in love all over again and made sure that she won. He would have done anything for her. They finished their game and walked down toward the shore.

"Let's go to the beach. Do you want to go swimming?" asked Gillian.

"Sure, but I need to buy a bathing suit first."

"Me too. Let's go shopping in town."

Gillian still liked black bikinis and bought one for herself. It was a lot like the one she had bought in Miami Beach years before, but now her body complemented it far better with her recently acquired hips. She could be a swimsuit model herself. She wasn't just a skinny kid anymore. They hit the beach and Gillian ran straight into the ocean. Jimmy raced in after her. They swam in the surf and playfully splashed water at each other. Jimmy dived under and disappeared for a few seconds. He came up between Gillian's legs and lifted her up on his shoulders. She let out a defiant yell when he threw her back in the water. The eyes of every man and boy on the beach were locked on her. Jimmy noticed and felt proud to be with her. They continued to swim for a while and then decided to warm up in the sun. They sat on a blanket watching the surf roll in and began to talk.

"Remember I started telling you yesterday about the trouble I got into?"

"Sure. I told you, I don't care what you did. You don't have to worry about it, Gee."

"There's more to it, Jimmy. There's things I haven't told you."

Jimmy listened and gazed into her eyes. He assured her again that he didn't care about her past.

Gillian decided it was time to engage in some creative story telling. "It was right after I split up with John and Lisa, about a year after I left you in Tulane."

Jimmy thought back to the day she left. He remembered her waving goodbye as she rode off down the road. He could still recall the pain in his heart as she disappeared around the bend.

"Oh, Jimmy. I should never have left that day."

"Well, you're here now."

Gillian smiled and took Jimmy's hand. She continued to tell her story. "I was at Ohio State and I met this guy named Mike. I went to a party with him at his frat house. I thought they were decent guys at first. But then they got me drunk and started suggesting I do things for them. You know I'm not like that. They started grabbing me and laughing. I just wanted to get out of there. They pushed me down on the bed and one of them held me down. Mike got on top of me and raped me. Then the others took their turn. There was nothing I could do. I was just seventeen then. It was hard for me to trust anyone after that. I just started hating people. I think that's why I'm the way I am now."

"I'm so sorry, Gee. It must have been horrible. But you seem to be okay now. We had a lot of fun today and you seem to be happy."

"Only on the outside. When I think back to that day, I just fill up with rage. I want to kill those guys."

"I can understand that. Anyone who could do that is a scumbag. They deserve to die."

"I don't know if I really want them dead, but I would like to get even somehow."

"I can imagine how you feel. Did you leave Ohio State after that?"

"Not right away. I was thinking about going to the cops, but I was afraid they might be able to tie me to some other things I had done. I didn't have anything to do with Mike and his frat buddies anymore but I saw them on campus a few times after that. Mike was dating this girl named Brittany. I thought about telling her what he did, but I decided not to. They would have just denied it and she wouldn't have believed me. I heard they got engaged right after that."

Jimmy felt the anger start to rise up inside him as she continued to tell him her story. He was ready to do anything for her. He would have liked to kill Mike himself.

"I googled his name and got about a hundred hits. After a while I was able to narrow it down. He lives in Albany now. He's a big deal in some software company. He's probably living a nice quiet life with his wife and kids like he never did anything wrong."

Gillian looked at Jimmy. She could see that he was becoming more and more upset with every new detail. "I thought about a way to get back at him, but I don't want to get anyone else in trouble."

"Tell me, Gee. What do you have in mind?"

"It's too dangerous, Jimmy. I could go to jail for a long time if I got caught."

"Tell me and I'll decide for myself if it's too dangerous.

"Mike Davis is his full name. He's a computer geek and he's a big deal for a company that makes software for financial institutions. If we could hack into the program, we could get him in some trouble."

"Sounds like a movie plot. Are you that good with computers?"

"Not really. Even if I were, I wouldn't have the privileges to change the program or make any transactions."

"So then what did you have in mind?"

"We would have to kidnap one of his clients."

Jimmy looked at her, uncertain if she was serious. She looked back at him and held his gaze with her eyes. His mind reeled as he began to realize that she wasn't kidding. "Why not just kidnap Mike? I could fuck him up pretty good. I'm not bad with my fists."

"That would only make people feel sorry for him. I want to fuck up his whole life. I want to disgrace him to his wife and family. I want his friends to think he's a total loser."

"I think I understand, Gee. You've really thought this out."

"You have no idea, Jimmy."

They continued to talk for the next hour and relaxed in the warm sunshine. Jimmy thought about the idea of helping her out. His own life just wasn't that exciting without Gillian in it. The idea seemed kind of sexy to him. The danger and the thought of sharing a bond with her began to intrigue him more and more. His thoughts went back to the day she had left him ten years earlier. Once again, he pictured her riding away and remembered how his heart had broken as she disappeared around the bend. Could he bear to lose her again? He wanted to spend as much time with her as he could.

"Have you thought at all about how you would pull this off?"

"Actually, I have. One of his clients is a bank executive with Lexington Finance in Boston. His name is Kevin Reardon. I'm sure he has the privileges to do a lot of things with that program."

"Tell me more."

Gillian smiled and said, "First, we would have to rent a house where we could keep him out of sight. We would keep him blindfolded so he wouldn't be able to identify us. Then we would have to get Internet access at the house and buy a computer. Also, we would need to buy some disposable cell phones and set up a phony bank account."

Jimmy listened and hung on her every word.

"We would get him to make a transfer to that account and make it look like Mike was responsible."

"Interesting. It might work at that."

"Yeah, but we're gonna need some money to do all these things. We'll talk more later. Let's go for another swim."

"Last one in has gorilla feet," joked Jimmy as he got up and started to run toward the ocean.

Gillian caught his foot with her hand and tripped Jimmy up. She got up and beat him to the water. "Who's got monkey feet?"

"You do," he said as he picked her up and tossed her into the ocean.

Gillian laughed and screamed as they frolicked in the water like two otters. They spent the rest of the day swimming and hanging at the beach. Later that evening they set out for Provincetown. They had dinner and that night they went to the National Sea Shore. They sat on a blanket and watched the ships sail by out on the ocean. It was an exceptionally warm day for June on the Cape and Gillian took her jacket off. "It's so beautiful. I could live here," said Gillian.

"So could I if I had a million dollars."

Gillian put her hand on his knee and began to move it gently back and forth. Jimmy looked at her, uncertain of her intentions. She laughed and pushed him down on the blanket. In seconds she had his shirt buttons undone. She put her lips on his mouth and kissed him passionately. She gave him her most provocative smile and said, "You can have anything you want, Jimmy. Anything."

Jimmy's mind was filled with love and lust as he began to make love to her. Gillian made sure he would never forget that night. She owned him now.

CHAPTER 31

Wednesday morning, June 16

Gillian woke up in their motel room and looked over at Jimmy, who was still asleep next to her. She snuggled up next to him and decided to give him some morning delight. Jimmy awoke to a dream that was far better than anything Morpheus could conjure. For the next hour Gillian did her best to satisfy his every lustful desire. Afterward they jumped into the shower together and Jimmy fulfilled another fantasy.

They spent the morning in Provincetown and found a nice restaurant on the beach where they had lunch. They continued to talk about their plan to exact revenge on Mike. Jimmy was now quite sure that Gillian was serious about carrying out her plan. He was beginning to recognize the wild animal inside of her. She reminded him of a dangerous jungle cat stalking her prey in the night with her emerald green eyes. It excited him even more. After what she had done for him in the last twenty hours, he was more than willing to do anything for her.

They finished lunch and Jimmy said, "Let me pay this time, Gee."

"No Jimmy. Let me. Save your money. We're gonna need it later."

She took out her credit card and Jimmy noticed it said Michelle Dennis.

He thought about the caller ID that came up when she had called him a few days earlier.

"So who is Michelle Dennis?" he asked.

There it was. Out in the open. She was going to have to explain. Was he ready to hear more?

"I guess I'll have to tell you now, Jimmy. I don't know what you're gonna think of me after this. Remember I told you how I was scamming people and stealing money?"

"Yeah. I told you that I'm okay with that."

"Well, there's more. I was in Rochester partying at this bar in a not so upscale neighborhood. I met this girl. She said she had just come up from Florida and didn't know anybody in town. We started talking and she hinted to me she made her money doing tricks. She seemed like a real easy mark. I mean, this girl was so naïve."

"So what happened?"

"I knew she was carrying a couple of hundred bucks with her. I pretended to be gay and that I wanted to hook up."

Jimmy smiled at the thought of Gillian with another girl. She noticed and smiled back at him.

"It was a beautiful day and I suggested we ride to a park outside of the city, where we could be alone. We got on the Harley and went to this place way out in the sticks. I planned on taking her bag and ditching her there."

Jimmy nodded as if he understood.

"She wasn't as timid as I thought. I'm pretty strong myself, and I usually don't have a problem getting the better of someone. Even against most guys. This girl surprised me. I told her I wanted to start fooling around and asked her to get undressed. She started taking off her clothes. While she wasn't paying attention, I started going through her bag. I took out her purse and took the money out, but she caught me. She flew into a rage. I didn't want to hurt her, Jimmy, but somehow, she got on top of me. She was tougher than I thought. She started yelling that she was going to call the cops and have me arrested. This girl was crazy. I tried to throw her off me, but she kept throwing punches. I didn't know what to do. I picked up a rock and hit her in the head with it. I watched as her eyes rolled back and then she went completely limp."

Jimmy just sat and listened. She excited him even more.

"She was dead, Jimmy. I buried her under a pile of rocks. I don't think she will ever be found."

"You did what you had to do. She didn't give you a choice. I would have done the same thing."

"I took her cell phone, her credit card and every other thing that could ID her. Even if she is found they won't be able to figure out who she was. I've been using her credit card for a while. I think I'm in the clear."

"Now I understand why you're so eager to pay for everything."

"The card probably won't work after a while, but I might as well use it for now."

"I feel like a whore, Gee. You're too good to me."

"Don't worry, Jimmy. You'll get the chance to make it up to me."

Jimmy was actually eager to prove that he would. They finished lunch and Gillian paid with Michelle's card as Jimmy looked on with amusement.

They spent the next few days riding up and down the coast and hanging out on the beach. Life was nonstop fun for Jimmy. Gillian diligently continued to craft her plan. She didn't mind spending time with Jimmy. She liked him well enough, almost like a girl would love a faithful dog.

The summer days continued to roll on. Gillian suggested that they stay in their motel for the rest of the month. Jimmy eagerly agreed. July Fourth arrived and they watched the fireworks over the bay. The feeling of patriotism was everywhere. The party atmosphere was spreading throughout the crowd. Gillian got drunk and flashed her boobs at more than just a few guys. Jimmy just laughed and got drunk along with her. They were having such a good time they decided to stay until September or as long as the credit card was still good. Gillian paid for everything.

As the days slipped by Gillian thought about how she would carry out her plan. Brick by brick it began to take shape in her mind. By the time August was turning to September, she had it worked out. The only thing left to do was convince Jimmy to do his part. She was sure she could.

One day in late August they were sitting on the beach enjoying the afternoon sun. Gillian let her mind wander and began to think about her future. Whatever reservations she had about carrying out her plan were fading fast.

If I'm going to go through with it, I might as well start now, she thought. She looked over at Jimmy and said, "I've had such a good time with you this summer. I wish it would never end."

"Me too, Gee. I'm so happy you called me that day. My whole life changed. I love you."

"Thanks, Jimmy. I love you too."

She moved closer to him on the blanket and gave him a kiss on the cheek. "Did you feel a little chill in the air last night?"

"Yeah. Now that you mention it."

"Summer's gonna end soon. We can't do this forever. What do you say we leave right before Labor Day? We could head back to Boston."

"What do you want to do there, Gee?"

"Remember what we were talking about earlier this summer? I still think about Mike and what happened to me. I want my revenge, Jimmy. It still gets me so angry."

Jimmy put his arm around her and said, "I can understand that. Fucking son of a bitch."

"I've been thinking about it. I'm sure we can pull it off. How much money do you have with you?"

THE NIGHT HAS GREEN EYES

"I've got a couple of hundred with me, but I could get a lot more. I have an account with a few grand in it."

"That will do for now but we're gonna need more. Let me handle that side of things."

"So what's your plan?"

"We would start by renting a house somewhere off in the woods outside of Boston. It wouldn't have to be anything special. Just someplace where nobody would bother us. Then we would have to find out where Reardon lives and start following him. We would have to figure out when he was alone and vulnerable. Of course, we would need a van. We couldn't be on motorcycles."

"No. I guess that wouldn't work out too well," said Jimmy, letting out a chuckle.

"Then we take him back to the house. We get him to transfer money to a phony account using Mike's user ID. That should fuck him up good. Of course, we couldn't let him see our faces."

"I'm with you all the way, Gee. I love you. We'll get it done."

Gillian threw her arms around him and said, "I knew I could count on you, Jimmy. I love you."

They spent another week enjoying the good weather and planning the details. Labor Day was approaching and they decided to leave on the first of the month, before the traffic built up. They arrived in Boston that afternoon and decided to stay at the same Days Inn where they had spent their first night together. Jimmy remembered how he had felt that night, how she had at first rejected his advances and how she had disappeared from his life years earlier. Gillian more than made up for it that night.

The next morning, they went to a diner for breakfast and searched through the papers for a house that could accommodate their needs. After several hours Gillian found a house just north of Westwood. The picture showed a modest two-bedroom house in what seemed to be a rural area.

"Let's check this one out, Jimmy. It looks perfect. I'll call and we can ride out there together this afternoon. You better rent the place with cash and use a phony name. We'll set up shop and get started."

The weather was still beautiful, and they rode out to Westwood and got together with the owner. He was an older man named O'Connell who said he had once used it as a glorified hunting cabin with his friends. Gillian asked if he wouldn't mind keeping his cable service and offered to pay him extra for it. The old man agreed. The first step of their plan was complete.

They went shopping and stocked the refrigerator with food and bought some wine and beer. Later they bought a TV, a computer, a printer and a router from Best Buy. That night they had a fire in the fireplace and sat on the floor drinking wine. They both agreed things couldn't get much better.

The following day they rented a car from Enterprise. It was an inconspicuous Ford Taurus. Michelle's credit card was still working but they had to pay for the house with cash. Jimmy had to hand over $3,000 for the first month's rent plus the deposit. They were running out of money and were going to need more. Gillian thought about how they could get more. She would have to get Jimmy to go along. None of her plans were going to work out without Jimmy. She had to make a move. She thought about the public service message she had seen months earlier at Boston College.

If you see something say something.

"We're starting to run out of money, Jimmy. We need a lot more before we snatch Reardon. We probably have to rent the house for at least October, maybe longer. I know how we could get some more, but it's risky. It's gonna take some guts. Are you in?"

"Of course, Gee. You know I'll do anything for you."

Jimmy was more than just willing. The idea of the two of them living dangerously excited him.

"We need to have some leverage if we're gonna pull this off."

"What did you have in mind?"

"I was looking on the Internet and I read about this chemist on Long Island. His name is James Carter. He claims you can make plastic explosives out of ordinary household materials. If we could get hold of some of that stuff and give Reardon a little demonstration, I think we could get him to do just about anything."

"I'll bet you're right. So tell me more."

"Why don't we take a little ride down to Long Island tomorrow and talk to Mr. Carter?"

Jimmy laughed and said, "You always have such a subtle way with words, Gee. I love it."

Gillian threw her arms around him and kissed him square on the mouth. "I love you, Jimmy. You're the best."

They spent the remainder of the day working out their plan.

"We should try to get hold of a gun, Jimmy. It'll make things a lot easier."

"Yeah. I don't think we're going to convince him with words, even though you are a pro."

"We're also gonna have to buy a bunch of M-80s and some long fuses."

"What do we need them for?"

"We have to test this stuff out and we need something to detonate it. An M-80 should do the trick."

Jimmy just smiled and said, "I'm impressed, Gee. You think of everything."

They drove around the neighborhood and asked several kids where they could get some. After offering top dollar, they finally were able to buy a few.

The following morning, they jumped in the Taurus and headed for Long Island.

"So how are we going to get hold of a gun?" asked Jimmy.

"I've got an idea. When we get to New York, head for the South Bronx. We can ask around. I'm pretty good at figuring out the right people to ask."

Three hours later they were pulling off the highway on Tremont Street. They cruised down the block and Gillian rolled down the window. There were several young Hispanic-looking boys hanging out on the corner wearing hooded sweatshirts.

"In the summer. Really? Stop here, Jimmy."

Gillian leaned her head out the window and asked them, "Hi fellas. Do any of you know how to get to Webster Avenue?"

They were all stunned to see such a pretty white girl in their neighborhood. They immediately ran to the window, stumbling over each other and barking out directions. Gillian started to laugh and flirt with them. After a few minutes went by they were practically friends. Then she dropped a bombshell on them.

"If a girl wants to buy a piece around here, who would she ask?"

For a moment they were stunned and just looked at one another. Eventually one of the younger boys said, "My brother knows where to get one." He seemed very eager to help her out.

"Where's your brother now?"

"He's probably down at the bar with his friends. Should I go tell him a pretty lady is looking to buy a gun?"

"I think that would be great."

"Before I go let me ask you, why's a girl like you wanna get a gun?"

"If you must know, a guy raped me and I wanna shoot his dick off."

The boy now seemed rather embarrassed that he had asked and said, "I'll be right back."

A few minutes later he returned with his brother. "This is my brother Roberto. Talk to him."

"I understand you're looking to buy yourself a piece. What were you looking to spend?" he said with a smile on his face.

"We were thinking about two hundred. We don't actually have it on us now but we can get it after you show us the gun. We need to go to an ATM. We can do the exchange then. And just so you know, my friend here is carrying so don't try anything cute."

Gillian stared at him with a look that could freeze a waterfall and she let him see her knife.

The smile left his face and Roberto stared back at her. He knew she meant business. "No ma'am. I've got a reputation to protect. Business is too good to fuck it up."

An hour later Robert returned with a Glock 19 and said "Two hundred and fifty dollars and it's all yours."

Gillian checked the weapon and made sure it was in good shape. "Do you have some ammo to go with it?" she asked.

Roberto gave her a handful and said, "On the house."

Jimmy went to the ATM and took out the money. They made the exchange and drove off toward the Throgs Neck Bridge and Long Island. Another step in their plan had fallen into place.

"Let's find a place to stay in Hempstead. That's where Carter teaches. We can find out more about him tomorrow. Labor Day weekend is coming up. That might fit right into our plans."

The next morning, they awoke and visited Hofstra University. Within half an hour they knew everything they needed to know about James Phillip Carter. The plan was unfolding nicely.

CHAPTER 32

September 3
Long Island

It was the Friday morning before Labor Day Weekend. Gillian and Jimmy woke up early in their motel room on Hempstead Turnpike. During their visit to Hofstra, they had learned that Professor Carter and his wife lived on Wilson Avenue in Westbury. It was a fifteen-minute drive from the motel. They cruised past the house and waited down the block.

"This is gonna take some planning, Jimmy. I'm guessing Carter will be much more willing to cooperate if he knows we have his wife. You could hold her hostage here at his house while I twist his arm and get him to do what we want. Everything depends on our getting that nitro."

"Whatever it takes, Gee. You know I'm in."

"We're going to need to buy all the right stuff first. I know we need nitric and sulfuric acid. He probably has all that stuff in his lab already but I want to make sure. The website said we also need skin lotion. It has to be the kind with glycerin in it."

"That shouldn't be any problem. I know where to get all that stuff."

"We'll need a cooler to keep it cold until we're ready to use it. We have to make sure we've got everything we need before we commit ourselves. That means we should grab Carter soon and find out if we need anything else. We only have until Monday night. After that the University will be too crowded."

The excitement was welling up inside Jimmy as he thought about actually pulling it off. He was about to take a leap across a border into a new life with Gillian. At 8:10 AM Carter emerged from his house and got into his Nissan Altima. Gillian wrote down the plate number. They followed him to Hofstra and watched as he walked into the science building.

"Tomorrow is Saturday and it's Labor Day weekend. There won't be many people on campus and I'm sure Carter can get into his chemistry lab. If we get here before sunrise, nobody will see us and we probably won't have any problems."

"I know we can pull this off, Gee. You're a smart girl. I like the way you think."

"Thanks, Jimmy. Oh, by the way, you do realize that if something goes wrong, we may have to off them, right?"

"Kidnapping means a life sentence anyway. I'll never let that happen to you. We'll do whatever it takes."

Gillian took out her phone and googled a map of Nassau County. There were several large green areas that appeared to be free of houses. "We should check out some of these places. We need to be familiar with them just in case we need to move fast."

"So where do we go now?"

"Let me google a description of them. Hang on."

Gillian googled a few areas that said preserve. They would be the most wild and isolated. She also googled Jones Beach State Park. She remembered reading about how the bodies of several prostitutes had been found dumped there in the marshland. The case was never solved.

"There's Massapequa Preserve, Muttontown Nature Preserve and Jones Beach. If we had to get rid of a body that would be the place to do it. Muttontown isn't far. Let's check that out first. I'll punch it in to the GPS."

Jimmy drove west on Hempstead Turnpike and then north on Route 106. They circled the preserve and took notice of an opening in the cyclone fence on the south side.

"Stop here, Jimmy."

Gillian got out of the car and began to walk into the preserve. She could see that the thick brush extended far into the woods on both sides of a narrow horse trail.

Perfect, she thought. Gillian knew that there was no way they would be able to let Carter and his wife live, but she didn't come right out and say it to Jimmy.

"Let's take a ride down to Jones Beach and drive down Ocean Parkway. I want to check it out. We need to test this stuff out and the shore in Suffolk County seems like a good place."

They drove south on Meadowbrook Parkway and reached Jones Beach. They turned east and drove along the water toward Oak Neck. Gillian could see the marshlands that extended out between the highway and the shore. It was perfect for what she had in mind.

"Okay, I'm happy. Let's go to Home Depot and pick up the things we need. There's one on Jericho Turnpike not far from Carter's house. Then we can hit a drugstore. We're gonna have to find out from Carter if we need anything else."

"What's your plan for grabbing Carter?"

"It would be easiest if we just take him at his house. That way his wife would already be there. Once we're inside he'll have to cooperate. I want to get started early Saturday so we should do it tonight. If it turns out we need some other things, I'll stay there and you can go out and get it Saturday morning. We'll have to wait until that night instead, but that's okay. We have to be done with this no later than Monday. After that Hofstra will be back in session."

Jimmy felt his toes begin to tingle.

"Let's get back to Hofstra and we'll follow him home from there. We can get him right before he walks into his house. He won't know what hit him. We can find out right then and there what we need to know. If his wife isn't alone, it could get complicated, so be on your toes."

Jimmy drove back to Hofstra and they waited for Carter. At just after five o'clock he walked out of the science building. Jimmy started the car and followed a few car lengths behind. They knew where he was going, so they didn't have to worry about losing him. They followed the same route they had driven earlier that morning. Butterflies were starting to flap in Jimmy's stomach. Gillian was as cool as ice.

She looked over at him and asked, "Are you sure you're ready for this?"

"Sure, Gee. I've got it together."

They continued to drive down Old Country Road and turned up Post Avenue. It wouldn't be long now. They made the turn onto Wilson and Carter parked in front of his house. Jimmy pulled up right behind him. Gillian looked up and down the block and made sure nobody was watching.

She jumped out of the car and quietly said, "Let's go, Jimmy. Put on your mask."

Carter didn't notice the two of them following behind as he walked up to his front door and opened it. Gillian ran up and pushed him inside. She and Jimmy quickly followed him inside and slammed the door shut behind them.

"What the fuck! Who the hell are you people?" shouted Carter.

"Just be cool and nothing's gonna happen," Gillian assured him as she put her knife up to his throat.

Jimmy held the gun on him.

An uneasy, apprehensive voice came from the kitchen, "What's going on, honey? Is somebody with you?"

"Tell her to be cool or I'll have to hurt her," said Gillian

"It's okay, Paula. Don't do anything."

Paula came running into the living room and saw the three of them standing by the front door.

She began to scream.

"Shut her up or I'll kill her. Tell the bitch to shut up," said Gillian.

"Be quiet, Paula. Do what they say."

Gillian pushed him into the living room and said, "Both of you sit down and shut up. If you do everything we say, you'll be telling your friends all about it one day."

That seemed to calm Paula down a little as she sat down and began to weep quietly.

"Zip-tie their hands to the chair and gag her," ordered Gillian.

Paula looked up with tears in her eyes, pleading not to be gagged. Jimmy just did what Gillian told him to do.

"What is it you people want?" demanded Carter, sounding somewhat angry and indignant.

"You're gonna help us make that nitro compound you were talking about on your website, James. After that, we let you go. Fair enough?" said Gillian, putting her face close to his.

"You're crazy. I'm not doing that."

Gillian slowly walked over to where Paula was sitting. She stared at James and cut her ear so that it started to bleed. "Oh no? I think maybe yes," she demanded with an icy stare.

James looked at her with a combination of hate and fear. "Okay. You win. So what do you want me to do?"

"You can begin by telling us what we need," said Gillian. "I think we have most of it. Understand, we're gonna have to try some of the finished product before we can let you go, so it better work."

"I'm going to need some special equipment. This stuff isn't that easy to make," said Carter.

"I'll bet you have everything you need at you lab at Hofstra."

"You've thought this out pretty well, haven't you?"

"I have my moments," said Gillian.

Jimmy just smiled.

"I have nitric and sulfuric acids at the lab. I'll need a source of glycerin like skin lotion, silicone gel, and sawdust to stabilize it. I'll also need a lot of dry ice."

"Where do we get sawdust?"

"You can use Spillfix instead. It's used to clean up oil spills. You can get it at automotive stores."

Gillian wrote it down.

"You got all this?" she asked Jimmy, careful not to use his name.

"Don't you realize that if something goes wrong while we're making it, the whole wing of the science building will come down?"

"Then you better not fuck up."

Carter just looked at her. *She's completely insane,* he thought. However, the fact that they were wearing masks gave him some hope that she didn't plan on killing them. Gillian was way ahead of him.

"Are you expecting company this weekend? Tell me now or things could get messy," demanded Gillian.

"No. We were supposed to go to Montauk for the weekend. Just the two of us."

"Good, good. That makes it simple. How much dry ice are we going to need?

"Ten pounds should do it. That's the most difficult part of it. Temperature is critical. Once it's mixed with sawdust and silicone gel it's much more stable. Still, it's extremely dangerous. You have to keep it cold."

"Thanks for the warning," said Gillian sarcastically.

"Tomorrow you've got to go out and get all this stuff," she said, looking at Jimmy. "It's too late now. First thing in the morning you go out and pick up the silicone and that Spillfix stuff. Later in the afternoon get twenty pounds of dry ice just to make sure. We'll have to make the stuff Saturday night."

"Sounds good to me," said Jimmy.

"We might as well all get comfortable. It's gonna be a long night," said Gillian. "Try and get some sleep, professor. We want you fresh tomorrow night. Don't want you making any mistakes."

The Carters just sat there looking anxiously at each other.

The danger was getting Jimmy all worked up. He wanted to take Gillian right there on the living room floor in front of the Carters, but she stayed focused and calmed him down.

"Wait until we get back home. I'll do anything you want. I promise. Get some sleep and wake me up in four hours."

Jimmy acquiesced and flopped down on the sofa. The night went on and Gillian took her turn to sleep. Neither of the Carters got a wink. The hours dragged on and morning finally arrived.

"Time to wake up," said Gillian, shaking Jimmy's shoulder. "You've got to go shopping."

Jimmy got himself together and gave Gillian a passionate kiss on the mouth. "I'll be right back, Gee," he whispered in her ear.

"Just stay cool, Jimmy. Everything is going to work out fine."

He walked out the door and paid another visit to Home Depot. Later that day he went to a beer distributer and bought the dry ice. By four o'clock they had everything they needed. The hours slipped by and soon it was dark.

"How long is all of this going to take, professor?"

"About two, maybe three, hours."

"Then we better get started. Let's go."

Jimmy cut the zip-ties on Carter's chair and pulled him to his feet. "Remember, no funny business. We've got your wife," he reminded him.

Gillian held the gun on him and said, "You're going to drive."

She carried the cooler out to his car, along with the acids and other materials. Carter looked back at his wife, who was still tied to the chair. The terror in her eyes was all it took to keep him in line.

They drove to the university and made their way to the chemistry lab without anybody seeing them. Carter began to set up the apparatus. Surprisingly, he began to explain to Gillian what he was doing and how it all worked. It was almost as if he took pride in his work. He began by refining the glycerin in a distilling flask. When it was pure enough, he inserted a thermometer in the solution so he could carefully monitor the temperature. He combined the two acids in just the right concentration and weighed out some of the Spillfix. When the solution hit – 40 degrees, he allowed the acid to titrate into the glycerin through a graduated column in tiny amounts. Gillian looked on with a degree of fascination. After two hours had elapsed the column was empty. Carter very slowly began to add the Spillfix in small amounts as he carefully watched the temperature. The solution began to gel. Keeping the temperature steady he emptied a tube of silicone into the mixture. Gillian watched as it turned into a gray rubbery substance. Carter took a knife and cut it into one-inch cubes. He breathed a sigh of relief as he said, "It's more stable now. Just keep it on ice. The colder the better."

"Thank you, professor. You've been very helpful."

"Can you drive me back home now?"

"We still have to try this stuff out. When I know it works, I'll drop you in a place where it's gonna take you a little time before you can get to the police. Then you can go back to your place and set your wife free."

Gillian let Carter carry the cooler as they walked back to his car. In just over half an hour they were nearing Oak Beach.

Gillian said, "Pull over. This is good."

She ordered Carter out of the car and took four small cubes of nitro out of the cooler.

"Follow me," she said. Carter obediently followed her out into the bog.

Gillian molded one of the cubes around an M-80 and they walked farther into the marshy terrain. She lit the fuse and the two of them took cover behind a sand dune. A minute later a powerful blast sent mud and sand flying in all directions.

"I'm satisfied," said Gillian. She smiled, pointed the gun at Carter and pumped three rounds into his chest.

Gillian took the wallet out of his pocket and put it in her own. She took the other three cubes of nitro and molded one of them around another M-80. She placed them underneath Carter's body. She lit the fuse and ran back toward the car. A minute later there was a thunderous explosion. She looked back into the bog where she had left Carter. There was no trace of his body anywhere. He had simply vanished into thin air. She got in the car and quickly drove away. Six years later DNA evidence would finally identify some of his bone fragments.

Gillian drove back north on the Wantagh Parkway and got back to Carter's house as fast as she could. She wiped off all traces of fingerprints from Carter's Altima and transferred the cooler to her Taurus. Jimmy was waiting for her at the door.

"Where's Carter?" he said.

She looked at Paula, who was desperately looking at her with tears in her eyes. *No need to complicate the situation,* she thought. "I've got him tied up in the woods. We can take her there and we'll ditch them both. That will give us plenty of time to get a jump on the cops."

Paula felt relieved that her ordeal might be coming to an end.

"Let's get her into the car."

Paula was eager to cooperate and went along quietly.

"Where do you have him stashed?"

"Remember the nature preserve in Muttontown we checked out yesterday? Go to that opening in the fence."

They arrived twenty minutes later, and Gillian ordered Paula to get out of the car. "Drive around the preserve and pick me up here in ten minutes, Jimmy," she said. Gillian took a flashlight and began to walk Mrs. Carter down the horse trail. After about fifty yards she pushed her off the trail and into the thick brush which bordered on each side. When they had gone about another thirty yards they came to a small clearing. Gillian was sure this was far enough. She took her knife from her jacket and grabbed Paula's hair.

Paula suddenly realized what was coming and all hope left her eyes. In a few seconds it was all over.

Gillian made her way back out of the brush and ran back down the horse trail. She jumped in the car and said, "Let's go, Jimmy."

"Everything go smoothly?"

"Like glass, Jimmy. Like glass."

In half an hour they were back on I-95, heading back toward Boston. Another step in Gillian's plan was complete.

By 9 o'clock AM they were back in Boston. They hadn't slept for hours and they were both exhausted. When they arrived at their house they immediately headed for bed. In seconds they were asleep. They both slept until three o'clock that afternoon. When they awoke, they decided just to stay home and sit on the porch in front of the house.

"So where do we go from here, Gee?"

"Getting that nitro was crucial. If we hadn't been able to pull that off, we'd never be able to carry out the rest of my plan."

"Do you think Carter or his wife will be able to identify us?"

A reptilian smile slowly curled across her lips. She looked at Jimmy with penetrating green eyes and said, "I don't think we have to worry about either of them."

Jimmy instantly understood her meaning. At that moment she looked more appealing to him than she ever had before. He saw a black panther, cold, calculating and deadly. He wanted her more than ever. Whatever it was inside Gillian that had stolen her soul was now intoxicating him as well. There was no turning back. Gillian watched as Jimmy began to slip away into darkness.

They sat on the front porch and continued to talk about what had taken place in the past few days.

Jimmy said, "What do you want to do tomorrow?

"I think we should start following Reardon soon. We have to figure out when he's alone and vulnerable. After we get him here, we give him a little demonstration of what Carter's magic love potion can do. You have to see this stuff, Jimmy. It's scary."

"How do we go about getting him here?"

"We have to find out where he lives. I tried to get it off the Internet, but it's not listed. We're going to have to follow him home from work. When we know his routine, we can work out a plan."

"Where do the explosives come in? What kind of leverage were you talking about?"

"After he sees what it can do, we threaten to level the Lexington Finance Building. I'm sure we can be very persuasive."

"What if he calls our bluff and refuses?"

"I'm not bluffing, but your point is well taken. The more leverage we have the better. Carter's wife seemed to be the difference yesterday. Maybe Reardon loves his wife just as much."

Jimmy looked at Gillian with a combination of intrigue and trepidation. Like the male of the species, he couldn't resist the temptation of his black widow mate.

"There's something else we have to move on, Jimmy. Remember I said we would need more money? In a few weeks we'll have to pay next month's rent."

"What do you want to do? Rob a store or a bank?"

"No. That's not my style. We've got to find a victim who's trusting and somewhat naïve. Someone who's got a lot of money and might not be missed right away."

Jimmy listened to her like a first-year apprentice would revere their master.

CHAPTER 33

Monday afternoon
Boston

The afternoon rolled on and Jimmy listened with increasing interest as they rocked back and forth on the porch swing.

"So who would make a good mark?"

"A new student. Someone who is away from home for the first time. Especially a foreign student. A rich girl from Europe or Asia. The loner type. We don't want a people person."

"Why someone like that?"

"They tend to be rebellious and headstrong. They're often eager to be independent and think their parents are a pain in the ass. They may not even have been in touch for months."

"Very smart, Gee. How would you find someone like that?"

"School is just starting up for the semester. Most universities have a student orientation program for freshmen in early September. There's also a special one for foreign students."

"So what's your plan?"

"We disorient them."

Jimmy let out a chuckle. "How?"

"We have to get them away from the other students before they make new friends."

"How will you know which one to go after?"

"Leave that up to me. I can single one out. I've had a lot of experience."

"Do you want to check out Boston College tomorrow and get started?"

"We could do that, but Boston College is very close to home. We don't want to be familiar faces on campus. I was thinking about Rhode Island University. It would only take a couple of days to find out what we need to know, but we've got to be discreet. We can't be seen hanging out with them on campus every day. After we find the right mark and get their trust, we talk them into visiting Cape Cod. We really hype it up. Then it's off to the races."

"Wouldn't it be easier just to rob someone?"

"That might get us a couple of hundred if we're lucky. We need at least a few grand."

Jimmy listened and began to fantasize about the hunt. He was beginning to love his new life. Later that day they looked up the address for Lexington Finance and decided to scope the place out. They located the building on Massachusetts Avenue and drove around, becoming familiar with the neighborhood. There was a coffee shop across from Lexington Finance and Gillian figured it was a good place to observe the front door. It was almost five o'clock and the two of them ordered coffee and sat by the window watching as people left the building. Gillian had a picture of Kevin Reardon from the newspaper. It was now just a question of time and patience. By six o'clock nobody resembling Reardon had come or gone and they called it a night. The next morning, they returned and waited in the coffee shop, watching the front door. When their prey had not shown up by nine o'clock, they decided to visit the Boston College campus. They spent some time in the student center and gathered information about The Foreign Students Association. Afterwards they gassed up the car at the Shell station, picked up some refreshments at the 7-11 and drove to Rhode Island to check out the university.

"Where do we begin?" asked Jimmy.

"We go to the student center and ask about upcoming events for foreign students or clubs we can join."

They walked over to the student center and Gillian found the information desk.

"Excuse me," she said. "I have a friend from Brazil who is a student here. She's interested in Samba dancing. I was wondering if you had a list of social events and dance clubs—that kind of thing."

"There is a website that has a list of all the clubs, dances and international events scheduled for the year. I can give you a printout for all the dances and events for September if you like."

"Oh good. Yes. That would be great. Thank you. Also, can you tell me if there's a place where the foreign students like to hang out?"

"You might talk to Simone Bernard. She's the president of the FSA. She's over in Barlow Hall. That's where most of the foreign students live. Maybe she knows a place off campus where they all go."

The receptionist printed out a list and handed it to Gillian with a smile.

"Thank you so much. This should help a lot."

Gillian and Jimmy grabbed something to eat at the snack bar and watched the students as they came and went.

"Keep your eyes and ears open. Watch for girls wearing expensive jeans, nice jackets and fancy shoes. Don't bother with any girls that are laughing with friends or walking in a group. Just look for girls by themselves and say hello. If they answer with an accent, try to keep the conversation going."

They sat at separate tables in the snack bar for another hour. Jimmy said hello to several girls who fit Gillian's criteria but none of them had a foreign accent. Only one guy had the balls to talk to Gillian.

"Let's go check out Barlow Hall. Maybe we'll have better luck there. Just keep saying hello to any girl who looks like she might have money. Sooner or later, we're going to find someone."

The two of them sat on a wall outside the entrance to Barlow Hall and waited. Each time a single girl walked by Jimmy would offer a friendly hello. Gillian sat a few feet away and would give him a nod if it was worth it to pursue the conversation.

A young girl emerged from the dormitory and walked past them.

"Hello," said Jimmy.

The girl answered, "Allo" with a distinct French accent. Gillian nodded to Jimmy.

"Are you a new student here?" Jimmy asked.

"Yes. I just arrived last week from Paris. And you?" she said with a cheerful, gregarious smile.

"I'm from Montreal. I just arrived last week myself."

"Ah, Montreal. I have some friends there. They are going to McGill University. I want to go up there next month to visit. I hear it's beautiful."

Gillian signaled Jimmy to end the chase. There was no point. She was too popular.

"I guess it's nice. A little cold in the winter, though, and the people suck."

Gillian had to stifle a laugh at his attempt to kill the conversation.

The girl started to walk away and said, "Au revoir. Have a nice day."

"You don't have to overdo it, Jimmy. But you get the idea."

They continued to hang out for a couple of hours, but they didn't meet anyone else who caught Gillian's attention.

"I want to be back in Boston and watch for Reardon before four o'clock. We can try again tomorrow."

They drove back to Boston and once again sat in the coffee shop watching the door to the Lexington building. Again, Reardon failed to show up and they went home for the night. Gillian could see the look of frustration on Jimmy's face. He wanted action.

"You've got to be patient," she reassured him. "Sooner or later, we'll jump. You've got to pick your prey carefully."

They followed the same routine for the next few days, to no avail, and the weekend arrived. It was Saturday, September 11, and Gillian thought about the significance of that day in history. Maybe she would have her day as well.

There was no point in watching for Reardon, so they drove straight down to Rhode Island and began to hunt. They started at the student center, where they would be less conspicuous. Gillian wore a baseball cap and tied her hair back. They ate breakfast at the snack bar in the morning and spent the next few hours shooting pool at the arcade. After lunch they decided to go to the Rathskeller for a beer. Jimmy put a couple of dollars in the jukebox, and they sat at a table going over the details of their plan.

"Remember. Your name is Roger. I'm your younger cousin Stephanie. We're from Montreal. You're starting a Master's degree in economics and I'm a freshman studying sociology. We live together off campus. You're supposed to be looking out for sweet, innocent little Stephanie. Got it?"

"Yeah. I got it."

After an hour a pretty girl with long, dark hair walked up to the bar and ordered a beer. Gillian's eyes followed her as she took a seat on the opposite side of the room. She had tight-fitting designer jeans and a nice-looking leather jacket. She took a book out of her handbag and opened it.

"Go check her out, Jimmy. You know what to say."

Jimmy casually walked across the room and slowly drifted toward her table. "Hello. Are you a new student here?" he said in a shy, hesitant voice.

She looked up from her book and said, "Yes. My name is Natasha. I am from Prague. Vaat is your name?"

"My name is Roger. Do you mind if I sit down?"

"Not at all. Please sit."

Jimmy sat down and began to talk small talk. "I'm from Montreal. I'm new here as well. What are you planning to study here?"

"I am studying psychology, and you?"

"I'm studying economics. I just started a Master's degree."

"Vel, that sounds interesting. Vaat do you vant to do later?"

"I think I would like to get a job on Wall Street in a couple of years."

"Oh! The Volf of Vall Street," she chuckled demurely.

"Yeah. Something like that. Ooooowwww," he howled, looking away with feigned humility.

"Call me Tasha. It is nice to meet with you."

Jimmy glanced over at Gillian and gave her a subtle nod.

"So, do you live here on campus?" Tasha asked.

"No. I share a house with my cousin. That's her over there in the corner," he said, pointing at Gillian.

"Oh. She is pretty girl."

"Are all the girls in Prague as pretty as you?"

Natasha looked away timidly and smiled. "I am not so beautiful, but many models come from Prague."

"Well, they overlooked you, Tasha."

Jimmy continued to flirt with her and after an hour he waved to Gillian to come over.

"Let me introduce you to my cousin. This is Stephanie. Stephanie, this is Tasha from Prague."

"It's nice to meet you, Tasha."

"Nice to meet you, too."

Gillian sat down and they all began to talk.

"So Roger vas telling me that you live together off campus together."

"Yes, my parents insisted that Roger look out for me my first year." Gillian rolled her eyes as if she resented their over-protection.

"I know vat you mean. My parents are the same vay. That is vye I come to America."

"Well, pretty girls should always be careful. You never know," said Jimmy.

Gillian kicked him under the table.

"If you are careful, I think it is okay. If you are stupid or you get drunk, then you get in trouble."

They continued to break the ice and Jimmy offered to buy another round of beers. Soon they were laughing and talking about American politics and a million other things. They each had another beer and as the hours went by Natasha was letting down the walls.

"Do you get along with your parents?" Gillian asked.

"They are okay, but they think I am small child. I have always to tell them I make my own mind."

"I know exactly how you feel," said Gillian. "They should just let us do what we want. We're not stupid."

Jimmy looked at his watch and said, "It's getting late, Steph. I've got some things to take care of. We should get going soon."

"All right, I'd like to hang out more, Tasha, but my guardian angel says it's time to go," said Gillian, looking at Jimmy with a pout. "Give me your number and I'll give you a call soon."

"Tell you what. Why don't we take a trip to Cape Cod one of these days soon, while the weather is still nice?" suggested Jimmy.

Natasha asked, "Vaat is Cape Cod?"

"That's where President Kennedy lived. It's really beautiful. It's only an hour or two away," Gillian explained. "We could pick you up early and go for the day. Have you heard of the Mayflower?"

"No. Vat is May Flower?"

"It's the ship that the first settlers sailed from England when they came to America. There are so many nice things to see there."

"Okay. I go. You call me."

Natasha gave them her number and they said so long. The trap was set.

They drove back to Boston and discussed the timing and worked out the details. Jimmy never had so much fun in all his life.

"We probably have to hold her for at least a week. An ATM won't let you take out more than a thousand a day. I figure she's worth at least five, maybe ten thousand. We can figure that out after we grab her."

"Why do we have to keep her for a week?"

"We have to monitor her cell phone. If nobody calls, it's probably safe to start tapping her bank account. But if she starts getting a lot of desperate phone calls, we have to weigh our options. They might be able to track us down. We might have to risk letting her answer her phone and make up a story. I'll be standing right behind her with a knife, of course."

"When do you think would be a good time to do this?"

"Next Saturday or Sunday. We don't want to give her time to make a lot of friends on campus or talk about us to other people, so the sooner the better. You can call her next Wednesday and set it up."

"So what do I say to her?"

"Tell her we're going to the Cape for the weekend and ask her if she wants to join us. Arrange to meet her Saturday morning off campus so that nobody sees us. Make it early, like seven o'clock."

Gillian googled a map of the university.

"Tell her the corner of Kingstown Road and Old North Road at seven sharp. Oh, and tell her to bring a bathing suit and a change of clothes."

"You're good, Gee. What do you want to do until then?"

"Tomorrow we just relax. Monday morning, we try to find out more about Reardon."

Jimmy kept looking over at Gillian. The thought of her artfully stalking her prey through the jungle was making the adrenalin pump through his veins. He imagined her sleek body moving silently through the night, planning to make a kill. It was getting him more excited every minute. Gillian could sense what was on his mind. She put her hand on his thigh and gave him a salacious smile. By the time they got home he was half insane with lust. Gillian immediately pulled him into the bedroom, pushed him down on the bed and attacked him. As she straddled his body, they began to tear at each other's clothes. It took only a few moments before they were both naked. Jimmy made an attempt to wrestle with her and gain control, but she held him down. Finally, he stopped resisting and Gillian took him like a wild animal.

CHAPTER 34

Monday, September 13, 7:30 PM

Gillian awoke early Monday morning and checked the cooler to make sure there was enough ice covering the nitro. She understood that if it was allowed to warm up it would be unstable. The slightest bump could set it off. She took a bag of ice from the freezer and laid it gently on top of the deadly explosive.

She woke up Jimmy and the two of them set out for the city. They returned to the coffee shop and began to watch the front doors of the Lexington Building. When Reardon had not shown up by 10 AM, they decided to visit the Blue Hills Nature Preserve in Milton. They spent the day walking in the woods, enjoying the warm fall weather. The following day they went through the same routine, to no avail. Jimmy was becoming impatient.

"Maybe we should take a more direct approach. We don't know if he's ever going to show up. It could take weeks before we spot him."

"Patience, Jimmy. He'll show up sooner or later. We can't tip our hand. If you start asking too many questions people get suspicious. We need to stay under the radar."

"Of course, Gee. I'm sorry. You know what you're doing."

On the morning of the fifteenth Jimmy called Natasha. "Hi Natasha. It's Roger. We met in the Rathskeller last Saturday."

"Yes. I remember. How are you?"

"I'm fine. Listen, my cousin and I are going to Cape Cod this weekend and we thought of you. We were wondering if you would like to join us."

"Oh yes. That voud be nice. Vil you come and get me?"

"Yes. We will meet you on the corner of Old North Road and Kingstown Road. It's right next to the campus. We want to get an early start and beat the traffic, so I'll pick you up at seven in the morning. Okay?"

"Yes, that voud be great."

"Oh yeah, we're going for the weekend so bring a bathing suit and a change of clothes and a toothbrush. We'll be back by Sunday night."

"Okay. I vill be vating for you Saturday at seven. This sounds great. Thank you, Roger."

"See you then, Tasha." He hung up and turned to Gillian. "It's all set, Gee. We're picking her up on Saturday."

"Nice work, Jimmy. Now we got to concentrate on Reardon."

Finally, on the morning of September 16 they spotted him as he arrived at work. They returned later in the afternoon and waited patiently in their car, keeping an eye on the front door of the Lexington Building. At 4:35 Reardon left the building and began walking toward his car.

"There he goes, Jimmy. Get ready."

Jimmy started the car and followed Reardon as he got into his black Mercedes. He started to drive away, and Jimmy lagged a few car-lengths behind. Half an hour later they knew exactly where he lived. Another brick had been cemented into Gillian's house.

The weather that September had been beautiful and Friday morning was no exception. The two of them decided to take a ride on their bikes, and Gillian noticed that her engine was running rough, so they dropped it off at the Chestnut Hill Shell station. She explained to the mechanic what the problem was and what she wanted done. Gillian smiled as she noticed him leering at her. She climbed on the back of Jimmy's ride and they rode off together. They spent the day at Boston College and later that afternoon Gillian picked up the Harley again. That evening they cruised by Reardon's house several times and tried to get more of an idea about his routine. They spotted his car in his driveway at just after six o'clock. When they returned an hour later the car was gone.

"I'll bet he takes his wife out to dinner. These rich types hardly ever cook for themselves," said Gillian.

"That sounds about right," agreed Jimmy.

Later that night they drove by one more time and the car had reappeared.

"Well, we know what their window is. They go out about seven and they take about two hours for dinner. We'll check them out a couple of more times before we make our move."

"You call the shots, Gee. I'm down with anything you want to do."

"Let's go home and get some sleep. We've got to be in Kingstown early tomorrow morning. We don't want to fuck this thing up."

Early the next morning they jumped in the Taurus and drove down to Rhode Island. They arrived at the corner where they had arranged to meet and a few minutes later Natasha showed up.

Gillian leaned out of the window and greeted her. "Hi Tasha. All set to go?"

"Yes. Vee are lucky it is such nice vetter."

Gillian opened the door and let her get into the back seat. "Did you remember your bathing suit?"

"Yes. I have it vith me."

"Then let's go, Rog."

Soon they were on their way back toward Boston. The three of them began to talk and Gillian tried her best to make Natasha comfortable on the way. There was no point in tipping their hand until they had to. They reached the junction in the highway where Cape Cod split off to the east, but they continued north toward Boston. Gillian hoped that Natasha would not notice, but she did. "Hey, the sign said Cape Cod vas dat vay."

"Oh. There's too much traffic that way, Tash. We know a shortcut. It will save us a half an hour," said Gillian

"Okay. You know the best."

In another half hour they were deep into a wooded area near their house. As the road began to narrow Natasha became increasingly suspicious. "Vare are you going? This is not the vay to the beach."

"We're just stopping at home to pick up some things. We'll be at the beach soon." Gillian could see that Natasha was becoming visibly uncomfortable and she continued to try to reassure her. After a few minutes they pulled into the driveway of their house. "Come on in, Tash. This is where we live. We won't be more than a few minutes."

Natasha did not feel at all comfortable and looked around to see if there were other houses in the area. Not wanting to upset her new friends, she reluctantly followed them into the house. The moment she was in the living room Jimmy produced some zip-ties and Gillian pushed her into a chair.

Natasha began to yell, and Jimmy said, "Shut up," and slapped her.

"Let her yell. Nobody can hear her."

Natasha began to cry now, realizing she was in danger. "Vat is it you vant?"

"Give us your bank card and tell us your password number," demanded Gillian.

Natasha looked at them and knew immediately that there was no point in fighting back. She could only hope that they would eventually let her go. She told them what they wanted to know.

"Let's go back to Rhode Island and try it out. If we use the card there it won't raise any flags."

They left Natasha tied up and drove back to Kingstown. Gillian wore her cowboy hat to conceal her face from the ATM cameras. She withdrew a thousand dollars and checked the balance. There was still $6,756 left in the checking account. They would have to keep Natasha for another week.

Every day for the next week, they drove down to Rhode Island and made further withdrawals from Natasha's account. In the evening they would drive by the Reardon's house and continue to familiarize themselves with their routine. It seemed that every night Reardon and his wife would go out to dinner at approximately seven o'clock and return sometime after nine o'clock. Gillian decided that Saturday night would be a good time to carry out their plan. On Friday, September 24, they had completely drained Natasha's bank account. She was of no more use to them.

"We're going to have to get rid of Natasha, Jimmy. You know we can't let her go, right?"

"Yeah. I figured that. How do you want to do it?"

"You know that preserve we went to the other day? The Blue Hills Reservation?"

"Yeah. I remember. There's some very thick woods out there. Kind of like that place on Long Island."

"Exactly. It's sort of on the way back to Rhode Island. We tell Natasha that we're going to take her back to her school, but we stop there on the way. The less she suspects the easier it will be to keep her calm and cooperative."

"When do you want to do this?"

"Tonight would be best. That way we have an empty house for the Reardons tomorrow night. Let's go back home and tell her we're going to let her go."

They returned home that afternoon and began to talk to Natasha, who was tied up in her chair. Gillian began to explain to her that they were going to let her go, but their plans hit an unexpected snag when there was a knock on the door.

"Shit. Jimmy, go see who it is. Don't say a word or you're dead, Natasha."

Jimmy got his gun and tucked it in his belt under his shirt. He went to the door and answered it.

A gray-haired man who looked to be in his mid-sixties stood before him with a curious expression.

"Can I help you?" said Jimmy.

"Yes. I was wondering if my friend Eric O'Connell was here. We used this place as a hunting lodge some years ago. I saw the car out front and thought maybe he was here."

"No. I rent this place with my girlfriend now. There's no Eric here."

Gillian held her hand over Natasha's mouth and kept her quiet.

Natasha sensed this might be her only chance and began to struggle. She bit Gillian on the finger and began to yell.

Gillian grabbed a towel and put it over her mouth to shut her up, but it was too late.

The man at the door became suspicious and said, "What's going on in there?" as he tried to look past Jimmy into the living room.

Natasha managed to let out a convincing scream and the man became alarmed. He turned to run but Jimmy clocked him over the head with his gun. He fell into a heap and remained motionless in the doorway.

Gillian ran to the door and said, "We're gonna have to get rid of this guy too, Jimmy. We don't have a choice."

"I hear ya, Gee."

"We've got to get rid of his car somewhere and find a place to dump him. We'll leave her tied up here in the meantime."

They bound his hands and feet with zip-ties and gagged him.

"There's a place called the Rocky Woods Reservation about twenty miles west of here. You drive his car. I'll follow you in the Taurus."

"Wouldn't it be easier to get rid of Natasha at the same time?"

"No, we'll come back for her later. Two people at the same time can get complicated."

They managed to get the elderly man into the back seat of his car and began to drive west. Half an hour later they arrived at the reservation. Jimmy pulled the man from the car and got him on his feet. Gillian cut the zip-ties and they began to walk him into the woods.

After they had walked for fifteen minutes Gillian said, "This is good. Stop here."

Jimmy watched as she cut his throat. He had never seen anyone die before. He watched as the man began to twitch in spasms while the blood sprayed from his neck. The kill had been swift and decisive. Jimmy was both horrified and fascinated by the violence of the struggle. When it was over, they dragged the body off the trail and began to cover it with rocks. It was something Gillian had done before. Jimmy felt a slight touch of nausea but it soon subsided. On the way back they passed an old dirt road and found a remote place to ditch the car. They removed the plates and Gillian wiped off all the fingerprints from the steering wheel and door handles. When they were satisfied they hadn't left any clues they drove back home. They still had one more loose end to deal with.

The sun had set, and it was beginning to get dark. Gillian once again tried to convince Natasha that they intended to let her go, but after what had happened, she wasn't buying it. They zip-tied her hands and feet, gagged her and got her into the car. Natasha fought them all the way. They got to the Blue Hills Reservation and parked the car on Unquity Road. It was after 8:30 and the area was almost deserted. Jimmy got out of the car and checked for headlights on the road.

"Coast is clear. Let's go," he said.

They pulled Natasha out of the car and quickly dragged her into the woods, where they were out of sight of the road. Natasha kicked and twisted with everything she had. Gillian ran back and locked up the car. They dragged her farther into the woods and Gillian cut the zip-ties that bound her ankles.

Jimmy pulled her up to her feet and said, "Start walking."

Natasha made an attempt to run but she couldn't break free from the two of them. She dragged her feet and made herself as heavy as possible, to no avail. After a long, arduous struggle, they were deep into the woods.

"This should be far enough. Nobody is gonna find her here."

Natasha's eyes filled with terror as Gillian continued to make her intentions clear. She made one final desperate attempt to run but Jimmy held on to her. He pushed her off her feet and on to her knees. Gillian pulled out her knife and came up behind her. Natasha tried to get up, but Gillian ended it quickly. This time Jimmy watched more with fascination than with horror. He was getting a stomach for it. A few seconds later Natasha lay motionless on the ground.

"Wait till she finishes bleeding out, Jimmy. Then drag her by her feet into those bushes. Try not to get any blood on yourself."

Five minutes later they were done. They started to make their way back to their car and Gillian began to talk about their plans for the following night. She went over every detail with Jimmy until she was sure she had it all covered. When they were almost back to the car Gillian began to curse. "God damn it. Shit."

"What? What's the matter, Gee?"

"We got a fucking parking ticket." Gillian grabbed it from under the wiper and said, "Let's get the fuck out of here."

"Do you think this is going to be a problem?"

"Probably not. I don't think anybody will ever find her out there. Even if they do eventually find her, they could never tie it to us. We've gotta ditch this car tonight though. We should get another one tomorrow from Avis or somewhere else."

"Is this going to throw a monkey wrench into our plans for tomorrow night?"

"How are your nerves?"

"I'm okay."

Gillian smiled at him and said, "Then we're good to go."

They drove back to their house and Jimmy picked up his motorcycle. He followed Gillian to the airport. She left the keys for the Taurus in the drop box.

"We should rent a van," she said. "It'll be more practical when we grab the Reardons. We want to keep them out of sight as much as possible. Another thing—I don't want to use Michelle's credit card for this, just in case. We should use yours. If they do tie the parking ticket to Michelle, we'll still be safe."

"You're right, Gee. Good thinking."

Jimmy used his credit card to rent a Honda Odyssey from Alamo, and Gillian followed him back home. They sat on the front porch for another hour and let the events of the day wind down in their minds. Once again, they went over the plans they had set for the next day. Before they went to bed Gillian made sure there was enough ice on the explosives in the cooler. They got a good night's sleep and woke up refreshed the next morning. Things were back on track.

CHAPTER 35

Saturday morning, September 25
Boston

Jimmy was filled with excitement and enthusiasm when he woke up Saturday morning. The thought of a new adventure with Gillian reminded him of when he was teenage boy buying his first motorcycle. He couldn't wait for the evening to come. Gillian picked up on it and was amused. They had breakfast in a diner on Chestnut Hill Avenue and spent most of the day on the Boston College Campus. They went over their checklist for things they would need that night.

"We've got zip-ties, mace, gags, cloth bags and masks. I think we're pretty much set," said Jimmy.

"Remember what happened yesterday. You've got to expect the unexpected, Jimmy. You never know."

"Yeah. That was bad luck, that fuckin' dude showing up at our door. That could have complicated things. Then that stupid parking ticket."

"That's why we needed the gun we bought. It gives us a definite edge and a better chance to get away if we have to."

"Yeah, but I don't know what scares them more, my gun or your knife."

"I know. They say people have a gut reaction to the sight of a sharp blade. There's something about the immediacy of cold steel. You can't see the bullets in a gun."

"You can definitely be a scary girl, Gee."

As the hours of the day passed the fever began to build inside Jimmy. It was now five o'clock in the afternoon and the sun was getting lower in the sky.

"Let's drive past Reardon's house and make sure his car is there. We want to make sure he's going to follow his normal routine. We should follow him to whatever restaurant he's going to and then follow him home after dinner. We know where he lives so we wouldn't have to be right on his ass."

"Then we take him when he gets out of his car?"

"Yeah, as long as the coast is clear. We get them in the van as quickly as possible. You keep the gun on them, and I'll zip-tie Reardon's hands. If he resists, knock him out with the gun. I'll have the mace ready just in case. Then we gag them and put the bags over their heads. Remember, we only have one chance at this. Everything we've done up until now is for nothing if we fuck this up."

"I'm sure we can do this. We've got it down."

"Let's switch plates with the ones we took off the old man's car yesterday. If things go wrong, we don't want some pain in the ass to get our plate number and have them trace the van back to Alamo."

"You've thought of everything, Gee. You are good."

They cruised down the street and saw Reardon's Mercedes parked in his driveway directly in front of his front door. The driveway was a horseshoe and was perfect for a quick getaway. The neighboring houses were far enough away that a minor commotion would not draw attention. "Let's wait down the block around the corner. He has to leave in that direction, so we can pick him up when he comes by. Don't follow too closely. It's not the end of the world if we lose him. We'll just have to wait here for him to come back."

"Don't worry, I won't lose him, and he won't see us. There're some things I'm pretty good at."

"I know you are. You've been great so far, Jimmy."

They drove down the block and turned the corner. They made a U-turn and waited for Reardon to come by. It was now seven o'clock and the sun had set. Half an hour later, Reardon had not yet come by.

"What if they're not going out tonight?"

"Then we try again tomorrow. Let's give it until eight o'clock."

At 7:45 Reardon's Mercedes turned the corner in front of them. Jimmy let him get a fifty-yard head-start and then began to follow at a distance. The Mercedes headed for the Back Bay Area and twenty minutes later pulled into the parking lot of one of Boston's finest restaurants. Jimmy pulled into the parking lot across the street. Kevin and Jennifer Reardon stepped out of their Mercedes and let the valet take the car.

"Well, we've got about an hour and a half wait," said Gillian. "Just sit back and relax."

Two hours later the Reardons emerged from the restaurant and got back in their car. Jimmy started the engine and pulled out in the direction of Reardon's house. He drove slowly and let the Mercedes pass him. It wouldn't be long now. Jimmy began to feel the butterflies again. Gillian became calm and focused.

The Mercedes approached the driveway and Jimmy closed the distance between them. His timing was perfect. The Reardons got out of their car and made a step toward the house. The Honda raced in from the opposite side of the horseshoe and blocked the Mercedes in. Gillian was out of the car in an instant, standing between them and the safety of their front door. She held up the knife and stared at Jennifer. Jimmy jumped out and pointed the gun at Kevin.

"On the ground, now," he ordered as he grabbed him by the arm.

Kevin began to resist, and Jimmy knocked him out. Jennifer began to scream but she was no match for Gillian. Within seconds she forced her into the van. Jimmy picked up Kevin and threw him into the back seat. He jumped in the driver's seat and made a quick exit from the driveway. Jennifer was becoming increasingly hysterical. Jimmy turned around and clocked her with the gun. He drove back toward Westwood while Gillian gagged them and tied up their hands and feet. Half an hour later they were home with their quarry. Jimmy dragged Reardon into the house and in minutes he had him tied to the chair where Natasha had been the day before. Gillian muscled Jennifer into the house and soon had her subdued as well.

"We did it, Jimmy. We're almost home."

They left the two of them gagged and tied up in the living room and retreated into the bedroom. They made passionate love and slept peacefully until the next morning.

Jimmy awoke and the events of the previous day rushed back into his mind. He pulled Gillian closer to him and kissed her forcefully on the mouth. "I love you, Gee."

Gillian sat up in bed. She stretched her arms above her head and smiled. She looked at Jimmy and thought, *He's my only real friend in the world. The only person who I can count on.*

Her feelings of friendship and gratitude were short lived, however, as she thought about why her two guests were tied and gagged in the living room. Her mind raced back in time to the house in Buffalo, where Frank and Angela had held her down and taken not only her flesh but her soul as well. The old feelings of hatred and betrayal stormed back into her mind like a rogue wave crushing everything in its path.

Most people are just garbage. They take whatever they want and then stab you in the back.

She began to think about Mike and Brittany and how she had stolen him away from her. The anger slowly began to well up inside of her again. *He betrayed me. He took what he wanted and threw me away like I was an old toy he no longer had interest in. I wonder if he's ever seen Chucky!*

She began to smile a different smile, not one of serenity but of vengeance. Her cold green eyes stared straight ahead, as if focused on some imaginary prey that had crossed her path. Jimmy could see her mood begin to change. He knew what was going through her mind.

He put his arm around her and said, "Don't worry, Gee. I'm with you all the way."

She threw her arms around him and the two of them made love until noon.

The Reardons were tied up and gagged facing away from each other in the living room. They could clearly hear the passionate sounds coming from the next room.

What are they after? Did I do something to make them angry? Reardon asked himself. *Do they want money? Are they holding us for ransom? My God. Jennifer. I can't let them hurt Jennifer.*

Kevin's mind raced, thinking about what to say and how to reason with them. He was totally prepared to give them anything they wanted to protect Jennifer.

After a while Gillian emerged from the bedroom. She began to circle around them, studying the fear in their eyes. Her cold stare sent chills down Jennifer's spine. Gillian took pleasure in toying with her captive audience. She continued to walk around them with a satisfied smile which spoke volumes. Clearly this was about more than just money. Kevin looked at her with pleading eyes.

Don't be fooled, she thought to herself. *They're all the same. Deep down inside, they only care about power and money. They care about themselves and other people like them. They don't care about people like me. They would fuck me in a second if it suited them.*

Gillian had succeeded in convincing Jimmy that Mike had raped her. After a while she began to believe it herself. In her mind it was not only Frank that had taken advantage of her, but Mike as well. There was a price he had to pay. Each day she drifted farther away from truth. The old Gillian was quickly disappearing.

Jimmy walked into the room and saw that Gillian was pleased with herself. He came up behind her and wrapped his arms around her shoulders. Together they stood in front of Reardon, staring at him. Kevin saw immediately that he wasn't going to get much sympathy from Jimmy either. He cast his eyes toward the ground in resignation.

Gillian walked over to Kevin and removed the gag from his mouth. Reardon took several deep breaths and cleared his head. He winced in pain as his senses began to return to him. His head was still throbbing from the pistol whipping he had received the night before.

He looked directly at Gillian and asked, "What is it you want from us?"

"In good time, Mr. Reardon." She looked at Jimmy and said, "I think it's time for a little demonstration."

She went to the cooler and took out a cube of nitro. She showed it to Reardon. "See how small this is? We have about sixty more just like it. Just keep that in mind, Mr. Reardon."

"What is that? What are you going to do?"

"Just relax. If you cooperate nothing's gonna happen. Untie him, Jimmy. Get him on his feet."

Jimmy knew the minute she called him by name there was no way she would let them go. He cut Reardon's zip-ties and pulled him to his feet.

"Let's go for a little walk, shall we? Just remember, I have a gun and we still have your wife, so don't get cute."

They walked Reardon to a place about a mile into the woods. Gillian wrapped the puttylike substance around the M-80 and showed it to him. "See? Just an ordinary blockbuster. Nothing that special."

She walked another fifty yards farther and placed the explosive in a hollow notch of a pine tree that measured about two feet in diameter. She lit the fuse and retreated toward where Jimmy and Reardon were waiting. "We better move back a little and take cover," suggested Gillian.

The three of them stood behind a large oak tree and waited. A minute later a powerful explosion sent a shock wave through the trees. Hundreds of birds took flight in a blind panic, and a storm of leaves fell to the ground. Splinters of wood flew in all directions. They heard the deep cracking sound of the pine tree and watched as it crashed to the ground with a tremendous thud.

"I hope you're properly impressed, Mr. Reardon, because unless you do exactly as we say I plan on leveling the Lexington Building. Of course, I could save a little for you and your wife to play with."

Jimmy laughed and said, "Holy shit. That was awesome."

"I told you this stuff is scary," said Gillian with a satisfied smile.

Jimmy marched Reardon back to the house and tied him to the chair again. Gillian stood in front of him and looked him square in the eye. "We mean business, Kevin," she said, trying to sound more personal.

"If it's money you want, I'll do everything I can to make it happen, but the minute you hurt my wife I'll do all I can to fuck you up. Are we clear?"

"Perfectly. Let's hope that won't be necessary. But there's something you don't understand. This isn't just about money. I have something special in mind."

"What would that be?"

"All in good time, Kevin."

Jimmy smiled as he watched the gears turn in Gillian's brain.

Reardon began to think their purpose was political and wondered how he would be useful to them. *Why am I so special? What could I do that someone else couldn't do better? There are people in government with a lot more pull than me.*

"Your company uses a program provided by Affirmed Software. I'm sure you're familiar with it, Kevin."

"Yes, of course. We use it for all our transactions. So this is about money."

"Yes and no. Just be patient. I'll explain."

"I don't know what you want me to do. I can make certain transactions, but I'm limited to a certain amount. I'm not sure I can help you."

"I want you to make certain changes to Affirmed's software, and I want it to appear that the changes were made through someone who works at Affirmed."

"That would be difficult. I would need the authorization code of someone who worked at Affirmed."

"I'm sure there's a way around that. You must know who their chief software engineer is."

"Yes, I do. It's a guy named Mike Davis."

Gillian pretended not to recognize the name. "Good. So you are familiar with their operation."

"Yes, to some extent, but I still don't know what you have in mind."

"Payback, Kevin. I want to fuck up this country as much as I can. They fucked me over. They fucked my whole family. By the time I'm done they're going to have a fiscal nightmare on their hands. You're going to help me create it."

"You're crazy. I won't do it."

Gillian smiled and drifted behind Jennifer with her knife in her hand. She knew just how to turn it in the light to make her point.

"Okay! Okay! I'll do what you want. Just don't hurt my wife."

"That's a good boy, Kevin. You learn quickly."

"I don't know what you want me to do. I don't have Davis's authorization code."

"When Lexington makes a transaction or request in which you are not directly involved, is there a universal company code that any of the higher executives can use?"

"No. There's nothing like that."

Gillian casually walked behind Jennifer again and put the knife up to her throat.

"Come on Kevin. Don't bullshit me. Are you sure there's no special code?"

She stared at Reardon. There was no mistake about the message she was sending.

Reardon sighed and said, " Okay. Yes, there is."

"Davis would be able to access that information, wouldn't he?"

"It's encrypted, but I'm sure he could find out. He wrote the program."

"So if he requested a transaction using that code it would go through, right?"

"Yes, but not without us knowing who requested it."

"That's not a problem for me."

"I don't understand your plan. Nobody would believe that Davis would try to get away with something like that. He'd get caught."

"All in good time, Kevin. The timing for this has to be perfect. We're going to send a little software update request to Affirmed Software through the New York office. I'm sure it will wind up on Davis's desk in Albany. You're going to request it using your company code."

"You've got this all worked out, don't you?"

"Most of it. You're going to supply me with the details I need."

"Then I guess you intend to keep us here for some time."

"Just get comfortable, Kevin. If you cooperate, you and your wife might even get some yard time."

Gillian motioned to Jimmy and the two of them walked outside. They sat on the porch swing and Gillian said, "How do you feel about living in Buenos Aires?"

Jimmy was surprised by her question.

"What do you mean, Gee?"

"We might have to get out of here in a hurry after this is over."

"Whatever happens I want to go where you go. You know that, right?"

"I do, Jimmy. I think everything is gonna work out just fine."

"So what's your plan?"

"Like I told you, I don't have to kill Mike Davis. I'll be happy with just destroying his life."

"How are you gonna do that?"

"First we get Reardon to make a bogus transaction to an account we set up and confirm that it took place."

"I'm with ya so far."

"Then we send a request to Affirmed for a software update. It will automatically wind up going to Mike. We eliminate the account the transfer was made to. It'll look like Mike was trying to embezzle money and covering his tracks. We're also going to create a lot of fiscal chaos and make it look like Affirmed screwed up. With any luck we could walk away with almost a hundred grand and at the same time destroy Mike's career. It will make him look like a total incompetent. Sooner or later, they'll figure out that he wasn't embezzling money, but his reputation as a software engineer will be ruined."

"Won't they be able to track the activity back to our computer? What about the Internet connection?"

"That's in O'Connell's name. The guy who rented us the house."

"How long is all this gonna take?"

"Hopefully no longer than a few weeks. Figure mid-October. We just leave one day without getting our deposit back or paying the rent. Nobody has our pictures. Nobody knows our names. We won't leave any fingerprints. We'll be in Argentina before anybody knows anything. The best they will be able to do is an artist's sketch."

"Maybe we should off the guy who rented us this house?"

"I've thought about that, but it would have to be on the day we left. That's complicated. If he came here to collect rent and he went missing, someone might come out here to check on him."

"You're right. You do the thinking, Gee."

"We have to start as soon as possible."

"What's our first step?"

"On Monday morning we have Reardon transfer ninety thousand dollars into the account we set up. We have to wait a few days to make sure it clears. After that we make a withdrawal of a small amount and make sure everything is kosher. If we keep the amount low, I doubt if it will raise any flags."

"Won't they be looking for Reardon and his wife?"

"My guess is that nobody is going to start worrying until Monday night, or even Tuesday. People like Reardon go off the radar on purpose sometimes. Even if they do suspect something, they're not going to start investigating a transaction of less than a hundred thousand right away. If we do this right, we might walk away with over eighty thousand. Timing is everything."

"So what do you want to do until tomorrow?"

"Why don't we start getting acquainted with the Reardons? They look like a lovely couple."

"You're bad, Gee."

"I know. I can't help it. It's in my nature," she said with a smile.

They walked back inside and Jimmy took a seat next to Kevin, staring at him with fixed eyes.

Gillian took out her knife. She stood behind Jennifer and began to play with her hair in an overtly suggestive way. She made sure Kevin could see the fear in Jennifer's eyes.

"Tomorrow morning you're going to do us a little favor, Kevin."

"All right. Tell me what you want."

"You're going to transfer ninety thousand dollars from Lexington to Affirmed Software using the company authorization code. You're going to make it look like it's a payment for services provided. Also, you're going to predate it with a time stamp that makes it look like the transaction happened last week."

"I don't know if I can do that."

"You can do it, Kevin. Don't bullshit me." Gillian gave Jennifer's hair a tug and put the knife up to her throat. "Then you're going to transfer that money to an account we have set up at Bank of America. That account is going to look like it's a personal expense account for an Affirmed employee. You have to set up that account through Affirmed."

"That's a little tricky. I'm not sure I can do that."

"Why would that be a problem? You're giving them money, not taking it."

"That's true, but I've never tried anything like that."

"What's more is you're going to do it in Davis's name."

"I see. Now I get it."

"One more thing."

"What?"

"If something goes wrong, we don't plan on being taken alive. We're just not the prison type, if you know what I mean. The minute a cop shows up in the driveway you and your pretty wife are dead."

"I don't think ninety thousand dollars is going to start a panic," said Reardon.

"No. But you and your wife disappearing will. Make sure you use the company authorization code and not your own."

Gillian smiled at Kevin with a look that sent a clear message. She was ready to kill.

CHAPTER 36

Monday, Sept. 27, 7:30 AM

Gillian awoke early in the morning and walked through the living room and straight into the kitchen.

"Anybody hungry?" she said, looking at her two captives with feigned sympathy.

Kevin and Jennifer looked blankly back at Gillian.

She walked over to Kevin, looked him straight in the eye, and said, "It's almost time to for you to do your thing. Remember what I said about cops showing up here. Don't roll the dice."

She walked over to Jennifer and untied her. "Anything you want to do? Now's the time."

Jennifer's legs were sore from having been tied up all day Sunday. She walked stiffly over to the bathroom and was grateful to be allowed some privacy.

Jimmy came in from the bedroom carrying the Glock and said, "It's five minutes to eight. Should we get Kevin to do his magic on the keyboard?"

"Why don't we let them get a little exercise? They'll be more relaxed and cooperative."

Jennifer came out of the bathroom and Gillian said, "If you want to walk around on the porch and stretch your legs, go right ahead. The fresh air will do you good. Just remember we still have your husband tied up. Besides, I'm sure I'm a lot faster than you so don't try to run. Should I make you some breakfast?"

Jennifer didn't know how to react to Gillian's sudden kindness. *It's like she's a totally different person. This is weird. She's completely insane, but brilliant at the same time.* "Thank you. Yes, I'm a little hungry. The only thing I've had to eat was that candy bar you gave me yesterday."

"I'm sorry. I'll try to make you more comfortable. If you want to take a shower there are some clean towels in the closet."

"I guess you plan on keeping us here for a long time."

"For a couple of weeks. First, we have to find out if the bank account was successfully set up. After that we start to withdraw the money. That should take about a week. As soon as we find out the account was deleted, we can make our getaway. We'll call the cops and tell them where to find you."

Jennifer hoped that was true but had her doubts.

Gillian accompanied her out to the porch and said, "Stretch out good. If you don't give us any problem, I'll let you out again this afternoon."

Jennifer was certain there was no chance of escape and did exactly as she was told. *Maybe we'll get a chance later on,* she hoped.

After ten minutes she brought Jennifer back inside and Jimmy zip-tied her to the chair. "Your turn, Kevin. Remember, your wife is tied up inside with me and my knife."

Jimmy held the gun on him and allowed him to use the bathroom. "Time for a little exercise. I'm sure you could use it after being tied up all yesterday."

"I'm okay. Just don't hurt my wife. Please."

"If you do everything we say, things will be just fine," Jimmy assured him.

It was now almost nine o'clock, and Jimmy walked Kevin back inside.

"Let's get started," Gillian said. "Bring the chair over to the computer and just tie his legs. Remember, Kevin, I'm watching everything you type in. Make sure you don't make any unintentional convenient mistakes."

Kevin began by accessing the Lexington website. He used the company authorization code to create an account at Affirmed and changed the time stamp to September 20. Gillian watched every keystroke with focused attention. The computer showed a message which confirmed the establishment of the account.

"So far so good, Kevin. Now transfer ninety thousand dollars from Lexington to that account."

Kevin dutifully did what she asked.

"Now transfer eighty thousand from that account to Bank of America with this routing number and account number. Make sure you time stamp that retroactively to September 20 as well. Be sure it's only eighty thousand. Not a penny more."

Kevin again did as he was told. The computer issued the message FUNDS TRANSFERRED.

Another brick was cemented into Gillian's house.

"Okay, log off. Make sure you're completely logged out of Lexington's website."

"You don't really expect to get away with this, do you?" said Kevin.

"Let us worry about that. I'll tell you what. Let's celebrate. Why don't we all sit down and have breakfast together."

Jimmy brought the chairs over to the kitchen table and Gillian made some scrambled eggs and toast. The four of them sat together and Gillian tried to make small talk. "We should play poker later. Do you guys know Texas Hold 'em?"

Her bizarre cavalier attitude made Jennifer more and more uncomfortable. *How could somebody be so detached from reality?* she thought.

"Let's get some fresh air," she said, looking at Jimmy. The two of them went out on the porch and sat on the swing. Jennifer could see them through the window laughing and talking to each other.

Where do people like this come from? she thought. *How do people get so twisted?*

"Were you serious when you asked them to play poker, Gee?"

Gillian laughed and said, "No, Jimmy. I want them to think I'm crazy."

"Why?"

"I want them to think I'm capable of doing anything. It makes them more cooperative. Being nice to them is even creepier than threatening them."

Jimmy laughed and said, "You're right about that. It's creeping me out."

An hour later Gillian walked back inside and said, "If you want to stretch out or if you need to use the bathroom, let us know. I'll make some lunch later on. Is there anything you would like to watch on TV?"

Kevin and Jennifer just looked at each other, not sure what to say.

After a moment Kevin said, "Sure. Why not? We could watch some TV. Right Jen?"

"Okay. Sure."

Gillian positioned the TV so that they could both see and said, "How about *Law & Order*?"

Jimmy, who had just walked back in, had to stifle a laugh and turned away.

"You might as well get comfortable. It's going to be at least two or three days till the money clears."

Kevin and Jennifer resigned themselves to their fate and began to watch the television.

"I'm going to ride into town and get a newspaper. I'll be back in an hour," said Gillian. "Anybody want anything?"

Again, Jimmy had to stifle a laugh.

"See you in an hour."

Gillian drove to the 7-11 on Chestnut Hill Ave and bought a copy of the *Boston Globe*. She also picked up a couple of Pepsis and a number of Payday candy bars. She paid with Michelle's credit card. Half an hour later she was back in Westwood. Kevin and Jennifer were half-heartedly watching the TV while Jimmy sat outside on the porch swing. Gillian untied Jennifer and again offered to let her shower. This time she accepted. The next day the routine was almost identical.

On Wednesday Gillian once again drove to the 7-11 and bought a copy of the *Globe*. The news of Reardon's disappearance was now on the front page. A smile came to her lips as the adrenalin rushed into her veins. She put the paper into her saddlebag and started back home. On the way she stopped at Bank of America and checked the balance of the account. The money had not yet cleared. Gillian arrived back at the house and showed the headlines to Jimmy.

"See? It took almost three days until it raised a flag. I figure we have at least another week or two to drain the account before they figure it out. Then we'll get Reardon to delete it and we're on the road. Timing is everything now."

• • • • •

Don Corlino sat at his desk at the FBI Regional Office. He took a sip of his coffee and read the headlines of the *Boston Globe*. The Reardon disappearance was the top story. George Barnett came from behind him and tossed a manila envelope on his desk.

"I see you're reading about your next assignment."

"You mean Jack is putting Tommy and me on this?"

"You got it."

"How many teams are on it?"

"Jack's got five other teams ready to go. The last time the Reardons were seen was on Saturday night. They were in Terrell's over in the Back Bay area. Their car was found in their driveway so we're guessing that's where they were abducted."

"Has anyone demanded any ransom?

"No. Nobody has any clue what's going on."

"Where's Tommy now?"

"Jack sent him out to Chicago this morning to track down one of Reardon's contacts. They had a meeting together there last week. Jack wants you to work on things here in Boston."

"Has anybody talked to Lexington yet?"

"We have a couple of teams out there now. They're checking his computer records. So far there's nothing that's setting off alarms. They checked all his transactions from Monday and Tuesday. If somebody is trying to extort money, it's not through the usual means. There's no record of any large sum of money being transferred that can't be accounted for. They checked every transaction that used his authorization code. Nothing."

"How about family and friends? Has anybody started interviewing them?"

"That's what Jack wants you to do. Here's a list for you to start with. There's other stuff in the envelope I just gave you. Good luck, Don."

Don began making phone calls and making arrangements to interview some of the Reardons' friends. It was going to be a long day.

CHAPTER 37

Thursday, September 30

Gillian awoke to the sound of rain pelting down on the roof. It was the first time it had rained all month. She walked out on the porch and breathed in the sweet country air. She called for Jimmy to join her outside on the swing. The two of them sat there for the next hour, enjoying the sound of the rain clattering down on the roof above them. By nine o'clock the weather showed no signs of lightening up. Gillian decided to make breakfast for her guests. The four of them sat at the table and Gillian began to play with Jennifer like a cat would play with a mouse.

She turned to her and said, "Don't you just love the rain? It makes everything so clean and fresh. I could just sit on the porch all day. It's so nice and cozy here. Don't you think?"

Jennifer looked to Kevin for support and then replied, "Yes. We love to walk in the rain."

"Oh good. Maybe we can go for a walk later. Just us girls. We can share some girl talk."

"Okay," Jennifer agreed nervously.

After breakfast Gillian allowed Jennifer and Kevin to use the bathroom and stretch their legs.

'You want to go for that walk now, Jennifer?" said Gillian with a friendly, upbeat voice.

Jennifer looked over at her husband, hoping for some sign of reassurance. Kevin wasn't sure what advice to give her.

She just made us breakfast. If she were going to kill us, why would she do that? he reasoned.

"Go ahead, honey. You girls have a nice talk." *Maybe if we bond with them, they'll let us go in the end.*

The rain had started to let up. Only a light drizzle was still coming down.

Gillian opened the front door and stepped out onto the porch.

"Come on, Jen. Let's go."

Jennifer looked back at Kevin with anxious eyes and reluctantly followed her outside.

"This feels so good. I love the rain on my face. Don't you?" said Gillian, drawing in a deep breath.

"Yes. I know what you mean. It's refreshing and clean. It's nice to get away from the city."

The two girls walked slowly down to the end of the driveway and turned left toward where the road came to a dead end. From there a path led into the woods.

"How long have you two been married?" Gillian asked casually.

"We got married in April about two and a half years ago."

"Do you go out to dinner every night?"

"Yes. Almost every night. How did you know that?"

Gillian just looked at her and smiled. "I'll bet Kevin really loves you. Doesn't he?"

"I'm sure he does. He treats me very well," said Jennifer, not quite sure where this was going.

"And I'll bet you love him, too."

"With all my heart." *Why is she asking me all these questions about Kevin? Why would she care about our marriage?*

The two of them continued to walk down the path farther into the woods.

"Did you meet in college?"

"No. He's almost ten years older than me. I met him at a party about five years ago. He asked me out and we dated for a while. When he was promoted at Lexington three years ago, he asked me to marry him."

"I guess it takes a lot of money to live where you do."

Jennifer suddenly realized how her answer sounded. "Oh. I didn't care about that. I would have married him either way."

"Don't you come from a rich family?"

"Yes, I do. My parents are part of the society clique. I find them boring. Kevin isn't like that."

The two of them continued to walk down the path, which was becoming less distinct with every step they took. Jennifer was starting to become more and more anxious and Gillian picked up on it.

"Are the two of you planning on having kids someday?" she asked in an earnest tone.

Jennifer felt oddly relieved when Gillian asked her that. She decided it would be best to open up to her. *Maybe she's got some feelings after all. Maybe I can make her care about me and Kevin.*

"That's all I think about. I want to have a little boy first, God willing. After that a little girl would be perfect. Just two kids. Then I think we're done. What about you?"

Gillian stopped walking and looked straight at Jennifer. A smile crossed her lips and she said, "I don't know if I would make such a good mother."

Jennifer froze and thought, *Was it a mistake to ask her that?*

Gillian could read her mind perfectly and decided to put her at ease again. "I may change my mind one day. Who knows what the future will bring? Maybe someday. Let's walk a little farther."

The path had all but disappeared and the terrain was becoming more rugged. Jennifer's mind was racing with apprehension.

"So what do you do all day, Jen? Do you have a job?"

"I work for PETA. I try to raise funds for the humane treatment of animals. I call people all day and try to organize local groups."

"Oh, that's great. I love cats. Dogs are cool too. I had a cat when I was little."

"So did I. It was the cutest thing. I have two dogs now. I want to get more but Kevin thinks two are already a handful. He's right, I guess. I'm just an animal nut, if you know what I mean."

"Yeah. I guess I am too. If I ever settle down, I'll probably get a dog and a cat."

They were now deep in the woods. They came to a small clearing that was surrounded by thickets of scrub pine. The rain was a bit steadier and Gillian stopped to look at Jennifer. "I guess this is far enough."

Jennifer's heart pounded as she looked back at Gillian.

"Why don't we head back? I think the rain is starting to pick up."

Jennifer breathed a sigh of relief. "Okay," she said in a timid, acquiescent voice.

The two girls started walking back the way they had come. By the time they were halfway the rain was coming down in earnest.

"We better run," said Gillian.

They took off running. Gillian was laughing as two of them burst through the front door, soaking wet. Jennifer brushed her hair aside and looked at Kevin, grateful just to see him one more time. Kevin looked back at her, encouraging her to stay positive.

"We have a dryer," said Gillian. "Why don't you get out of that dress and I'll loan you a pair of jeans. We're about the same size. I have a shirt for you too."

Half an hour later Jennifer was sitting in a chair facing Kevin. She was wearing Gillian's clothes. Even Jimmy seemed puzzled about what was going on.

Jennifer and Kevin just looked at each other, uncertain what to expect.

"Why don't you two talk to each other? I'm going to pick up a paper and check the bank again. I'll be back in an hour or two."

Gillian drove her Harley to the 7-11 and picked up the paper. The Reardon disappearance was again on the front page. She felt another rush of adrenalin. The thought of getting away clean and making it to Argentina was becoming more realistic in her mind. On the way home she again stopped at Bank of America. This time a balance of $86,542 appeared on the screen. Gillian withdrew $1,000. She tried a second time but was denied.

Oh well. Can't blame a girl for trying. We might have to withdraw the money in person. Gillian had opened the account with Michelle Dennis's identification. She had given her Rochester address as her permanent residence. Eventually their luck would run out. Things had to move fast if they were going to get away with it. She rode back to the house.

Gillian walked back inside and found the three of them watching *Law & Order* on television. Things seemed calm enough. Jennifer looked at her hoping to rekindle the fledgling bond they had shared that morning. Gillian gave her a faint smile.

"Why don't we go outside for a while and sit on the porch, Jimmy? We'll let these two love birds have some alone time."

"Okay with me." Jimmy followed Gillian on to the porch and they sat on the swing. "What was that all about this morning, Gee? Why did you take that walk her? In the rain, no less. I thought for sure I wasn't going to see her again."

"A little psychology, Jimmy. Believe me, I have my reasons."

"You're the boss."

"Good news, Jimmy. The money cleared. The only thing is we might have to withdraw the money in person. We can only get a thousand a day through the ATM. That's going to take too long."

"When do you plan on doing that?" asked Jimmy uncertainly.

"Let's try to get a few more thousand from the ATM over the next couple of days. We can also get cash back on purchases we make at stores. I think we should wait until next week to try to make a large withdrawal. It's risky, Jimmy. We may have to bolt if things go wrong."

"I understand, Gee."

It was late afternoon and a chill descended on their little paradise.

"Let's go back inside and start up a fire. We can all get comfortable and watch TV."

"Sounds like a plan," he agreed.

· · · · ·

After having interviewed twelve different acquaintances of the Reardons, Don Corlino returned to his office. He had recorded several of the conversations with Reardon's friends and associates. He began to enter some of the facts into his computer. He created a basic timeline of the events preceding Saturday night. He also drew a map of relationships between their friends. George Barnett walked over to him and asked, "Anything?"

"Nothing that screams at you. I have the feeling this is going to be a tough one."

"I have to say it does seem a bit unusual. No bodies. No ransom note. You ever heard of something like this before?"

"No George. No, I have not."

Don put his elbows on his desk, put his fingers to his temples and rested his head on his palms.

CHAPTER 38

Friday, Oct. 1, 7:30 AM

Don was already at his desk at 7:30 in the morning. He had gotten the names of a few more people he wanted to talk to from the interviews he had conducted the previous day. He began to make phone calls.

George came over to his desk and said, "Jack wants to know if you've made any progress."

"Believe me, you and Jack will be the very first people I talk to if I find something."

"I know, Don. He doesn't want to push, but you know how things are in a high profile case. It's no easier for him."

"I know. I know. I'm just not looking forward to this right now. I promised Cheryl I'd spend more time with her. I don't want to look like a liar."

"No one said this job was easy. Sometimes your life isn't your own."

"Explain that to Cheryl."

"She worries about you."

"I know. She's actually been a pretty good sport about it."

"Well, check in with me even if you don't come up with anything. What are you doing now?"

"I have several names I'm going to follow up on. There's really nothing else right now."

"Good luck, then."

Don picked up the phone again and began to schedule times to interview potential leads.

At nine o'clock he hit the road. By lunch time he had interviewed four different parties. He was no further along in trying to put the pieces together. There were no pieces. Only two missing people.

· · · · ·

Gillian awoke early Friday morning, thrilled that her plan to set up the phony account through Affirmed had worked out. She sat up in bed and stretched her arms out over her head with a smile of satisfaction and accomplishment. She woke up Jimmy and gave him a big hug and kissed him on the cheek.

"We did it, Jimmy. We should at least be able to get enough money to make our getaway. It's time to launch the next part of our plan and fuck up Mike good. Let's go wake up our friends."

Gillian got dressed and walked into the living room. "Rise and shine, Kevin. I've got another little job for you."

Jimmy walked in and untied Kevin while Gillian kept the gun on him. He led him to the chair in front of the computer.

"Take a seat, Kevin. Log back into Lexington. We're going to make a few more transactions."

"Okay. Tell me what you want me to do."

"Pull up the list of all your clients who have loans over ten million dollars from Lexington."

Kevin pulled up a list of several major contractors and government agencies.

"All right. Set up accounts in each company and start doling out the money. Make sure the amounts are less than ninety thousand each. Route each one through Affirmed Software and make sure the accounts are in their name. And don't forget, use your generic code."

"I'll do my best but I'm not making any guarantees."

"It better be your best," said Gillian, smiling and looking at Jennifer.

Kevin started tapping the keys. A message came up on the computer screen:

TRANSFER COMPLETE

A smile curled up on Gillian's lips. Jimmy started to laugh and said, "Yes."

"Keep going. Do the same for everyone on the list."

Kevin had no choice but to comply. Half an hour later they were done.

Gillian smiled and said, "Now go to your smaller accounts and issue a notice that their loans are being called. Make sure the request is routed through Affirmed."

"But they'll just call Lexington and find out it's not true," argued Kevin.

"I know. I'm just hoping to cause some trouble for Affirmed. I want it to look like a computer glitch."

Kevin did what she asked.

When they were finished Gillian suggested that they all have breakfast together.

"Oh, thank you. I'm starved," pleaded Jennifer.

"I could use something to eat myself," said Jimmy.

Just after breakfast Gillian took her Harley to the 7-11 and picked up the newspaper and a few more candy bars. She made another stop at Bank of America and tried to withdraw another thousand dollars. A message appeared on the screen: Maximum withdrawal allowed $200.

What the fuck? What the hell is this? she whispered to herself. Gillian withdrew $200 and tried a second time. Her request was denied. *God damn it. Fuck.*

She got back on her Harley and flew back home. The minute she got there she motioned to Jimmy to come out on the porch.

"We got a problem, Jimmy."

"What's the matter, Gee?"

"The fucking ATM won't let me take out more than two hundred. That means the bank probably won't let us make a major withdrawal either. I don't know what changed. It could be that Affirmed has a weekly withdrawal limit for that type of account. Maybe you have to get direct approval from the company after you've withdrawn a certain amount. I just don't know."

"What do you want to do?"

"I want to fuck Mike over."

"Yeah. I know. Maybe he's still going to get screwed for this."

"No. We didn't steal enough. I'll bet he's the one who put the safeguard in the software. It probably means that our other plans to discredit Affirmed and fuck up Mike aren't going to work either."

"So what's our next move?"

Gillian thought for a moment and said, "Maybe we should try a more direct approach. How do you feel about another kidnapping?"

Jimmy smiled and looked her straight in the eye. "I'm getting bored sitting around here. Anything you want to do is cool with me."

"I was hoping you'd say that."

"When do we get started?"

"We better move quickly. Things are starting to heat up. Mike lives out in Albany with his wife and kids. That's about three hours away. I want to go there and scope the place out first. You should stay here and watch our guests. I'm going to be at least a few days."

"Why don't we just get rid of these two first and I'll come with you?"

"No. These two could still be useful."

"Okay. Just call me and let me know how things are."

"When I figure things out, we can take the car out there and snatch them."

"Okay."

"By the way, keep them both tied up. Get the *Globe* every morning and stay on top of things. Call me if something important comes up."

"When are you leaving?"

"I'm going to take a ride out to Albany right now. I'm sure I would still recognize him right away. I'll follow him home and then start watching the house "

"Be careful, Gee."

"Don't worry about me. Just keep an eye on these two. And make sure there's enough ice in that cooler."

Gillian jumped on her Harley and drove off. Half an hour later she was riding down I-90 west. She began to think about how Mike had dumped her like she was just so much trash. Once again, the anger started to build up inside her.

Does he still remember me? What if I walked past him? Would he even recognize me? I never stood a chance. He just used me and then tossed me aside. He's no different than Frank or Angela or George. I was only seventeen then. That's statutory rape. He should have gone to jail. Now I understand why there are laws against fucking seventeen-year–old, innocent little girls.

With every mile she put behind her the anger grew. She hit the throttle hard and the Harley responded. It sprang forward with a roar of defiant anger and raced down the highway. By the time she reached Albany she was ready to kill.

It was early afternoon when Gillian pulled into the parking lot across the street from Affirmed Software. As fate would have it, a blue Subaru pulled into the lot in front of Affirmed at that exact moment. Mike stepped out, accompanied by two girls.

Holy shit. That's him. After all this time. I would know him a mile away.

She watched as Mike disappeared into the building with his two companions. Gillian rode her bike across the street and got a quick look at his license plate.

He'll probably leave around five o'clock. It's Friday. I'll come back at four to make sure I don't miss him.

Gillian took a ride and found a comfortable diner to pass the time and read the *Globe*. The Reardon mystery was still a top story. The main article stated that the FBI and police had few leads and that there were no witnesses who could explain their sudden disappearance. Gillian smiled as she continued to read. Authorities were asking for the public's help and urging anyone with information to come forward.

We'll still be safe for at least another week or two. They don't have a clue, she thought to herself. Gillian waited until five o'clock and then returned to the Affirmed parking lot to wait for Mike. Just after six o'clock she watched him leave the building and get into his car. She started up the Harley and waited for Mike to get on the road. She followed about a hundred yards behind. Five minutes later they were on I-90 West. Gillian continued to follow at a safe distance. She watched as Mike pulled off the highway and headed for Forest Park. The streets became narrower and more rural as they got farther away from the highway. Gillian took notice of the majestic green hills in the distance. They were getting into a very small, out-of-the-way community. She stopped following and turned the Harley around.

I'll come back later and look for his car. No point in arousing suspicion.

An hour later Gillian returned to the area and located Mike's car in front of his house on Birch Street.

There's no way I can watch this place from the street, she thought. *I'm sure the neighbors would call the cops. I'll have to find a good vantage point from those hills behind the house.*

She drove around and got familiar with the area. There was a dirt road at the end of the development that led into the hills.

If I get a pair of binoculars I can hike up into the hills and check things out from there.

Gillian figured there wasn't much more she could find out until the next day so she found a motel on the highway and called it a day. As she got ready for bed, she caught a glimpse of herself as she walked past the mirror. She paused and looked hard at the girl standing in front of her. It was someone she hardly recognized. The person she had been six months earlier no longer existed. At first, she had a moment of doubt but it was short-lived. She smiled at her reflection. She was beginning to like who she had become. She walked over to the bed and lay down. She began to make plans.

The next morning, she went to a sporting goods store and bought a pair of binoculars. She wanted to begin watching Mike's house but the weather had other plans. A steady rain was beginning to fall. Reluctantly she returned to her motel room and called Jimmy.

"Yeah, Gee. How's it going?"

"So far so good. I know where Mike lives. I just have to figure out their routine. How's everything on your end?"

"Nothing different. We just watch TV all day. Reardon isn't going to take any chances with me pointing a gun at his wife. I let them take turns walking around. It helps to keep them calm. I read in the paper that the cops have no clue what happened to them."

"Yeah. Things are going to be all right. I'll be back on Tuesday night. I should know enough by then."

"Good. I miss you already."

Early Sunday morning Gillian drove her Harley back to Forest Park and rode up the dirt road into the hills. She got off her bike and found a good spot to watch Mike's house. She made herself comfortable and took out the binoculars. Just after nine o'clock the rear door swung open and a yellow lab came charging out and headed straight for the hills. The dog was followed by two little girls who frantically chased after it. A moment later Mike appeared with a girl who was almost certainly Brittany. A spike of jealousy hit Gillian in her stomach and her head at the same time. She watched as Mike put his arm around her and kissed her on the cheek. The anger began to build up inside.

Will ya just look at the happy couple. Beautiful house. A couple of sweet little girls. A dog. Just the perfect family. The temperature started to rise again in Gillian's brain. She had a sudden urge to run down the hill and plunge a knife into Brittany's heart while Mike watched. *Why should they be so happy? It's so unfair? They're no better than me. That should be me down there.*

Gillian was almost ready to act, but she caught herself in time. *Patience. All in good time. Stick to the plan.*

She watched as the two of them began to climb the hill. She could hear Brittany shout for the kids to wait for them, apparently to no avail. Gillian adjusted her binoculars and watched them all as they walked along the ridge. Several times the dog ran far ahead and then returned to accompany the girls.

Good dog. Make sure they're safe. You never know what's out there, Gillian laughed to herself.

Well, they're probably going to be gone for most of the day. I might as well get something to eat and come back later.

• • • • •

Jimmy sat on the couch with his Glock next to him on the coffee table. He hit the remote and switched the TV to an episode of *Crossing Jordan*.

"This show okay with you guys?" he said to his two captives. "I'm going into town for a little while. Either of you need the bathroom before I go? I'll be back in about an hour."

Jennifer shook her head.

"How about you, Kevin? You gotta go?"

"No. I can wait till you get back," he said, knowing it was pointless to try anything.

Jimmy made sure the zip-ties were tight enough and the chairs were securely tied to the table. He looked at them both one more time and walked outside. Kevin and Jennifer heard the roar of the Harley when Jimmy started it up. They listened as the sound began to wane as the bike rode off down the road. They were alone for the first time since their ordeal began a week earlier. Jennifer looked at Kevin with tears in her eyes and a look of desperation.

"What are we going to do? Is there any way you can free yourself, Kevin?"

"I can't move an inch. The chair won't budge and these ties are too tight."

"Maybe somebody will come to the house while that guy is gone."

"We've been here almost a week. The chance of somebody showing up here is a hundred to one. We're pretty far out in the woods. Our friends seem to have planned this out pretty well."

"I know. She's pretty smart. What do you think they're going to do with us?"

Kevin didn't want to tell her what he really thought. He began to think. *If their plan was to frame Mike for embezzlement and discredit*

Affirmed, they could never leave us as witnesses. We would just clear him in the end. That means their plan was to kill us all along. I don't think she ever considered holding us for ransom. Jennifer's right. This girl is too smart for that. What can I tell Jen to make her feel better? God, I just want to hold her close and tell her everything will be okay.

"I think our best chance is to be friendly and make them see us as people. Think about it. I think she might feel some connection with you. She gave you her jeans and shirt so you could be more comfortable. Why would she do that? It's funny. I think she might actually like you."

"I hope you're right. She scares the hell out of me."

Me too, thought Kevin. *Those green eyes look right through you. One minute she's being nice. The next she's like ice. It's like her soul just left her body. God only knows what's there in its place.*

"Be brave, Jen. Just keep on being friendly. Try to get close to her. It's our best chance."

• • • • •

Gillian picked up a copy of the *Times Union* and the *New York Post*. She went to a diner and ordered coffee and a bagel. She began to read the headlines and looked for any reference to the Reardon kidnapping. Apparently, the story wasn't big news in New York City or Albany. She decided to call Jimmy and find out how things were going.

"Nothing has changed, Gee. The paper still mentions the Reardons, but it's not even front page anymore. I think things are starting to quiet down a bit."

"Don't let your guard down. The papers might be losing interest but I'm sure the FBI is still hot to trot. I'm going to stay here for two more days and nail down Mike's routine. I have to figure out if Sunday or a weekday is a better time to pull this off. I'll call you tomorrow."

Gillian sipped her coffee and continued to read the paper. It was still too early to go back to Mike's house.

They're probably going to be gone for most of the afternoon, she thought. *I'll wait until four o'clock and then go back.*

Gillian took a ride on her bike and thought about paying a visit to the state university.

Why not? It's been almost three months. I doubt anyone would recognize me. I've got nothing to kill but time.

Gillian returned to the SUNY campus and walked around, thinking about the events that had led up to the murder of George Weston.

That guy was a total asshole. He got exactly what he deserved. People aren't what they appear to be. Frank and Angela were no different. I'll bet more than half the people in the world would commit rape or murder if they thought they could get away with it. I wonder what Mike's wife is really like. I'll bet she's got a dark side. I wonder if Mike really knows her at all.

Gillian spent the next few hours justifying all the things she had done since that night in Buffalo. *Everybody has their demons. It was just a matter of chance where they wound up. Some people were just luckier than others. Put a loaded gun in someone's hands at the wrong time and just sit back and enjoy the fireworks. I'm no different than anyone else.*

At three o'clock Gillian headed back to Forest Park. She parked her bike on the same dirt road and hiked back up to her vantage point on the hill. It was just after five o'clock when Mike and his family returned from their outing. Gillian watched as Brittany and the girls went back inside. She was about to get up and leave when the dog started to bark and run nervously back and forth. It ran directly in her direction and stared at where she was hiding. Gillian kept her head down and stayed out of sight.

She heard Mike yell out, "Come back, girl. What's out there, girl? Is there a bear? A raccoon? Come on, girl. Get inside."

Reluctantly the dog obeyed and went inside. Mike closed the door behind them. Gillian breathed a sigh of relief and went back to her motel.

The next morning Gillian rode her Harley back to Forest Park and walked up into the hills. It was just after 8:15 when Mike, Brittany and the girls emerged from the house. Mike kissed them all, got in his car and drove away. Gillian took note of the time. The girls walked down the block and got on the school bus. Brittany went back inside. An hour later she came back out and drove away in her car. Again, Gillian took note of the time.

• • • • •

At 7:30 Monday morning Don was at his desk again. George tossed the manila envelope describing the murder of Jane Doe in Milford on to his desk. After he had finished looking at the pictures, he talked with George about the likelihood that it was Jennifer Reardon. He got McGowan's name as the lead detective and raced off to the Medical Examiner's office to meet with Erika Konig. She gave him the news that it wasn't Jennifer Reardon.

Another dead end, he thought.

But was it?

The wheels began to turn in Don's head.

• • • • •

Gillian decided to take a ride out to Affirmed and figure out Mike's daily routine. She was almost positive that Forest Park was a much better place to kidnap Mike and his family. As a matter of fact, she wasn't sure that kidnapping Mike was even necessary.

Maybe it would be better just to take his wife and kids. Send him a message that I'm in control.

At six o'clock she watched as Mike left Affirmed. She began to follow him again. When Mike reached the highway, she once again began to follow behind at a safe distance.

Let's have a little fun, she thought. *I haven't seen him up close in years. He can't see my face with this helmet on. Let's fuck with his head.*

She gunned the Harley and raced up directly behind Mike's Subaru. She made sure Mike saw her in the rearview mirror. She backed off a bit and then raced up on his left side. She stared at Mike, who mouthed an unwarranted apology to her. She fell back again and then raced up on the passenger side. She gave him a not so subtle finger. Again, she could see Mike try to apologize, *I'm sorry.*

It was like sweet wine on her lips to see him apologize. Gillian broke off her pursuit and decided to call it a day. On her way back to her motel she bought herself a bottle of Sauvignon Blanc. With a definite sense of accomplishment and satisfaction, she got good and drunk.

$$\bullet \ \bullet \ \bullet \ \bullet \ \bullet$$

The next morning Gillian woke up with a hangover. She decided it wasn't necessary to check out Mike's house in the morning. She was sure they all had the same routine every day.

Kids usually get home from school after two o'clock. I'm sure the school bus will drop them off safe and sound in front of their house. I just need to know exactly what time. I wonder if their sweet mother will be waiting there to pick them up. I'll know everything I need to know this afternoon.

Gillian went to her favorite diner and once again got a copy of the local paper and the *New York Post*. Again, there was no mention of the Reardon disappearance. She ordered coffee and breakfast and began to read. At just before 10 AM her phone rang. It was Jimmy.

"Yeah, hi Jimmy."

"Hi. Some bad news, Gee."

"What's up?"

"I read in the *Globe* this morning they found Tasha."

"Fuck! God fucking damn it. That's not good, Jimmy. Fuck! They're going to start checking out everything to do with the area. They'll probably track our rental car with that ticket we got. I won't be able to use Michelle's card anymore."

"Do you still want to go through with your plan to kidnap Mike?"

"Maybe. I'm not sure. I've got to think."

"Are you still coming back tonight?"

"I'll probably be home by nine o'clock."

"Okay, Gee. Can't wait to see you."

Gillian sat and thought about how to proceed. She still wanted to get back at Mike but things were beginning to get more complicated.

I better hit up Bank of America for as much as I can while I'm out here. I doubt they'll figure out anything about Michelle right away, but why tempt fate?

Gillian rode around on her bike until one o'clock and then headed out for Forest Park. She parked her Harley on the dirt road and took her place on the hill. She took out her binoculars and focused on the street where the school bus had picked up the girls on Monday morning.

At 2:45 the bus pulled up just down the block from Mike's house. Three little girls and one boy got off the bus. The boy ran across the street while the three girls began to walk slowly down the block. Gillian recognized two of them as Mike's kids. They continued to walk until they came to a blue house with white trim. Gillian made a note of it. She watched as the three of them disappeared through the front door.

At just after 4:24 Brittany arrived home and parked in her driveway. She walked into her house and a few minutes later reappeared wearing blue jeans and a casual shirt. She walked down the block and went to the house where the three girls had just gone. At 4:35 she walked back home with her two little girls in tow. It wasn't until seven o'clock that Mike arrived and went inside. Gillian knew everything she needed to know.

Gillian jumped on her Harley and headed back toward Boston. By ten o'clock that night she arrived back in her secret hole in the wall. Jimmy had missed her in more ways than one and couldn't wait to get her alone. Gillian had to fight him off with both claws.

"I'm too tired, Jimmy. Maybe tomorrow morning. I've been riding all night."

• • • • •

Don had met Eddie and Rob at the Medical Examiner's Office the previous day. They had come to an agreement to cooperate in the investigation. Don began to pursue the case with the mindset of a profiler. He concentrated on what type of person might commit this kind of murder. He focused on the method and similarity to other cases. Eddie and Rob concentrated on the physical evidence. They began with videotapes and parking tickets.

By Tuesday afternoon Don was deep into his investigation of the disappearance of James Carter and the murder of his wife Paula. He had uncovered a possible tie to terrorism. Eddie and Rob were still treading water chasing down dead ends. They all felt a sense of urgency. The trail was getting colder.

CHAPTER 39

Wednesday, Oct. 6
Westwood

Gillian awoke to the touch of Jimmy's hand on her hip. He pulled her closer and kissed her on the lips. She felt his hand move slowly toward her breast and she tried to turn away. Maybe it was her recent encounter with Mike that was on her mind, but for the moment she had no interest in Jimmy. At least in that way. Jimmy persisted with his advances and once more pulled her body closer. Gillian was still half asleep as she felt him push inside her. Reluctantly she allowed him to take what he wanted. She still needed him but Jimmy could sense that something had changed.

What's wrong? Did something happen while she was gone? I don't know what I would do if she didn't want me anymore. I have to keep her happy.

When Jimmy had finished making love to her, Gillian said, "I think we should ride out to Albany Friday morning. We have to start moving quickly. We might only have a week or two before they start putting things together. It might be easier if we just take his wife and kids. Mike can be a handful from what I remember. A little bit of leverage might be enough."

"You make the plans, Gee. That's what you're good at."

Gillian could sense that he was trying extra hard to please her. She really did have some honest feelings for Jimmy, but she had stronger ones about Mike. The anger sparked inside her again and she tried to repress it. *Just be cool. Don't lose it now.*

"I'm going to town for the paper. I'll stop at the bank and then do some food shopping. I'll be back soon."

Before she left, Gillian walked over to Jennifer and asked, "Is there anything special I can get for you? I'm thinking about grilling some steaks tonight. Is that okay with you?"

Jennifer looked at her and just said, "Sure. That will be fine. Thanks."

In spite of Gillian's polite and caring demeanor Jennifer was far more afraid of her than she was of Jimmy. Her constantly changing moods were unnerving. She knew it was Gillian who called the shots. Undoubtedly, she was the one who planned their kidnapping. Jimmy was just an obedient pawn in her game. Their lives were in her hands.

"How about you, Kevin? Anything special?"

"No. Whatever you're having is just fine."

"Okay then. I'll be back to make lunch in an hour. Sit tight."

Jimmy let out an exaggerated laugh, trying to show his appreciation for her sense of humor.

"Okay. I'll keep an eye on these two again."

An hour later Gillian was back. She carefully put more ice in the cooler and put the steaks in the refrigerator.

"Who's ready for a walk? How about you, Jen? Want to stretch your legs?"

"Sure, I definitely could use a walk." *If I can make friends with her, maybe we can get out of this alive,* she thought.

Jimmy cut her ties and the two of them walked outside together.

"Why don't we walk the way we did the other day? It's so beautiful there," Gillian suggested.

"Okay. That sounds good. It's such a nice day."

They walked to the end of the road and started down the path into the woods.

"Where did you go to college?" asked Gillian.

"I went to Amherst. I studied public relations."

She thought about asking Gillian if she went to college but was worried that she might offend her. Gillian decided to offer the information herself.

"I never went to college. At least I never attended any classes. But I did spend a lot of time at several different schools. I just sort of fit in on campus."

"Did you ever want to study anything?"

"I once thought about being a medical examiner or a forensic analyst. You know, like those shows where they track down the bad guys with DNA and other clues."

"Yeah. I like those shows too," said Jennifer nervously. *Is she for real or messing with my head? Just be friendly and try to make it personal.*

"Did you have a lot of boyfriends while you were in college, Jen?"

"A few. I wasn't really serious about anyone until I met Kevin. He stole my heart. How about you?"

"Quite a few, actually."

"I'm not surprised. You're a very pretty girl."

"Thanks. So are you, Jen. Don't you think we look a little bit alike?"

"I can see that. We're about the same age. We both have dark hair and the same figure. Your jeans fit me perfectly."

"Did anybody ever take advantage of you while you were in college? I mean did a guy ever force himself on you?"

"No, but I had a philosophy professor who was very suggestive, if you know what I mean. He called me into his office and said I could improve my grade a lot if I was willing to participate in some extra-curricular activities."

"Is that how the bastard put it? Some men are total pigs."

"I know. That will never change, but Kevin would never do something like that. Why? Did anybody ever try something like that with you?"

"They more than tried. I was gang-raped at a frat party when I was seventeen." That wasn't the actual truth, but over the past few months Gillian had convinced herself that it was. *If I hadn't willingly given myself to Mike, he would have just taken what he wanted anyway. He's no different than any other guy. If they think they can get away with something, they'll do whatever they want.*

Gillian repressed the truth that she was actually the one who would use men to get what she wanted. Even when she met Mike for the first time, her main intent was to find a place to stay and maybe get a few free meals. But in her mind she was the innocent victim in a world of deceit and betrayal.

"That's awful. Did you report it to the police or the university?" Jennifer asked. She was honestly sympathetic. All girls could imagine the anguish of going through something like that.

"No. They would never believe someone like me. You know how guys stick together."

Jennifer looked at her and wanted to give her a hug. She actually felt sincere compassion. She began to see Gillian as a young girl who had lost her way long ago. *She probably ran away from home as a teenager. I'll bet her father abused her. That's why she doesn't trust men. She's a damaged soul.* "Some guys are assholes. That's for sure. I can imagine the hell you must have gone through. I can totally understand why you feel the way you do. Just try to remember, not everyone is a bad person. There are lots of people who care. They would listen and be on your side."

Jennifer was hoping to appeal to the wounded vulnerable little girl inside of her. "How well did you know the guys who did that to you? Do you know their names?"

"Funny you should bring that up. One of them was a guy named Mike Davis. He wrote the software for Lexington's financial transactions. I met him at Ohio State University. My original plan was to frame him for embezzlement. I needed your husband to set that up. That's why you're here. Unfortunately, there's a limit on the amount I can withdraw, so now it's plan B."

"I saw the two of you on the computer. My husband mentioned something about Mike Davis the other day. We talked when you and Jimmy were both gone. Now I understand why you hate him," said Jennifer, trying her best to sound like an ally.

"Tell me, what makes people like you and Kevin different from Mike Davis and his wife?"

Jennifer thought carefully about what to say. Finally, she said, "I don't know. I never met either of them. I guess we can never truly understand what goes on in someone else's mind." *Should I try to reason with her? Would she let us go if I told her we would help her get even with Mike? The statute of limitations is up on his crime, but we might be able to get him fired. Kevin's got a lot of pull. Maybe we could ask the authorities to show mercy.*

They continued walking deeper into the woods. Jennifer felt that she had at least begun to form the basis of a friendship with Gillian, at least on some level. She didn't feel the sense of doom she had felt the last time they had walked this way. She was still terrified of Gillian's erratic changes in personality but now she felt there was hope.

Gillian allowed Jennifer to walk a few steps ahead of her. She unzipped her jacket and let it hang open loosely around her shoulders. She felt the knife close to her breast in her inside pocket.

I know I have to kill her sooner or later. There's no way I can just let them go. It really is too bad. I think in a different world I might actually have even been friends with her.

Jennifer continued to walk ahead of her, looking up at the colorful leaves of the maple trees above. The air was crisp and clean. Each breath was filled with the promise of a new day. Through the trees she could see white puffy clouds that dotted the blue sky far above.

• • • • •

Earlier that day Don had left Long Island and was now busy helping the Danbury Police track down clues in the Patricia Nelson murder. He had accompanied detective Edelman to Duncan Smith's house and was now aware of the name Eddie Lubin. Later that afternoon he would have him in custody.

Rob Morrow and Eddie McGowan were busy following up on a parking ticket given to a rental car in the Blue Hills Reservation. They learned it had been rented to a girl named Michelle Dennis of Rochester, New York. Later that day they tracked down a ticket given to a car registered to an Adam Roach on which the plates did not match the vehicle. At the end of the day, all of that had been explained. They still didn't have any clear direction to take. They wound up at Zan's later that night.

• • • • •

Mike and Brittany were still at work. They were looking forward to their family trip to Lake Placid with the girls the following day. Later that evening they would be busy packing and making last-minute arrangements with the neighbors.

• • • • •

Gillian continued to walk slowly behind Jennifer. She unsnapped the clasp on her knife sheath and thought, *She actually trusts me. People who trust other people so easily are usually trustworthy themselves. It's hard to believe after what I put them through. She must be a nice person. I actually like her. I don't have to kill her right now. Who knows what's going to happen? I guess I can wait another day or two. She's a lot smarter than Jimmy and I like our little walks in the woods.*

"Do you want to keep walking or should we turn around and go back?" asked Gillian.

"I could walk a little more. It's up to you. To tell you the truth, my legs feel a lot better now that I've been walking, and I was never a big fan of TV."

Gillian had to laugh. *At least she's got a sense of humor,* she thought.

The more time I spend alone with her, the better chance I have of getting her sympathy. If she's made up her mind to kill us, there's not a lot I can do about it anyway.

"Okay. Let's keep going for another ten minutes and then we'll go back."

The two of them continued to talk about nature and all the places they wanted to visit. By the time they had walked another ten minutes they had both agreed that horses and dogs were better than people and that winter snow was overrated.

"I know you probably don't want to give me your real name, but it would be nice if I knew what to call you. I heard your friend call you Gee. Is there a name I could call you by?" *I should try to make things as personal as I can. I need her to care about us.*

Gillian thought for a moment and then smiled. She turned to Jennifer and said, "Sure. You can call me Grace."

"That's a beautiful name. It suits you."

"Thanks. I always liked it, too."

Jennifer's mind was racing. She felt like a sailor trying to navigate through treacherous waters.

Should I offer to help her settle her score with Mike? What would she do? Would she think I was trying to trick her? I need her to trust me. God, what should I do?

She decided to play it safe and wait. Half an hour later they arrived back at the house. Kevin was relieved to see Jennifer walk back through the door.

"I don't think we have to tie up Jennifer. She's not going to run, but keep the gun handy just in case. We can trust you, right Jen?"

"I'll do anything you ask."

Gillian motioned Jimmy out on the porch.

"We should probably get rid of the Honda and rent a bigger van. We want to bring the bikes with us. It'll be better for what we need to do in Albany. We may have to kidnap all four of them. The Honda won't work. You should go do it now. I'll stay here and entertain our friends. Let me have the gun."

"Okay, Gee. I'll be back soon." He gave the gun to Gillian.

"Get some more zip-ties and some more ice," she yelled after him.

Jimmy took off in the Honda and Gillian went back inside to watch Kevin and Jennifer.

The three of them sat and began watching television.

Kevin looked at Gillian and thought about what to say.

"I can tell from the way you've been acting that your plan isn't working out the way you wanted. If you let us go, I promise I won't identify you to the police. I can even get you a lot of money if you let me get to a bank. All I want is for my wife to be safe. I give you my word."

"Kevin. Wait, Kevin. There's something you need to know. I don't think this is just about money." Jennifer looked at Gillian with sympathetic eyes and said, "Grace explained to me what happened to her. That guy you mentioned, the one who works for Affirmed Software. Mike Davis is a real jerk."

Jennifer looked at Kevin, trying to get him to play along.

"Grace. So I finally know your name," said Kevin. "If Mike Davis did something to you, I'm sure I can make life difficult for him. If you let us go, I promise I'll do everything I can to even the score. I'll tell the police not to press any kidnapping charges. All I want is for Jennifer to be safe."

"I'll think about it, Kevin," Gillian said. "Maybe we can work something out. Either of you two hungry? I can cook up some macaroni and cheese."

Gillian went to the kitchen and put a pot of water on the stove.

Jennifer and Kevin just looked at each other, not quite sure of where they stood.

Jimmy returned an hour later with more ice and another package of zip-ties. Gillian placed the ice carefully in the cooler and the four of them watched TV for the rest of the day. That night Gillian lay in bed with Jimmy and went over their plans for the next day. She decided Thursday might be a better day to drive to Albany. It would give her more flexibility in her plan.

CHAPTER 40

Thursday Morning, Oct. 7

Gillian walked into the living room and turned on the television set. She turned it to the news and waited for the weather report.

"Good morning, Jen," she said with a smile. "Sorry to wake you up so early. I'm trying to get a fix on the weather."

"Good morning, Grace. That's okay. Do you think you could cut these ties? I could really use the bathroom."

"Sure. No problem." Gillian pulled the knife from her jacket and cut the zip-ties.

Jennifer painfully flexed her wrists and pushed herself up to her feet. "I hope we're going for another walk today. My legs are really stiff."

"That depends on the weather. I may have an errand to run today."

Kevin awoke to the conversation and said, "Good morning, girls." He immediately regretted saying it. *Girls? What am I thinking? Maybe I shouldn't overdo it.*

Gillian laughed to herself and said, "Good morning, Kevin. I'll untie you just as soon as Jen is done with the bathroom."

"Thanks. Take your time, honey. I'm just fine."

The weather report came on and predicted heavy rain for Friday afternoon and evening.

I guess that rules out my plans until next week, thought Gillian. "Looks like you got your wish, Jen. I'm not going anywhere until Monday. What do you guys want for breakfast?"

"Anything you want is fine with us," said Kevin.

Gillian threw some bacon into a frying pan and whipped up some scrambled eggs.

"Where do you girls go when you take your walk?" asked Kevin, trying to start up some friendly conversation.

"Just a couple of miles into the woods. A little farther than that place I showed you last week."

Kevin recalled the little demonstration Gillian had given him and was sorry he asked.

Jimmy awoke and walked into the living room and said, "Mmm. Smells good. I'm hungry."

"It'll be done in a couple of minutes. Just break out some plates for us."

"Sure thing."

The four of them sat down to eat and Gillian tried to start up some friendly conversation. "The news said we're getting a storm tomorrow. I love storms, don't you, Jen?"

"Yeah. I guess so. It depends on what I have to do at the time."

"How about you, Kevin?"

"Yeah. Definitely. I've always wanted to see a huge tornado from afar."

Kevin reflected on how completely surreal their situation had become. All he could do was continue with his plan to be agreeable and friendly. He looked over at Jennifer and held her eyes with his own. Jennifer knew he was trying to give her comfort and express his complete devotion. She tried her best to show him that she understood what he was trying to say.

After breakfast Gillian said, "Are you ready for our walk, Jen?"

"Sure. It looks like the rain is going to hold off for a while."

The two girls set out on their hike while Jimmy and Kevin stayed behind and watched television.

"Any preference for what you want to watch, Kevin?"

"Not really. Anything you put on will be just fine."

A couple of hours later Gillian and Jennifer returned. Kevin was, of course, relieved to see them come back together.

"How was your hike?" asked Kevin, looking at each of them in turn.

"Really nice," they both said at the same time.

"Let me make some lunch. I'm hungry from all that walking. How about you, Jen?"

"I could eat."

"Wanna help me make lunch? We could make cheeseburgers on the grill. Why don't we have a picnic?"

"That's a great idea, Grace. I think Kevin could use some fresh air."

"Grace? thought Jimmy, looking at Gillian with a wry smile. *Where did she get that from?*

Gillian caught Jimmy's reaction. She smiled and shot a sarcastic look back in his direction.

Jimmy cut Kevin's tie wraps and allowed him to stretch his legs. The four of them sat at a wooden table in the front yard and ate lunch together. Once again, they took turns making small talk and went on all afternoon like they were best friends.

After lunch Gillian called Jimmy to the side and said, "I can't use Michelle's phone anymore. They may be able to put two and two together and track us down. I'm going to have to ditch it and get a couple of burner phones. I'm going to Boston. I'll pick some up at the Apple store. I'll be back this evening."

"Okay. I'll stay here and watch these two."

Gillian rode off on her Harley. First, she hit the Apple store and purchased three burner phones. Next, she picked up the paper at the 7-11 and bought her usual stock of candy bars and a can of Pepsi. She took Michelle's cell phone from her pocket and was about to toss it in the garbage.

Wait a minute. I think maybe a bit of misdirection is in order just in case the cops do figure it out.

She used Michelle's phone and googled *Low Income areas in Boston.* Several choices came up. Mattapan was close by and seemed to fit the bill. She rode her Harley down to one of the government housing complexes and got off her bike. She walked around for a half an hour and found an alley where she could conveniently ditch the phone.

Now if they track down the phone, they'll think Michelle lived down here. They'll waste a lot of time running in the wrong direction.

Gillian looked around her and noticed there were no windows facing the alley. There was only one door that accessed the alley from the apartment complex, and there was no clear view from the road. It was almost completely desolate. She walked to the end of the alley and discovered a small gap between the buildings. It was barely a foot wide. She took off her leather jacket and squeezed through to the other side. She recognized the courtyard she had passed by minutes earlier. It was a shortcut back to where she had parked her Harley. She went back through the opening and looked for a place to ditch the phone. There was a row of dumpsters lined up against the wall. Gillian opened one of them and was immediately repulsed by the rank smell when she lifted the lid. Obviously, It hadn't been emptied in over a week.

Boy, if I wanted to kill somebody, this would be the perfect place. If the cops find the phone, they might figure Michelle ran into some kind of trouble here.

Gillian took out Michelle's phone and checked her contact list. She found the number for Maxine and sent her a message that she was in Boston visiting friends. She then made several random calls to numbers with that area code. Instead of tossing the phone into the trash she placed it behind one of the dumpsters and drove back to Westwood.

Gillian and Jennifer cooked dinner for everyone and they spent the rest of evening watching television. Gillian offered everyone a Snickers bar for dessert before they all retired for the night.

• • • • •

Earlier that day, Don had driven to Rochester. He had talked to Maxine and collected the DNA evidence from Michelle Dennis's hairbrush. Later that night he was in Buffalo, ready to meet with Detective Arnold the next day.

McGowan and Morrow had spent the day staking out the house on Beacon Street and were very grateful to finally be sitting at Zan's.

Mike and Brittany had finished their dinner at The View restaurant and were now resting up for the next day's hike up Cascade Mountain.

• • • • •

Gillian awoke the next morning before Jimmy. She jumped out of bed, showered and got herself dressed. Jimmy began to wonder why she was being distant.

She is moody sometimes. Maybe it'll just pass.

Jimmy certainly hoped so.

The long Columbus Day weekend had arrived. Friday went by without incident. Gillian picked up the paper after breakfast, went to the bank and took her afternoon walk with Jennifer. They spent another evening watching TV.

On the other hand, it had been a busy day for Don. He had met with Detective Arnold and visited the murder scene where Leslie Anne, Angela and Frank had drawn their final breaths. He had learned about Miss Google Eyes and had sent Michelle's DNA samples to the lab in Boston. He went to sleep that night eager to get started on the hunt the next day.

Eddie and Rob had endured the boredom of the Beacon Street stake-out. Rob had made his date with Meriam. They had once again wound up at Zan's that evening, and Rob was looking forward to Saturday night.

Mike and Brittany had climbed Cascade Mountain. They had enjoyed an excellent meal at The View that evening and fell asleep almost instantly.

• • • • •

Saturday came and went. For Gillian and her companions, it was another uneventful day. Gillian continued to make plans and coached Jimmy on how things should go down. Everything was set for the following Friday.

With the help of Miss Google Eyes, Don and Paul Arnold had figured out the identity of Motorcycle Man. They had apprehended and interviewed him and Don had pretty much eliminated him as a suspect in the three murders. He also learned that Michelle Dennis was not the Jane Doe in the Boston morgue. He had driven back to Rochester and informed Maxine of that fact. Maxine explained to Don that she had received a text message from Michelle on Thursday telling her that she was in Boston visiting friends. She thanked Don again for his concern and dedication. Don had his doubts that the text actually came from Michelle.

Eddie and Rob spent the morning in the police station and called it an early day. Rob went on his date with Meriam that evening and was beginning to fall in love.

Mike, Brittany and the two girls had enjoyed a relaxing day at the movies. That evening they had dinner at The View and watched the sun set over Mirror Lake. They were looking forward to another day hiking in the mountains.

• • • • •

Sunday was just another day in the woods for Gillian. It was becoming routine. Jimmy was becoming antsy and couldn't wait for Friday to arrive. Gillian picked up on his restlessness and decided to show him a little more attention. It worked and Jimmy began to settle down. All her plans depended on Jimmy staying focused. Gillian knew just how to handle him. The hours passed by and soon the day was over.

• • • • •

Don had met with Detective Connelly in Albany and was still no closer to an answer than he was six days earlier. Sunday night he drove to Boston and was back in Cheryl's arms.

Eddie and Rob had taken the day off. They were also no closer to solving anything. Rob was busy thinking about Meriam and Eddie was spending time at home with his wife Lisa.

Mike, Brittany and the kids had climbed several mountains and had no idea that they had just dodged a bullet.

CHAPTER 41

Monday morning, October 11

Monday had begun for Gillian the same as it had the past few days. After breakfast she had picked up the newspaper and gone to the bank. She was almost home when her Harley began to run rough again. The bike sputtered and barked at her.

God damn. I'm gonna have to take it back to that Shell station.

When she got back home, she called Jimmy over and said, "You've got to follow me back to Boston. My Harley is acting up again."

"Sure, Gee. Let me tie up Jen and we'll be on our way."

Jimmy followed Gillian back to the Shell station. It was a holiday and the mechanic wasn't available. They arranged to pick up the bike following day at five o'clock. They returned home and sat on the porch swing.

"If we're going to pull this off, Friday would be the best time. Mike and his family wouldn't be missed at work or school until after the weekend. The trail would be colder and we'd have a better chance of getting away with it," said Gillian.

"You make the plans. It sounds good to me, said Jimmy, trying his best to make her happy. "You've done pretty well so far."

"Thanks, Jimmy. You've been great."

Jimmy began to feel better about his relationship with Gillian. He shook off the feelings of rejection he had felt a few days earlier. *We're back on track*, he thought.

· · · · ·

Don had agreed that Eddie and Rob should continue to track down leads on Jane Doe and Michelle Dennis. He explained that Maxine had received a text message from Michelle's phone, but had some doubts that it was actually from Michelle. He would concentrate on the terrorist angle. He spent most of the day checking Wyatt's list of usual suspects.

Eddie and Rob convinced Sarah to help them get info on Michelle Dennis. They had gotten her mother's maiden name and were able to get a list of her recent credit card transactions. They were out canvassing the Chestnut Hill Avenue area.

Mike and Brittany were on the top of Whiteface mountain and looking out over the beautiful hills below. Jamie and Ronnie were in awe when their father pointed out the mountains they had hiked over the weekend.

· · · · ·

Gillian got up from the porch swing and walked back inside. "Do you want to keep me company while I go for walk, Jen?"

"Sure. I'm always down with that."

The two girls set out on their walk into the woods.

It was early in the evening and the light was beginning to fade. Gillian and Jennifer had still not returned. Kevin was beginning to worry. Just as the final glow of twilight had disappeared, they came walking through the door.

"You were gone for a long time," said Kevin. "I was beginning to worry."

"We were having fun. Grace is a very interesting girl. It turns out we have a lot to talk about."

"Yeah, you know us girls when we get together. We just never shut up," laughed Gillian, looking at Kevin with a vexing smile. Kevin felt a chill run down his spine. Part of Gillian did actually like Jennifer. She didn't want to kill her. *What would my chances be if I just called the police and told them where to find her? Could I still make a run for it and make it to Argentina? Decisions, decisions.*

Gillian and Jennifer made dinner and they all sat at the table again sharing stories. The day ended with them watching old movies on TV.

• • • • •

Don had agreed to meet Eddie and Rob at Zan's. The three of them began to discuss the case and realized immediately they had already covered the same things more than once. They sat back and knocked down several drinks and went home.

• • • • •

Mike and his family had arrived back home from the Adirondacks. Brittany was too tired to cook dinner so they ordered a pizza and just relaxed in front of the TV. They all agreed it was one of the best weekends ever.

CHAPTER 42

Tuesday morning, Oct. 12

Gillian sat on the porch swing and rocked back and forth. She collected her thoughts and began to think. *This Michelle thing really screwed us up. It's the only thing that worries me. If they check the calls on her phone, they might be able to tie it to us. I called Jimmy a couple of times. That was a mistake. Damn it! How did they find Tasha's body so quickly? Will Jimmy hold up if the cops question him? So far, they don't even know I exist. We've probably got a couple of days before they can put it all together. It's not likely that they would suspect a girl of being involved in Tasha's murder.*

Jimmy walked out on the porch and said, "Hey, Gee. What's on your mind?"

"I've got to pick up the Harley at five o'clock so there's no point in going to town now. We can pick up the paper and hit the ATM later. I'm just going to sit here and work out a plan. I just can't believe they found Tasha's body so quickly. I mean, what are the odds?"

"I know, Gee. That was really bad luck. We should have been totally free and clear."

"It's going to take some time for the cops and the FBI to figure it all out but we better start moving quickly. I called your number with Michelle's phone. If they get a warrant, they might track us down. You called O'Connell on your phone when we got this place."

"So what should we do?"

"I'm sure Michelle isn't the number one lead that they're following up on. She's probably still low priority as a suspect. So far, I haven't read anything in the paper about the cops making an ID on Tasha. They may figure Michelle Dennis was their victim. They could be asking a lot of questions in Rochester. Sooner or later, they'll figure out it wasn't Michelle. Hopefully they'll stop looking in that direction. Right now, I think we're still okay."

"Then you still want to make the grab on Friday?"

"Yeah. We're still on track for Friday afternoon."

The hours went by and it was now late afternoon. It was time to pick up Gillian's Harley. Jimmy made sure that Kevin and Jennifer were tied up securely and they decided to take the van to town. On the way Gillian stopped at the ATM and withdrew another $200.

It was almost five o'clock when they pulled into the Shell station. The mechanic was still working on the bike.

Gillian walked over to him and asked, "Is my bike going to be finished soon?"

He looked Gillian up and down with a wanton smile on his face. "Almost done. Just torquing it down now."

"What was wrong with it?"

"Blowback was fouling the spark plug. I put in new seals. Should be just fine now."

Jimmy paid the damages and the two of them were on their way.

"Why don't we have dinner in town? It's been a long time since we enjoyed something special," suggested Gillian.

"Sure. Why not? Let's party."

They took a walk around the Chestnut Hill Reservoir to build up an appetite and later went to the restaurant where Gillian had been months earlier. They split a bottle of wine and enjoyed the view of the lake. It was about nine thirty when they left the restaurant.

"Shoot! We forgot to buy the paper. I'm gonna stop at the 7-11. Follow me over there. Maybe they'll still have one," said Gillian.

It was misty and a light fog swirled just above the road. Gillian eased her Harley down Chestnut Hill Avenue and pulled into the 7-11 parking lot. Jimmy pulled in right behind her. She jumped off her bike and walked through the door. Jimmy waited in the van. A man she did not recognize approached her and held up a picture of a girl.

"Good evening, miss. I'm a detective with the Boston Police Department. Can you tell me if you have seen this girl?" He showed her Michelle's picture.

Gillian recognized it immediately. She had been carrying it in her pocket for the last few months. She looked at the photograph and quickly said, "No."

"Could you take a closer look, please," persisted Rob. "Her name is Michelle. We've been trying to locate her for the past week. Are you sure you don't recognize her?"

She looked at it again and said, "Sorry. No, I haven't."

The detective persisted and said, "Could you look again?"

Gillian looked a little longer this time, hoping it would make him happy and once again said, "No. No, I haven't. Sorry."

She picked up the last copy of the *Boston Globe* from the rack, went to the snack aisle and got a couple of Payday peanut bars and a bag of potato chips. She then walked to the cooler and got a Pepsi. She took a sideways glance at the detective, trying not to be obvious. He was eying her suspiciously. She watched him as he walked to the window. He appeared to be staring at her Harley. Gillian walked to the counter and paid for her items. As she began to walk out the detective suddenly stepped in front of her.

He looked her square in the eyes and said, "Could you look at this picture one more time? You barely gave it any thought."

Gillian remained cool but she could see the detective was taking an interest in her. She sidestepped him and emphatically said, "No. I told you. She doesn't look familiar."

Gillian walked out of the store and started walking toward her Harley. On the way she looked over at Jimmy, who was waiting in the van. She motioned towards the detective with her eyes. Jimmy caught on immediately. She climbed back on the bike and began to slowly ride down Chestnut Hill Avenue. She watched behind in her rear-view mirror and could see the detective as he quickly jumped in his car and began to follow her. She continued down the road and then turned left on Clinton Street. She watched as the detective's car followed her around the corner.

Gillian decided to pull over and call Jimmy. She now had a burner phone and wasn't worried about leaving a trail.

Jimmy picked up and said, "Yeah, Gee. You were right. That guy is following you."

"I know, Jimmy. I'm on Clinton Street. He pulled over about fifty yards behind me. He's got his lights off. I don't know how but I think he's got me pegged as Michelle. He probably wants to find out where I live. We might have to get rid of this guy before he gets any closer. I'm heading for Mattapan. I know the perfect place. Keep following us. I'll call you later."

"Okay. I saw where you turned. I'm just down the road on Chestnut."

"I'm getting back on the road. Give it about a half a minute. I'll start out slow so you can catch up."

"Gotcha, Gee."

Gillian headed for Mattapan, making sure the detective was still behind her. When she got to the housing project she pulled over and got off her bike. The night air was cool and damp and a light drizzle made it difficult to see. An eerie glow shrouded the streetlamps. She took her knife from her saddlebag and concealed it inside her jacket. She noticed as the detective's car turned the corner and pulled over down the road. She began to walk slowly toward the buildings, being careful not to look back.

I'm sure he's gonna follow me, she thought.

She got to the courtyard and casually looked to her right as she walked slowly toward the gap between the buildings. She caught a glimpse of the detective, who ducked back behind the corner.

Gillian smiled. It was all going according to plan. She took off her jacket and began to ease her body between the buildings. The bricks were cold and moist against her skin and it was more difficult to squeeze through than it had been a few days earlier. When she got through to the other side, she jumped up on the brick overhang and lay on top of it like a panther waiting for her prey.

I'm sure he's going to come through the alley and come out right underneath me. All I have to do now is wait.

After a few minutes she heard the faint sound of footsteps on the other side of the overhang. She anticipated the detective crouching down and poking his head through the opening just beneath her. Gillian got herself ready. She held the knife firmly in her hand. A few seconds later it was all over. The detective lay flat on the ground clutching his throat. She could see the look of complete surprise in his eyes. She waited until the bleeding stopped and jumped down from the overhang. She called Jimmy on the burner phone.

"Yeah, Gee."

"Did you see where I parked my bike?"

"Yeah. I'm right down the street."

"I'll be there in a minute. I'm going to need your help with something."

"Okay, Gee."

Gillian went back through the buildings and led Jimmy back to the alley. This time she went the way the detective had come so Jimmy could get through.

"You gotta help me get his body into the dumpster. The longer it takes for someone to find him, the better it will be for us."

Gillian took the car keys, cell phone and wallet from his pocket. She looked at his identification and read the name out loud.

"Robert Morrow. Well, sorry, Mr. Morrow. I guess you shouldn't have been so nosy."

They opened one of the dumpsters and threw his body in.

"Let's cover him up with some trash from one of the other dumpsters," suggested Gillian.

Jimmy opened up one of the other dumpsters and winced. "Jesus. That stinks. Doesn't anybody empty these things?"

"Hopefully not for a few more days. We should also move his car at least a few blocks away."

Gillian retrieved Michelle's cell phone from behind the dumpster. *Don't want to leave this behind and remove all doubt,* she thought.

Jimmy drove Morrow's car to the other side of the projects. Gillian followed him on her Harley and drove him back to the van.

Two hours later they were sitting on the porch swing talking about what had happened earlier that evening.

"We should probably change our plans. Things are getting too hot. If we're going to pull this thing off, we should do it tomorrow. Are you up to it?"

"Sure, Gee. Whatever you want."

"Good. Let's get some sleep."

CHAPTER 43

Wednesday morning, Oct. 13

Gillian got up early the next morning and woke up Jimmy. "We've got a lot to do today. We better get started."

After breakfast they loaded Gillian's Harley into the van and secured it with rope ties.

"Let's get all of our things together. We may not be coming back here, Jimmy."

Jennifer noticed that they were packing up all their belongings and became apprehensive about what was going to happen. Kevin looked at her and picked up on her thoughts.

When they had finished loading their stuff into the van, Gillian took the remaining ice from the freezer and carefully placed it in the cooler.

"What do you want to do with these two?" asked Jimmy.

The moment of decision had come.

Jennifer looked pleadingly at Gillian. Tears were beginning to well up in her eyes.

Gillian looked back at Jennifer. Whatever was left of her soul was fighting a battle. She thought for a moment and said, "We'll leave them here for the time being. We might be able to use them as a bargaining chip if something goes wrong."

Jennifer breathed a sigh of relief.

Gillian walked outside with the cooler, placed it carefully in the van and tied it down securely.

She walked back inside and said, "We're all set, Jimmy. Let's hit the road."

"Are you sure about leaving these two behind?"

"Yeah. For the moment they're still of use to us. You two lovebirds stay cool. We'll let the police know where you are when we're free and clear."

Kevin looked at her with some doubt.

Jimmy walked outside and Gillian gave Jennifer one more look. She then walked out and closed the door behind her.

"Were you serious about calling the police?" asked Jimmy.

"Maybe. I haven't decided yet. Maybe we could just let fate decide. The police might find them in time."

"Okay, Gee. You make the plans."

Secretly Gillian knew that the police would get the tape from the 7-11 and be able to ID her. They might also be able to get a plate number for her Harley. Sooner or later, they would be able to track her down. After almost ten years, the Harley was still registered in Jimmy's name. Killing the Reardons served no real purpose. She also figured they would get Jimmy's phone records and eventually connect them to O'Connell and the house, but she kept her thoughts to herself. Her only reason for killing the detective was to buy time so she could carry out her revenge on Mike Davis, irrational as it was.

Gillian got in the van and headed for I-90. Jimmy followed her on his bike. Three hours later they were in Albany. Gillian pulled into the parking lot of the motel she had stayed at two weeks earlier. They got a room and brought the cooler inside. They unloaded Gillian's Harley and kept it out of sight from the main road. When they had finished, they drove to Forest Park so that Jimmy could become familiar with the area. By the time they were done it was almost one o'clock. They decided to grab some lunch and go over the final details of their plan.

• • • • •

As soon as Eddie had viewed the 7-11 tape and discovered that Rob had been there the previous evening, he called Jimmy Dugan. An APB was put out on Rob's car. Eddie had gone to the video lab at the FBI building and he and Don had just reviewed the tape from the Shell station. They now had a name to go with the motorcycle.

James Gordon.

Don called Jack Sullivan. "Hi Jack. We're gonna need a court order for Michelle Dennis's phone records. There's another person of interest named James Gordon. We're gonna need his phone records for the past two months as well. Tell the judge STAT. Explain that lives may be at stake."

"Understood, Don. I'm on it."

Within minutes a fax came through from the phone company.

"We've got a couple of calls from Michelle Dennis to Gordon. He also called her a few times. There's a whole bunch of calls from Michelle's phone to numbers in Rochester a few days ago," said Don.

"That doesn't make a lot of sense," said Eddie. "Michelle was probably dead by that time. We know for sure she wasn't in possession of her phone. I don't think our suspect is likely to know a lot of people in Rochester."

Don thought for a moment and said, "She's pretty smart. She's trying to confuse us and waste our time. Concentrate on the other calls."

"There's only a couple of calls from Gordon's phone other than Michelle's number. One is to a bank in Ohio. There's also one to someone named Eric O'Connell. He lives locally here in Boston."

"Let's call him right away and see how he knows Gordon," said Don.

He dialed the number and waited. Voicemail answered with the usual message.

Eric O'Connell is unavailable. Please leave a message at the beep.

"Damn it. Find out his address. We need to find him now." At that very moment Don got a phone call from Greg in Missing Persons. "Yeah, Greg. What's up?"

"We've got a positive ID on Jane Doe. Her name is Natasha Dvorak. She's a foreign student from Czechoslovakia. She was last seen at Rhode Island University. Her parents reported her missing a few days ago. Erika confirmed that she is definitely our Jane Doe. Apparently, her bank account was drained of over six thousand dollars."

"Okay. Thanks Greg. That explains things. It was about money."

Don hung up and told Eddie what he had learned.

"If it wasn't for those kids, we would have never found her."

"Yeah. But Rob wouldn't be missing."

"I know, Eddie. I'm sorry. Let's stay optimistic. We should take a ride out to O'Connell's house and see if he's there. Let's see what we can find out. Every minute counts."

Eddie and Don took a drive out to O'Connell's house and knocked on the door. There was no answer.

"Shit. We could really use a break right now," cursed Eddie. "Try calling him again."

Don punched in the number and again it went to voicemail.

Don left a message and identified himself as an FBI agent and informed him of the urgency. He needed to know about James Gordon as soon as possible.

Eddie thought about stopping at Charlie's to tell Meriam about Rob, but figured it was better to wait until they knew more.

"We should call Rob's parents and tell them what's going on," said Eddie.

"Let's wait. I want to chase down as many leads as possible while they're still hot. We don't have time to deal with relatives right now."

"Why don't we ask some of O'Connell's neighbors if they know where he is?"

They spent the next half hour knocking on doors and asking questions, to no avail. Nobody knew much about Eric O'Connell other than that he was an older man who kept to himself.

Frustrated, the detectives decided to pay a visit to the Shell station and ask some questions.

Before they got there Eddie got a phone call from Jimmy Dugan. "Yeah, Jimmy. What's up?"

"They found Rob's car abandoned in a housing project in Mattapan. I've ordered every available man down there to search the area. You might want to go down there and help them out."

"Okay Jimmy, thanks for letting us know. We're on our way." He turned to Don. "They found Rob's car in Mattapan. Let's head down there."

Don hit the gas and turned on the siren. They reached Mattapan in less than twelve minutes.

Eddie immediately found one of the policeman who was searching the area. He asked where he could find Rob's car. The officer showed him the way.

Eddie took out a handkerchief and opened the door. He carefully looked around the car for anything that might give them a clue. "Has anybody taken anything from the car?"

"I'm not sure. You might want to ask that officer over there."

He pointed to an officer standing close by and called out, "Hey Pete. Come over here a second. This is Detective Morrow's partner. He wants to ask you some questions."

The officer walked over to Eddie and said, "You're Eddie McGowan, right?"

"That's right," said Eddie, extending his hand. "This is Don Corlino. He's with the FBI."

The officer introduced himself as Peter Molson. "Dugan had me in charge of things but now that you're here, you can call the shots," he said.

"Have you guys taken anything from the car?"

"No. We haven't touched it. We're waiting for a forensic team."

"Have you searched the dumpsters in the area?" asked Eddie.

"We looked into some of them but there was nothing obvious."

"We're going to need several teams down here. We have to empty all these dumpsters and go through every one of them with a fine-tooth comb."

"I'll get on it right away, detective."

Eddie called Jimmy Dugan and requested more forensic personnel.

The officer spread the word to the other policemen who were searching the area.

"Let's start looking around, Don."

· · · · ·

It was now four o'clock and Brittany was preparing to leave her office. She called Mike and asked him when he expected to be home. They agreed that dinner would be at about seven o'clock. She then called Mrs. Cooper to ask how her new website was working out. When it went to voicemail, she left a brief message and decided to try again later.

• • • • •

Gillian and Jimmy returned briefly to their motel room and got ready to carry out their plan. They went over the details one more time. Gillian was satisfied that everything was going smoothly. At four o'clock they set out for Forest Park.

• • • • •

Eddie was coordinating the efforts of the forensic teams at the housing project in Mattapan. They had examined the contents of several dumpsters closest to where Rob's car had been found. It was quarter to five when a solemn looking officer walked up to Eddie.

"I'm sorry, Detective McGowan. We just found Detective Morrow's body a few blocks from here. He was found in a dumpster behind the building on Phillip's Court. It was a little out of the way and we almost missed it."

"Show me the way," demanded Eddie.

The two detectives followed the officer to the alley behind the building. Eddie prepared himself for what he was about to see. Rob was more than just a partner. He was also a close friend. They had to crouch down as they went under the overhang the way Morrow had done the night before. The smell of the week-old garbage was overpowering.

Eddie emerged into the alley and got to his feet. Several forensic personnel were examining the body. They stopped what they were doing when they saw Eddie.

"We're so sorry, Detective," said Doug Morse.

He recognized the forensic team immediately. They were the same team that had worked the crime scene in Milton. Eddie looked down at Rob's body. He had been placed on his back looking up. He saw the deep cut to his throat. The image of Rob's face raced away from him and then rushed right back at him like a bad acid trip. It was almost too much for Eddie to bear. He had to look away. There was no doubt about who had committed the murder, and the anger started to build up inside of him.

All Don could say was, "I'm sorry, Eddie."

There were no words that could help at that moment.

"Let's go hunt her down," Eddie said coldly, looking Don straight in the eye.

· · · · ·

Brittany turned on to Birch Street and cruised down the block. She took no special notice of the blue van parked just down the street from her house. It was now four thirty in the afternoon. Gillian watched closely as Brittany got out of her car and walked inside. She had seen it all several times before.

"She should be coming out in about five minutes," she said to Jimmy.

Jimmy just nodded and said, "I'm ready."

"She's going to pick up her two little girls and start walking back home. That's when we take them."

They watched as Brittany emerged from her house and started walking down the block in their direction. She had her cell phone in her hand and appeared completely unaware of them. Brittany walked up to the house and knocked on the door. A woman appeared in the doorway with Mike's two little girls and another little girl. Gillian watched as they had a brief conversation. Brittany then began to walk away with her two little girls in tow.

"Get ready, Jimmy. This can't take more than a few seconds."

Gillian watched from her passenger side window and said, "Now, Jimmy."

Jimmy began to roll down the block, following close behind them. Gillian made sure no one was on the street.

When they had caught up to Brittany and the kids she said, "Stop."

She jumped out of the van. In an instant she stood between Brittany and the safety of her house. She had her knife out and saw the look of terror on Brittany's face.

"Get in the van," she said quietly.

When Brittany hesitated, she said, "Get in the van, now. All of you."

She made sure they knew she meant business.

The three of them complied.

"Get out of here, Jimmy. Let's go."

A minute later they were heading down Route 50 and out of sight. Gillian turned around and looked at her captives in the back seat. One of the little girls was trying to get something out of her backpack.

"Give me that," demanded Gillian. She grabbed the backpack.

Gillian noticed Brittany with her hand in her jacket pocket and said, "Take off your jacket and give it to me." With a cold stare, she looked Brittany dead in the eyes. "Right now. I'm not fucking around."

"Get your hand out of your pocket. Fuck. Show me your hands."

Jimmy turned around with the Glock in his hand.

"Blue Dodge van. South on Route 50. A man and a woman. Late twenties," Brittany managed to get out.

Jimmy knocked her out with the gun.

Gillian took the cell phone out of Brittany's pocket and checked the call log. She looked at the last call and said, "I wonder who Delores Cooper is."

They continued driving down Route 50 and farther into the country. Jamie and Roni were crying.

"Mommy, wake up," Roni sobbed.

"Your mom is gonna be fine. Just be quiet."

Half an hour later Brittany regained consciousness with a splitting headache.

Gillian looked at her and said, "Who is Delores Cooper?"

"What?" said Brittany, not quite sure what she was talking about.

"The last call you made on your phone. Delores Cooper. Who is she?"

Through the fog in her brain Brittany suddenly remembered that her last call was to old Mrs. Cooper and not Mike. Her heart sank and she began to despair. Mike wouldn't suspect anything was wrong for at least another hour. By then they could be anywhere.

PART III

CHAPTER 44

Oct. 13, 4:50 PM
Clifton Park

Sergeant Nichols was at his desk at the Clifton Park police station. His shift was about to end and he was starting to wrap things up for the day. He took another look at the call log and made a note of the issues that had not yet been resolved. He would leave a memo for Sergeant McNeil, who was due to take over at five o'clock. Just as he was getting up to leave, the phone rang and he answered it. "Clifton Park Police. Sergeant Nichols speaking."

He was greeted by the raspy voice of an old lady and an incoherent din on the other end of the line. She was yelling frantically into the phone.

"Yes. Yes. Hello. It's my friend. I think she may have been kidnapped. I just got a phone call from her. I mean it was on voicemail. It was about twenty minutes ago. She says they have her in a Dodge van. They're heading south on Route 50. You've got to save her."

Sergeant Nichols listened to her incoherent ravings and said, "Slow down, ma'am. Let's start with your name."

"My name is Delores Cooper. She says a man and a woman have her in…."

Nichols cut her off and asked, "How old are you, ma'am?"

"What! What difference does that make? We may not have a lot of time."

Nichols began to smile and asked, "Where do you live?"

"Why is that important? You're wasting time, Sergeant! You have to do something now!"

Nichol's voice took on a sarcastic tone. "Now. How old did you say your friend is, sweetheart?"

Mrs. Cooper could tell he was not taking her seriously. By this time in her life, she was fed up with being dismissed as a senile old lady. "Listen, you pompous asshole. My friend may be in real danger. You better start taking me seriously. If anything happens to her, you're going to be in deep, deep dog shit. I'm recording this whole conversation."

Nichols almost dropped the phone. The sudden change in her tone took him by surprise. He didn't expect that kind of language from an old lady. *Maybe I should start taking her more seriously,* he thought. "I'm sorry, Mrs. Cooper, but I have to know more before I can help you."

He asked her again, "How old is your friend?"

"She's in her late twenties. I think she has her kids with her. Listen, this is urgent. You've got to put out an alert on a blue Dodge van right away."

"Now take it easy. Calm down. I can't just turn the whole world upside down without something more solid to go on. What's your friend's name?"

"Brittany Davis. She lives in Forest Park. I know her through her business."

Mrs. Cooper was becoming less frantic and Nichols began to take her more seriously.

"I'll tell you what, Mrs. Cooper. There's a way you can forward the voicemail message directly to me. If I hear the message, I might be able to do more. Tap on the voicemail your friend sent to you."

Mrs. Cooper followed his instructions and said, "Okay. Now what?"

"Now hit the SHARE button on the top right. It's a box with an arrow pointing up. There will be some options for you."

Again, she did what he asked. "Okay."

"Now send it to my number."

A few seconds later Sergeant Nichols had Brittany's voicemail. *Maybe she's not as lost as I thought,* he began to think.

He listened to the desperate voice of the woman on the phone. It was just as Mrs. Cooper had described.

He listened more closely and clearly heard her say, "Blue Dodge van heading south on Route 50. A man and a woman in their late twenties." He then heard the voice of a second woman cursing and demanding that she get her hands out of her pockets.

"Mrs. Cooper, I'm going to send this voicemail to the FBI in Albany. They'll know what to do with it. If they decide it's for real, I'm sure they'll jump on it."

"Okay. Thank you, Sergeant. I'm sorry I called you an asshole."

"That's okay. I'll call the police department over in Schenectady. I'll tell them to keep an eye out for a blue Dodge van that might be acting suspiciously. Do you have a phone number for your friend?"

Mrs. Cooper gave him Brittany's number.

"I'll keep trying her number. That's the best I can do for now."

"Okay, but do me a favor and call me back. Let me know what the FBI is doing about it."

"Very well, Mrs. Cooper. I'll call you back as soon as I know anything."

Sergeant Nichols called the FBI in Albany and sent them the voicemail.

• • • • •

Gillian made sure that Brittany and the two little girls were sufficiently restrained with zip-ties. They drove back in the direction of the motel where they had booked a room earlier that day.

Gillian turned around in her seat and glared at Brittany with fire in her eyes and said, "I don't know who that Cooper lady is. My guess is that you were trying to call someone else. Probably your husband. He was second on the call log. So who is she, Mrs. Davis?"

Gillian pulled the gag down from Brittany's mouth.

"She's just a business client. I hardly know her."

"We should probably ditch the van, Jimmy. We can't take any chances. We'll pick up my Harley again and put it back in the van. We've got to do this quickly. Davis is going to be leaving his office at about six o'clock. You can follow me there on your bike. After we get there, I'll find a place to get rid of the van. Let's get moving before things get too hot."

With those words Brittany became even more desperate. She knew Mike would be alone. He wouldn't be able to do anything to help. No one would even miss them until the next day.

After Jimmy loaded the Harley back into the van, they headed toward Albany and Mike's office. At five thirty they arrived at the parking lot of Affirmed Software. Gillian was pleased to see that Mike's car was still there. Jimmy left his bike behind the building across the street and joined Gillian in the van.

"This changes our plans a little, Jimmy, but we're still on for tonight," said Gillian.

"Whatever you want to do. I'm down," said Jimmy.

"We'll wait until Mike walks out the door. You pull the gun on him and push him back inside. It should be dark by then. After you're inside, I'll bring in his wife and kids."

"Sounds good to me."

They sat back and waited.

• • • • •

Mike sat at his desk and pulled the stack of manila envelopes closer to him. He picked up the Lexington file and began to read it. *I'll just skim over it quickly and start on it tomorrow.*

It was just after five o'clock and Diane and Donna had left for the day.

By the time he finished reviewing it was almost 6 o'clock. *Let me call Brittany and let her know I'm on my way.* Mike called her on his cell. When there was no answer, he decided to stay for a few minutes and try again later. He tried calling Jamie and Roni. Again, there was no answer. *Maybe she's over at Dawn's house with the kids. I'll try calling there.*

Mrs. Avery answered the phone. "Oh. Hi Mike," she said, a bit surprised to hear from him. "How are you? Did one of the girls forget something?"

"No, Dawn. Did Brittany pick up the kids today?"

"Yes. About an hour and a half ago. Isn't she home?"

"I don't know, Dawn. She was supposed to be. She's not answering her phone. Jamie and Roni aren't picking up either. "

"Maybe she went to the store for something and didn't want to pick up while she was driving."

"Maybe, but I doubt it. Could you do me a favor?"

"Sure, Mike."

"Could you run down to my house and check on Brittany and the girls?"

"Of course, Mike. I'll call you back in a couple of minutes."

Three minutes later Mike's phone rang.

"Hi Mike. I'm at your house. The door was unlocked so I walked inside. I yelled out for Brittany and the girls. There's nobody here. Just Kardashian, who's barking like crazy."

"Could you go in the back yard and call out towards the woods? Maybe they're outside."

Dawn walked outside and called Brittany's name again. Nothing. "Sorry, Mike. She's not out there either."

"Okay. Thanks Dawn. Could you call me if you see her or hear anything?"

"Of course, Mike. I'm going over to the Hendersons' house. Maybe she's there."

"Okay. Thanks, Dawn. Goodbye."

Mike was beginning to worry. *Where is she? She wouldn't just wander off somewhere. She would have called me if there was an emergency or if something happened to the girls.*

At twenty minutes after six his phone rang. It was an unfamiliar number.

"Yes."

"Mr. Davis, this is Detective Anderson. I'm with the FBI in Albany."

Mike's heart jumped up into his throat. "Yes? What's going on?"

"We got your number through the phone company. We don't know anything for sure yet. Someone named Delores Cooper recorded a voicemail that came from your wife's phone. We don't want to alarm you unnecessarily but we just want to check something out. Have you spoken to your wife in the past few hours?"

"No, I haven't. I've been trying to reach her but she's not picking up her phone. She's supposed to be at home but she's not there. Neither are my kids. I had my neighbor go over to check on them. They're all supposed to be there."

Mike was now going crazy.

"Okay. Try to stay calm, Mr. Davis. There are a few questions I have to ask you."

"All right. Go ahead."

"Do you know anybody who owns a blue Dodge van?"

Mike thought for a moment and said, "No. I don't think so."

"The voicemail described a man and a woman, possibly in their late twenties. Does that ring any bells?"

"Not really. There are lots of people we know of that age."

"What is your current occupation and place of employment?"

"I'm a software engineer. I work for a company called Affirmed Software."

"Have there been any problems at your place of employment?"

Mike quickly said no and then a lightning bolt hit him. "Detective Anderson, wait. An important client of mine disappeared along with his wife a few weeks ago. His name is Reardon. He's an executive with Lexington Finance in Boston. I got a request about a software upgrade from Lexington a couple of days ago. I don't know for sure but there's a possibility that might have something to do with this."

"Where are you now, Mr. Davis?"

"I'm at my office."

"I'm going to send a patrol car to pick you up and bring you to our headquarters here in Albany. I don't want you driving right now."

"Forget it. I'm on my way. I'll be there in about half an hour."

• • • • •

Don and Eddie left the Mattapan housing project at just after six o'clock. The forensic teams had turned up nothing. They began to discuss their options.

Aside from the APB on Gillian's Harley, the phone call James Gordon made to Eric O'Connell was probably the only lead they had to go on.

"We should call every car-rental company in the Boston area and see if there were any rentals in James Gordon's name," said Don.

"Good idea. I'll call Dugan and have someone get on it right away."

"We should also start trying to find out about Eric O'Connell."

Don called Greg Phillips at Missing Persons. "Greg, we need to know everything about a guy named Eric O'Connell. Please. This is urgent. Lives are at stake. Call Jack with any info you can give him."

"Of course, Don. I'll get on it immediately."

"Thanks, Greg. I gotta run now."

• • • • •

At 6:25 Mike stepped outside the Affirmed Building with a desperate look on his face. Before he could lock the door, Jimmy was out of the van and blocking his way. He pulled out the gun and said, "Get back inside, Mr. Davis. We have your wife and kids in the van. Don't do anything stupid."

Mike looked at the van and remembered what Detective Anderson had said about a blue Dodge van. He hesitated for a moment and then reluctantly went back inside, looking desperately in the direction of the van. Jimmy pushed him along and shoved him into a chair in the lobby. Gillian waited until Jimmy and Mike were inside, then cut the zip-ties from Brittany's hands and legs.

"Let's go, Mrs. Davis. We're going inside. Just remember. Your kids are still in the car, so don't try anything. If you cooperate all this will be over soon."

Brittany hoped that was true.

Gillian kept the knife out just in case and quickly hustled Brittany toward the door.

The second they were inside Mike saw Brittany and wanted to go to her. Jimmy pushed him back in the chair and held the gun on him.

"Sit down, Mr. Davis."

Mike looked at Brittany. The anguish in her eyes was almost too much for him to bear. He knew she was thinking about Jamie and Roni. He did his best to give her hope and reassure her.

"Let's take them into one of the back rooms. We'll keep them tied up there while I ditch the van," said Gillian.

After Jimmy made sure they were both tied up Gillian brought in the two girls. She then went back for the cooler. She opened it and noticed the ice was almost all melted. She brought it inside.

I'm sure it will be all right for at least a few more hours.

She walked over to Mike and went through his pockets. She found his cell phone and took it from him.

"I'm going to ditch the van, Jimmy. I'll be back in about a half hour."

"Okay. Be careful. I'll keep my eyes on our guests."

$$\bullet \ \bullet \ \bullet \ \bullet \ \bullet$$

At 6:35 Don got a call from Jack Sullivan.

"Yeah, Jack."

"Listen, Don. We just got a call from our Albany office. They just informed us that there's been a possible kidnapping that may be connected to the Reardon disappearance. A guy named Mike Davis works for Affirmed Software. Their software handles all the Lexington financial transactions. We haven't gotten any ransom demands but there's strong evidence that someone abducted his wife and kids a couple of hours ago. I'm going to have a chopper fly you out there. I want you to check in with a detective by the name of Anderson. He'll bring you up to speed. There will be a car available for you when you get there."

"Okay, Jack. I'll be right there. I want Eddie McGowan to come with me. He's already very familiar with the case."

"Sure, Don. No problem. The chopper will be waiting for you."

Don hit the gas and they took off for FBI headquarters. On the way he filled in Eddie about the kidnapping. Fifteen minutes later they were in the air heading for Albany.

• • • • •

It was 6:45 when Gillian rolled her Harley out the back of the van and headed back south. She parked it behind the building where Jimmy had left his bike, out of view of the street. At 7:05 she was back inside the Affirmed Building with Jimmy, Mike and Brittany.

"I should get rid of Davis's car too. I'm going to move it across the street behind the building. We want this place to look like a ghost town. Turn off that light and pull down the shade, Jimmy. Just keep the desk lamp on."

Gillian took Mike's keys and moved his car to where they had left the bikes. Gillian went back across the street. It was 7:10.

• • • • •

At 7:15 Don and Eddie walked into the Albany FBI building. They went to the receptionist and identified themselves.

"We need to speak with Detective Anderson," said Don.

"He's expecting you. Please follow me."

The receptionist led them to a conference room where Detective Anderson was on the phone.

"Please be seated, detectives. I'll be with you in a moment."

Don and Eddie sat down and waited for Anderson to finish his call.

"That was the state police. We've got an APB on that Dodge van in five states. I'm Detective Anderson," he said, extending his hand.

"Don Corlino. I'm FBI as well."

"Detective McGowan. Boston PD," said Eddie.

"I think we should start with the voicemail we got from Mrs. Davis's phone. Let me play it back for you."

Eddie and Don listened to the desperate voice of Mrs. Davis as she tried her best to give a description of the van and her abductors. They could hear the children crying in the background. They then heard the other girl curse at her.

The anger began to rise in Eddie as he realized it was most likely the voice of the person who murdered Rob. Don picked up on it.

"Who was the voicemail sent to?" asked Don.

"That's the funny thing. It was to an old lady named Mrs. Cooper. She's 85 years old. She reported it to the Clifton Park Police Department and they sent the voicemail to us. We don't know why Mrs. Davis called her."

"She probably wasn't looking at her phone. The girl was yelling at her, telling her to take her hands out of her pockets. I think she was dialing blind and just desperate to get through to somebody," said Don.

"That's a good bet," agreed Eddie.

"In any case if it wasn't for that old lady, we might not even know about it yet."

"Did you get the phone company to track Mrs. Davis's phone and locate it?" asked Don.

"Yes. We're waiting for them to get back to us."

"I imagine you've talked to Mr. Davis," said Don.

"Yes. I spoke with him. He's on his way here now. He confirmed that his wife's not answering her phone. She was supposed to be at home but she's not."

Anderson's phone rang and he answered. "Detective Anderson."

Don and Eddie listened to the one-sided conversation.

"They found the Dodge van about thirty miles north of here. They're questioning possible witnesses now."

"Either they switched vehicles or they're holding Mrs. Davis in a motel or some other building," said Eddie.

"We have pictures of James Gordon from the Ohio Department of Motor Vehicles. We also have pictures of his female accomplice from the 7-11 tape you sent us. We can have the local police start showing their pictures at the motels in the area," said Anderson.

"See if you can get it on the 11 o'clock news as well," added Don.

• • • • •

Gillian pulled a chair over to where Mike was tied up and turned it so it was facing away from him. She straddled it and sat down with her arms resting on the back of the chair. She smiled directly at Mike. *I wonder if he recognizes me yet.*

Mike looked back at her, wondering why she was smiling. *What kind of game is she playing? Am I supposed to figure something out?*

Gillian continued to smile at him. It had been a long time but slowly he began to recognize her.

The long black hair, the white skin and that smile.

Ten years earlier Gillian went by the name Jennifer.

"Jennifer?" he managed to get out.

"Very good, Mike. You remembered."

Gillian continued to smile at Mike, savoring every moment. She looked around the room and noticed the picture of Brittany and his two daughters on the desk. "Nice pictures, Mike. I guess this is your office."

"What is it you want, Jennifer?"

Gillian began to laugh. "There's a little favor I want you to do for me, Mike."

Mike could already guess what that was.

Gillian stood up and wheeled Mike's chair over to the desk. "Cut his ties, Jimmy. I think he wants to play the piano for us."

Jimmy laughed and cut the ties.

"Pull up the Lexington software. We're going to have a little fun."

· · · · ·

Don drummed his fingers impatiently on the arms of his chair. He stood up and began pacing around the room. He knew that every minute was critical if they were going to find Mrs. Davis alive. He looked at Detective Anderson.

"You said Mr. Davis was on his way over here, Detective. How long ago was that?"

"That was about an hour ago. I told him I was going to have a patrol car pick him up and drive him over here, but he insisted on driving himself. He should be here any minute. His office is in Rotterdam. That's only about twenty miles west of here, but with rush hour traffic it could take a while."

"Let's not take anything for granted. Why don't you give him a call?"

Anderson dialed the number. It went to voicemail.

"He's not picking up," said Anderson.

"Call the local police and have a patrol car check out the Affirmed Building. We should check with the DMV and find out what Davis is driving and get the plate number. See if the car is still in the parking lot."

Anderson called the DMV and got the information. He then called the Rotterdam police.

"What else can we do while we're waiting?" asked Don, hoping for suggestions.

"Why don't you try calling Eric O'Connell again?" suggested Eddie.

Don knew that George Barnett was trying to call O'Connell every five minutes but decided to try anyway. He called the number and waited. Again, it went to voicemail. Frustration was beginning to eat at him.

After ten minutes Anderson's phone rang and he picked up.

Again, Don and Eddie listened to the one-sided conversation.

"That was the Rotterdam police. The Affirmed Building appears to be locked up tight. There are no lights on and there are no vehicles in the parking lot."

"They had to get rid of the Dodge van," said Eddie. They may have carjacked Davis when he tried to leave the building. The Subaru is big enough for all of them."

"That's certainly a possibility," said Don. "We better put out an APB on that Subaru."

Anderson called the State Police and gave them the information. "What now?" said Anderson.

"Try calling Davis again," said Don. "If he doesn't pick up, have the phone company track and locate his phone as well."

Anderson was about to make the call when his phone rang. After a brief conversation he ended the call and looked at Don and Eddie.

"We just located Mrs. Davis's cell phone in that Dodge van they found abandoned. It was in a backpack with three other phones."

"I'm sure they've thought of all these things ahead of time. They're not stupid. If they have Mr. Davis too, they probably got rid of his phone somewhere on the road," said Eddie.

"Try calling him again anyway. What can it hurt?"

Anderson dialed the number. Again, it went to voicemail.

CHAPTER 45

Oct. 13
Rotterdam, Affirmed Building

Gillian walked back and forth behind Brittany, smiling and playing with her knife in a cavalier way. She stroked Brittany's hair and whispered in her ear, making sure Mike was watching.

"How we doing, Mike? You almost done?"

"I'm working as fast as I can. It's more complicated than you think."

"Well, you better finish quick. We want to be out of here in less than half an hour."

Gillian whispered in Brittany's ear again, keeping her eyes on Mike.

Brittany turned her head away in revulsion. *Thank God the girls aren't in the room. At least they don't have to watch this,* she thought.

Mike continued to work on Gillian's demands, trying his best to stall for time. *I wonder how long it will take before Detective Anderson suspects something and sends someone out here. It may be our only chance.* "It's going to take at least half an hour. I can't get into the deeper algorithms without disabling other functions first. The whole system could crash."

Gillian held her knife to Brittany's throat and shouted, "Don't fuck with me, Mike. You better make it happen! Quick!"

"Okay. Okay. I'm working as fast as I can."

Brittany could hear Roni starting to cry in the room down the hall.

• • • • •

It was now 7:45 at FBI headquarters. Don looked at Anderson with desperation and urgency in his eyes.

"Are there state troopers watching all the key roads heading out of Rotterdam? They should have spotted Davis's Subaru by now."

"Nothing so far. We have a statewide BOLO on the Subaru. There's no way they can get out of the state. We have every local police force within 200 miles of here on alert," Anderson assured him.

Don began to think and said, "Is that patrol car still over at the Affirmed Building?"

"I'll check with the Rotterdam Police again," said Anderson.

"Have them station a patrol car in the parking lot, and get them to scour the area for that Subaru. I have the feeling they may still be holed up inside the Affirmed Building."

"Very possible. They could have ditched the Subaru close by and made sure it was out of sight," agreed Eddie.

"How long would it take us to drive to Rotterdam, Detective?" asked Don.

"At least twenty-five minutes. It depends on the traffic. Could take as much as forty minutes at this hour," said Anderson.

"Is that chopper still here?" asked Don.

"Yeah. It's all set to go."

"We're going to take a little trip out to Rotterdam. Let's go, Eddie."

"I'll keep you posted if anything new comes up, detectives," said Anderson.

Eddie and Don raced out the door and ran toward the helipad.

• • • • •

It was now ten minutes to eight. Mike continued to carry out the sabotage Gillian had ordered him to inflict.

"Eight o'clock, Mike. You have until eight or things are going to start getting ugly," warned Gillian.

"The laws of physics are not going to change just to make you happy, Jennifer. If you want me to do everything you asked, it's going to take at least another twenty or thirty minutes."

Gillian motioned to Jimmy and they stepped out of the room. "We've got to be out of here soon. I have the feeling things are going to heat up. We have to be far away from here in the next few hours."

"So what's the plan, Gee?"

"We jump on the bikes and head south. We hijack a car, preferably an SUV with a single woman driving. Then we keep heading south on the back roads. Hopefully nobody will report her missing for at least a couple of hours. After that we split up and make our way to Texas. We have to change the way we look. We're too obvious traveling together. We'll meet up in El Paso and get across the river there. The border guards have their hands full with all the illegals coming in from Mexico. I doubt they'll have time to deal with anyone going the other way. With any luck we could be in Argentina a week from now."

"What about Davis and his wife?"

"No witnesses this time, Jimmy. I'll take care of that."

"What about money?"

"I'll make sure the money has been transferred to Bank of America. He's setting up a linked account where the money will automatically be transferred after two days. They won't be able to trace it. It will take them a while to figure it all out. There won't be any restrictions on withdrawals and we'll have almost two hundred thousand to keep us happy."

"I like it, Gee. Hanging with you is a blast."

Gillian laughed and said, "You ain't seen nothin' yet, Jimmy."

The two of them walked back inside the office where Mike was still busy making changes to the software.

Brittany felt her flesh crawl as Gillian walked slowly back and forth behind her.

It was now almost eight o'clock and Mike knew time was running out. He had no way of knowing that the FBI already knew the identity of one of their abductors or that they had pictures that could identify the girl he had known as Jennifer ten years earlier.

I'm sure she plans to kill us. There's no way she can leave any witnesses. If I were still alive, I could just undo all the changes I made to the software.

"It's eight o'clock, Mike," shouted Gillian.

"The money has been transferred to your bank account. In a few minutes I'll be done with the rest of the changes you wanted."

"Check it out, Jimmy. Get on your phone and log into our account."

Jimmy got on the Bank of America website and logged on.

"The money is there, Gee. The original ninety thousand minus the money you withdrew. Plus another ninety thousand. There's a total of a hundred and seventy eight thousand."

Mike judged the likelihood that he could overpower Jimmy and wrestle the gun away from him. He looked at Brittany and thought about Jamie and Roni.

It's too risky, he thought. *But I've got to try something.*

Brittany had the same thoughts and looked at Mike. She tried to telegraph her thoughts to him.

Mike looked back at her and nodded in agreement.

It's now or never, thought Brittany.

She planted her feet firmly on the floor and pushed off as hard as she could, sending her backwards and knocking Gillian off her feet.

Mike picked up the lamp from his desk and whirled around, knocking the gun from Jimmy's hand. He punched him hard in the throat and shoved him across the room.

Jimmy gasped for air and stumbled backwards over a chair.

If I go for the gun Brittany is dead. There's only one chance.

Mike raced over to Gillian, who was just getting to her feet and still off balance. He grabbed her by the arm and spun her around, slamming her hard into the wall. Gillian's head hit the wall with an audible crack. Mike could see her eyes roll back as she almost lost consciousness. Mike grabbed the knife from Gillian and quickly cut the ties from Brittany's chair. Jimmy was getting up and heading for the gun.

"Let's go, Brit. Run."

Mike and Brittany ran down the hall and into the office where Jamie and Roni were tied up.

Mike locked the door and said, "Help me push this desk over here."

Together they pushed the desk so it blocked the door.

Jamie and Roni were frantic and practically jumping out of their chairs as they watched what was going on. Brittany took Gillian's knife and cut their ties.

Outside they could hear Gillian cursing.

Mike picked up a floor lamp and jammed the stand between the desk and the wall so the door couldn't be opened.

"Stay away from the door," Mike shouted as he hustled them out of the way.

Seconds later four bullets flew through the door and blew away the lock.

Jimmy tried to open the door, but it wouldn't budge.

"Fuck. We don't have time for this, Jimmy. We've got to get the fuck out of here now," cursed Gillian. "I'm going to get the cooler."

Gillian took out most of the explosives and placed the cubes in the hallway outside the office where Mike and his family were hiding. She put the rest in a satchel.

"I'll save a couple of cubes and toss them in with an M-80 after we're on the bikes. That should give us plenty of time before it goes off." She put the satchel over her shoulder.

The two of them raced out the front door.

• • • • •

Don tapped the chopper pilot on the shoulder and asked, "How much longer?"

"We're almost there. That's the Affirmed Building down below."

"Okay. Put her down a block away in that parking lot."

The pilot began to take the chopper down and prepared to land in the parking lot.

As they were about to land Eddie noticed two figures race out of the front door of the Affirmed Building and run across the parking lot.

"What do you make of that, Don?" asked Eddie.

"Looks like a man and a woman. Most likely our suspects, but let's not jump the gun. It could be Davis and his wife."

• • • • •

Mike looked at Brittany and said, "I don't hear them out there anymore. I want you to stay here with the girls. I'm going to take a peek."

He pulled the desk away, opened the door ever so slightly and peered into the hallway. What he saw filled him with terror. The gray cubes lining the baseboard could only be one thing.

"We've got to get out of here, now." He pushed the door wide open and pulled Brittany and his daughters into the hallway. "Go out the back door and get as far away from the building as you can. I'm going to check the front parking lot."

"Come with us, Mike. Let the police handle this."

"I'll be careful. I promise."

"Come with us, Daddy," screamed Roni. "Don't go."

"Please, Brit. Take the girls and go now."

Reluctantly Brittany took the girls by the hand and rushed out the back door, looking back, hoping that Mike would follow her.

Mike headed quickly for the front door and looked out into the parking lot. There was no sign of Jimmy or Gillian. He opened the door and stepped outside. He could hear the chopper as it set down in the parking lot down the block.

He watched as two men jumped from the chopper. *Probably FBI. Detective Anderson must have sent them.*

● ● ● ● ●

Gillian also heard the chopper set down.

She turned to Jimmy and said, "This is going to be close. You ready?"

"Let's do it, Gee."

Gillian and Jimmy got on their bikes and emerged from behind the building where they had hidden the Subaru.

Gillian turned her Harley around, revved the engine and tore across the parking lot directly toward Mike, still carrying the explosives in her satchel. The bike began to sputter and cough. The misfires slowed her down just enough to give Don and Eddie time to reach the parking lot. Gillian was now only sixty or seventy yards from where Mike was standing.

The adrenaline must be kicking in, thought Eddie. *I haven't run this fast in years.*

He saw the Harley as it sped toward Mike.

Eddie got on one knee, took careful aim and squeezed off several rounds in her direction.

Don did the same.

One bullet hit the rear tire.

Too late, Gillian recognized her vulnerability. The bike went into a skid and Gillian lost control. It slammed sideways into a concrete lighting fixture. A second later the bike exploded, setting off the C4 in the satchel as well. With a brilliant flash the Harley disappeared, along with Gillian.

The shock wave knocked Eddie backwards on his ass.

The front wheel, soaked with gasoline, continued to bounce along past Mike and across the street.

Eddie and Don watched in silent awe as small pieces of Gillian began to rain down in the parking lot.

It was over.

At least for Gillian it was.

Jimmy watched in anguish as everything he cared about vanished before his eyes. He took out his gun, revved the Harley and raced toward Eddie and Don.

Jimmy died in a hail of bullets just feet from where Gillian had met her end.

Mike began to walk toward the two detectives, holding his hands in the air. "I'm Mike Davis," he shouted, trying to be heard above the din of the helicopter.

Eddie and Don holstered their weapons and identified themselves.

"My wife and kids are somewhere close by. I told them to get as far from the building as possible. I think the whole place is wired with C4 or something. You probably want to call in some pros from the bomb squad."

Don got on his phone and called Anderson to explain the situation.

"We better move away from the building as well," suggested Don.

The three of them began to run away from the building toward the helicopter.

"Could you arrange for a patrol car to look for my wife and kids? I'm sure they're not far away. She must have heard the explosion. I want her to know I'm all right."

"Of course, Mr. Davis."

Don called the Rotterdam Police Department and arranged for several patrol cars to search the area.

"Did you recognize either of the two people who kidnapped your wife and kids, Mr. Davis?" asked Don.

"I don't know who the guy is but I knew the girl about ten years ago when I was at Ohio State. Her name is Jennifer."

"If that's her real name. I doubt it. She's a suspect in several homicides, including a Boston Police detective," said Eddie.

"Do you have any idea why she would want to get revenge on Lexington Finance or your family?" asked Don.

"Not a clue," said Mike, shaking his head. "Not a clue."

"I'm not sure but I don't think this was just about money, Mr. Davis. She must have known there was a limit to what she could get. The rewards just don't warrant the risk. I think it may have been personal in nature," suggested Don.

Mike thought about it. It was hard to believe someone could carry a grudge for that long.

"What can you tell us about Reardon and his wife? They're still listed as missing but I'm not too optimistic about finding them alive," said Don "Can you think of anything that could help us?"

"No. Not really. I never met with Reardon but I knew who he was. I can't imagine how they would be involved."

"It's possible you were the real target all along, Mr. Davis," explained Don.

Mike just shook his head in disbelief.

A few minutes later a squad car pulled up next to them and Brittany jumped out with the kids. She raced over to Mike and threw her arms around him. Jamie and Roni grabbed hold as well.

"It's all over, girls. Everything is going to be all right."

Roni's eyes filled with tears of joy and relief. "I love you, Daddy," she sobbed.

"Thank God, Mike. When we heard the explosion, we didn't know what to think."

Brittany and Jamie began to cry as well.

Don and Eddie looked on, glad that they had gotten there in time.

It was hard for Eddie to smile, knowing that his partner was dead, but at least something worked out for the best.

Brittany continued to hug Mike with all her strength and asked, "What happened to that awful woman? Did the police arrest those two?"

"They're both dead, Brit. They won't be bothering us again."

"I'm sure you would all like to go home and be alone right now," said Don. "I know you're all a bit stressed out. I don't think it would be a good idea for you to drive, Mr. Davis. You're going to have to give an official statement but I think that can wait until tomorrow. How would you like a ride home in a helicopter? You can pick up your car later."

"I think we've all had enough excitement for one day, Mike." Brittany looked at Don and asked, "Can we just get a ride home in a nice, boring police car?"

Don laughed and said, "Of course, Mrs. Davis. I'll arrange for it right away."

Five minutes later Mike, Brittany and their two little girls were headed back toward Forest Park.

Needless to say, it was a day none of them would ever forget.

CHAPTER 46

Thursday Oct. 14, 9 AM
FBI Albany

Don and Eddie were busy writing out their reports about what had occurred at the Affirmed Building the night before. Don's phone rang. It was Jack Sullivan. "Yes, Jack. What's up?"

"You're not going to believe it, Don. We did a thorough check into Eric O'Connell. We found out he owns a small house in Westwood and sent a patrol car out there. Guess who we found tied up inside."

Don hesitated for a moment and said, "Kevin Reardon and his wife?"

"That's right. They were a little sore and thirsty but otherwise okay."

"That's fantastic news, Jack. Let me tell Eddie." Don turned to Eddie and said, "They found Reardon and his wife. They're alive."

Eddie said, "That's great, Don." But quietly he was thinking to himself, *I wish Rob could be here to celebrate the good news.*

Don picked up on Eddie's thoughts. "Eddie and I are finishing things up here in Albany, Jack. I'll probably be back tomorrow." He ended the call and turned to Eddie with a look of compassion and understanding. "If you want to fly back to Boston right now and talk to Rob's family, I understand. I can handle things here."

"If you're sure you don't mind, I would like to get back and talk to some of his friends. I doubt the news about Rob has hit the papers yet."

"You go on ahead. I'll meet with you sometime tomorrow."

• • • • •

Eddie took the helicopter back to Boston and made his way to Charlie's. Meriam was surprised to see him walk through the door by himself. She waved to Eddie and smiled hello, but it faded quickly when she saw the serious expression on his face. One look said it all. Meriam set down the tray she was carrying and ran over to him.

All Eddie could do was look at her and say, "I'm so sorry, Meriam. Rob is gone."

Meriam's eyes welled up with tears as the reality of Eddie's words began to sink in. It was one of the hardest things Eddie ever had to do. Meriam collapsed into the booth behind her and began to sob uncontrollably. Eddie sat down across from her and tried his best to console her, but there wasn't much he could think of that would help.

He briefly explained what had happened and told her that if it hadn't been for Rob several innocent people would most likely have lost their lives, including two little girls.

Meriam listened and tried her best to understand. Eddie stayed with her for the next ten minutes, trying to do whatever he could that might help.

Finally, he said, "I have to go and talk to Rob's parents, Meriam. I should probably go now."

Meriam stood up and hugged Eddie. "Please let me know about any services that they have planned."

"I'll do that, Meriam."

Eddie walked out the door into the rain.

CHAPTER 47

Friday, Oct. 15, 10 AM
Boston FBI Building

Kevin and Jennifer Reardon waited in one of the conference rooms at FBI headquarters in Boston. They were told a detective would be with them soon to interview them and take a statement. The FBI had identified the male kidnapper as James Gordon from Ohio. They were still trying to obtain information that could identify his female companion.

"I can't believe they let us live, Jen," said Kevin. "I heard they had the Affirmed Building rigged with explosives and were about to set it off when the police showed up. Davis and his family barely made it out of there. We were so lucky."

"I don't know for sure but I think I actually made a bond with her. I think she was a very damaged person. Something terrible must have happened to her at some point in her life. You were right when you told me to try and make friends with her. I can't put my finger on it, but I think she actually envied my relationship with you. I think she identified with me in a way."

"Whatever the reason... what you did saved both our lives. She was completely unpredictable. It's almost like she was two different people."

A chill went through Jennifer as she thought about the conversations she had while walking in the woods with her captor. How close had she come to death? It could have turned on a dime. One wrong word and it could have all ended right there.

Don walked into the room, pulled up a chair and introduced himself. "First, I'd like to say that I'm very happy that you're both all right."

"Thank you, Detective Corlino. I heard you were an important reason that they found us in time. We're both very grateful. I heard a Boston Police Detective lost his life during the investigation."

"Unfortunately, that's true. He was a very brave man. He was the reason we were able to track down the girl who abducted you."

"I would like to personally sponsor a fund in his name. Do you know if he has a family to support? Whatever I can do to help. I'm sure Lexington will be happy to make the same offer."

"That's very generous of you, Mr. Reardon. I'll see what I can do to set it up. Right now, what I would like to concentrate on is determining the identity of the girl. We still have no clue who she was or where she was from."

"We don't know anything, really. We only know that she knew Mike Davis at some point in her life. I'm not sure exactly why, but I think she was trying to exact some revenge for something he had done," explained Jennifer.

"I met Mr. Davis. He seems like a decent family guy. From her actions, I doubt that her thoughts were particularly rational," suggested Don.

Kevin looked at Don and raised an eyebrow. "I'll have to agree with you there, detective."

"We have someone interviewing Mr. Davis as we speak. We're hoping he can help to identify her. The only other things we have to go on are her connection to James Gordon and some videotapes. There's no body to identify. The crime lab did manage to get some tissue samples. DNA analysis determined that her ancestry was mostly English or Irish, partly Italian and some Eastern European."

Jennifer shuddered when she learned how she had died. "I think she said something about growing up in the mid-west somewhere. Maybe Indiana," Jennifer added.

Don wrote it down in his notes.

"Mr. Davis said that he knew her briefly ten years ago when he went to Ohio State University. He knew her as Jennifer but couldn't remember her last name," explained Don.

Jennifer took a deep breath and gave Kevin a knowing look. It confirmed her theory that she somehow identified with her. "She told us her name was Grace. Her boyfriend just called her Gee."

"I doubt she ever went by her real name. She was probably living her life on the run for many years. It's possible we may never figure out who she really was," said Don with a slight tone of disappointment in his voice.

"Why would such a beautiful girl turn to such a desperate life, Detective?" asked Jennifer. "It just doesn't make a lot of sense to me. She had so much to live for."

"I can't answer that, Mrs. Reardon. In spite of her irrational behavior, she was actually a very smart girl. If it hadn't been for a couple of teenage kids and an eighty-five year old lady, we may never have been able to catch up with her."

After another half hour, Don was satisfied he had learned all he could from the Reardons and concluded the interview. Six months later the FBI was still trying to figure out Gillian's true identity.

· · · · ·

Later that month Don took Cheryl to Hawaii for an extended month-long vacation. They visited the Big Island and Maui. Later they went on to Oahu.

They climbed Diamond Head together and when they got to the top, Don dropped to one knee and asked Cheryl to marry him.

• • • • •

Meanwhile Mrs. Cooper instantly became one of Mike and Brittany's favorite people. In the years to come they invited her over for dinner on many occasions. Mrs. Cooper's Christmas cards became an overnight success story. She was a millionaire by the time she turned ninety.

ACKNOWLEDGEMENTS

I would like to thank Don Alesi for his advice on making this book as true to life as possible. As a former FBI agent his knowledge of the JTTF and official police procedures was very helpful. I chose him as the model for the main character in this book.

I would also like to thank Rich Aebly for his input about computer software and programming.

In addition I would like to thank the Blue Hills Reservation and the Boston Police Department for their cooperation during my research.